The VIOLINIST *of* VENICE

The VIOLINIST *of* VENICE

A STORY OF VIVALDI

ALYSSA PALOMBO

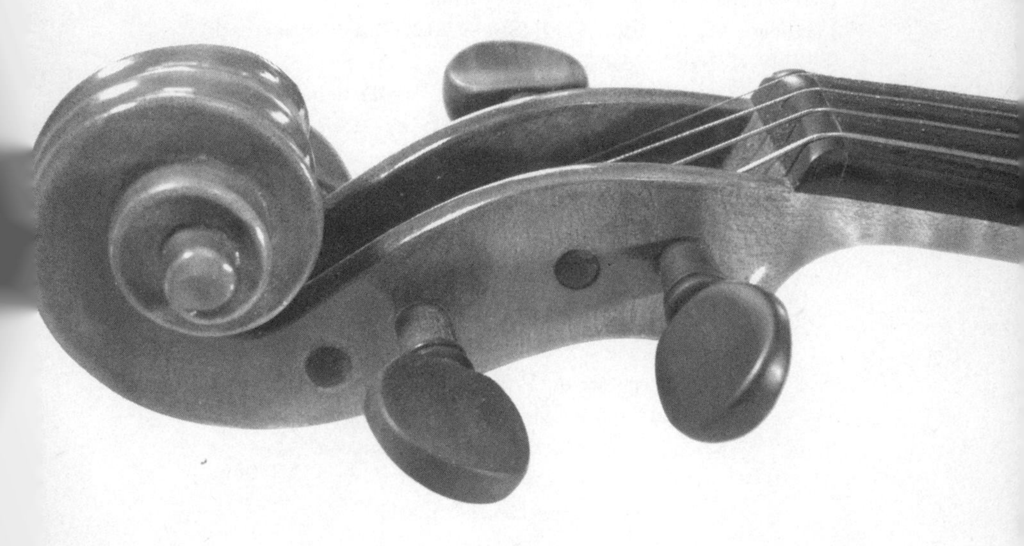

 St. Martin's Griffin New York

This is a work of fiction. All of the characters, organizations, and events portrayed in this novel are either products of the author's imagination or are used fictitiously.

For information, address St. Martin's Press, 175 Fifth Avenue, New York, N.Y. 10010.

www.stmartins.com

Designed by Molly Rose Murphy

Library of Congress Cataloging-in-Publication Data

Names: Palombo, Alyssa.
Title: The violinist of Venice : a story of Vivaldi / Alyssa Palombo.
Description: New York : St. Martin's Griffin, 2015.
Identifiers: LCCN 2015035712| ISBN 9781250071491 (paperback) | ISBN 9781466882638 (e-book)
Subjects: LCSH: Vivaldi, Antonio, 1678–1741—Fiction. | Violinists—Fiction. | Venice (Italy)—History—18th century—Fiction. | BISAC: FICTION / Historical. | FICTION / Romance / Historical. | GSAFD: Historical fiction.
Classification: LCC PS3619.A3564 V56 2015 | DDC 813/.6—dc23
LC record available at http://lccn.loc.gov/2015035712

Our books may be purchased in bulk for promotional, educational, or business use. Please contact your local bookseller or the Macmillan Corporate and Premium Sales Department at (800) 221-7945, extension 5442, or by e-mail at MacmillanSpecialMarkets@macmillan.com.

First Edition: December 2015

10 9 8 7 6 5 4 3 2 1

For my mom, Debbie Palombo,
who crossed an ocean with me so I could tell this story,
and who always, always believed

SINFONIA

Flames. That is how I remember Antonio Vivaldi: the flames of his red hair; the flames of the candles that flickered determinedly around him as he composed late at night; the fires he would kindle in the grate in the cold, dark winter, the red-orange glow lighting his bare skin; the passion with which he played the violin, such passion that I would not have been surprised had the strings, the bow, caught fire.

Music is a singular kind of passion; it envelops, surrounds, obsesses. To share that passion with another soul is to amplify it, to create a sort of intimacy unlike anything else.

Vivaldi gave my life fire, passion, heat. There was a time when—without him—I was frozen; when I was like a corpse interred in a tomb of ice.

And now that he is gone, the world is cold once again. Yet he is not gone forever. He lives on in the music he wrote; and in my memories. But with the pleasure of remembering, it seems, always comes pain; and if there is one thing I have learned in my life in Venice—this beautiful, incomparable city of water and music and masks and deception—it is that we must live through both pleasure and pain as best we can.

MOVEMENT ONE

IL PRETE ROSSO

April–September 1710

1

THE MAESTRO

The gondola sliced silently through the dark water of the canal. My hired gondolier pressed the craft close against the wall of one of the buildings that lined the waterway, allowing another boat to pass us.

"Ciao, Luca!" he called to the other gondolier, his voice echoing loudly off the stones of the narrow canal, causing me to start.

I drew the hood of my cloak closer about my face, hiding it as we passed the other gondola.

We drew up to a bridge, and I spied a set of stone steps leading up to the street—*the* street. "Stop," I said, my voice low from within the hood. "Let me out here, *per favore*."

The gondolier obliged, bringing the boat close to the steps and stopping so that I could gather my skirts and step out, giving me his hand to assist me. I pressed some coins into his palm, and he nodded to me. "*Grazie, signorina. Buona notte.*"

I started down the street, peering at the houses, looking for the one where the man I sought was said to reside. I crossed a bridge over another small canal, the water beneath looking deep enough to swallow both my secrets and me and leave no trace of either.

Just beyond the bridge I found it. I took a deep breath, banishing the last of my nervousness, pushed open the door and, without knocking, boldly stepped inside.

The room I entered was not large, and appeared even smaller by its clutter. Sheets of parchment covered the table a few paces in front of me, some written upon, some blank, and many with bars of music scrawled on them. A harpsichord sat against one wall, scarcely recognizable beneath the papers heaped on it. I counted three instrument cases throughout the room that each looked to be the right size to hold a violin, or perhaps a viola d'amore. A lit lamp sat on the table amongst the papers, and another on the desk against the wall to my right. These, plus the slowly dying fire in the grate to my left, were the only sources of light in the dim room.

At the desk, bent over a piece of parchment, quill in hand, sat a man in worn-looking clerical robes. He looked up, startled, and I was able to get my first good look at him. He had hair as red as the embers in the hearth and wide dark eyes that, when they caught sight of me, narrowed on my face in anger, then bewilderment. From what I had heard, he was only in his early thirties, yet the strain of childhood illness and—or so I guessed—the trials that life had seen fit to deliver him had given him the weary demeanor of a still older man. And yet beneath his somewhat haggard appearance there was a spark of liveliness, of fire, that made him appealing all the same.

"Who are you? What do you want?" he demanded, scowling as he rose from his chair.

I took another step forward into the room, pushing my hood back from my face. "I seek Maestro Antonio Vivaldi," I said. "The man they call *il Prete Rosso*." The Red Priest.

"Hmph." He snorted derisively. "You have found him, although I do not know that I rightly deserve the title maestro anymore. After all, I have been sacked."

"I know," I said. All of Venice knew that about a year ago, Maestro Vivaldi had been removed, for reasons largely unknown, from his position as violin master and composer at the Conservatorio dell'Ospedale della Pietà, the foundling home renowned for its superb, solely female orchestra and choir. He had spent the past year since his dismissal traveling throughout Europe—or so the gossip said. Having heard of his return, I took the first opportunity I could to seek him out. "I was thinking that as you are currently out of a job, you might be willing to take on a private student."

His gaze narrowed on me again. "I might be," he said.

Clearly he was expecting me to bargain. The corners of my mouth curled up slightly into a smile as I reached beneath my cloak and extracted a cloth purse that was heavy with coins. I closed the remaining distance between us and handed it to the maestro. His eyes widened as he felt its weight, and grew round with disbelief as he opened it and saw how much gold was within.

"I trust that will be sufficient for my first month of lessons," I said, "as well as your discretion."

He looked back up at me. "Who are you?" he asked again. When I failed to answer immediately, he went on. "If you can afford to pay me so much, then surely you can afford to have some perfumed, mincing fop or other come to you in the comfort of your own palazzo and teach you. Why come here—in the middle of the night, no less—to seek me out?"

"That is quite a lengthy tale, padre," I answered. "Suffice it to say that I have heard that there is no better violinist in all of Venice than yourself, and that is why I have gone to such lengths to find you."

He frowned, not satisfied with so vague an explanation, but he let the matter rest. "You wish to learn the violin, then?" he asked.

I nodded. "I used to play, years ago . . ." I shook my head. "It has been a very long time." Five years, to be exact; five years since my mother had died and taken all the music in our house with her.

Vivaldi nodded absently, then turned to remove a violin and bow—which I took to be his own—from a case that sat open on the floor next to the desk. He handed them to me. "Show me what you know," he said.

Oh, it had been so long since I'd held a violin in my hands, had felt the smoothness of the wood beneath my fingers, had smelled the faint, spicy scent of the varnish. I had not practiced before coming to see the maestro, thinking it best not to tempt fate before I could secure his help. I closed my eyes, savoring the feeling of being reunited with an old friend I had believed I might never see again. Then I began.

I started with the simplest scales: C major and A minor. My fingers were stiff and clumsy on the strings, but after playing each scale twice, the old patterns and habits began to return. When I felt more comfortable, I began to play a simple but pretty melody I remembered playing when I was younger. My memory was imperfect; there were several points where I forgot what note came next and simply skipped ahead to the next one that I could recall. It was rather unimpressive, but it was all I could think of to play. When I came to the end, I began again, this time improvising to repair the sections I'd forgotten. So intoxicated was I with simply playing a violin again that I forgot Vivaldi's presence altogether, until he lightly placed a hand on my shoulder to stop me.

"Good," he said, more to himself than to me. "Good; not bad at all. I can tell that you have a natural talent. And you certainly play with passion." He smiled, and the expression transformed his face. "I shall teach you. I assume you have an instrument of your own?"

I nodded, thinking of the untouched violin I had stolen from my brother Claudio's room. It had been given to him as a gift and was of the finest craftsmanship, though he had never played or shown any interest in learning. "Yes, I do," I answered. "Though it will be . . . difficult for me to bring it here with me."

The maestro waved this aside. "I have one that you may use. You wish to come here for your lessons, then?"

"Yes," I replied quickly. "Yes, if that suits."

"Very well," he said, his eyes bright with curiosity. "Shall we say two days hence, around midday? If that is agreeable to you?"

I thought for a moment. I could perhaps get away unnoticed for a time then. "Yes, that is agreeable."

"Though I do not suppose you will tell me the reasons behind such need for discretion?" he asked.

I smiled. "As I said, that is quite the long story, padre, and one that would be better saved for another time." *Or never.*

"I see," he said.

"Two days hence, then," I said, moving toward the door.

"Wait," he said, and I stopped. "May I at least learn your name, signorina?"

I glanced at him over my shoulder. "Adriana," I said. I could not risk him recognizing my surname; so, before he could press me further, I pulled my hood over my face again and stepped outside into the late April rain, leaving him to think what he would.

2

ALLEGRO

In the two days before I was to return to Maestro Vivaldi's house for my first lesson, I tried to practice as much as I was able, which was unfortunately not a great deal. The morning after my visit to the maestro, I ordered all of the servants to keep away from my rooms and not disturb me, claiming I had a pounding pain in my head and must rest in absolute silence. It was a display worthy of an opera house diva, and I was obeyed, which was all that mattered. When I was certain no one would hear, I took my brother's violin from its hiding place beneath my bed—which I acknowledge as being less than creative—and played all the scales and arpeggios I knew. I forced myself to play them until they were technically smooth and pitch-perfect before allowing myself to move on to the melody I had played for Maestro Vivaldi.

The next day, not being able to use the same excuse, I took every chance I could to barricade myself in my bedchamber and silently practice my fingering, as well as shifting positions. What had taken me years to learn as a child came back to me quickly, as though the knowledge had lain sleeping in my mind, waiting for me to call upon it again.

When the day of my lesson came, I feigned a return of my headache after my maid had dressed me, begging to be left alone again for the afternoon. As soon as she was gone, I slipped on my hooded cloak and a Carnevale half mask of white lace—Easter had long since passed and Carnevale resumed again—and slipped out of my rooms. I carefully locked the door behind me—my heart swelling in my throat at the thought of my father finding out—and trembling with fear, with excitement, made my way down the back staircase and out the rear door into the street that ran behind the palazzo. I saw no one, and I was certain no one saw me.

I was foolhardy, perhaps, but the burning flame that music kindled in me, once lit, could not be ignored, for fear that it would consume me.

I was thankful that I had left myself plenty of time to get to the maestro's house, as I made several wrong turns along the way. To say that Venice was a maze of narrow walkways, streets, bridges, and small waterways running off the Grand Canal was an understatement. I had never been out, unescorted, among the common people, and it took me some time to make my way through the crowds as they pushed and shoved all about me, on their way to the markets at the Rialto, to their employment, to Mass.

I crossed the same bridge I had a few nights ago, and today the water beneath it sparkled a jewel-bright green as the sun shone on it. It was far too early in the year for the heat to bring with it the stink of the canals and all the rubbish they contained, so one could smell only the faintest hint of the sea throughout the city.

Once I arrived, I knocked twice before letting myself in, knowing that he would be expecting me. As I removed my mask, he came down the staircase at the rear of the room, dressed this time in a less worn-looking priest's cassock. His unruly red hair was neatly combed and had been tied back with a piece of black cord. "Signorina Ad[illegible]ana," he greeted me, smiling. "I have been looking forward t[illegible]ginning your musical instruction today."

Apparently the maestro was much more personable when one did not unexpectedly burst in upon him late at night, I thought wryly. "I thank you for such kind words, maestro," I said. "I, too, have been looking forward to this day."

"How long before you must depart?" he asked, somewhat awkwardly.

"I must be back within two hours, no later," I answered.

"Very good," he said. "Let us begin, then, so that we may make the most of our time."

He produced the spare violin which he had promised for my use—not so fine as the one I had stolen from my brother, yet it was clear that this one had been played a bit more—and placed it in my hands. He began by asking me to play as many scales as I knew, and I obliged, pleased that even in the course of my limited practicing I had been able to recall most of them. After the scales, we moved on to arpeggios, and I was able to play them nearly perfectly, but for a few notes that went slightly sharp.

"Do not hold the bow so tightly," he admonished, stopping me in the middle of one arpeggio. He placed his fingers on top of mine and gently loosened their grip. He gave me a crooked sort of smile. "It is not going anywhere, you know."

I nodded and relaxed my fingers, knowing there was no way that I could explain to the maestro that, for me, each moment with the violin was a stolen one.

He stepped back and motioned for me to play the arpeggio over again. This time, the bow slid much more smoothly over the strings, and the sound that resulted was much brighter and more vibrant, and the pitch did not falter. I smiled to let him know I heard the difference.

Once we finished with the arpeggios, he asked me to return to e song I had played for him two evenings ago. "I would like to hear play that again, if you will, signorina," he said. "As much of it as n remember."

I obeyed, placing the bow on the strings and beginning the song. I closed my eyes briefly as I felt the music begin to fill the air around me, falling with feather-light touches onto my skin.

Not halfway into the song, he stopped me, again placing a gentle hand on my shoulder to get my attention. When I opened my eyes, he was standing quite near me. "Straighten your wrist," he said. He reached out and let his fingers encircle the slender bones of my left wrist, pressing lightly on the back of my hand, which had bent at an angle. "This must be perfectly straight in order to properly support the instrument, and make the fingering easier."

This time, the simple touch of his hand on my wrist caused a heated flush to spread from my cheeks down to my chest. My embarrassment as I realized this no doubt only caused the color that had risen in my skin to deepen.

Dio mio, I snapped at myself, *he is a priest. Get hold of yourself, Adriana.*

"Do you realize," he was saying, even as I struggled to compose myself, "that when you were playing the scales or the arpeggios, your wrist was perfectly straight and your posture correct? Yet the moment you began to play this song, your posture changed."

"Ah," I responded. "I had not realized, no."

He smiled and stepped back. "I thought not. Otherwise you would not be doing it, no? But I think when you are playing something more . . . formal and structured, shall we say, like a scale, you hold yourself more rigidly, more controlled. Then, when you begin to play a melody, you seek to play the music itself, and not just the notes. You try to get at the emotion of the piece, at what it is saying, and in so doing allow your technique to fall away."

I bit my lip, chagrined by my lapse, but also feeling rather exposed and defenseless. How had he managed to deduce all of that from just a few measures of a melody? "My apologies. I must try to correct that in the future."

"No, no," the maestro hurriedly contradicted. "You misunderstand me. In a violin player, in a true musician, that is exactly what one wants. I can teach you to have the most superb, flawless technique imaginable, yet the emotion I cannot teach. If you cannot reach the emotion of the music on your own, then there is nothing I can do. It is this that separates the true musicians, the true artists, from the mere . . . instrumentalists." As he spoke, his pale skin became slightly flushed, and it was clear to which category Vivaldi himself belonged.

I heard the words tumbling from my mouth before I could stop them. "Would you play something for me?"

His lips parted slightly in surprise as he silently regarded me.

I found myself stammering, "It is just, as I told you, everyone says that you are the finest violinist in Venice, yet I have never heard you play, and I . . ." I trailed off, unable to tell him what I really wanted to say: *I want to hear for myself if you are all that they say you are, if you are really that skilled, that brilliant. I want to know if we are both speaking the same language, for I think we are.*

The surprise vanished from his face, and with a quick nod he crossed the room and removed his violin from its case on his desk. He set the instrument into position, lifted his bow, and began to play.

Oh, the music that came pouring from the Red Priest's violin. Though he was the only one playing, the music seemed to swell and build and fill the entire room, until it sounded as though it must be coming from a full orchestra, instead of just one man. The piece he played was both rapid and lively, yet there was a passionate, desperate edge to it. And for all the music's strident sort of quickness, he played it smoothly, so that the sound was rich and full.

And what a sound it was. It did not seem possible that an ordinary violin, played by a seemingly ordinary man, was capable of singing with such beauty. And I thought that if one could somehow *hear* pure gold, this was exactly what it would sound like.

It called to mind the tale of Orfeo and how his music had been able to make the very rocks and trees move and dance. I had always thought it a silly story, yet hearing Vivaldi play, I believed, if just for a moment, that such a thing was possible.

I do not know how long he played; it seemed that he played forever, the glorious melody circling back on itself again and again, without end. My heart seemed to speed up, so that it beat in time with the music.

Yet when he played the final notes and removed his bow from the strings, I felt as though it had not been nearly long enough, and that I could have listened to him play for an eternity.

As soon as he stopped, his attention returned to me. I found myself staring at him silently. And even though I feared he was misinterpreting my reaction, I could not summon any words to accurately describe what I was feeling.

Finally, as though he could no longer bear the silence, he spoke. "And so?" he asked, his voice echoing dully off the walls. "Do I live up to your expectations?"

My voice came out scratchy and unused. "What *was* that?"

His body stiffened as he misunderstood my meaning. "It is part of one of my own compositions."

"It was magnificent," I gushed. "I don't think I have ever heard anything more beautiful."

Relaxing, he chuckled as he put his violin back into its case. "You do me too much honor, signorina."

"It is true!" I insisted. "Surely you know without my telling you that it was—"

"Very well," he interrupted, smiling. "I shall accept your praise, if you insist. I am rather fond of that piece myself, truth be told."

I shook my head. "I do not feel the least bit worthy of learning from you."

"Nonsense," he said, his tone now sharp. "You appreciated what you just heard, did you not? Not everyone would, as I know from experience." His eyes met mine. "You understand, I think."

I felt a strange and uncomfortable flush of heat at these words. "Yes," I replied. "I think that I may. That I will."

We held each other's gaze just an instant too long, then he looked away and nodded toward my borrowed violin. "Let us see if you can play that melody again, and keep your wrist straight this time," he said. "Emotion may be the most critical aspect of music, but the trick is to be able to combine that with perfect technique."

I picked up my violin. "Very well," I said. "I will try again."

Playing the violin again ignited a permanent glow that I carried inside me, which burned gently and steadily just beneath my breastbone. Before I left Maestro Vivaldi's house, we agreed I should return at noon in three days' time, but I knew my frequent comings and goings would not go unremarked upon for long. I was tempting *il destino,* but I couldn't stop. I thought of it constantly; no matter what else I was doing, in my head I was making music. Bursts of color were beginning to flower in the unending gray that had dominated my world for years.

Yet what haunted me most of all, in those few days following my first lesson, was the music Vivaldi had played. I heard it over and over again in my head, as though I could not forget it even if I had wanted to, and I began to feel that the music had changed something within me, though I did not know what.

3

APPASSIONATA

"Faster, Signorina Adriana! You must play it faster!" Vivaldi shouted for the second time, causing me to stop in the middle of the piece I was playing.

"I am still becoming familiar with the piece," I protested. "This is only the third time I have gone through it, after all."

Vivaldi was shaking his head before I had finished speaking. "You are thinking about it too much," he told me. "You are perfectly capable of playing this without familiarizing yourself with it. Do not let your head get in the way of what your hands are doing; simply do it." He motioned toward the bow dangling limply from my right hand. "Try it again."

I lifted the bow to the strings, took a deep breath, and closed my eyes briefly. *Do not let your head get in the way of what your hands are doing.* I thought I knew what the maestro meant; but knowing and doing are very different things.

I opened my eyes and focused on the sheet of music in front of me, then began to play. I tried to take in the notes written on the page and send them directly on to the tips of my fingers, only letting them pass through my mind for an instant. Amazingly, it worked, somehow; and when I reached the point where Vivaldi had stopped me just moments before, where he had demanded that I play it faster, I heard the music spill from my violin at the perfect speed, fast enough yet not too fast. I broke into a smile as I glided through it. From there I played on to the end without pause, holding out the last note perhaps half a beat too long, savoring it. When I finally looked up, I saw that Maestro Vivaldi's eyes were bright with approval.

"You see?" he said. "I told you that you could do it. It is that simple."

I smiled at his praise, and then, hesitating slightly, asked, "Did you write this?"

"I did."

"It is wonderful," I said, hoping that he could hear my sincerity.

"It is made even more so by your playing of it," he said.

That same strange and welcome warmth as before flared within me, starting somewhere in my stomach and creeping up to my face. Knowing his eyes were upon me, I was forced to bow my head to collect myself.

When I looked up again, he had turned away and was shuffling through a stack of parchment.

"I have another for you to try," he said, his back to me. He straightened up with another sheaf of papers in his hand and frowned. "Yet you are still not keeping your wrist precisely straight when you play," he said, his voice a bit more stern now. "We have a little more time yet; let us see if we cannot correct that once and for all. It will make reaching each note much easier."

I shook my head slightly, as if to clear it, and set my violin into position again, waiting for him to tell me when to begin.

I made it safely home again that afternoon without being detected. Yet just as I had ensconced myself in a seat by a window in my rooms with a volume of Petrarch's sonnets, one of the maids appeared at my door, telling me that my father required me to dine with him that evening.

My father was, more often than not, much occupied with business, and lately I had been—very happily—left to my own devices as a result. But I knew that the servants would report to him all of my doings, as needed. It had happened before; when I was about fourteen, I had slipped out of the palazzo one Carnevale night at dusk to watch the revelers, and dream of joining them. I had not strayed far; I even made it safely back inside without being seen. Yet about a half hour later, my father burst into my room, delivering a ferocious lecture as well as a backhand across my face. I never discovered which of the servants told, but since then I knew better than to trust them.

As my maid, Meneghina, dressed me in a presentable gown for dinner that evening, I briefly entertained the idea that this unexpected summons meant my father had discovered my secret trips. But I knew better. If he'd learned of my disobedience, he would have taken me to task in a display of unrestrained rage that would shake the walls. I shivered thinking of it.

He was already seated when I entered the dining room. "Adriana," he said in his deep voice, nodding formally in my direction.

"Father," I replied, before resuming my silence.

Servants brought out our soup, and one filled my wineglass with one of the crisp white wines that was produced on the mainland of the Veneto.

I had almost finished my soup—a salty broth with white fish—when my father finally spoke again. "I have some news for you," he said. "I am leaving the day after tomorrow to assist your brother with some business matters in Florence."

My elder brother, Claudio, had moved to Florence a few years ago to take charge of the d'Amato business offices there. As head of the company, my father made periodic trips there to ensure everything was to his satisfaction.

"While I am gone," he continued as the servants removed our

soup dishes, "your Zia Gianna will be staying here with you. We may expect her tomorrow."

"And how long will you be gone?" I asked.

"I plan to spend the summer there," he said as the servants brought out the next course.

I forced myself to temper my smile. My father's departure provided just the freedom I needed to continue my lessons. If the servants noticed anything during his absence—and Fortuna, that most capricious of goddesses, smiled on me—they would forget it by the time he returned.

My father put a piece of chicken into his mouth and chewed, scrutinizing me. He swallowed. "And when I return I shall focus on finding a husband for you."

My stomach lurched, as when one slips and narrowly misses tumbling into a canal. I had known that this would be coming soon: a few months ago, my father had sent away my tutor and stopped my daily lessons, saying I was eighteen and had learned all that was proper for a woman and more than enough to be a patrician wife and run a nobleman's household. Yet hearing it aloud gave it life outside of my own mind.

My father chuckled. "Surely this cannot be a surprise to you, Adriana. It is time you had a husband and, given the position of our family and your dowry, we shall have Venice's finest to choose from."

He had said "we," but I was not fooled. When I did not respond, he said, "Well, you have the rest of the summer to accustom yourself to the idea. I am expecting you to do well in marriage, Adriana, and to bring honor to our family. It is a woman's duty," he added, an edge of warning in his voice.

I bowed my head and nodded at my plate, my meal suddenly losing all appeal. "Yes, Father," I said quietly. There was nothing else to say.

4

THE CROSS I BEAR

"Stop, Signorina Adriana. Stop for a moment."

So intensely was I trying to unravel what seemed to be a very complicated section of music that I did not immediately register the maestro's words. It was not until he placed a gentle hand on my shoulder that I felt myself pulled abruptly back into the cluttered front room of his house.

"My apologies, maestro," I said, flustered and disoriented, not immediately realizing that he let his hand linger upon my shoulder longer than necessary. "I was just thinking . . . that is, I cannot seem to—"

He waved my attempted apologies aside. "You do not seem quite in your usual spirits today, Signorina Adriana, if I may presume to say so. Is anything amiss?"

I opened my mouth to reply, to tell him that I was quite well, that everything was fine, I was just tired, or it was the heat—for it was unseasonably warm that day. But instead, "It is my father," I blurted out. "He has just gone to Florence on business for the summer, but when he comes back, he is going to find a husband for me." I looked down, away from the Red Priest's penetrating stare. "I am sorry,"

I said. "I do not know why I told you. You certainly do not care about such trivial matters. I should—"

Vivaldi shook his head. "On the contrary. It is not trivial, and I do care. But I must confess I do not fully understand. I thought most young ladies wished to make a good marriage, if they are able?"

I studied him disbelievingly, but there was nothing but sincerity in his open gaze. "I suppose it is mostly that I do not want a marriage with the kind of man my father will choose for me," I said. "He cares little for my happiness, you see . . ." I trailed off, unable to put eighteen years' worth of anxiety and mistrust into words.

Vivaldi did not say anything. Then he motioned to my violin. "Put that away for now," he told me. He turned and disappeared through a door at the back of the room, emerging a moment later with a bottle of white wine and two glasses. "Music serves to cure all ills, yet a bit of wine never goes amiss either, no?"

I smiled, accepting the glass of wine he poured me. As soon as I tasted it, I knew it was cheaper than I was used to, but I enjoyed it all the same. It was sweet and soothing.

I sat in the tattered armchair near the fireplace, and he took the other, angling it in my direction. "So tell me, Signorina Adriana," he said, "what would you do with your life, if you could? If you did not have to marry?"

It was a question no one else would dare ask; a question I had barely dared to ask myself. Yet my answer was immediate. "I would play music. It is the one thing I have loved in my life, yet for so long I have been cut off from it. But even if my father let me"—Vivaldi's eyebrows lifted in curiosity—"there is no call for female instrumentalists, only singers in the opera." I paused, taking a sip of wine. "And I know I have to marry someone, someday, but I want my husband to be someone I love, that I choose for myself . . ." I trailed off and glanced at the maestro again, then looked down into my wineglass. "You are very kind to listen," I said. "But I do not wish to burden you with my troubles, nor do I expect you to understand the cares and wishes of a silly young woman."

"I am afraid I must contradict you again, signorina," he replied, a trace of emotion beneath his words. "You speak of music; who better to understand than I? What is more," he added, almost reluctantly, "I, too, know what it is to have a path chosen for you which is not what you would have desired."

I glanced back up, surprised.

"I am the eldest son of a family which was never particularly well off," he continued. "And so my parents decided the best chance I would have to advance in the world was the Church." He took another sip, staring at a spot on the wall behind me, as though he were seeing people and places and events long in the past. "I was a boy of fifteen when I was accepted into the minor orders for the priesthood; what was I to do? I was too young to have any idea of what I wanted. I still did not know ten years later, when I was ordained; but even if I did, by then it was too late. Even if I had realized what I know now." He shook his head, sighing.

I struggled to find my voice, spellbound by this side of him I never knew existed. "And what is it that you know now?" I asked softly.

His eyes snapped back to my face, almost surprised, as though he had forgotten I was there. "I am not at all suited for the priesthood," he said wryly. "I am the wrong sort of man altogether. My passions are not limited solely to serving our Heavenly Father, I am afraid." He smiled and looked away. "Strange," he said, more to himself than to me.

"What is strange?" I asked.

His eyes met mine again, an odd curiosity in them. "I do not believe I have ever told anybody that before," he said. "Only said it to myself, countless times, over and over again."

I remained frozen where I was, silent, unsure how to respond. *Why me?* a part of me wanted to ask. *Why tell me, of all people?*

"Still," he added, breaking what had turned into a long silence, "being a man of the cloth has had its advantages. Were I not a priest, I would never have been able to teach at the Pietà, or write music for them." He laughed. "For as long as that lasted." He tipped his head back, draining the rest of his glass. "At least I am not required to say Mass," he said. "A chest ailment," he explained, in response to my questioning look. "A breathing problem that plagued me greatly as a boy, but seems to have mostly sorted itself out as I have grown older. Nothing serious. A convenient excuse," he added with a smile, "though I expect the bishop was glad to be rid of me, as I got into a persistent habit of leaving the altar during Mass if an idea for a new composition struck me."

I laughed aloud at this.

Noticing my wine was gone as well, he refilled my glass, then his, without a word. He lifted his glass. "To us, Signorina Adriana. Perhaps the fact that we already know what our lives lack will at the very least keep us from spending our years wondering what is missing."

I touched my glass lightly to his, smiling.

"But one thing, maestro," I said, after we drank our toast. "That is enough of this 'signorina' nonsense. You must call me Adriana."

He nodded. "Yet I fear I must presume upon this familiarity a bit further. Would it do so much harm if you told me your surname?"

I considered this. Surely it could do no harm now.

"Just to sate my curiosity," he added.

"D'Amato," I confessed finally. "Adriana d'Amato."

His eyes widened. "Surely not," he breathed. "Then you are the mysterious daughter that Enrico d'Amato keeps under such close guard."

I flushed. "I had not realized that all of Venice knew of my circumstances," I said. "But yes."

He gave me a crooked sort of smile. "Never underestimate the might of the Venetian gossips, my girl."

"Then you understand why your discretion is of the utmost

importance," I said. "Nobody—especially my father—can know I've been coming here."

His face closed off slightly. "Is it your own reputation you guard so closely, or his?" he asked coolly.

"It is my skin I am guarding," I retorted. "And I mean that in the most literal sense you can imagine. My father has forbidden me to study music. Were he to discover that I had disobeyed him . . ." My voice wavered. "It would not go well for me."

Vivaldi sighed. "Forgive me, Adriana. Of course your secret is safe with me." We sat in silence for several moments before he spoke again. "Perhaps we had best finish our wine, and leave it at that for the day."

I agreed. As I drank the last of my wine, I was surprised by the degree to which unburdening myself—and hearing the maestro's confidences in return—had lifted my spirits. I took my leave soon after, glowing at how he had said my name, *Adriana*. It was as if he were saying the name of a favorite composition.

5

SPELLBOUND

During my father's absence, I was able to go to the maestro's house more often. Zia Gianna—my father's elder sister—had become a very wealthy widow upon the death of her much older husband some years ago. She had inherited a huge palazzo and estate in Mantua, and so far as I knew spent most of her time skulking about the place, upset that she lived there rather than in the fashionable city of Venice. As such, she scarcely paid me any attention, preferring instead to spend her time with her Venetian friends at parties, the opera, or visiting the shops at the Rialto. Indeed, she was so seldom actually present in our palazzo that I thought my father could have saved himself the trouble of sending for her at all.

The lessons were pure joy. Each day I could feel my fingers regaining their old strength and suppleness. Such were my enthusiasm, dedication, and—perhaps—talent, that I was soon able to play any piece of music Vivaldi put in front of me at first glance. However, sensing the fast progress I was making, the maestro began giving me much more difficult music—often his own compositions, along with those of others. He also took to instructing me on points of composition and the theory behind it; how music was and should be put together.

"See here," he said, while we were discussing phrasing one afternoon. "All music must return to where it began—the root of the scale, no?" Picking up his own violin, he played a quick C-major scale, upward and down again. "It always moves back to the beginning. If I were to begin the scale but then stop on the fourth note"—he paused, moving quickly up through the first four notes and then abruptly stopping—"it feels incomplete, and the listener is unsettled."

I nodded.

"The same is true of a piece of music, be it melody or harmony. This here, for instance"—he pointed with his bow to the sheet of music, a sonata by the old master Corelli—"if I play it like this . . ." He began to play the first bars of the sonata, then stopped at a random point, though he executed a customary rallentando before stopping. "It simply does not feel right, because I did not end on the tonic chord. Even those who have no understanding of music would feel that this is wrong and somehow incomplete. And again, the listener is unsettled."

"Yes, completely," I answered. Despite slowing as he reached his stopping point, it still had not felt final. It had put me almost physically off balance, a feeling not unlike reaching for the back of a chair to steady yourself, only to find the chair was much farther away than you thought.

He smiled, pleased I had grasped his point. "There are rules by which music must abide, even when you are not aware of them. Without such rules, it would be chaos, and one cannot convey much of anything in chaos. This is why you must consider more carefully which notes the music is moving toward, so that you may phrase the melody in a more meaningful way."

I spent much of the summer thus at the maestro's house, playing and listening and learning from a teacher whom I knew was second to none. Vivaldi was always pleased to see me, to hear me play, to give me a new piece of music. I thought that if I could spend my entire life this way—living, it seemed, always inside a song—I would be perfectly, absolutely content; happy, even, and would never ask for anything more.

One day in early September, I arrived at the Red Priest's house in a melancholy state: my father was due back in the next day or two. And almost as if he had known my spirits would be down, Vivaldi had something a bit different planned.

"Come in, come in," he said when I opened the door. "I have been waiting for you. I need your assistance."

My eyebrows rose. "My assistance?"

He nodded. "Here." He gestured to two music stands he had placed side by side.

I stepped closer and examined the sheets of music on them. It was a largo, a slow movement, for two solo violins.

Vivaldi moved to stand beside me, and when I turned to face him I saw his violin was already in his hand. "It is something I have been working on," he explained. "A concerto for two violins, in A minor, as you can see. I have heard this movement in my head for some time now, but I need to hear it aloud, with both parts played together." He smiled. "We shall have to imagine the rest of the orchestra, however."

"Are you sure you want me to play this?" I asked incredulously. "I am not sure if I—"

He interrupted, shaking his head vehemently. "You must not doubt yourself, Adriana," he said. "You are more than capable of playing this." He paused. "I *need* you to play it."

I had no idea what to say. I hesitated briefly before taking my violin and bow from the case and setting the instrument into position. I took my place, glancing at the maestro, awaiting his signal to begin. With a single brisk nod, we played the opening together: a series of simple unison notes. At another quick nod from Vivaldi, I took the first violin part, beginning the beautiful cantabile melody that seemed to drift effortlessly from the strings of my violin, almost like falling snow. After another four measures, Vivaldi came in, echoing what I had just played. His next measure consisted of a long F, and from there the melody tumbled into another gentle cascade of notes. I came in above him, on a high B flat, and from there our respective lines of music twined around each other in a tightly and inextricably bound duet.

I kept my eyes on the music, fearful of making a mistake, of spoiling this perfect tapestry of sound that we were creating; yet even so I could sense that every now and then Vivaldi would take his gaze from his own score and watch me.

Dio mio, *this is beautiful, more beautiful than anything I have ever heard*. Dimly I realized that I had stopped breathing for a moment.

The long strands of notes continued on, entwining and embracing one another like lovers, rising and falling like a sigh, like a breath. They fit together so perfectly that it did not seem as though Vivaldi could have written it; rather, he must have *found* it, fully formed; must have plucked this exquisite music from thin air, from some enormous body of music that already existed around us, audible only to those who sought it.

The tenderness of the minor melodies was so heart-wrenching, so painfully beautiful, as to make playing it almost terrifyingly intimate, as if in doing so I was seeing the maestro's naked soul, and he could see mine. I shivered slightly, pressing the feelings of fear and exposure into the bow hairs, the strings; let it bleed into the music.

As we neared the end of the movement, I could see that the last few measures were simply a repetition of the chords at the beginning. As we entered those final measures, I tore my eyes from the music and turned to look at Vivaldi, only to find his warm, dark eyes already seeking mine as we ended the piece together in perfect unison.

We stood, eyes locked, until the last traces of the music faded completely and we were only ourselves again, but somehow not quite the same as we had been only minutes before.

Finally he lowered his instrument, and, exhaling shakily, I did the same. Breaking the loud silence that always seems to follow a powerful piece of music, he said, keeping his eyes on mine, "It is just as I have always said. You play the *music*, Adriana, not just some notes on a page, but something far greater."

"I . . ." I did not know what to say, nor could I bear his gaze any longer. I looked down at the floor. "Surely I . . ."

He did not seem to hear my barely formed protests. My heart quickened as he stepped closer, reaching out and placing a hand gently beneath my chin, tilting my face to meet his eyes again. "It is as if you were able to read my thoughts, to know what I was feeling as I wrote this . . ." He trailed off, and slowly, carefully, his hand began tracing the line of my jawbone, caressing the curve of my cheek.

I was frozen, unable to move, unwilling to do so. Unthinkingly, I closed my eyes and leaned ever so slightly into his touch, into the feverish heat of where his skin met mine. He drew nearer to me, the cloth of our clothing whispering as it brushed together, and his fingers trailed lightly down my neck, resting at the nape, drawing me gently toward him. Our lips were almost touching. I could feel his breath caressing my skin as I inhaled his scent. I could hear his heart beating, or was that my own? My existence shrank down to the pounding in my ears, and his lips, just a hairsbreadth from mine.

Some part of me knew I could close the distance between us with little more than a breath. Instead I waited there for him, suspended, wanting the tide to draw me under or cast me out to sea. I felt certain, somehow, that I was going to drown.

Suddenly, he pulled back and moved away, putting several long paces between us. "I am sorry," he said, looking away and running his fingers through his hair. "I should not have—"

"No, no," I assured him. "I—" I broke off, not having the slightest idea of what I meant to say next. That I liked his touch? That I wished he had continued? That I wanted him to kiss me?

Did I?

A heavy, uncomfortable silence stretched between us, and I felt as if it were stifling me, leaving me alone, too alone, with my thoughts.

Finally Vivaldi spoke. "Perhaps you should go," he said, still not looking at me. "I do not think . . ." He trailed off awkwardly.

Struggling to find my voice, I nodded. "Yes, I believe you are right," I said, putting my violin and bow back in their case. I walked quickly to the door, stopping just as I reached it. "Shall we say . . . three days hence, at the same time?" I ventured. Vivaldi nodded in response. With that, I took my leave, only to spend the rest of that day—and the next, and the one after—trying to understand what, exactly, had happened.

6

MODULATION

Two days later, my father returned from Florence. All at once, the atmosphere of the house changed from peaceful to full of tension and gloom—or perhaps I was the only one who felt that way.

In the furor that the master's return had sent the servants into, I almost missed a familiar face in the bustle of the entrance hall: Giuseppe Rivalli, my brother's manservant, looking a bit worn and dusty from the long journey.

I smiled at the sight of him; glad, as always, to see him. Though he had long been in the service of my brother, it was I with whom he was closest. Giuseppe and I had grown up together; his mother had been a servant in the household, and my parents—especially my mother—had taken a liking to him as a boy. He was two years younger than Claudio, and always had the time for me that my brother, believing himself at six years older than me to be too important to be bothered with a tangle-headed younger sister, did not.

After my mother's death of a fever, my father finally decreed it was no longer proper for me to spend so much time with a servant—especially a male servant. Giuseppe was given permanent duties in

Claudio's household, and we were not able to see each other as often—and then not at all, when he moved to Florence with Claudio.

"Giuseppe," I said, approaching him with a warm smile. Upon seeing me, he bowed courteously. "To what do I owe the pleasure? Has Claudio come back to Venice, then?"

He sighed, his weariness showing on his face. He had smooth skin, tanned from running errands in the sun, and his hair was a rich dark brown. His brown eyes were wide and striking, and his face hovered between rounded and angular. Had I not known him since childhood, I would no doubt have been forced to concede that he was a very handsome man.

"No, Claudio is not with us," Giuseppe said. "He has dismissed me, as a matter of fact."

"What?"

"Yes," he said, with a somewhat crooked smile. "Said he preferred to have a manservant who was a Florentine. Why this should bother him after all these years, I know not." He shrugged. "So Don d'Amato brought me back with him, as you see. He said he would find some work for me here."

"*Grazie a Dio,*" I said. "I am so happy you will be back in Venice!"

He smiled again. "I am happy to be home, as well."

"Where is Father?" I asked, not without apprehension.

"He is downstairs at the water entrance, supervising the unloading of the luggage," Giuseppe said.

I nodded. "I shall make myself scarce, then, until I am summoned." I gathered up my skirts, preparing to dash upstairs to my rooms, but Giuseppe put a light hand on my arm to prevent me.

"Wait," he said softly. "How are you, Madonna Adriana?" His eyes searched mine. "You have been keeping out of trouble, yes?"

I knew what he really meant: *You are not doing anything for which your father will feel the need to punish you, are you?* I bit my lip, unable to lie to Giuseppe, but unwilling to tell him the whole truth.

Yet having him in Venice was a boon I had not expected. He could be of help to me.

His look changed to one of concern and almost disapproval. "What are you on about now, madonna?" he asked.

I shook my head. "Nothing, Giuseppe. Nothing you need concern yourself with."

He released my arm, watching me carefully. "Take care, madonna," he said. "You *will* take care, yes?"

I nodded. "Of course. Please do not worry about me."

"I shall try not to," he said, smiling slightly.

As expected, I received a summons to dine that evening with my father and Zia Gianna, who would be returning to Mantua the next day. Meneghina dressed me in a pale pink gown trimmed with lace, slightly more formal than I would normally wear, but not too formal for a family dinner.

"Well, Adriana," my father said, once the three of us were seated and the servants had brought our pasta course, "you are looking quite well. Gianna tells me that everything here went very smoothly."

His dark, sharp eyes held a veiled threat that said in no uncertain terms that, should he hear otherwise from anyone else, I would be the one who would pay for it. "Indeed it did, Father," I said.

"Good," he said. "I am glad to hear it."

"And I trust your business in Florence went well? And that Claudio is well?" I inquired, not because I cared, but because it was expected that I ask.

"Well enough," he answered. "Claudio is much the same as ever." My brother was apparently still making as much time for drinking, gambling, and whoring as he had in Venice. He smiled first at me, then at his sister. "Though I shall not bore you ladies with business talk. Gianna, I trust you enjoyed a pleasant stay?"

Zia Gianna launched into a recitation of everything she had done in Venice, the goods she had purchased, the people she had seen, and what each of them had been wearing. I could see quite plainly that my father didn't care, but it would have been discourteous to cut her off.

In the course of my aunt's tedious tirade, I felt myself slip into memory. I found myself remembering Vivaldi's hand on my face, my neck, the heat of his skin against mine; how close he had come to kissing me, how I wondered what might have happened had he not stopped. The heat in my face began to spread down through the rest of my body.

Much to my horror, I heard my father calling my name. I abruptly pulled myself from my daydream. "Yes, Father?" I asked, struggling to keep my voice even. "Forgive me, my mind was wandering."

He eyed me suspiciously. "Your aunt complimented you on your modesty, Adriana," he told me.

"I—oh," I said, looking across the table at Zia Gianna. She was nodding.

"Truly, Enrico, I never heard a word out of her when she was not spoken to," she said. "I cannot see why you are always going on about her willfulness."

"I thank you for saying so, Zia," I said.

My father, meanwhile, was still studying me. "Your face is quite red, Adriana," he said. "You are not taking ill, I hope?"

"No, no," I assured him. "I was just not expecting such a compliment."

"I see," he said. Then Zia Gianna claimed his attention again, and he was forced to let me be.

When the servants brought in the *dolci* a bit later, there was a lull in the conversation, and I took the opportunity. "I see that Giuseppe Rivalli has come back to Venice, Father," I said casually, before taking a bite of my custard with strawberries.

"Yes, Claudio no longer required his services," my father said. "I am sure we can find something for him to do here."

"Perhaps he could act as my personal footman," I suggested. "I have known him since we were both children, after all, and he has always served me well—when he was not busy serving my brother, that is. And I should hate for him to feel like he was not needed."

My father chuckled. "You have a good heart, Adriana." I could hear the second part of the sentence, the part that he could not bring himself to say aloud: *just like your mother.* "That is just as well. I suppose it is time you had your own footman to take you about in the gondola, or to the shops and whatnot."

I smiled. "Thank you, Father."

7

DECEPTIVE CADENCE

The following day, when I was due to return to Vivaldi's house for my next lesson, I let Giuseppe in—somewhat—on my secret. I had him take me to the shops at the Rialto and instructed him to wait there, and that I would return in no more than two hours' time.

He eyed me reproachfully. "What are you on about, Madonna?" he asked. "Where are you going? What are you doing there?"

I laughed. "Goodness, Giuseppe, you need not sound as though it is so dire. It is nothing to worry about; I am not doing anything dangerous or scandalous." Yet I found myself thinking twice as I spoke that last word, remembering again that almost-kiss.

"If it is nothing questionable, why can you not tell me?"

I sighed. "Because if you do not know where I am going, then you will not be lying if you need to tell my father so."

"If it is something of which your father would not approve, then it *is* dangerous—for both of us," he told me. "You know this. And what if something were to happen to you? What if you did not return?"

I wondered what exactly Giuseppe thought I was going off to do.

"You need not worry," I said. "I will be perfectly safe. You *must* trust me."

"I only wish—"

"Please, Giuseppe," I said. "Do not press me." I paused, pointing to a small café situated in a lovely spot on the Grand Canal. "Go sit there, have a glass of wine, or a brandy. I will meet you there." With that, I set off, melting into the crowd of people before he could say anything else.

Upon my arrival, the lesson began as usual. Vivaldi made no mention of what happened the last time. The only change—if I was not imagining it—was that when he lightly touched my fingers or wrist to correct my position, he did so briefly, and did not let his touch linger, as he had in times past. Indeed, so casual was his behavior that I found myself wondering whether or not he had even remembered, or if he had simply put it out of his mind as soon as I left. That did not seem quite fair; that something that had so haunted me for the past few days should not have had the same effect on him. That beautiful, somehow vulnerable music we had played, and that moment after—brief and fleeting though it was—had changed something in me. What, I did not know; but what did seem obvious was that he had managed to remain entirely indifferent.

Perhaps it is because you are a silly, inexperienced girl who knows nothing of the world, whereas he is a grown man, a voice in my head hissed at me, even as I was fighting my way through a difficult E-major concerto he had put before me. *And he is a priest.* But I thought of him as a man first, a musician second, and a priest last.

No, that same nagging, irritating little voice contradicted me. *You began to think of him as a man only three days ago . . .*

I abruptly stopped playing, heaving a loud sigh of frustration—at both my uncomfortable thoughts, which were sticking in my skin like burrs caught in my gown, and at my inability to play the music that was before me. "I cannot do this!" I cried.

As soon as the words left my mouth, I recognized how impetuously childish I sounded. I sighed again, this time in repentance, and transferred my bow to the same hand that held my violin, rubbing my forehead with the other. "I am sorry, maestro. I do not know what has come over me today."

I was so weary of lying all the time, about how I felt, what I thought, where I was going, what I wanted. I was always lying to someone: my father, the servants, Giuseppe, and now Vivaldi. Vivaldi, the one person whom I had thought I would not have to lie to.

He frowned and moved forward, as if to take the music from the stand. "Perhaps you are right," he said. "Perhaps this is too difficult. Maybe it is best left for another time . . ."

I shook my head firmly. "No," I said, irritated that he would say such a thing; especially after the last lesson, when he had said I played so beautifully. Or had he forgotten that as well? "I can play it," I told him.

Setting my violin into position once more, I took a moment to glance over the notes on the page once before beginning again. I would ignore him, I resolved; I would ignore him and play as though he were not in the room, as though I were playing for just myself. There would be only music in my mind.

I put my bow to the strings and began to play the opening notes, tentatively at first, then with mounting confidence as I progressed. Before long I was furiously attacking each measure, picking my way through the thorny clumps of notes on the staves without hesitation, flying through them with an almost reckless abandon; but, instead of making an absolute disaster of the piece and a fool of myself—as I had half expected—I was playing it *correctly*. And better than correctly. It was almost . . . lovely. It was as though some other, more competent violinist had stepped into my body and begun to play for me, showing the maestro that I *could* play it, and well. That was when

I realized I was not ignoring him at all; rather, I was intensely aware of where he stood, several paces away from me, watching and listening carefully. But instead of allowing him to confuse and fluster me, I was pouring my very frustration into the music—which was just where it belonged. If my true feelings, my true thoughts, could have no other expression than through the strings of my violin, then I would play them louder and more boldly than I would ever dream of speaking them.

By the time I brought the piece to a close, I was breathing heavily from exertion, and beads of sweat had gathered on my forehead. I allowed myself a moment in which to catch my breath, then turned to face Vivaldi, curious to see his reaction but unwilling to appear so.

His expression was that of a man trying to stop an enormous grin from spreading across his face. "Well done, Adriana," he said. He threw his hands up in surrender. "I see that I am proved quite wrong."

It was somewhat infuriating to realize that voicing his doubts over whether or not I could play the piece had been intended to have exactly this effect: to challenge and prod and even anger me into playing it as well as—possibly better than—he knew I could.

"Now I must put my mind to finding something that will truly challenge you, *cara*," he said.

I froze, startled. *Cara*. Dear one.

He quickly turned away from me and walked to his desk, hunting through the stacks of music there.

I watched him shuffle through the sheaves of parchment, and without thinking, I said, "Maestro . . ."

He straightened and turned to face me. "Yes?"

I opened my mouth, yet this time no words came out, although the ones I would have liked to say were not far to seek: *Why did you nearly kiss me a few days ago? Do you wish you had? Do you still wish to? Is that why you have scarcely looked me in the eye all day?*

But when he continued to look at me expectantly, I sighed and simply said, "It is nothing."

8

IMPROVISATION

In the first week that my father was home, I heard nothing of potential suitors. I knew better than to take heart from this, for my father simply needed some time to settle back into business in Venice after his absence. It was a temporary stay of execution. The axe would fall eventually; it was just a matter of when.

For the time being I went about my business, carefully sneaking out to Vivaldi's house for lessons, and trying to practice behind closed—and locked—doors whenever possible. The music that the maestro was now giving me made it essential that I practice as much as possible, so that I did not disgrace myself under his discerning ear. Giuseppe continued to assist me in leaving the palazzo, though he was not happy about it. I still had not told him where I was going, nor did I intend to.

Then, in the second week after my father's return, I got the news I had been dreading.

I was just dressing for the day when my father's manservant appeared to tell me that I was to report to his study immediately. Meneghina finished lacing my gown and quickly pinned up my hair, then left.

Remaining seated at my dressing table, I stared at my reflection in the gilt-framed Murano glass mirror, gathering my courage. I smiled, practicing for the moment when my father delivered me news of some suitor about whom I must pretend to be happy; yet even to me, the smile looked fake, forced, fragile.

I took a deep breath and rose, knowing I could delay this no longer.

I made my way to my father's study, which was on the floor below my rooms. The door was already open, and I halted in the doorway, awaiting permission to enter. When he looked up from the papers on his desk and caught sight of me, he waved me forward.

"Adriana," he said, as I came in and sat in one of the silk-upholstered chairs facing his desk. "I wanted to give you fair warning. I shall be hosting a party here a week hence, and I shall need you to play hostess. The guests will be largely my business associates and investors and their wives—also their sons." His expression became stern. "Needless to say, I am hoping you may find a potential suitor or two among them, and as such, I will require your full cooperation, and will expect you to look your best."

"Yes, Father," I said, because it seemed that I was expected to say *something*.

My father tended to keep me shut away in my rooms when he had company over, citing the loose morals of Venetian society. Yet now that a husband was needed, he was forced to loosen his hold, if only slightly. Under the circumstances, though, I realized that I much preferred the role of cloistered virgin to chattel for sale.

"Very good," he said, turning his attention back to the documents before him. "I am glad we understand each other." There was a brief pause, and he glanced back up at me, as though surprised to find me still sitting before him. "That is all. You may go."

I rose wordlessly to take my leave.

I swept back down the hall and up the stairs to my rooms, jaw clenched tightly to prevent the ugly, jagged emotions I felt from spilling onto my face. When I reached my bedchamber, I locked the door behind me and removed my violin from its hiding place beneath the bed. My fingers itched to play; it was the only thing that could bring me any modicum of solace at this particular moment, and damn any who might hear me.

My fingers scurried up and down the fingerboard to match the speed of my bow, picking out a rough melody that was not beautiful or soothing, but harsh and prickly, and perhaps the more powerful for it. I leaped between notes, sprinkling in dissonant chords as I went. The melody seemed to slide from the strings, curling itself up my arm and twining around my body, a sinuous serpent that held me in its grasp.

When the melody—or whatever it had been—finally came to an end, I felt a great deal calmer. My emotions receded and the musician in me came forward, wondering what it was that I had played. Yet as I put the bow to the strings to try to play it again—more slowly this time, so I could study it—nothing came. It had slipped through the cracks in my mind, and though I stood there and tried and tried, I could not remember it. The melody was gone.

The party my father gave was more or less what I had anticipated. Meneghina laced me into a gown chosen by my father: one that was cut to show off my figure just enough but not too much, one that was fine—of green silk and lace at the neckline, bodice, and sleeves—but not the finest that I owned. My dark curls had been tamed and hung halfway down my back. I did look rather lovely, I thought, but this caused me to grow more despondent, as those who would see me were not ones for whom I would have chosen to look beautiful.

The evening began in the large ballroom of the *piano nobile*, where my father received his guests and introduced them to me. It was a blur of names and faces: business associates and members of the Grand Council and their wives, as well as a member of the

Signoria and his son. The young man—Lorenzo or Luca Morosini, some such thing—was seated beside me at dinner, where he proceeded to regale me with his views on such varied topics as Venice's Jews—who, he felt, were treated much too leniently—as well as his dislike for the opera. He found it distasteful to see the divas wearing so much makeup and such scandalous costumes, for only whores would put themselves on such display. In fact, according to young Don Morosini, women should not be encouraged to engage in the arts at all.

"Take that ridiculous woman artist, for instance; what is her name?" he asked, nodding imperiously at the servant who had appeared to refill his wineglass. "Rosalba. Stealing commissions away from the rest of the artists in Europe, men who have trained and studied for years, all to be passed over in favor of a *woman*."

He was as old-fashioned as the most elderly grandfather of the republic. My father would adore him. I had to hope that they did not get a chance to converse later in the evening, or I might wake to find myself betrothed to the monster.

The only respite I had was from the man seated on my other side, Senator Giacomo Baldovino, and he was hardly any better. He was old, older than my father, with a belly that suggested he partook of the finest foods and beverages without *quite* overindulging. He was apparently a lifelong bachelor, and he went on at length about his family palazzo, which was much in need of renovations and, he hinted, a woman's touch—all while glancing obviously and appreciatively at the hint of bosom revealed by my gown's neckline.

Later that night, once everyone had finally, *finally* departed, my father followed me up the stairs to my rooms and settled himself in one of the chairs in my sitting room. "Senator Morosini's son seemed rather taken with you," he said. "He is a younger son, of course, but to marry into a senatorial family is a high honor for a girl without noble blood."

Exhaustion made me blunt. "And does it matter that I was not in the least taken with him?" I asked.

His eyes darkened and his smile hardened. "No, it does not," he said. "You are a girl of eighteen. How can you be expected to know what sort of man will be best for you?" He lapsed into silence for a moment before continuing. "Senator Baldovino was also quite taken with you," he said. "He expressed a wish to call on you."

I gave him a disgusted look. "He is older than you are, Father."

He laughed. "I am well aware, *figlia*. I anticipate there will be better prospects yet for you—and younger ones, as well. Senator Baldovino comes from a minor noble family, and owes his seat in the Senate more to the accomplishments of his esteemed late father than to any political talents of his own. Still, he is an old friend, and is powerful enough in his own right, so it would hardly do to offend him. And you should consider yourself honored that a senator wishes to pay court to you." He rose from his chair. "High time you slept, I think. *Buona notte, figlia*."

"*Buona notte*," I said woodenly. It was all I could do not to slam the door behind him.

9

DISSONANCE

Senator Baldovino came to call on me a week after the party. As we drank wine in the parlor, he spoke of people in Venetian society whom I did not know, and tedious governmental happenings I could not bring myself to care about. I replied when necessary, and was perfectly polite, even though inside I was screaming. He took his leave before long, thankfully.

I had other matters on my mind by then as well. It was almost the beginning of October, and I would need to pay Maestro Vivaldi for my next month of lessons. I would wait until Thursday of the following week. Among his other business interests, my father owned a share in one of the glassworks on Murano, and went there most Thursdays to check on production and consult with the other investors.

After lunch on the appointed day, I was reading in one of the window seats in the library when I saw my father step out onto the dock in front of the palazzo and get into his gondola to make the journey across the lagoon. I had to act quickly, before my courage failed me.

I set my book aside and headed for his study, hoping I need not be forced to explain myself to any of the servants. I opened the unlocked door—one of the maids would be in to clean soon—stepped inside, and closed it behind me. I went to the desk and opened the top right drawer, where beneath a great many papers was the small wooden box that held the key to the safe.

I crossed the room and removed the painting of the Grand Canal from where it hung on the wall; behind it, built into the wall, was the safe, which I unlocked. Inside were piles of gold ducats, important papers, and some of my mother's more costly jewels.

I extracted a small velvet pouch from the bodice of my dress and counted out the ducats I would need into it. I drew the drawstrings tightly closed and was just closing the safe when the door to the study opened behind me.

I whirled around in fright, one hand over my furiously pounding heart and the other clutching the purse of coins, to see my father standing in the doorway, looking like the very personification of wrath, his favorite of all the deadly sins.

He must have returned for something he had forgotten, not that it mattered now. He had discovered me. There was nothing I could do about it, no way I could explain myself, nothing to stop the storm that was about to break over and crush me as surely as a ship dashed against the rocks.

"Father," I said. "I—"

Without bothering to speak, he crossed the room to where I stood in three long, angry strides and struck me, the back of his hand crashing against my cheek with such force that I went tumbling to the ground, the pouch of coins falling from my hand.

"What in God's name do you think you are doing!" he roared. "Stealing from me! From your father! In my own house!"

Clutching the stinging side of my face, I got to my feet, backing away from him. "You do not understand," I said, thinking wildly for some explanation I could give.

He hit me across the face again, sending me stumbling into the wall behind me. "Oh, I know very well what you were doing, and why!" he shouted, spraying me with spittle. "Do you think I do not? Do you think I am a fool?"

"No, Father," I said, shrinking into the wall as he advanced on me. "That is, I do not—"

He seized me roughly by the shoulder, his fingers digging so hard into my flesh that I cried out in pain. He dragged me away from the wall and flung me across the room, into his desk. My other shoulder, as well as my back, slammed into the wood of the heavy desk as I fell, causing me to cry out again. Tears stung my eyes at the sharp pain, but I bit my lip, determined to hold them back. I would be damned if I gave him the satisfaction of seeing me cry.

"Yes, I know exactly what you have been on about!" he yelled, standing over me where I was slumped against the desk, so I could not rise to my feet. "I have heard the violin music coming from your chambers. Do you think I am deaf as well as blind?" He reached down and grabbed me by my hair at the scalp, pulling it loose from the few pins that had been holding it in place, and yanked me to my feet. He thrust his face close to mine. "At first I told myself I was imagining it, that I must be mistaken; that *my* daughter would never dare to disobey me, that she would never even think of it—" He twisted the clump of hair he held in his hand, and I felt my eyes water anew at the pain. I bit down so hard on my tongue to stop from making a sound that it began to bleed. "Because she would know the consequences that awaited her."

I did not even try to speak. It would have been futile, and I would sooner die than beg him to stop.

"And yet, what do I find?" he asked, with a low, dangerous whisper in my ear. "I find that very daughter of mine, to whom I have given the world on a golden plate, sneaking behind my back and stealing from me!" By the end of the sentence, he was shouting again and, with these angry words ringing in my ears, he took a step back, still holding me by the hair, and delivered one last, mighty blow to

my face with the back of his hand. I felt a wrenching in my n
my head snapped to one side, and bright sparks filled my vision.

He then wrapped his large hand around the back of my neck a
shoved me toward the door of his study. "Now get out of my sight,
and God help you if I so much as lay eyes on you again the rest of this day!" he bellowed, pushing me out into the hallway with such force that I stumbled and fell to my knees on the carpet. "You are never to touch a violin again while you are under my roof! And you are to stay away from whatever frittering fool you have convinced to teach you that confounded instrument!" he added. "God only knows what else he has been doing with you besides teaching you *music.*" He spat the last word. "And if I ever discover that you have disobeyed me again, Adriana, I shall not be responsible for what I do!" With that, he slammed the door of his study so hard the walls rattled.

I remained crumpled on the floor, fighting to compose myself. Then I slowly dragged myself to my feet, feeling acutely every last budding bruise, every last inch of my body that throbbed with pain. Several of the servants were peeking around doorways, having been summoned by the commotion. My face grew hot with shame.

Nevertheless, I would give them nothing further to gossip about. With my shoulders back, looking straight ahead, I walked down the hallway and to the staircase that would take me up to my rooms.

As I reached the staircase, I saw Giuseppe hurrying toward me from the opposite direction. His look of concern changed to one of shock and alarm as he saw me. "Madonna!" he cried. "Are you all right? Please, I—"

"Leave me, Giuseppe," I said, not looking at him as I began to climb the stairs.

"Please, madonna, let me—"

"I said leave me!" I shouted, picking up my skirts and practically running the rest of the way up the staircase to my rooms.

adonna!" I heard him call after me, but he did not follow. I ed into my sitting room and closed the door behind me. Then I ntinued into my bedchamber, where I shut and bolted the door be- ore sinking down onto the bed, my whole body trembling. But I did not cry. I would not cry. I refused.

MOVEMENT TWO

THE POINT OF NO RETURN

September 1710–December 1710

10

WITHOUT FEAR

Eventually I rose from the bed to go sit at my dressing table. I pulled the dangling, loosened pins from my hair and carefully picked out the knots with my fingers while staring blankly at my reflection in the mirror.

So my father had discovered my secret, the one I had been trying so desperately to hide, and his reaction had been exactly what I expected. He had exacted the punishment from my very flesh with that monstrous temper of his. Foolishly, I had thought that he would never hear me practicing—he was usually out during the day. Since he had never confronted me about it, I had assumed that my secret was still safe.

I had grown careless.

At least the punishment was over. But what now?

After everything, would I bend to my father's will? Would I, once and for all, have to give up music? And, more importantly, could I?

But I had no choice. I would not be able to procure any more money to pay Vivaldi for his tutelage, and leaving the house would be more difficult now.

hought of never playing music again—of never playing again—felt as if someone had taken a knife and thrust it n my ribs. It was more painful than any of the injuries my er had inflicted on me. To never again coax a glorious cascade of otes from the strings, to never again lose myself in the music, in that place that was not wholly of this world. My life would be empty and cold, a sepulcher housing a living corpse.

And to never again see Vivaldi, and have him look straight into me as if he understood everything, even the things I'd never spoken aloud to anyone.

My heart cracked at the thought. I had not imagined anything could be more painful than being cut off from music, yet somehow this last thought was. In a way, both thoughts were one and the same. I would miss Vivaldi and the spellbinding, excruciatingly beautiful music he wrote, and the music he was able to draw forth from me, which was beyond anything I ever thought myself capable of.

Vivaldi. I simply could not stop seeing him without explanation. He *had* to know. And I could not face the long, musicless days ahead without seeing him one last time.

And maybe, just maybe, there was still some way out of this. Maybe he would see something that I could not—another way out.

As soon as night fell, I would steal away one last time. I had to see him just once more.

I knocked as loudly as I dared on the door of Vivaldi's house, my violin tucked under my cloak to keep it out of the rain that had begun to fall. The skies had opened up not long after I left the palazzo; my cloak and hood were beginning to soak through, and my hair was plastered against my face and neck.

The front room of the house was dark, and there was no sign of anyone within. What if he was not even home?

"Maestro!" I hissed. "Maestro, please open the door!" I knocked louder as the rain began to fall harder. Lightning flashed, ing the narrow street for less than a second.

Finally, I saw him descend the stairs at the back of the carrying a lit lamp and squinting irritably out into the dark. He obviously dressed in haste, as he was wearing a plain black pair of breeches and an untucked white linen shirt.

He peered out the window and, seeing me, hastened to open the door. "Adriana?" he asked, letting me in, clearly confused by my presence at such an hour, and in such weather. "What in the name of—" He gasped as I pulled back the hood of my cloak upon entering, exposing my bruised and swollen face to the dim light. "*Mater Dei,* what has happened to you?"

I opened my mouth to explain, but the words caught in my throat as I saw the range of emotions that flickered across his face in the lamplight: horror, anger, surprise, indignation, concern. "My father," was all I managed to choke out.

Vivaldi's eyes widened in shock. "*Gesù Cristo,*" he breathed. "Your father did this to you?"

I nodded, unsure how to go on.

"Come, sit down, sit," he said, helping me out of my sodden cloak and leading me to a chair by the fire. He had me sit while he went about kindling a blaze in the grate. "We must get you warm," he muttered to himself.

"I . . . I am sorry to come so late, and to wake you, but I had to tell you," I said, once he had taken the chair beside mine. I set my violin on the small table between us. "My father found out that I was sneaking away for music lessons, that I had disobeyed his order that I am not to study music. He . . ." I looked down, away from his eyes, so full of worry and sympathy that I could weep. "He was not pleased with me. As you can see."

"Oh, *cara.*" He made a move as though to touch my cheek, and I felt a twinge of disappointment when he thought better of it. "I had no idea it was this bad."

.d. "And so I have come to tell you that I cannot study with .onger. I will not be able to get the money with which to pay out I could not simply stop coming without ever telling you y . . ." My voice broke. Oh, God, this was unbearable, worse than . had thought it would be. How had I thought I could cut him out of my life and leave no wound behind? "And I brought you my violin," I said. "I did not want my father to find it; he would destroy it if he did. I thought I might ask you to keep it safe. And you will have much more use for it than I will."

"Oh, Adriana," he breathed. He reached out and covered my hand with his, as though he could not resist any longer. He traced the outlines of my fingers with his, and I could feel the calluses that had formed on his fingertips from years of the playing the violin.

I knew that now I should rise and take my leave. But I couldn't. I remained where I was, closing my eyes and savoring his light touch.

Finally he broke the long silence. "I will continue to teach you, *cara,*" he said. He removed his hand from mine and ran his fingers across the strings of the violin on the table, making them hum. "Money or no. But it is your safety that concerns me, if I were to do so."

A flush spread through my entire body at his words. "Why?" I asked, unable to help myself. "Why do that for me?"

He smiled. "I must admit, the money did help me quite a bit of late. But if I am entirely truthful, I would miss your company most of all." He added hastily, "And, of course, you are one of the most gifted violinists I have met. It would be criminal for you to stop studying." His eyes met mine. "And I think I am right in saying that, for you, a life without music would be one not worth living, *sì?*"

"Yes," I said, surprised at his frankness. "There is nothing more my father can do to me, not truly. But if he succeeds in taking music from me, then I may as well be dead. I knew that you, maestro, of all people, would understand."

He sighed. "I do, though I have never been made to face such a choice, thanks be to God." He shook his head. "To think, if you were but a poor, orphaned foundling in this city, you would be able to study and play music freely, and perform it as well. Yet you have every luxury imaginable, except the one thing you truly desire. It makes one wonder who the truly lucky ones are, does it not?"

"I have thought the same thing often enough." We both fell silent for a moment before I spoke again. "Yet I could not ask you to teach me without any payment," I said. "It would not be right."

He reached out, without hesitating, and squeezed my hand. "Do not concern yourself with that," he said softly. "I will be here for you, when it is safe for you to seek me out again."

I turned my hand over and laced my fingers with his. Then, realizing what I was doing, I withdrew. "I should go," I said reluctantly, rising.

He hesitated. "You cannot go out into the storm," he said. "You will fall ill, walking all the way in such rain. Stay until it passes."

Every instinct was telling me to go, that the longer I was away, the greater my chances of discovery. Yet my desire to stay was far stronger. "I suppose you are right," I said, a quiet thrill running up my spine as I sat back down.

He stared into the fire, the corners of his lips twitching slightly upward. "When I was a boy," he said, "every time there was a storm such as this, I would leave the house and walk all the way to the Riva degli Schiavoni to watch the lightning over the lagoon." He glanced up at me and smiled. "It is quite a sight to behold."

"Would that we could go now and do just that," I said. "But you are right; we would no doubt catch our deaths."

He laughed. "I nearly did catch my death once or twice," he said. "I was often ill as a child, and such wanderings in the rain did not help matters in the least."

Outside, the rain continued to pound against the stone and splash into the canals, and thunder rumbled overhead. I shivered, moving my chair closer to the fire.

He jumped out of his chair instantly. "How careless of me," he murmured. He quickly disappeared upstairs, and then returned, carrying a thin wool blanket. He stepped behind me and gently moved my wet hair aside, so that he could drape the blanket over my shoulders. His fingers lingered on the back of my neck, then my shoulders, as he wrapped the blanket around me. I found myself wishing there was nothing between his hands and my skin. I shivered again, but this time it had nothing to do with the cold or damp.

Do not stop, I silently admonished him and, as if he heard me, his hands remained for just a moment before withdrawing.

I closed my eyes and leaned my head back against the chair, attempting to master myself.

"Perhaps you would like to rest for a bit? Upstairs?" he asked, mistaking my expression for one of exhaustion. His face turned slightly pink. "I did not mean . . . that is, I will, of course, remain down here."

I rose, letting the blanket fall from my shoulders. "You need not stay downstairs," I said, sounding braver than I felt. I stepped close to him, so that our bodies were only a breath apart, and laid my hand against his cheek. "You could join me."

A shudder ran through his body, and his hands reached up to cup my face. "Adriana," he whispered. Then, suddenly, he moved away from me and pressed his hands to his forehead. "Oh, God. No. We cannot. This cannot be. I am a man of God, and you—"

"Antonio," I said, the first time I had used his given name. He looked up at me, startled, and I could see the desire that had ignited in his eyes. "You are a man, and I am a woman. God need have nothing to do with it."

"You are a virgin." It was not a question.

Sweat began to coat my palms as I wondered how I possibly thought I could see this through. "What of it?" I asked, as though it did not matter, when in truth it did; it mattered more than anything in the world, that I *was* a virgin and was willing not to be, for him.

"Am I to believe that you have never been with a woman before?" I raised an eyebrow.

He threw me a glance heavy with desire and frustration and anger. "I have not always been a priest," he said, a touch sardonically, by way of answer.

When he said nothing further, I looked away from him, mortification seeping in and threatening to choke me. "Do you wish me to go?" I asked. I was beginning to feel I had made a horrible mistake, one I had no idea how to fix. If it was indeed possible to fix it.

"No," he bit out, looking angry with himself for saying it. "Yes . . . *Sancta Maria,* I do not know."

Shame and embarrassment washed over me. *He does not want me. I should not be doing this to him.* "I am sorry," I said aloud. "I will go." I took my wet cloak from where it hung near the fire, put it on, and began to walk to the door, keeping my head down so I would not have to look at him.

I had just reached the door when he seized me by the waist, spun me to face him, and kissed me; a passionate, bruising kiss that pressed my back up against the door so that I was pinned between it and his body.

I wrapped my arms tightly around him and kissed him in return, my mouth opening beneath his, and for a long moment we stayed locked in that strange embrace, the virgin and the priest. Then he drew back, took my hand, and led me up the stairs to his bedchamber.

Once inside, he shut the door behind us and turned back to me. Hands shaking, I unfastened my cloak again, letting it fall to the floor. I looked up at him, and my helplessness and anxiety must have been quite plain on my face, for he closed the distance between us and took me into his arms, pressing his lips to mine again. He then turned me so that my back was to him and began to unlace my gown, then my corset, until I was wearing only my linen shift. In the dim light of the only lit candle in the room, the bruises that had formed where my father's fingers had dug cruelly into my flesh were revealed. Vivaldi bent his head to kiss the swollen, discolored skin. I sighed and tilted my head to one side, and he moved to kiss the side of my neck. I felt a pleasurable throbbing between my legs as his lips touched the tender skin.

I drew away, turning to face him, and pulled the shift off over my head, dropping it to the floor. Now there was nothing between his gaze and me, but for as bold as I had been before, I was now unable to meet his eyes.

Gently he placed a hand under my chin and lifted it, so that I had to look at him. "Do not look away, *cara*," he murmured. "You are beautiful." He kissed me again, this time guiding me back into the bed behind me.

I slid beneath the coverlet, grateful to no longer be so exposed. Standing beside the bed, he removed his shirt and breeches, then got into the bed and took me in his arms.

Sensing my nervousness—had it been only moments ago that I so brazenly offered myself to him?—he began to speak as his hands moved over my bare skin, as though doing his best to put me more at ease. "You do not know," he murmured in my ear, "you can have no idea of how many times I have dreamt of this very moment. Night after night I would lie awake and think of this, imagine every last, beautiful detail. And each time I would tell myself that it must be the last, that I must not think such things again, only to dream them again the next night."

He kissed my neck again, his lips moving down my chest to the hollow between my breasts. I closed my eyes and arched my body beneath his mouth, heat prickling my skin.

I did not know what he expected or wanted; yet he seemed to know exactly the things I wanted, ached for, even though I did not know myself. When I, inexperienced as I was, returned his touch and kisses, he groaned and shifted himself atop me, one hand reaching down to caress my inner thigh. My heart rate sped up as my breathing quickened.

He paused. "Are you afraid?" he asked.

If I said yes, I knew he would stop. And that was the last thing I wanted him to do. I reached up to take his face in my hands. "No, Antonio," I said, my voice shaking and heavy with desire. "Of all the people in the world, I could never be afraid of you."

It was painful, with a bit of blood, as I had heard rumors of. But it did not matter. What mattered were his hands on my body, hungry yet gentle at the same time, as though I were something sacred, to be revered. What mattered was the feeling of being close, so close, to this man I loved in ways I was just beginning to understand. And what mattered were the words he whispered in my ear: that he was mine and I was his, that he would never hurt me, that I would be safe with him, always. That he loved me. And I believed his words as others believe in God: hoping that they would be what saved me.

11

END OF THE DREAM

I woke when dawn was only a few hours off, when the sky was still pitch-black. The rain had stopped. Slipping from bed quietly, I picked up my clothes from the floor and pulled them on as best I could, tying my corset and gown loosely. As I dressed, I studied the small room around me. It was plain and nondescript, with just the large bed, a window with simple linen curtains that looked out onto the street, a wardrobe—though his clothes were strewn about rather haphazardly—and a wooden crucifix hanging on the wall opposite the window. Even in the dark, I fancied that the crucified Christ's eyes watched me reproachfully. I turned my back on it.

I heard Vivaldi stir behind me. Eyes adjusted to the darkness, I saw that he had pulled himself into a sitting position and was watching me. "Where are you going?" he asked, his voice raspy with sleep.

"Home," I said, brushing my long, tousled hair away from my face. "I must get back before anyone discovers I am missing." I shuddered. "If they have not already."

"At this hour?" he asked. "You cannot simply go strolling through the streets of Venice alone. It is far too dangerous."

"I arrived here safely," I pointed out, scooping up my cloak—still damp—from the floor and settling it about my shoulders. "And it would be far more dangerous for me if it were to become known that I had left in the middle of the night."

He sighed, and I could see that he was rubbing his forehead in consternation. "Oh, *cara,*" he said. "What have we done? We—"

I crossed to him and placed a finger on his lips. "No," I whispered. "Please. I beg of you." I paused and drew a deep, unsteady breath as I tried to get the words out. "These past few hours have been the most beautiful of my life. Please do not ruin them with regrets and fear of consequences. There will be time enough for all that, if need be. Just . . ." I trailed off and looked at him beseechingly. "Please."

He sighed, then turned his head to kiss the palm of my hand. "Yes," he said softly. "You are right."

He got out of bed. "I will go with you," he said. "Just to see you home." I opened my mouth to protest, but he cut me off. "It is far too dangerous for you at this time of night, as I said." He began to hunt about in the dark for his own discarded clothes.

"What if someone should see you with me?" I asked him, a near panic rising to claw at my throat. "What if—God and the Holy Virgin forbid—what if my father was to see you with me?"

"And if your father caught you returning to the house at this hour, would it matter much whether or not there was a man with you?"

I considered this as he dressed himself. "No," I admitted. "But it is not myself for whom I am concerned."

"Nor am I concerned for myself," he said, looking for his shoes. "So we are perfectly matched."

Once he was suitably attired against the night air, we left, with me leading him through the maze of streets and canals to my family's palazzo. Fortunately, we met no one to impede us on our way. When we came within sight of the back entrance, I motioned for him to keep to the shadows, lest some vigilant servant should happen to be keeping watch.

I heard Vivaldi draw in his breath sharply as we drew nearer. "So this is Ca' d'Amato," he whispered.

"Yes," I said, "and were it up to me, I would never set foot inside again."

I turned to him in the shadows, only to find that he was moving to take me in his arms. Boldly, he bent his head to kiss me, pressing my back against the palazzo's stone wall. I kissed him back, mindful of what would befall us should anyone see, yet unable to stop.

"When should I return to you?" I asked as we broke apart.

Even in the darkness, I saw the look of uncertainty and chagrin that flashed across his face, leaving me terrified, for a brief and vivid moment, that he would tell me I could not return. "Two nights hence," he said, drawing back only a few inches, so that I could still feel the heat of his breath on my face as he spoke. "If you can get away."

"I shall if it is the last thing I do," I swore.

"And I will pray that it is not," he said. He kissed me one last time. "*Buona notte, cara.* May you sleep well."

I smiled, happily doubting that I would be able to do any such thing.

12

MEA CULPA

The next morning, as Meneghina was dressing me, my father barged in without warning. "Father," I said coolly, my tone belying the fear that was pumping through my veins. Had he discovered I left the night before?

"Give me that violin of yours," he said. "You will have no further need for it."

"I gave it to Giuseppe yesterday, and told him to destroy it, in accordance with your wishes," I said. Giuseppe would have his wits about him enough to lie for me if my father should question him before I could speak to him.

My father narrowed his eyes. "Oh, you did, did you?"

I widened my eyes. "I assumed you wanted it destroyed, so that it would not present any further temptation for me."

"Hmph." My father grunted in displeasure. I knew perfectly well that he had intended to destroy the instrument himself—or sell it, perhaps—after taking it from me. "Very well, then," he said. He began to walk toward the door, then stopped and turned back to me. "I trust that you will not forget what we spoke about yesterday, Adriana," he said.

Or, rather, that I will not forget what you beat into me yesterday. "No, Father," I said. "Rest assured I will not forget."

"Good." With that, he left my chambers, and I allowed myself to exhale, ever so slightly.

Each hour of that day, and the one that followed, seemed to crawl by at the speed of one of the slowest barges on the Grand Canal. I lived for nothing but the moment when I would be able to slip away again and return to Antonio. Even the dull pain between my legs served only to make the memories and longing even sharper.

I moved through those two days like a ghost, *uno fantasma*, keeping to myself, getting in nobody's way, unwilling to pull myself from the world within my head.

Yet the longer I was away from Antonio, the more my fears grew. I remembered how he had begun to voice his doubts, when we had awoken. And had he not hesitated when I had asked him when I should return? In my absence, might he not have come to regret his actions all the more? Now that he had time to think, away from me? I was almost paralyzed with fear at the thought that he would never wish to see me again, imagining him remorseful and angry and . . . *ashamed*. Then at other times I would tell myself I was being foolish; after all, he had told me to return, had he not? And how he had kissed me just outside the door of the palazzo . . .

And so my vicious cycle of doubt and reassurance went on. I barely ate. Sleep was all but impossible.

Finally, the appointed night arrived, and I again left the palazzo as soon as quiet began to settle over it. The possibility of being discovered was no less real or likely than it had been the first time, yet wrapped in a love-struck haze that was a potent mixture of fear, desire, anxiety, and anticipation, I did not dwell on it.

I arrived safely at Vivaldi's house, and knocked softly two times before going in. The state in which I found him was unfortunately more or less what I had feared.

He had evidently been pacing the floor, waiting for me, and stopped to look up when he saw me. "Adriana," he said. "Come in. I must speak with you."

I stepped into the dim light of the room and undid my cloak, trying not to let him see my shaking hands. "What is the matter?" I asked. But God help me, I already knew.

He began pacing again, as though unsure how to say what he wanted. I knew with a crushing certainty that I would not like it, whatever it was.

"I cannot countenance what I have done," he said at last, stopping and looking at me. Just as suddenly, he looked away, running his fingers through his loose, unruly hair. "I have defiled a virgin. I have broken my vows as a priest. I have put you in grave danger. I have . . ." He trailed off. "Ah, God!" he cried, his voice vibrating with anguish. "*Domine Deus,* how I have sinned . . ."

My breath froze in my lungs as I listened to him.

No . . . please, God, stop him saying these things. Does he not see? Oh God, Mother Mary, let me have this one thing, this one thing in all my wretched life.

Yet as fervent as my prayers were, I was uncomfortably aware that I was likely the last person God and His virgin mother were likely to hear. Surely the prayers of a lustful sinner were not answered, not when she was praying to sin again? But why should wishing for love and happiness be a sin?

"I must beg your pardon, Adriana," he said, collecting himself. "For the wrong I have done you. We must both seek penance, and not allow ourselves to be so tempted again."

I shook my head, as if to ward off his words.

"Please," I whispered, my eyes downcast. "Do not do this."

"Adriana." My name came out half sigh, half groan. "How can I not?" He began pacing again. "Do you not see what could befall us? What could befall you?" He stopped. "I could have gotten you with child," he said, not looking at me. "What would become of you then? As it is, I may have already ruined your chances for marriage and a respectable future—"

"But I do not *want* any of that," I argued.

He sighed. "You do not know what you want. You do not understand—"

"I do not understand?" I cried. "I understood perfectly well two nights ago, when you were making love to me."

He flinched. "Adriana, please—"

"I do not *want* to make a good marriage and refresh some nobleman's coffers and bear his children," I spat. "You know that, Antonio. I only want—"

"Do not say it," he cut me off. "Merciful God, do not say it. I will not be able to bear it if you do."

"Say what?" I demanded. "Say that I want only you? That you are the first beautiful thing that has happened to me since I can remember? That—"

"Yes! That!" he cried. "Do you not see? You cannot want these things! They can lead nowhere except to pain and despair and ruin!"

"I would have left," I told him, my voice low. "If you had told me to. If you had not stopped me. Remember that, Antonio, before you blame me for what's happened. I would have walked through that door if you had wanted me to."

"I am not blaming you," he said. "Not in the way that you think. Not—" He broke off and turned away from me. "It is both of us," he said at last. "We are both to blame."

Neither of us spoke or moved; we simply stayed locked in our silent struggle, standing halfway across the room from each other, not knowing how to draw closer or move farther away.

I finally broke the silence. "What now, then?" I asked, calling on all my strength to keep my voice from breaking, to hide everything inside me that was beginning to splinter. "What do we do now?" I continued, taking another step toward him. "Is this what you want? Because if it is, I . . ." I closed my eyes. "I will go, and never seek you out again."

He turned his head to look at me. "I do not know what else to do," he said, his voice rough. "I cannot protect you if I am your lover. This is the only way I can think of to keep you safe."

"Safe from what?" I whispered.

"Safe from . . . ah, God, from everything!" Without warning, he strode across the room to where I stood and seized me by the shoulders. "No good can come of this, do you understand? None!" He shook me slightly. "This can only lead to you being disgraced and dishonored, or me, or both of us! And what is worse . . ." He gently caressed my cheek, where the bruises left by my father's blows had begun to fade to an ugly greenish-yellow color. "I saw what your father did to you—and just for daring to learn music! I can see the marks from where he struck you yet," he went on, his fingers still outlining the marks. "What would he do if he were to learn that you had a lover? And one such as myself at that?" Tenderly he cupped my face in his hands. "He would kill you, Adriana. Even I can see that. A man who is capable of inflicting such brutal punishment on his own daughter is surely capable of anything."

At his words I felt joy and hope, fragile and daring as spring's first flower, begin to blossom in my heart. If he thought that his fear for my safety and honor would succeed in driving me away, he was wrong, for it was having precisely the opposite effect.

"Oh, Antonio," I said, reaching up to rest my hand against his face. "Do you not know that there are some things that are worth dying for?"

At these words, he violently clutched me to him, holding me in a tight, almost suffocating embrace. "Please do not, *cara,*" he whispered in my ear. "Please." He drew back slightly, so that he could see my face. "Listen to me—"

"No!" I cried, shoving him away roughly. "You listen!" I recognized how childish I sounded, so I took a deep breath, trying to calm myself. "Maybe . . ." I scrambled to gather my frantic, jumbled thoughts. "Perhaps none of those things—the dangers or shame or whatever it is that may lie at the end of this road—matters. Perhaps the good in this—the good which you said could not be—is simply what is here, now, between us, and is comprised of nothing greater than ourselves." I looked up to meet his gaze, startled by what I saw there: it was as if he wanted so desperately to believe me, yet a part of him still resisted. "Maybe . . ." I trailed off again, trying to think of how to make him understand. "Maybe it is not doing homage to some stern, unknown, unseen God that is the holiest of things one can do," I said, never taking my eyes from his. "After all, is it God or man who keeps such tallies of sin and virtuousness? Perhaps it is love which is sacred above all things, of God and man alike. And I do not believe, *amore mio*, that any God worthy of worship will condemn us for thinking so."

He stared at me for a long time. "Do you truly believe this, then?" he asked finally.

I returned his stare evenly, though inwardly I had reached my breaking point. I longed to scream at him, to beg him. Instead, I replied, "I have never believed in anything more."

"So now you will seduce me with your words, your beautiful words," he whispered, reaching out and brushing a strand of hair away from my face.

"I seduce no one," I said. "I would have you come to me of your own free will, or not at all."

Then, just as suddenly and violently as before, he crushed me to him. I could feel every line of his body, and he of mine. His lips brushed my hair. "This is madness," he whispered. His hands traveled downward, over my body, possessively caressing every curve. "Madness! You know that, yes?"

I nodded, my head buried against his shoulder. "Yes. But even knowing that cannot change how I feel."

"Nor I." I thought I heard him whisper, under his breath, something that sounded like the words *miserere nobis,* yet I could not be certain. But then his lips were seeking mine, and he was leading me to his bedchamber, and I returned to that world of passion and light and joy that I had recalled in my mind over and over throughout the past few days. I felt the ghost I had been disappear, and again I knew myself to be real, made of flesh and sensation and feeling.

13

ADAGIO

Again Vivaldi saw me home in the small hours of the morning, and I made it back to my rooms undetected. We planned to meet again in another two days' time, but I feared what his state of mind would be then. Would his resolve to end our relationship have returned, or had his doubts been effectively silenced? The only thing I could do was wait, and so I waited, beginning the torture all over again, like a prisoner counting the minutes until her release.

When the awaited night came at long last, my heart pounded as I reached his house. What man would I find looking out at me from his eyes tonight?

When I arrived, breathless, he was again pacing the room, waiting. I froze, certain he was about to unleash another litany of regrets, but upon seeing me, he crossed the room and in an instant had me in his arms. Wordlessly we returned to his bed, and he made love to me with an excruciating slowness that both tortured me and caused me to cry out with pleasure. *So this is what everyone whispers and writes and sings of,* I thought, before being consumed by sensation. I felt him smile against my mouth as he kissed me, and I clung tightly to him, hoping that this glorious fall would never end.

We did not know how many nights, how many hours, we might have together, and so each moment, each tick of the clock, had to be made to last. And he made it last exquisitely.

Afterward, neither of us slept, so we lay together in the bed, holding each other and talking, when we had something to say, and embracing the silence when we did not, hands lightly exploring each other's skin.

Eventually he asked me, "Why did your father forbid you to study music?" One hand absentmindedly caressed the curve of my waist. "I know that he did, of course, but you never told me why."

I shifted a bit, turning toward him. "It has something to do with my mother," I told him. "She was a famous singer, a soprano." I glanced up at him in the dark. "Lucrezia della Pietà."

He drew in his breath sharply in surprise. "She is your mother?" he asked.

I nodded against his shoulder. "My father heard her sing when he was a young man, and fell so in love with her just in hearing her voice that he made her an offer of marriage." I laughed. "That is the story, in any case. Whether it was really quite so romantic, I could not say."

"Incredible," he said. "She is still much talked of at the Pietà, one of the greatest, they say. I never heard her sing myself."

"Her voice was . . ." I paused. "To call it beautiful would not do it justice. As I child I thought that all of God's angels together could not sing as magnificently as she."

"But she was never allowed to perform again once she married," he said, knowing even better than I the restrictions that governed the wards of the Pietà. He sighed. "A waste. But what had this to do with you, and your father?"

"When I was about six, and it was plain that I had not inherited her voice, she hired a violin teacher to come to the palazzo to teach me," I went on. "It was the instrument she had always wanted to play, but never had the aptitude for. And, clearly, I turned out to have quite the affinity for it." I smiled. "She always called me her little *miracolo,* for after Claudio was born the midwife told her the birth had so damaged her that she would never bear another child. Yet I was born all the same.

"She died of a fever when I was thirteen, and my father stopped my music lessons. I suppose I do not really know why," I said, considering it all anew. "He says it is unseemly for a woman to learn music, which is certainly not how he felt when he met my mother; and of course, he is in the minority in his belief. Perhaps it is just that after my mother died, he could no longer bear to hear music anymore, could not bear the sound of anything beautiful." My fingers traced the lines of his chest as I spoke. "Perhaps it would have been different if I had been a singer like her; if I had inherited her voice. Then maybe he would have felt that there was a part of her he could still keep." I smiled. "But alas, I was only born to be a violin player, it seems."

"Then I thank heaven for that, *cara mia,*" he murmured in my ear. "For that is what brought you to me."

My whole body flushed with happiness at his words. I tilted my face to look at him, smiling. "And now it is my turn to ask you something," I said.

"Ask away."

My smile faded slightly as I spoke, my expression growing serious. "Why were you dismissed from the Pietà?"

He sighed heavily. "I did not much care for their rules," he said bluntly. "Rules for performing, for practicing, for the types of music that could be performed. It is hard to create in a place such as that. But the governors of the Pietà did not see it that way, and I disagreed with them, strenuously and often. Eventually they decided I was not worth the trouble, I suppose.

"And I miss it, in truth," he went on. "The skill, the talent of those girls, and the music they were capable of making . . ."

There was a part of me that, as his lover, could not help but be jealous to hear him speak so of these faceless, cloistered young women, whom few people were permitted to lay eyes on. Yet the musician in me was impressed and intrigued by the reverence with which he spoke of their abilities. "I have not heard the *coro* of the Pietà for many years, not since my mother would take me to Mass there," I said. "I doubt I would be allowed to go now."

Vivaldi raised an eyebrow at me. "Your father will not let you go to Mass?" he asked.

"He will not go to the Pietà—it is too painful for him—and in his current mood I do not think he would let me go alone, or with one of the servants," I said. "No doubt he would suspect me of some trickery."

"Then I do not suppose he would let you attend an opera, either?" Vivaldi asked.

I laughed. "It is quite doubtful. Why do you ask?"

"I know you would enjoy it immensely, even if none of the divas sing as beautifully as Lucrezia della Pietà. And perhaps," he admitted, with an almost sheepish smile, "it was a bit of a self-serving question as well, for I have been playing as the soloist for the orchestra at the Teatro Sant' Angelo for several weeks now."

"Aha," I said playfully. "Now I discover your true aim, *amore mio*. Rest assured I would come just to hear you play, but I fear the chances of that are nonexistent at present." As I spoke, sadness began to descend on me. "Let us not talk about this anymore," I said, my voice wavering slightly. I closed my eyes, resting my head against his shoulder.

I felt his lips brush my tousled hair. "Do you think things would be different for you if your mother still lived?"

I had no answer. So much had happened since she died that I had become accustomed to thinking of my life as divided into two separate, almost unrelated lives: the one before her death and the one after.

If she had lived, there would always have been music, and my father would not be so bitter and angry.

I struggled to pull my voice from where it had retreated, deep down inside me. "Yes," I whispered. "Yes, I daresay things would be different."

He sighed and rested his cheek against the top of my head. "If only there was some way," he murmured. "Something I could do to change things—"

"Please, let us not speak of such things," I said, cutting him off.

He looked as though he meant to argue, so I pressed my lips against his to silence him. After a moment, he pulled away, albeit regretfully. "Should we not be getting you home?" he asked.

I smiled and shifted my position, drawing him atop me. "Not yet, my love. We were quite successful at this a short time ago, no? I am anxious to see if we can repeat that success . . . Oh." I sighed as our bodies fitted together once more, and everything else was forgotten.

14

WHAT HAVE YOU DONE

Later that night, I watched Vivaldi slip away from my palazzo, waiting until he was safely out of sight before stepping into the small hallway. I waited a moment for my eyes to adjust to the darkness before carefully making my way through the sleeping house.

I had reached the first landing on the back stairs and was turning the corner to climb the next flight when I collided with someone. A scream rose to my lips as I stumbled back against the wall. A small choking sound came from my throat as I stifled it, and my heart quadrupled its pace, beating so hard and fast it was almost painful.

I quickly tried to run by the shadowy figure. But before I could get very far, my apprehender reached out and seized my shoulders in a strong grip, preventing me.

"Adriana!" he hissed as I struggled against him as silently as I could. "Adriana! Stop! It is me! Giuseppe!"

I stopped fighting and peered at his face in the darkness. "Giuseppe?" I sagged against him, all the fear immediately draining from my body. "Oh, thank God."

"I would not relax quite yet," he growled. "What in the name of heaven and all the saints are you doing? Where have you been? What—"

"Shhh! Not here, for God's sake." I grabbed his hand to lead him up the stairs. "Come with me."

"Where?"

"To my rooms, where do you think? I will tell you everything there, I swear, but please, just follow me before we wake the entire house!"

He acquiesced, and followed me to my rooms. I glanced furtively around the hall outside my door, but there was no one about. I closed and locked the sitting room door behind us, then led the way into the bedchamber, where I did the same. I turned from my task to find Giuseppe staring hard at me, his face white with anger, his lips set in a tight, thin line. He did not speak; he merely faced me, silently, waiting for my explanation.

I removed my cloak and walked past him to the wardrobe to hang it up. I was completely at a loss as to how to begin, to explain what I needed to without making myself seem like . . . well, a whore. I felt rather like a child squirming before an irate schoolmaster.

I cleared my throat, unable to quite meet his eye. "I—"

Again I was surprised as Giuseppe abruptly cut me off. "Good Christ, Adriana," he said. "Where on God's green earth have you been? I saw you leave," he said, causing my mouth to drop open. I started to speak again, but he held up a hand to silence me, as though he were the master and I the servant. "Yes, I saw you sneaking out the back entrance from the window in my room, and I have waited up all night for you to return. I saw you with him," he added, his voice hard, accusing. "Whoever he is." He threw up his hands. "What is the matter with you, Adriana? Was the beating your father gave you not enough to make you more prudent?" His voice rose, in spite of himself. "What can you be thinking? What—"

"First of all," I interjected, in a much softer tone, "keep your voice down. You will most certainly *not* help me—which I am interpreting as your true aim, as opposed to insulting me—by alerting the rest of the household to the fact that I left earlier, and have only just now returned."

Giuseppe had the grace to look slightly embarrassed.

"Secondly," I continued, "I promised that I would tell you all, if only you would give me a chance to explain. And," I added, "no matter how much you approve or disapprove of my actions, I need not answer to you for anything I do."

He looked as though he might argue, but he simply nodded and said, "I understand. My apologies, madonna."

I took a deep breath and thought carefully about how to proceed. Giuseppe might be quite useful when let in on my secret, although getting him to actually agree to help me was another matter entirely.

"I have been with a man, it is true," I began. "It is not what you think," I protested as he made a noise of disgust. "I . . . I love him."

"Love," Giuseppe spat. "Yes, I am sure that is what it is."

"How dare you—"

"Perhaps it is love for you, but it is likely not for him," Giuseppe said. "How can you be so foolish and naïve?"

"You do not understand!"

"Like hell I do not!" he said, in the loudest whisper I had ever heard. "I am a man. I know the sorts of lies men will tell women in order to get—"

"Please!" I cried. "You told me you would give me a chance to explain, and so far you have not done so."

He sighed at this, but remained silent.

"I love him," I repeated, my voice stronger now. "And I believe that he loves me. He cares for me, deeply, that I know. And he is concerned for me. He knows what manner of man my father is, and all that has passed between him and me of late."

"If he is so concerned," Giuseppe asked, "then why does he not do the honorable thing and ask for your hand?"

I laughed aloud at this. "He is not the sort of man I could marry. He cannot marry me."

"He is already married, then?" When I did not reply, Giuseppe sighed. "Who is it, Adriana? I will not tell, I swear—you know I would not do that to you." He shook his head. "Not even for your own good, which I have no doubt putting a stop to this would be. Just tell me his name."

I hesitated.

"Who is it?" he asked again, in a whisper this time.

I sighed. "His name is Antonio Vivaldi."

"*Madre di Dio!*" Giuseppe all but shouted. "Not the Red Priest?"

"Quiet!" I hissed. "Yes."

Giuseppe walked around the bed and seized me again by the shoulders, shaking me. "*Dio mio,* Adriana, the man is a priest!" he cried, shaking me again. "What is the matter with you? Do you have any idea what would happen if the two of you were found out?" Abruptly he released me and stepped back, trembling in consternation. "By the Virgin . . . the consequences would be catastrophic!"

"Do you think I do not know this?" I demanded. "Do you think he does not? I do not need you to remind me."

"Apparently you do," Giuseppe retorted, "for the knowledge alone has not been enough to stop you."

"It is not that simple!"

"Oh, Adriana," he said, his shoulders slumping as his large, sturdy body seemed to fold inward on itself. "What have you done this time? How is it that you cannot see the danger of your actions?"

"I can see it," I said. "Believe me, I can see it. I just do not care."

"That is even worse."

"There are some things, Giuseppe, that you risk everything for," I said. "And I need not—I *will* not—answer to you, nor do I care what you may think of me."

He laughed, a short, harsh sound. "But you do," he said. "You must, for you need me to help you, do you not?"

"I do not *need* your help," I said. "I do not deny that this would be easier that way, but even if you refuse, that will not stop me."

He sank down to sit on the bed. I did not protest the familiarity of the action; we were far past standing on propriety now. "God help us both," he said finally, after a long pause. "This is madness, you know. Utter madness."

His words echoed the ones Vivaldi had spoken two nights ago. *Yes, yes, we are all aware that sanity is something this venture is altogether lacking,* I thought with a tinge of humor. *At least everyone is in accord on that count.* "So will you help me?" I asked.

He shook his head, disbelieving. "Yes, God forgive me," he said. "I will. I will, even though I think this will be the ruin of us both, and of your Maestro Vivaldi as well, because I think that whatever slim chance we do have of coming through this lies in my helping you."

I smiled, allowing my relief to show. "Thank you, my friend," I said.

"Tell me this," Giuseppe said, rising to his feet. "Is it to him you have been going, all those times you had me wait for you near the Rialto? Has it been going on that long?"

"I have been going to him all along, yes, but it had not . . ." I was surprised to find myself blushing. "We were not lovers until last week."

"Then why . . ." Suddenly a look of comprehension crossed his face. "The violinist," he said. "He was the one giving you music lessons. That is how it started."

"Yes."

He laughed. "If only Don d'Amato knew what effect his discipline truly had."

"Let us pray that he never finds out."

"Oh, I shall," Giuseppe said, moving toward the door. "Believe me, I shall pray for that above all else. We will likely require divine intervention to come through this in one piece."

"If God exists as they say He does, then I am the last one He would be willing to help," I said.

Giuseppe laughed, in spite of himself. "It is better not to remind ourselves of that fact." He opened the door that led to the sitting room and paused in the doorway. "Good night, then, madonna. We will talk more tomorrow. Sleep well."

"Good night, Giuseppe," I said. "And . . . thank you."

He shook his head. "Do not thank me for anything just yet. Who knows what may become of us before this is over?" On that ominous note, he turned and left, shutting the door behind him.

15

LARGO

The next day, I set out to see an herb-woman whose name I had procured from Meneghina, under the pretense of needing a concoction for my skin. If I was going to carry on such a dangerous love affair, I could under no circumstances conceive a child. I had Giuseppe escort me to see the woman, and was given some herbs and instructed to mix a pinch of it into my tea or wine after each time I was with my lover. At least one worry was put to rest.

The following day, I was summoned to my father's study, where I was informed that we had received an invitation to a large party being given by the Foscari family to mark the end of the festival season in late November, when all the revelry of Venice would pause for Advent before resuming again on St. Stephen's Day.

The Foscari family was one of the premier noble families of Venice, having produced at least one doge, as well as managing to hold on to their vast wealth at a time when much of the Venetian nobility was losing their fortunes. Everyone of importance in Venetian society would be there—as my father wasted no time in informing me—and, naturally, it was assumed I would meet my future husband there.

"This promises to be a profitable evening for our family," my father said. "And I trust you will behave with the perfect decorum and grace that our family name demands." He did not add "or else," but the threat was implied. "You are to have a new gown," he added. "The dressmaker is coming tomorrow to fit you for it."

I replied with my customary "Yes, Father" and, when he dismissed me, rose and took my leave calmly.

I had dreaded the fitting, but by the end the dressmaker had given me a fairly vivid idea of what the gown was to look like, and I was looking forward, in spite of myself, to trying on the finished product—much as I did not like its intended purpose. It was to be made of a pale blue silk, trimmed with silver lace and embroidered with silver thread. The skirt would be slashed to reveal a petticoat of cloth of silver that was being specially made as well. The overall effect would no doubt be stunning, which both excited and depressed me.

Later that same night was to be my next tryst with Vivaldi, so once the dressmaker had left I summoned Giuseppe to my rooms.

"Tonight you will accompany me to his house, so that you know the way," I told him, my voice low. "Then you may go wherever you please, so long as you return for me after three hours."

He nodded, his expression betraying his discomfort. "As you wish, madonna," was all he said in reply.

I had been expecting a reprisal of his tirade from a few nights ago, not to mention all of the new arguments and reasons why I was utterly mad that he had no doubt thought of since. This resigned acquiescence was certainly much more welcome. "Very well," I said. "Return for me here at midnight. I shall be waiting for you."

He bowed and left the room without saying anything further.

That night, Giuseppe came for me at the appointed time, and I led him through the labyrinth of streets and canals to Vivaldi's house, telling him to make note of the way.

"Here it is," I said, as we drew within sight of our destination. "You will be able to find your way back here?"

He nodded.

"Very well," I said. "Remember, three hours."

"*Sì*, madonna." With that, he turned and retreated the way we had come.

I opened the door and slipped inside.

"Who was that you were speaking to?" Vivaldi asked, his voice hushed, taking my arm when I entered and drawing me further into the room, away from the windows. "Did someone follow you here?"

"No, no," I replied quickly. "You need not worry. That was Giuseppe Rivalli, my servant. He is to return later so he can take me home, and—"

"You told someone about this?" he demanded. "Adriana, what were you thinking? No one must know, no one! Do you know—"

"I had no choice!" I cried. "He caught me coming home the last time—and be thankful that it was him, believe me, for if it had been anyone else, my father would doubtlessly have beaten me bloody by now."

He flinched at my words.

"He will not betray us, *caro mio*," I said, stepping closer to him and cupping his face in my hands. "Have no fear. I would trust him with my life, and yours."

He reached up and took my hands firmly in his. "Are you certain?"

I nodded.

He sighed. "Very well, then. If you say so, *cara*."

Neither of us could sleep that night. We lay awake, hoping Giuseppe would never return.

"I have a question for you, Tonio," I said finally, turning to him.

He glanced at me, raising his eyebrows expectantly. "*Sì?*"

"I have been wondering when I shall get to play the violin again," I said. I grinned mischievously. "I have, after all, tendered you your payment thus far."

He winced. "Do not say that," he said. "You make yourself sound like a . . ." He trailed off.

"A whore," I finished for him.

He nodded uncomfortably. "Nor does it make me sound much better."

I shrugged. "I would rather be your whore than the wife of some insipid patrician."

He looked mildly scandalized by my words. "You should not say such things."

"Why not? It is true."

"Yes, but . . . even so," he said, apparently unable to tell me exactly why I should not say such things. He sighed. "So you wish to play, do you?"

I nodded eagerly, a child's wide grin spreading across my face.

He smiled in return. "Good," he said, rising from the bed. "Get up and dress yourself, and we will play."

Once we were both dressed, we went downstairs, where Vivaldi located my violin and handed it to me, smiling.

I immediately ran through a scale, happy to hear the rich, lovely sound coming from the strings. "I am afraid that I will get terribly out of practice now that I cannot play at home."

He plucked several sheets of parchment from his desk and set them on the music stand in front of me. "The only way to avoid that problem, then, is for you to come here more often, *cara*." He gestured to the pages before me—an A-minor concerto. "This is something I have been working on. Try it."

After glancing over it once, I took a deep breath to steady myself and began to play, noting how quickly the piece started out. I found that it never let up: it was one rapid succession of notes after another, leaping higher and then plunging back down. I knew Vivaldi and his music well enough to know that no one else could have written it.

Much as I tried not to think about what I was doing, what I was playing, I found myself forced to slow down at several points to work my way through certain tangles of notes; even so, I made a few small mistakes along the way, my fingers clumsy from disuse. I had a good idea of what the maestro would have to say when I was done, but so be it.

When I reached the end of the piece and glanced at Vivaldi, he gazed back at me impassively and said, "Play it again."

I complied, my fingers becoming much looser this time, my playing smoother. Once finished, I started again, determined to play it through perfectly. The third time was the best yet; I was able to play it as fast as was required, though I did make perhaps two or three noticeable mistakes. When I finally stopped, out of breath and invigorated, I admitted, "That may take a bit more practice."

He nodded, selecting another sheaf of papers from the table. "Yes," he agreed distractedly. "Leave that for now, and try the next movement, the largo." He placed the pages upon the stand and motioned for me to begin.

This movement was much slower, more languid. I moved through it with relative ease, playing it smoothly and cleanly. Once I had finished, I looked up triumphantly, expecting him to exclaim over how well I had played it. Instead, he merely shook his head and, with a scowl, said, "Dreadful."

In my shock, it took me a moment to find my voice. I stuttered, "What? . . . Why?"

"Dreadful," he repeated, his voice even. "I had not expected you of all people to fall into this particular trap, but you did. I thought you knew better, Adriana. What have I been teaching you all this time?"

"What do you mean?" I demanded, bewildered and slightly hurt.

"You played the allegro much better," he informed me. "Do you know why?"

"But I made several mistakes in the allegro," I reminded him. "I made no mistakes at all in the second movement."

He shook his head. "It is not about whether you made mistakes or not. It is about the *emotion* of the music, Adriana, and the feeling with which you play it."

I waited silently for him to elaborate.

He sighed at my inability to grasp what he was saying. "Think of how you played the allegro. You made mistakes, yes, and you were frustrated. You wanted very much to be able to play it perfectly, and because of that desire, that frustration, you played with hunger, and gave a liveliness and edge to the music." He moved across the room to where his own violin was kept and removed it from its case. "But because the largo is slower, and you had more time to think about each note, and how you would get to the next one, you did not pay as much attention to them, nor to the piece as a whole. I could hear the place in each and every long, drawn-out note where you gave up on it, where you stopped caring about it."

I opened my mouth reflexively to protest, but he was right, and I knew it.

He set his violin into position and lifted the bow. "Listen." Without so much as glancing at the music on the stand, he began to play.

It sounded like a different piece of music altogether from what I had just played. He held out each note lovingly, gently, tenderly, moving on to the next one with a certain reluctance, as though unwilling to let the previous one go. It sounded almost like a love song, wistful whispers tinged with sadness, as when one is thinking of one's beloved, yet cannot go to them. The thought was irresistible: *Had he written this for me?*

Yet the slow, languorous, sensuous strings of notes also made me think of the sun shimmering on the many glassy waterways of Venice, of the summer heat hanging low over the canals. Perhaps it was just as much a love song for this beautiful city, where one breathed in music from the air.

When he finished, he looked up and met my eyes. "Now do you see?" he asked softly, as though to speak any louder would be to disturb the spell the music had cast over the room. Over me. "There is more to it than just the music, just the notes—there must be, if it is to be worth listening to. I have told you that there is more to virtuosity than technique. I know that you love music more than anything, so you must let that *passione* infuse every note you play. You must let your listener hear it."

"Yes," I replied, my own voice hushed. "Yes, I see."

He nodded. "Then play it. Play it like the virtuoso that you are."

So I did.

This time I paid close attention to each and every note, to its sound and cadence and meaning, its place in the larger context of the melody. I began by playing carefully, gently, as if each note were a fragile, hesitant breath drawn in the silence. As I went on, I let my bow sink ever so slightly into the strings, giving each note a sense of urgency I hadn't heard before, that I hadn't seen hiding between all of the markings on the staff. The longer notes cried out for a bold, vivid crescendo that would make the room ring, but each time I resisted, allowing the sound to swell ever so slightly before returning it to the place of almost unbearable softness where it had started.

When I reached the end of the piece, I remained still for a moment, eyes closed, until the last note faded completely from the air. Only then did I open my eyes and slowly lower my instrument.

The look on Vivaldi's face was one of pride and gratification and affection. It was a long time before he spoke, yet there was no need for words just then. "Yes," he said finally. "That is what music is."

The spell was abruptly broken by several sharp raps on the door. I almost jumped out of my skin before seeing Giuseppe through the window. I let out a sigh of relief and motioned for him to come inside.

I turned back to Vivaldi. "I must go, I am afraid," I said, handing my violin back to him.

He took it, nodding. "Next time you come, we play again."

I smiled. "Of course."

His gaze shifted to Giuseppe, who was standing awkwardly yet defiantly inside the doorway. He nodded tightly. "Signor Rivalli."

Giuseppe inclined his head in acknowledgment. "Don Vivaldi."

I had the uncomfortable feeling that there was much more they wished to say to each other, yet thankfully each held his tongue. I fetched my cloak from the chair where I had left it, facing Vivaldi as I settled it about my shoulders. "Two nights hence, then, *amore mio?*" I asked, my voice low.

He nodded. I could tell that he wanted to take me in his arms and bid me a proper good night, but did not because of Giuseppe's presence. "*Si. Addio, cara.*"

16

L'ESTRO ARMONICO

And so we fell into a routine, if such an ordinary, pedestrian word can be applied to something so heavenly. We would make love, then spend the rest of the night playing music; or sometimes we would begin with music that would turn into lovemaking. I did not know which I loved more.

Vivaldi continued to give me some insight into the composition process, and how music and chords and notes must be put together, often using his own compositions as examples.

Soon enough, I was able to play the allegro of the A-minor concerto almost as well as Vivaldi, or so I fancied. The third movement, another allegro, was equally difficult, but I loved it just as much as I had the first. "I may have to name this 'Adriana's Concerto,'" he joked one night.

I laughed. "I am honored. But I do not think that that would help our bid for secrecy very much, do you?"

"Perhaps not," he said, smiling.

"Since you are satisfied with my progress on this concerto, then, what will you give me to play next?" I asked, dropping into one of the chairs by the fire.

He laughed. "So demanding! You learn faster than I can write, *cara.*"

I scowled at him.

"I see I will have to come up with something for you next time," he said, sitting in the other chair beside me.

"You shall have plenty of time, for it will not be for several nights," I reminded him unhappily. "My father is dragging me to that atrocious marriage market masquerading as a ball."

A troubled look entered his eyes. We had never said it aloud, but both of us knew that my marriage, whenever it should occur, would be the end of our love affair.

I quickly changed the subject. "There is something else I would like to learn to play, Tonio."

He raised his eyebrows. "And what might that be?"

"Do you remember the first lesson I had with you, when I asked you to play for me?"

He nodded. "*Si.*"

"Do you remember what you played that day?"

He nodded immediately. "*Si,* I do."

"I would like to play that."

"Why?" he asked. "Why that one?"

I tried to think of how to explain. "It was more than beautiful, it was . . . captivating. Brilliant. Consuming. How long will you sit there grinning at me like a fool as I try to think of more words?"

He laughed aloud. "I was just thinking . . . it is interesting. And strange."

"How so?"

"Of all the concertos I have written, I believe that one is my favorite," he told me. "I suppose that is why I played it for you that day." He paused, considering. "It is written for four solo violins and cello continuo, but I can teach you certain sections of it, if you wish."

Suddenly I was not so sure. "I do not know. Perhaps I would rather hear you play it again."

He laughed. "You do not wish to play it yourself?"

"I do not know if I can do it justice," I said. The bold, passionate melody swept through my memory again. What if I could not play his favorite concerto as well as he wished?

He sighed. "You can, Adriana. I know you can." Yet all the same, he rose and went to fetch his violin from its case. "However, since you ask it, I shall play it for you, my lady," he said, sweeping me a gallant bow.

It was just as breathtaking as I remembered it—perhaps more so, now that I was hearing it again in all its liveliness and color and resonance, and not just in a pale memory. The piece had so much life, so much intensity when played by one violin that I could not imagine how immense it would sound when played by four, with an entire orchestra surrounding it. It was intricate, but certainly not more difficult than anything else he had given me to play. But I was afraid that, were I to attempt it, it would lose some of its spellbinding magic, some of the power it had over me to quicken my heart and still my breathing. If I tried to unravel it, note by note, surely it would no longer affect me thus.

I would leave it precisely where it was: in Vivaldi's capable hands.

When he ended the piece, I rose from my chair, stepped close to him, and kissed him. "I will leave it to you, *amore*," I said. "No one will ever be able to play it quite the way you do, and I do not wish to try."

He set his instrument on the table behind him and took me fully in his arms. "Far be it for me to argue with a beautiful woman," he murmured.

"Then do not." I drew away from him, loosening the laces on the back of my gown as I moved toward the staircase, pulling it seductively down to reveal my bare shoulders. "Follow me, and do exactly as I say."

"What will you do with all these concerti, then?" I asked later, as we lay in bed together. "Will you have them performed, or published, or . . ."

"Some of them have already been performed by the *coro* at the Pietà," he said. "Others are newer. I am looking into having them published, though, yes."

"Truly?"

"*Sì*. There is a group of twelve—several of which you have already played—that go quite well together, or so I like to think. Our favorite is one of them," he added.

"And what will you call this collection?" I asked.

"Well, if I cannot call it *I concerti d'Adriana*," he teased, "then I suppose it is fortunate that I have another title I like. I was thinking of calling it *L'estro armonico*."

L'estro armonico. The harmonic inspiration. "The name suits," I said, smiling.

"I am glad you think so."

"Oh, I do. And furthermore," I added, "I think that that name shall become quite well known—not just in Venice, but throughout Europe."

"You truly believe that?" he asked.

"I know it," I said. "And I thought you knew better than to argue with a beautiful woman . . . *especially* one who is naked in bed with you . . ."

He wrapped his arms around me and shifted me so that I was straddling him. "My mistake," he said. "You must help me to make sure that I never make it again, *mia bella*."

17

PARTITA

The dreaded evening of the *festa* at Ca' Foscari arrived, and the preparations for it commenced as soon as I rose that day. Meneghina drew me a bath and washed my long hair; once it dried, she arranged it in as stylish and elaborate a fashion as she could manage. She braided many small locks of hair and wound them around my head like a crown, leaving the rest of my hair to fall in loose curls down my back. Through the crown of braids she wove several delicate silver chains set with diamonds, which my father had ordered for the occasion. At my insistence, Meneghina then used only the barest traces of cosmetics on my face. I had no desire to be as thickly painted as a clown upon the stage.

The gown, which my father had gone to such pains and expense to have made for me, had arrived several days before, and I adored it in spite of myself. It was every bit as beautiful as the dressmaker had promised, with its froths of silver lace and embroidery. It looked as though it had been breathed from the very winter air.

Once my hair and makeup were complete, Meneghina laced me into my corset, petticoats, and finally the gown. The finishing touch was a necklace of elaborately worked silver set with sapphires, and earrings to match—a gift from my father to my mother many years ago.

My father was called in. As he entered my bedchamber and saw me standing before the dressing table, he stopped dead, an almost stricken look on his face. "Adriana," he said. "You look . . . you look just as beautiful as your mother. She would be very proud."

I was taken aback by his words. I must have looked very much like my mother for him to mention her. "Thank you, Father," I said sincerely.

Extending his arm to me, he said, "Shall I escort you down to the gondola, *figlia mia?*"

Meneghina settled my fur wrap about my shoulders, and I crossed the room to him and took his arm. He led me down the stairs to the ground floor and out to the dock, where the gondola bobbed patiently.

As my father helped me into the gondola, I felt my pessimistic spirits lift a bit. My father was being so cordial, and I was wearing the most beautiful gown I had ever set eyes on, about to go to a party given by members of Venetian high society, the likes of which I had never before been permitted to attend. I was weary of being shut up in my gloomy palazzo, seeing nothing of my city or those who inhabited it. That had changed once I had started venturing to Vivaldi's house, and it would change again tonight, though in a different way.

As our gondola carried us up the Grand Canal to Ca' Foscari, I peered through the curtains of the *felze,* which created a sheltered space in the gondola and protected us from the elements. It was an uncommonly mild night for late November, and I would just as soon have ridden out in the open air, that I might gaze upon the bright, cold stars.

A liveried footman was waiting on the dock just outside Ca' Foscari. He assisted me in stepping out of the gondola, then I took my father's arm and allowed him to lead me into the brightly lit palazzo. Another footman was waiting to lead us through the entrance hall and up the stairs to the *piano nobile*, serving this evening as a ballroom, with an orchestra in one corner and an enormous table laden with food at the other end of the room. Yet another table held wine and spirits, manned by a veritable legion of servants. None of the guests would have to lift a finger for anything.

Waiting just inside the tall mahogany doors to welcome us was our hostess, Donna Foscari. A woman of perhaps fifty or so, she was dressed in a festive red gown trimmed with gold lace, and diamonds dripped from her throat, ears, and fingers. On any other woman, such a display would have looked excessive and vulgar; however, Donna Foscari's regal bearing—aided by her rather tall height—made it look natural, stunning.

"Don d'Amato," she purred as we drew nearer. She held out her hand for my father to kiss. "*Benvenuto*."

"My dear Donna Foscari," he said, bowing, oozing charm and warmth. "You are dazzling, this evening and always."

She laughed. "You are too kind, signore."

"May I present my daughter," my father said, drawing me forward. "Adriana."

I inclined my head in a respectful nod. "It is an honor, Donna Foscari."

"Likewise, my dear," she said. "My, but you are a beauty, child."

I felt my face flush. "*Grazie*, madonna. And I thank you for inviting us into your home."

She waved a heavily ringed hand. "Not at all. I trust you will enjoy yourselves this evening. There are a great many handsome young men who will no doubt be in a fever to make your acquaintance in particular, Donna Adriana. I would introduce you about myself, if my duties as hostess permitted, but alas." She sighed. "When I see my husband, I shall send him to introduce you to a few eligible young men." She glanced at my father, raising her eyebrows inquisitively. "If that is agreeable to you, Don d'Amato."

He bowed again. "Perfectly agreeable."

"Benissimo," she said. "Now do enjoy *la festa,* you two."

"What a boon it would be, if Don Foscari were to introduce you to some of his acquaintances," my father whispered in my ear as we walked in. "The Foscaris also have a younger son who is about your age. His parents are no doubt hoping for a girl of noble birth for him, but perhaps for a second son a girl of impeccable breeding with a very generous dowry will suit."

I wanted to laugh at this, but restrained myself. "Do you truly believe that the Foscari family would make an offer for my hand?"

For once, my insolent tone did not bother him. "And why not? We are much wealthier than most noble families in Venice; that is all that matters. There is no reason why you could not marry into this family."

I shook my head. Surely now my father was aiming too high. It was hardly a secret that most of the noble families were burning through their wealth at an alarming rate, and that the preferred method of replenishing the coffers was through marriage to a girl who would bring a sizable dowry; however, the Foscari family fortune was in no need of replenishing, and all of Venice knew it.

Suddenly I became aware that I was attracting glances from many of the young men in attendance. They pretended not to be looking; I caught the eye of several and smiled politely, only to have them quickly turn away and whisper to a companion, perhaps to inquire who I was.

"Ah, now, there is an acquaintance of ours," my father said, steering me toward Senator Baldovino, bedecked in his purple senator's robes and looking as aged and portly as ever.

"Enrico!" the senator cried jovially. "Good to see you!"

"And you, Senator," my father said. "You remember my daughter, Adriana, surely?"

The senator's eyes darted very quickly up my person, from the hem of my gown to my waist, then lingering just momentarily upon my décolletage before moving on to my face. His smile widened as he took my hand, bending to kiss it. "A pleasure to see you again, Donna Adriana. You look more beautiful than ever."

"The pleasure is all mine, Senator," I replied, although I did not mean it.

"So you have finally let her out, Enrico," he said, addressing my father while keeping his eyes fixed on me. "You keep her quite locked away in that palazzo of yours. I know of no one in all of Venetian society who has claimed to have seen her out before tonight!"

My father smiled tightly. "Perhaps I am a bit overprotective," he said, "however, it is all in the interest of modesty. Young women these days are far too loose and wild—even those who have been bred to know better."

I smiled inwardly, not daring to let my amusement show. Little did my father know that his crown jewel, the most important item he had on the auction block, was used goods.

"*Allora,* that is perfectly understandable," Senator Baldovino replied. He turned his full attention back to me. "Shall I get you a glass of wine, madonna?"

I flashed him a bright, artificial smile. "You are most obliging, Senator," I said. He bowed and moved off through the crowd.

Before he returned, a man about my father's age and dressed in the black of a nobleman approached us. "Enrico! I had hoped to see you here! How have you been, my friend?"

"As well as ever, Daniele," he said. He drew me forward. "May I present my daughter, Adriana."

"Ah!" the man said, his eyes lighting up at the sight of me. "Charmed, madonna, I assure you."

"Adriana, this is Daniele Giordano, an old friend of mine," my father said. "He is one of the governors of the Pietà."

You are one of the ones who fired Antonio. "An honor, Don Giordano."

"The honor is all mine, madonna. I must confess that I came over here hoping to be introduced to you, and that I might present my son to you and your esteemed father." With a wave of his white, aristocratic hand, Don Giordano beckoned forth a tall, lanky boy. "My son, Daniele Giordano the younger. Daniele, meet Don Enrico d'Amato, of whom you have heard me speak, and his lovely daughter, Adriana."

Daniele bowed politely to my father and me. Although his height and slender frame made him appear somewhat awkward, he moved surprisingly gracefully. His brown hair was shot through with gold, gleaming in the light from the immense chandelier. "A pleasure, Don d'Amato, Donna Adriana." He turned to me and offered his hand. "Would you do me the honor of dancing with me, madonna?"

I smiled and placed my hand in his. "The honor would be all mine," I said, wryly wondering how many times I was going to utter that phrase this evening.

As we walked away, I could hear Don Giordano saying to my father, "They strike a fine figure, do they not?" I could not hear my father's reply, but had no doubt that it was a positive one. Daniele Giordano was just the sort of man my father wanted me to marry: the eldest son of a nobleman who would one day take his father's place on the Grand Council; a future patron of institutions such as the Pietà; and just wealthy enough to be envied and respected, but not so wealthy that he could not use my dowry.

Joining the other dancers, Don Daniele took my left hand in his right, and placed his other hand on my waist, guiding me seamlessly into the dance.

"You look positively breathtaking this evening, Donna Adriana," he said after a moment had passed. "A vision. If I may presume to say so."

I smiled. "Thank you, good signore. I do not believe there is a lady alive who would find such a compliment too presumptuous."

He laughed, but then did not speak again for the rest of the dance. He was a fine dancer, and handsome, certainly, but I found myself wishing he was more talkative. It was likely he was one of those men who did not feel that a woman was a worthy partner for conversation.

Once the dance ended, he led me back to our fathers. Don Giordano was conversing animatedly with another man, and my father was speaking to a gentleman on his other side; another acquaintance whose son was waiting patiently beside him. My father drew me away from Don Daniele—who looked rather annoyed at this turn of events—and insisted I meet the illustrious Senator Such-and-such and his son, and so it started all over again.

I danced with several more young men, all with noble and prominent fathers, until I laughingly begged to be excused from dancing in order to catch my breath. At some point, Senator Baldovino made his way back with the promised glass of wine, but was quickly shunted to one side by the small crowd growing around me. It was slowly becoming clear to me that I had just as sizable an entourage as any other eligible lady in the ballroom—perhaps more so. That Don Foscari had never appeared to make the hoped-for introductions did not matter. There were the young men I had already danced with—some of whom sought to keep my attention by telling jokes and relating stories of their exploits—and still others who sought to secure an introduction. It seemed that with every other breath one of them was offering to fetch me wine, champagne, fruit, or chocolates, to lead me to dance again, or to find me a chair if I wished to rest. No service, it seemed, was too much for the young lady who had apparently become, within the hour, Venice's most desirable prize.

The air of mystery was part of my allure; it seemed the entire republic knew that I had been essentially locked away in my family's palazzo until this evening. The d'Amato wealth was equally to thank for such attention. Yet no woman is immune to handsome suitors telling her she is beautiful, and whispering poetry in her ear.

Every so often I would catch a glimpse of my father, and though his expression in no way betrayed him—he was too good a businessman for that—I knew that he was delighted at the way the evening was unfolding.

Surely somewhere in this crush is a suitor he will find acceptable. My future husband is here, among the finest Venice has to offer. The wine dulled the despair I would normally have felt; instead, it became a game: I would attempt to imagine myself as this one's wife, or that one's, and found I simply could not imagine any of it.

"Adriana." My father's voice at my elbow roused me from my perverse pastime. I looked up to see he had another familiar face in tow. "You remember Don Lorenzo Morosini?"

It was my distasteful dinner partner of some nights ago. He bowed, a sickly smile on his angular face. "It is a delight to see you again, Donna Adriana. I have wanted very much to call on you these weeks past, but my father keeps me very busy assisting him with his business interests."

"Indeed," I said. "It is lovely to see you again, Don Lorenzo."

He offered me his arm. "Would you take a turn about the room with me, madonna?" he asked, just loudly enough for the rest of my entourage to hear. "It is quite crowded in this particular spot."

I reluctantly obliged. "Why, thank you, good signore."

We began to circle the outer perimeter of the great room. "I have mentioned you to my father, madonna," he said. I was slightly startled to note a slight slur that I had not heard before. "Of course, he met you at the dinner your father so kindly hosted, but I have brought your name up to him since then."

"Oh?" I asked. "Surely a member of our most noble Signoria can have no interest in a simple merchant's daughter."

He smiled indulgently at what he took to be my inability to comprehend his statement. "He remembers you as being a most gracious young woman, and so encouraged me to seek further intercourse—that is, *discourse*—with you."

I started slightly at his slip of the tongue. "I am flattered," I said, making no effort to sound as though I meant it.

"Yes, well," he said. He stopped and drew me into a quiet corner of the room, stumbling slightly as he did so. "I am planning to come to call on you, Madonna Adriana. I shall speak to your father before this night is over, to make sure he is agreeable—"

"Yes," I said distractedly, my spine stiffening as he moved closer to me. I stepped back, only to find myself with my back against the wall. "Perhaps, signore, you might consider whether your actions at the present moment are likely to endear you to him—or to me."

He smiled again and reached out to take my arm, his hand brushing against my breast as he did so. "I flatter myself that my suit will be very well received—"

I slapped his hand away, horrified. "Then you deceive yourself," I snapped. He took a step closer to me. "How dare you—"

"Don Lorenzo Morosini, is it not?"

I looked up and beheld the handsomest man I had seen all evening. He was about my age, perhaps a few years older; tall, with a head of neatly tamed chestnut curls and light brown eyes that seemed made to hold laughter and warmth. They were rather hard just then, though, as they regarded Don Lorenzo.

"Why, yes," Don Lorenzo said, turning to size up the intruder. "I would have expected you to know 'tis not gentlemanly to interrupt a private conversation, Don Tommaso."

"I would have expected *you* to know it is not gentlemanly to accost a lady in the corner of a ballroom," he returned sharply. "I would not wish to put words in the lady's mouth, of course, but I would hazard a guess that you are making her quite uncomfortable."

"This is none of your affair, Foscari," Don Lorenzo slurred, roughly grabbing my arm. "I am courting this lady—"

"I knew not that courtship involved such insults and untoward actions," I said, pulling away from his grip. "If this is the case, then may our good Lord preserve me from all suitors! I shall take myself to a convent at first light."

At this, Don Tommaso—Don Tommaso *Foscari*, if I had heard

correctly—smiled broadly, and I felt a strange lightness in my heart at the sight. "Come, madonna," he said, offering me his arm. "If you are willing, I shall endeavor to change your negative opinion of my sex, though I quite understand that this may prove to be an insurmountable task."

I smiled back at him and took his arm.

"This—this is an outrage," Don Lorenzo sputtered behind us as we moved away, all but forgetting him.

"I owe you my thanks," I began, but Don Tommaso waved my words aside.

"Not at all. I could not turn away from a lady in distress—though I do not doubt that you would have extricated yourself from the situation admirably without my help," he said.

"I thank you just the same," I said. "He was dreadful."

"Then perhaps I may persuade you to favor me with a dance, as my reward," he said, turning the full force of his smile and his warm brown eyes on me. My traitorous heart fluttered again.

"It would be only fair," I agreed, and Don Tommaso led me smoothly into the circle of dancers as the musicians began a new tune.

"I suppose that I should formally introduce myself," he said as we began to dance. "I am Tommaso Foscari, the youngest son of the family."

So this was the second son my father had spoken of so covetously. "I am Adriana d'Amato," I said. "My father is Enrico d'Amato."

"I have heard your name spoken often tonight," Don Tommaso said. "I had planned to seek a formal introduction, but I hope your father will forgive me for securing one in a rather unconventional manner."

I laughed. "And now I see your true aim in rescuing me, Don Tommaso. You sought to play the role of the knight in a fairy story, and thus secure the maiden's favor."

To my surprise, he blushed and grinned sheepishly. "If only I were so clever as that! Truly, I wished only to help, and yet if my good deed *does* win me the favor of so fair a maiden, then I can hardly complain."

Now it was my turn to blush, but just then Don Tommaso changed the subject, as though fearing he was making me uncomfortable. "You are here with your father, then?"

"Yes," I said. "My father was speaking with some friends just that way," I said, nodding in the direction of where I had last seen him.

Don Tommaso smiled. "We shall trust that he is enjoying himself." He lowered his voice just slightly. "Though he cannot be enjoying himself as much as I am, for I have the privilege of dancing with the most beautiful woman in Venice."

I was thrown off by the earnestness in his gaze. I knew the fashionable thing to do would be to reply with some witty, self-deprecating comment, thus forcing him to counter with even loftier comments. Yet in the face of his sincerity, I merely blushed again and looked away.

Just then I caught sight of my father watching us from across the *piano nobile*. His face held surprise and even bewilderment, but they were both overshadowed by a look of triumph. Then another couple stepped in front of my line of sight, and I could no longer see him.

"The orchestra is exquisite," I ventured after a few moments. Personally, I felt them to be merely adequate—their rhythm was impeccable, but they had no sense of phrasing—yet I was curious to learn the young Foscari's thoughts on music.

He glanced briefly at them over his shoulder. "They are well enough, though not of the quality that my parents could perhaps have procured had they taken more care." He smiled. "Though you must forgive me for being rude enough to contradict a lady."

I could not stop a wide grin from spreading over my face.

Don Tommaso smiled slightly in response. "What have I said to so amuse, Donna Adriana?"

For some reason, I found myself telling him the truth. "It is just that I don't *truly* think the orchestra is 'exquisite,'" I confessed. "I simply wanted to see what you would say."

He looked quite surprised for a moment, then threw back his head and laughed. "I think you and I will get on quite well, Donna Adriana," he said. "You enjoy music, then?"

I nodded. "Oh, yes. Very much."

"And have you been taught to sing, or to play some instrument, as so many young ladies are?"

"I was taught to play the violin when I was a child," I told him, adhering to the truth as it was known to my father. "I have not had a lesson since the age of perhaps thirteen."

"And so you enjoy music primarily as a listener, then," he said. "As I do."

I nodded, pinning a false smile to my face. "Precisely."

The dance ended then, and we drew apart, him with a bow, me with a curtsy, as was required. "I thank you for the privilege, Donna Adriana," he said. "Now, if you will allow me to return you to your father, and be so good as to present me to him. I must ask his forgiveness for not asking him for an introduction to you first."

"No doubt under the circumstances, he will be most understanding," I said. "Father," I called out as we approached where he stood, speaking again to Senator Baldovino. My father turned toward me with the biggest and most brilliant smile I had ever seen on his face. "May I present Don Tommaso Foscari."

Don Tommaso swept my father a bow. "An honor, Don d'Amato," he said, his voice ringing with sincerity. "I hope you will forgive me for stealing your lovely daughter away for a dance without first securing your permission."

My father clapped him on the shoulder. "Not at all, Don Tommaso, not at all," he said. "My daughter and I are both honored."

Don Tommaso took my hand and kissed it. "I shall fetch you a glass of wine, madonna, so that you may refresh yourself after our dance," he said gallantly. "And I hope that I may persuade you to reserve yet another dance for me this evening."

"With pleasure," I said. He bowed again, then went off to seek the promised glass of wine.

As soon as he was out of earshot, my father leaned down to whisper to me. "What luck!" he crowed. "I had not hoped that Tommaso Foscari would himself seek an introduction. Yet behold! He appears to be quite enchanted with you."

"Take care, Father," I said. "Do not begin counting marriage proposals before they have been made."

"I count nothing before it is right in front of me," he said. "Yet this is certainly a promising start. I can see for myself that he is quite taken with you."

I said nothing. Though I did not wish to be married—since I could not be married to the person I wanted—it was hard not to be drawn in by Tommaso Foscari, by his handsome face, by his attentive and courteous manner, by his clever banter, by his compliments. He could have his pick of the wealthy, beautiful women of Venice, yet he was choosing to spend the evening with *me*.

Be careful, Adriana. You are in danger of more than the wine going to your head this evening.

"You dance quite well, Donna Adriana," a voice to my right said. I turned to see Senator Baldovino beside me.

I inclined my head graciously. "I thank you for saying so, Senator."

"I have not danced for many years," he mused aloud. "But I daresay I could be persuaded if I had a partner as lovely as yourself." He offered me his arm. "Would you do me the honor?"

"Oh . . ." I thought wildly for some excuse. "Don Tommaso Foscari has just gone to fetch me some wine. I should not wish him to return and find me gone."

"Never mind that," the senator said brusquely. "If he has an ounce of sense in that pretty head of his, he will wait."

Left without a choice, I took his arm and allowed myself to be led to the dance floor.

I well believed that he had not danced for years, as his lack of practice showed. He was awkward and clumsy, and frequently fell out of time with the music. I attempted several times to guide him back into sync with the other dancers, but soon I gave up, devoting my attention to praying for the end of the dance to come swiftly.

When it did come, he led me back to where I had been standing with my father. Don Tommaso was, just as the senator had predicted, waiting for me with a glass of chilled white wine, smiling patiently.

"Well done, Senator," Don Tommaso said. "I need not tell you that you have been most wise in your choice of a dance partner."

"No, indeed," Senator Baldovino said. "I will leave her to you, young man." With that, he withdrew from the group.

Don Tommaso presented me with the wine. "Now you are doubly in need of refreshment, Donna Adriana."

"Indeed, Don Tommaso. I thank you."

"Please call me Tommaso," he invited.

"If you insist," I answered, deliberately not extending the same privilege to him. It was probably better to keep him at a distance.

"You have told me that you enjoy music, Donna Adriana," he said as I sipped my wine, "but do you enjoy the opera?"

"I have never seen one," I answered, "and so I cannot say."

"What! A native of Venice who has never seen an opera?" Tommaso demanded with a smile. "How can this be?"

"My father does not care for the opera," I explained. "And so I have never been presented with the opportunity to attend."

"It is fortunate that I have come along, then," he said. "For you see, my elder brother is possessed of a large box at the Teatro Sant' Angelo, and Friday next he has invited me to join him and his wife for the performance. It would be my great honor and privilege if you would accompany me."

A wide, excited smile broke across my face. The Teatro Sant' Angelo was the theater where Vivaldi played as a soloist. Now I would be able to see him play, just as I had wished to. "Oh, yes!" I exclaimed. "I should be delighted."

Tommaso laughed. "I am glad," he said. "Though I confess a curiosity as to whether your enthusiastic acceptance is due more to your love of music, or to a desire for my company."

This time I hit instantly on the perfect witty, noncommittal reply. "I have not yet heard the music, my good signore," I said, with a smile and a toss of my head. "Ask me again once I have heard the music."

18

SE TU M'AMI

"I have a surprise for you, *caro mio,*" I said to Vivaldi two days later—in the afternoon, this time—as we dressed in preparation to go downstairs and play music.

He raised an eyebrow at me expectantly. "And what might that be?"

I smiled. "On Friday night, I shall be attending the opera at the Teatro Sant' Angelo."

His entire countenance became illuminated at my news. "*Eccellente!* Have you managed to persuade your father to attend, then?"

"It is not my father who shall be accompanying me." I hesitated. "It is a suitor with whom I shall be attending." I rolled my eyes, as though the whole affair were completely ridiculous.

"Oh?" he said, trying to sound nonchalant, though I could see him struggling to hide his consternation. "And who might the lucky bachelor be?"

"His name is Tommaso Foscari," I said, as though I were naming a young man of no importance, as opposed to the son of the premier family of Venice. "His family owns a box at the theater, I believe."

"What!" Vivaldi shouted. "You are being courted by a Foscari?"

"I only just met him," I said. "At the ball on Monday. We danced, and he asked if I would accompany him to the opera. And of course I said yes—to see you."

"Adriana," he said, crossing the room and taking me by the shoulders. "Listen to me. If he makes you an offer, you are to accept him, do you understand me? You must accept him!"

"Let go of me," I said, tearing myself out of his grasp. "I already have my father directing me as to whom I can and should marry; the last thing I need is for you to do the same!"

"Why do you persist in this blindness?" he asked, throwing up his hands. "Do you not see that you must marry someone, someday? Your father will not have it any other way, and besides, what other future can there be for you?"

I opened my mouth to interject, but he held up a hand to silence me.

"I am not finished," he said coldly. "Tommaso Foscari will be able to give you the world, and then some. If he asks for your hand, you must accept him without thinking twice about me. Are you so blind and stubborn that you cannot see all of this for yourself?"

"Listen to you!" I cried. "If you are so anxious to be rid of me, then perhaps I should just leave now, and let that be an end to it!"

"That is not what I meant," he said. "Not at all. But what we have cannot last forever. You must acknowledge that."

"I have acknowledged it," I retorted. "But that does not mean I am in any rush to be married to a man I have just met."

Neither of us spoke again for a time, locked in a silent confrontation, each of us refusing to back down. Finally he broke the silence. "If you wish to leave, I will not stop you."

I took a deep breath, steadying myself. "I do not *wish* to leave," I said. "But I thought that you wanted me to—"

"No," he cut me off quickly. "No. I just hope that you might still have a chance for an ordinary, respectable future after all this. Even though . . ." He trailed off and sighed. "Even though it may be too late."

I remained silent.

"Ah, *cara*." He crossed the room to me and took me in his arms. I closed my eyes and let myself sink into him. I felt his lips brush against my hair. "What is this life we are living, where we cannot bring ourselves to think of the future?"

"I do not know," I murmured. "All I know is that I cannot bear to think of any future that does not include you."

He released me, cupping my face gently in his hands. "You know that I wish things could be different, *sì*?" he asked. "You know that I wish I could be the man who wakes up beside you every day, and that we need have nothing to fear?"

My breath caught in my throat. He had never said such things to me before, not even in our most tender moments. And these things he said he wished for were exactly what I wished for as well, in the deepest hollows of my heart, that place that I tried not to examine too closely for fear of what I might find.

In that moment, I could see this entire future before me, and it seemed so easy. It seemed, right then, that if we wanted it badly enough, all we had to do was reach out and take it.

I could do it. I could open my mouth right now and ask him to renounce the Church, so that things can *be different, as we both wish them to be.* But even though it seemed such a simple thing, I did not do it. For it was not simple. He was risking so much for me already that I could not bring myself to ask him this one, final thing. I could not ask him to give up the only life he knew for a future that now seemed to be evanescing before my eyes as rapidly as a beautiful dream does when the sun's rays fall upon it.

He slid his hands down to my shoulders, then my waist, and withdrew them. "But it cannot be," he went on. "I have nothing to offer you—I cannot even offer you myself, not completely. Yet for what it is worth . . ." His eyes searched my face. "I love you, Adriana. I do. But I love you enough that I want what is best for you, and unfortunately that does not include me."

My more sensible, realistic—perhaps bitter—side recognized the truth of his words. Love was simply not going to be enough.

"I know," I said finally, looking back up to meet his eyes. "But that is the kind of love that hurts."

A knock on the door downstairs startled us, causing us both to flinch away from each other. A few seconds later, we heard the door open, and Giuseppe's voice calling out tentatively, "Madonna?" Then, slightly louder, "Adriana?"

"Coming, Giuseppe," I called. I reached for my cloak and pulled it on. "I must go," I said. I suddenly found myself unable to look at him. "I am sorry."

"You have nothing to be sorry for." He stepped forward and lightly kissed my forehead. "May you get home safely, *cara*."

"I will see you two nights hence at the theater," I said, desperate for this afternoon not to leave a bitter, somber taste in our mouths.

He smiled, as I had hoped he would. "Of course," he said. "I will look for you in the grandest box of them all."

"I will be there," I promised as I moved toward the door, "with eyes only for you."

Later, as I walked beside Giuseppe on our way home, I could not help but mull over our argument. My troubled thoughts must have been evident, for Giuseppe, after stealing several sideways glances at me, asked, "You seem out of sorts, madonna. Is anything amiss?"

We had to press our way through a bit of a crowd in the narrow street just then. I waited until Giuseppe drew near me again before replying. "No, I am well enough, Giuseppe. Thank you for asking."

We moved onto a bridge over a narrow canal, and Giuseppe gently took my elbow and steered me toward the railing, away from anyone who might overhear. "Are you certain? Because you seem to be rather upset."

I sighed, realizing he knew me entirely too well to be put off with such vague replies. "It is just that . . . he makes me so angry sometimes!" I burst out. "I love him, yet . . . one moment I want nothing more than to be with him, and the next I could slap him! The things he says, sometimes . . . he confuses me. I know not what to think or even to feel half the time."

To my surprise, Giuseppe chuckled. "Based on my experience, that certainly sounds like an apt description of love. Not the one the poets prefer, of course, but accurate nonetheless."

I stared at him in astonishment. "So I am not altogether mad?" I asked.

"Well, you may be, but that is a separate matter entirely," he teased.

"Truly, Giuseppe, what do you mean?" I pressed. "Love is supposed to be like this?"

He leaned his forearms on the iron railing of the bridge and looked out over the water of the canal before us, reflecting the dirty façades of the stone buildings surrounding it. "I do not claim to know how love is supposed to be. I can only tell you what it is—what it has been—for me." He paused. "I think the people we love cause such violent changes in our emotions because we are so vulnerable to them. When you love someone, you give them power over you, so perhaps it is mostly fear that causes us to react with anger, as we sometimes do—fear that they will misuse the power we have given them, knowingly or not." He looked up and met my eyes. "I have found this applies not just to romantic love, but also to more friendly or familial attachments as well."

His words gave me the chance to blurt out the question I had been longing to ask for years. "Why are you so good to me, Giuseppe?" I asked. "What is it that makes you feel so . . ." I paused. "Responsible for me?"

"That is a question that you must ask your father," he said, straightening.

"What does my *father* have to do with this?" I demanded.

He chuckled and moved away from the railing. "More than you know."

Frowning, I followed him as he began to lead the way back home. "I have not the slightest idea what you mean," I said.

"And it is not my place to enlighten you on this point."

My first instinct was to press him on the matter, yet something held me back. If it was something he felt he had no right to tell me, then he must have a good reason. After all, when had Giuseppe ever refused me?

So instead I remained silent, and we walked the rest of the way back to the palazzo without speaking further.

19

OPERA AND CONCERTO

On Friday night Tommaso came to call for me, as planned. I met him wearing a gown of dark red velvet trimmed with gold thread. My father had bought me a gold and ruby pendant with earrings to match, and carefully selected strands of my hair were held back with a gold hairpin. In my hand I carried a fan of the same fabric as my gown, edged in lace.

Tommaso's eyes caught sight of me as soon as I appeared on the staircase, and never left me as I descended the stairs and stopped before him. He immediately kissed my hand, still keeping his eyes on mine. "After you left *la festa,* I thought I could only have imagined so beautiful a creature as you," he said, by way of greeting. "But now I see that memory and imagination alike have failed me, for you are far lovelier than I remembered."

I blushed. Nearby, my father had a smile on his face that was wider than the most ridiculous Carnevale mask.

Without giving me a chance to respond, Tommaso offered me his arm and, with a warm smile, asked, "Shall we be off, madonna?"

I took his arm and smiled in return.

"I thank you again for permitting your daughter to accompany

me, Don d'Amato," Tommaso said. "Her comfort and safety will b
my utmost priority."

"Good. I am glad to hear you say so," my father replied, apparently feeling he had to play the stern, reluctant parent at least briefly.

"You need not fear, sir," Tommaso said. "I shall return her to you as soon as the evening's entertainment has ended."

"Good-bye, Father," I called as we moved toward the door, intensely relieved and elated to be away from his watchful eye for a few hours without worrying about secrecy.

Tommaso stepped into his gondola, then reached up to assist me in doing the same. Once we were both comfortable Tommaso called to his gondolier to take us to the theater.

"I confess to being somewhat surprised that your father did not insist on a chaperone," Tommaso said as soon as we were away from the dock.

I felt slightly alarmed at such a comment. "I believe he felt that, as a gentleman, you could be trusted in my company without one," I said coolly.

He laughed. "I did not mean to make you ill at ease," he said. "I have heard that Enrico d'Amato is unusually protective of his daughter, especially in so lax a city as Venice. Not to mention that, before my parents' ball, no one could rightly recall ever having seen you in public before." He smiled. "I have been making some inquiries, you see."

"Oh?" I said, my tone uncaring, yet truthfully I was nervous—I had so very much to hide. "And what else have you learned?"

"Let me see," he began, smiling. "I know your mother was Lucrezia della Pietà, and that she had one of the finest voices of any of the Pietà's foundlings, ever. I also know that she died several years ago, and that your father has never remarried. I know that you have an elder brother named Claudio who is the heir apparent to the d'Amato firm. And I also know," he added, his voice dropping to just above a whisper and leaning closer to me, "that you are the most beautiful woman I have ever seen." Just as abruptly, he sat back again. "Now tell me, is there anything else you think I should know?"

I smiled and looked away from him. "Not at the moment."

As we passed one of the great houses on the Grand Canal, I heard snatches of a lovely melody, accompanied by a lute. I pulled back the curtains of the *felze* and peered out.

A young man stood in a gondola beneath the balcony of a palazzo, playing the lute and singing a song about a lady of such beauty that Venus blushed in her presence, and that Zeus himself would be jealous of the man who held her affections. On and on the song went, praising the beauty and grace of the unnamed lady, whom I assumed resided in that palazzo. As the young man reached the end of his song, spectators in nearby boats applauded. Then the balcony doors opened and a lady appeared, dressed in evening finery, and blew a kiss to the ardent young man below.

"Ah, yes," I heard Tommaso say behind me. "Donna Grimaldi will never want for admirers, it would seem."

Based on the glimpse of Donna Grimaldi that I had seen—she was possessed of hair that shone like gold, a heart-shaped face, and a figure for which women would sell their souls—I could only agree.

"The young man is her suitor, then?" I asked.

Tommaso laughed. "I should hope not, for the lady is married to Senator Grimaldi. He is a friend of my brother's."

I raised my eyebrows incredulously. "And yet a man dares pay court to her anyway?"

He smiled. "I forget that you have not been out and about in society. It is very much the custom for men and women to play at courtly love, to exchange poems and songs and small gifts, whether they be married to others or not. Likely that young man—or another young man like him—escorts Donna Grimaldi to the opera and the Ridotto and to parties."

"And her husband does not mind?"

Tommaso grinned. "Hardly. He will take it as a compliment that another man should so admire his wife. Sometimes such a *cavaliere servente* might also be a woman's lover, but these things are usually chaste."

I was silent as I turned this new information over in my head. The idea of love as a game played purely for show, for display, for the consumption of others, was completely contrary to my experience of it. And yet if I was to make my way through Venetian society and keep my secrets, I must learn to play the game, and play it well.

"I have a confession to make," Tommaso said as he drew near to the theater. "I instructed my gondolier to bring us here the long way around, so that I might have a bit more time alone with you."

I smiled, a tad uncomfortable but unwilling to show it. "It was a lovely ride."

Once we docked, Tommaso helped me from the gondola himself, and we joined the large, milling crowd gathered outside the theater. There were many finely dressed ladies and gentlemen: patricians, wealthy businessmen, foreign dignitaries, all manner of members of the privileged class. I also noticed several courtesans on the arms of wealthy men, their dresses cut low enough that their bare breasts were exposed to the night air. Then there were theatergoers who were neither noble nor wealthy, identifiable by their plain manner of dress: just ordinary Venetians indulging in their love of music.

When we stepped inside the theater, Tommaso had a brief conversation with the concierge, and then led me up several flights of stairs until we reached the box.

The Foscari box was easily the grandest in the theater; it was positioned directly opposite the stage, allowing for an unobstructed view. A chandelier made of thousands of sparkling pieces of Murano glass hung from the gilt ceiling above us, a ceiling that boasted an almost overwhelming display of frescoes and carvings.

I spread my fan, using it to hide the wonder and delight on my face as I took a seat at the front of the box and looked around. It was beautiful, this temple devoted solely to music. I knew that there were other, more richly decorated opera houses in Venice, but this one had a claim on my affections before I had even seen it.

This was Vivaldi's theater.

I felt my excitement growing almost unbearably as I looked down at the orchestra. Though his distinguishing red hair was hidden by a powdered white wig, I recognized Vivaldi at once. As if he could feel my gaze, he turned and scanned the row of boxes until he saw me, a smile stretching across his face. He shifted in his seat and audaciously raised his bow, pointing in my direction, a salute.

My wide answering grin was hidden by my fan, so instead I winked boldly in reply.

Beside me, I was startled to hear Tommaso say, "I wonder who the Red Priest knows up in the boxes?"

I lowered my fan and gave him a look of wide-eyed innocence. "Who?"

He nodded down at the orchestra. "The solo violinist," he said. "His name is Antonio Vivaldi. They call him *il Prete Rosso,* because of his red hair. Have you never heard of him?"

I shook my head, maintaining a look of polite bewilderment.

He smiled. "Well, then, as a former violinist yourself, you will certainly appreciate his skill. He is phenomenal; if there is a better violinist in Venice, I have not heard him. Anyway, just a moment ago, he gestured to someone in one of the boxes, and I simply wondered who it was that he knows. Probably some wealthy patron he is courting. He is a composer as well, or so I hear."

"No doubt," I said vaguely. I raised my fan again and snapped it open to hide the smile that had crept back onto my face.

We had not been in the box long before several of Tommaso's friends and acquaintances came in to greet us, and we moved to the seats in the back section of the box to speak with them. Tommaso introduced me to all of them, in a flurry of names that I could not quite keep straight. There was Bernardo Contarini, about Tommaso's age, and heir to another of Venice's most powerful families. He introduced us to Count Sandro Farnese, visiting from Rome. There was elderly Senator Guicciardi and his wife, who begged Tommaso to give their regards to his father. Then came Tommaso's friend Giovanni Somebody-or-other, who had on his arm a woman I suspected of being a courtesan, as her dress was cut perilously low and Giovanni did not introduce her.

We were also visited by a close friend of Tommaso's, Paolo Cornaro—or was it Corner? He bowed over my hand and paid extravagant compliments to my beauty, much to the displeasure of his new bride, a girl named Silvia, who would have been a raving beauty had it not been for the seemingly permanent sour look on her face.

"I declare, Donna Adriana," she said to me, as Paolo and Tommaso were rapidly conversing about a friend of theirs who was apparently in dire straits after too much gambling at the Ridotto—honestly, and the sin of gossiping is laid primarily at the door of women—"I have heard your name spoken, of course, but cannot recall ever crossing your path in society."

"Nor would you, donna," I replied, "for I have not been about in society until very recently. My mother died several years ago, you see, and it has made my father somewhat overprotective."

"I see." She sniffed, snapped open her fan and began languidly fanning herself, as if the very action bored her. "Well, men do love a mystery—while it lasts, that is."

I drew back as though she had slapped me.

Fortunately, I was saved by the arrival of Tommaso's brother, Alvise, and his wife, Beatrice. Since I had not been introduced to them at the ball, Tommaso quickly made the introductions. Alvise was a quiet, serious, reticent man; a man many considered in line to be elected doge someday. Beatrice was kind yet reserved; Tommaso later whispered in my ear that his sister-in-law had always been shy, and was much warmer once she knew someone better.

From the floor of the theater, I could hear the sounds of the orchestra tuning as one, ostensibly in preparation to begin, and it sent excitement scurrying through my veins. I glanced up at Tommaso, assuming we would be going to take our seats now.

"You would do me a great honor, both of you, if you would join me in a hand of cards," Paolo was saying to Tommaso and his brother.

Tommaso reached for my hand. "I would, *amico mio,* but this time I must decline," he said. "Unfashionable though I know it is, I would very much like to see at least *some* of the opera." He turned and smiled at me, which I must confess caused my knees to weaken just a bit. "And I daresay that my lovely companion feels the same way."

"We can hardly blame my brother for eschewing our company in favor of that of Donna Adriana," Alvise Foscari said, bestowing on us what I sensed was a rare smile. "In that case, I shall certainly oblige you, Don Cornaro." So that was Paolo's surname; his family, too, had produced several doges over the years. "I will be ordering dinner for us shortly, *fratello,*" he said to Tommaso. "Hopefully the two of you can be persuaded to join us?"

"Of course," Tommaso said. "Do fetch us when the time comes." He led me back through the curtain separating the seats from the rear of the box and helped me into a chair.

"The fashionable practice," he explained to me, "is to spend one's time at the opera doing anything but watching the opera—except, of course, when one's favorite singer is onstage, or when one of the characters is about to die a dramatic death." He grinned. "I seem to be the only one in my circle of acquaintances who actually comes to the opera with the intention of seeing most of the performance and hearing the music." The look he gave me then was a companionable one, as if we were coconspirators. "And I believe that you feel the same way, yes?"

My answering smile was genuine and warm. "Yes," I said. "To ignore such music and spectacle, why, it seems almost sinful."

"That it does," Tommaso said, "and we can only hope that all these poor souls will confess as much to their priest tomorrow." With that, he settled back into his seat for the beginning of the opera.

I realized, with a certainty that made my entire body go cold, that Vivaldi had been right, in a way. Of all the men in Venice whom my father would consider serious contenders for my hand, Tommaso Foscari was the one best suited for me—perhaps perfect for me. And I genuinely enjoyed his company. But this only made me want to push him further away.

The moment the opera began, however, I forgot everything except the music. The *prima donna* strutted onto the stage to thunderous applause as the orchestra struck up the lively opening bars. She was arrayed in an elaborate Grecian costume, and weighed down with so much gold jewelry that she positively sparkled in the light from the stage lamps. She inclined her head regally in acknowledgment of the applause, then launched into the first aria.

Her voice was strong and full, yet also light. She would reach the highest notes in impossibly rapid passages, only to embellish them with a series of trills and ornaments. The cadenza at the end of her aria earned her a round of near-deafening applause.

With the conclusion of her aria, other singers came out onstage, and the plot of the opera began to unfold. I was lost in the music, the intricate arias, the back-and-forth banter of recitative, the tender love duets and elaborate ensemble numbers. But unsurprisingly, it was the orchestra and Vivaldi in particular that truly enthralled me.

It was new and somewhat strange to see Vivaldi playing for an audience, and in the service of a much larger whole, rather than hearing him play when we were alone, when he played just for me. I had never played in such a way before, and the tricks of blending and balancing intrigued me as I watched him.

When, after over two hours, the curtains fell, signaling the end of the first act, the audience applauded, and everyone rose from their seats to seek out their friends and acquaintances during the intermission.

"Tommaso, *fratello,*" Alvise Foscari called, poking his head through the curtains that separated the seats from the rest of the box, "I have held off on our dinner as long as possible, but we will wait no longer for you, I am afraid!"

I began to rise, but Tommaso placed his hand atop mine to keep me where I was.

"Stay," he murmured. "You will want to hear this." To his brother, he called, "Just a few more minutes, Alvise. The lady and I wish to hear the concerto."

I threw him a questioning look.

"At the intermission, it is customary for the orchestra's soloist to play a concerto, or some such thing," he explained. "Remember what I was telling you about this man Vivaldi? Now you will see what he is truly capable of."

"I have been watching him through much of the performance thus far," I said. "It seems he is just as skilled as you say."

"You would know better than I," Tommaso said.

Just then, as if on cue, Vivaldi rose from his seat and began to play.

I drew my breath in sharply when I heard the opening notes; I recognized them instantly. It was the first movement, the allegro, of the A-minor concerto he had taught me to play.

I glanced quickly at Tommaso, afraid that perhaps he had noticed my reaction, but his attention was fully on Vivaldi. I gratefully turned my gaze to the same place, feeling my heart beginning to thrum excitedly in my chest.

Vivaldi played it a thousand times better than I could ever dream of playing it, or so it seemed to my ears. And as though it were not an exquisite piece of music already, he embellished it a great deal, adding impossibly rapid ornaments and difficult cadenzas throughout, just as the singers did in their arias.

Once he reached the end of the allegro, he paused just briefly before beginning the next movement, the largo. It would always sound like a love song to me, whether he played it just for me or I for him, or whether he played it in an opera house before hundreds of people, bold and unafraid in its quiet simplicity.

As he reached the end of the movement, I realized I had been holding my breath; when he paused again, I let go a small, soft sigh, hoping Tommaso had not noticed.

The third movement, also an allegro, he played with a seemingly impossible speed and ferocity. Again he included elaborate ornamentation throughout, and toward the end he added a long, complicated cadenza that caused my breath to catch in my throat once more, as though I could see the notes falling through the air and was left to wonder where they would land.

As he finished and took his bow, I noted the substantial volume of applause that his performance received. Though most operagoers seemed to consider the social aspect of the experience the most important, they at least knew remarkable, exceptional music when they heard it. They—we—were Venetians, after all.

Once I awoke from the beautiful spell that Vivaldi's music had cast over me, like a maiden in a fairy story awakening from an enchanted sleep, I found Tommaso watching me expectantly, waiting for my reaction.

I smiled, flattered by his obvious desire that all I saw and heard should be pleasing to me. "Incredible," I said.

He smiled in return, then reached over and took my hand between his, squeezing it gently. "I am so glad that you are enjoying yourself this evening," he said.

I was saved from further intimacy by Paolo, who stuck his head through the curtains just then. "We have started eating without you, lovebirds!" he called. I heard Beatrice shriek at his impropriety, and I felt myself flush with embarrassment as I realized what we looked like. What if Vivaldi had looked up to see my reaction to his performance and saw us, the color in my cheeks and my hand in Tommaso's?

There was no help for it now; I rose and followed Tommaso into the back section of the box, where a table had been set up and a veritable feast laid out. We all sat to eat, and I was soon quite lost, trying to follow a flurry of gossip about people I did not know. Tommaso, bless him, kept up a whispered commentary for my benefit, explaining who each person they spoke of was and how each was acquainted with him or her.

Our dinner lasted through much of the second act, until Tommaso begged his companions to excuse us so that we might see the finale. To my surprise, the entire party rose and filed out into the front of the box to watch the end.

When the opera concluded and the singers came out onstage to take their bows, I enthusiastically rose to my feet with the rest of the audience to applaud. The *prima donna* received a shower of flowers, and small pieces of parchment—no doubt love notes and poems. As the members of the orchestra got to their feet in turn to be acknowledged, I applauded even louder, unable to stop an enormous smile from stretching across my face.

Once the applause had ended and the performers had begun to leave the stage, Tommaso turned to me. "So what say you, now that you have seen an opera?"

"It was wonderful," I said. "I shall never forgive my father for having deprived me of this particular pleasure for so long."

Tommaso laughed. "You need depend on him no longer," he said, "for I shall escort you to any opera in the city, any time you wish to attend."

"That is very kind of you," I said, both grateful for and unsettled by his offer.

"But now you must answer a question of mine," he said, as we left the box and moved toward the lobby. "Do you remember what I asked you at the ball, when first you agreed to accompany me tonight?"

"Yes," I replied, knowing what was coming.

"Then now that you have seen an opera, I would beg you to revisit that question," he said.

I was silent, considering my reply. I had guessed that he would bring this up, yet still I had not prepared a suitable answer. "Certainly the prospect of hearing such excellent music—and so well performed—will play a part in my desire to attend such events in the future," I said truthfully. "Yet to be quite frank, I enjoyed your company this evening, and find you to be a perfect gentleman."

He grinned boyishly. "I thank you for your compliments, madonna," he said. "And please know I found your company absolutely enchanting, and that I think you the most gracious and elegant of women."

I smiled demurely at this and looked away, realizing uneasily that he appeared to be quite smitten with me.

Yet it is one thing to be smitten, and quite another to propose marriage, I quickly reminded myself as we went out to the dock where his gondola was waiting. *I should not alarm myself, not yet.*

"There are a great many parties and such this evening that we might attend," Tommaso told me once we were settled into the gondola, "but I think it best that I deliver you straight home tonight." He smiled wryly. "I would not want your father to find fault with me, and therefore deprive me of your company in the future."

It was all I could do not to roll my eyes. *As long as your surname is Foscari, I have no doubt that you could get me with child, and my father would still not find fault with you.* "Very well," I said aloud.

That night the city was full of revelers, as it often is; cheers, shouting, singing, laughing, and the occasional strain of violins or flutes could be heard coming from other boats and from the streets and buildings around us.

As I listened to the opera of *la Serenissima* herself that echoed around us, I could feel Tommaso watching me, silently and unobtrusively, yet he seemed to know I did not wish to talk just then. Out of the corner of my eye I saw him lean back and listen along with me.

20

SCARLET

After I had risen, dressed, and broken my fast the next morning, I sent for Giuseppe. "I am going to him tonight," I said.

Startled, he asked, "So soon? You were next to meet tomorrow night, *sì*?"

"Yes," I said, "but I cannot wait that long. I must see him tonight." I tried to hide the wide grin that threatened as I remembered him playing the concerto, playing it for *me,* before the whole theater, as though declaring to them all that I was his.

"And what if he is not home?"

"Then he is not home, and we will return."

Giuseppe hesitated, as though to say something else, but he merely bowed and said, "As you wish, madonna."

As we drew near Vivaldi's house just after midnight, I could see the flickering light of candles and perhaps a fire behind the curtains. "He is home," I said to Giuseppe, my voice low. "Return for me at four o'clock." My blood heated at the thought of so much time with him.

"As you wish, madonna," Giuseppe said. He turned and made his way back up the street, leaving me with the feeling that that phrase signified he had something he wished to say but was not planning to say it. I found I did not much care for it.

I pushed these thoughts aside, knocking once to alert Vivaldi to my presence, then let myself in. "Tonio, I—"

I stopped dead, the door slamming behind me, when I saw—disaster of disasters—he was not alone. The man sitting in the second chair before the fire looked startled and confused, studying me quickly before turning a questioning gaze to Vivaldi.

"I am so sorry," I said, taking a step backward and bumping into the door. "I did not realize that . . . you had a guest." I could feel my face burning, and my stomach roiled so that I was certain I would vomit.

We were found out. We had been discovered, and it was my fault.

"Adriana," Vivaldi said, quickly rising from his chair. The panicked, stricken look on his face no doubt mirrored mine. "I was not expecting you this evening."

"Antonio," the stranger said, rising from his chair. He was a bit taller than Vivaldi, and a great deal older as well. His hair was gray, and his face had the worn look of a man who had toiled many years for very little. "What goes on here?"

Like the consummate performer that he was, Vivaldi immediately collected himself. "Signorina Adriana," he said formally, "may I introduce my father, Giovanni Battista Vivaldi."

Shock and shame seemed about to drown me, but I composed myself, wondering how in the name of God and all the saints we were going to explain ourselves—and if we should even go to the trouble. "A pleasure to meet you, signore," I said, stepping into the light from the fire.

"And this, Father, is Adriana," Vivaldi continued. "She studies the violin with me."

My breath caught in my throat as I hoped, prayed. Not quite a lie. But hardly the complete truth.

"The pleasure is all mine, signorina," Signor Vivaldi said, though his courteous response was belied by his suspicious tone and the frown creasing his brow. "But a violin lesson, so late?" He looked from me to his son and back again. "Surely this is not a safe or seemly hour for a young woman to be out and about in Venice alone?"

"I am a servant in one of the noble houses, signore," I said, squirming uncomfortably. "It is only once my mistress releases me from my duties that I am able to come for a lesson, and Maestro Vivaldi has most graciously agreed to accommodate me. I show some small talent for the instrument, you see."

"A great deal of talent," Vivaldi corrected, just as a teacher would do for a favorite student.

I marveled at the ease with which the lies rolled off our tongues. "And I did not come alone. My brother is a manservant in the house where I am employed as well," I went on, "and so he accompanies me and then returns to fetch me home." I dipped my head slightly, deferentially. "I thank you for your concern, though, signore."

He nodded, still frowning. "Well, do not let me keep you from your lesson, then, signorina. I came to dine with my son and have stayed later than I meant to."

"No—no," I said hurriedly. "I . . . I fear that I have mistaken the date of my lesson." I looked at Vivaldi. "It is tomorrow, maestro, no? My apologies. I—"

"Do not leave on my account," Signor Vivaldi said shortly. "As I said, it is past time for me to take my leave."

I was unsure as to whether it would be more or less suspicious to protest further, so in the end I kept silent.

"Yes, stay, signorina," Vivaldi said finally. "Your brother has no doubt already departed and cannot be fetched back to see you safely home."

Signor Vivaldi shrugged on his cloak. "I think I will come by tomorrow, Antonio, if that is agreeable," he said. "You quite forgot to show me that new concerto you spoke of."

The look he gave his son, however, was one with which I, possessed of a disapproving father myself, was all too familiar. "Yes . . . of course," Vivaldi said. "*Buona notte, padre.*"

He saw his father to the door and watched, body rigid, until the older man had moved out of sight. He slumped against the door frame in relief.

I could barely summon my voice from the depths of horror and mortification to which it had sunk. "Tonio, I . . . I am so sorry. I did not know—"

"No, of course you did not," he said, spinning to face me, eyes blazing angrily. "Why do you think that we arrange nights to meet, Adriana? Do you think I see no one but you? Do you think no one comes here to seek me but you?"

I felt that I could die of shame and regret; a part of me wished I would. "No, of course not. I only wanted to see you, after—"

"I am not some plaything for your pleasure, to be at your beck and call whenever you grow bored with the view from your palazzo," he cut me off, advancing on me. "I have a life that does not include you, and the two must stay separate!"

"That is not fair, and you know it," I said, my voice small.

He ignored me. "This will be the undoing of everything! You know that, do you not? It is catastrophic!" His hands were balled into fists as though he wanted to strike something. He pushed past me and began pacing in front of the fire.

"Perhaps he believed us," I ventured.

The look Vivaldi gave me was one of utter contempt. "He did not believe us. He knows. He knows the truth about us. About me."

"And so?" I asked. "He is your father. Surely he will not tell anyone. Surely he would not do that to you."

"It is not that," he said, stopping and facing me. "Can you not see, you foolish girl? *No one* was to know of this, least of all my father!"

"You speak as though you are ashamed of me," I said.

"Of course I am ashamed!" he shouted, causing me to flinch.

"How can I not be? I am a priest with a mistress! Of course I am ashamed of you, of all of this!"

I could not have been more shocked had he slapped me across the face. Yet soon enough my own anger allowed me to recover my voice. "And yet you have been sinning quite joyfully these past few months, I notice," I spat. "How dare you say such things to me, as though I am some common whore whom you pay to spend the night?"

"We are both of us whores," he shot back. "Is this what you wanted, Adriana? Is this what you were dreaming of in your silly romantic fantasies? An illicit, tawdry love affair with a musician before you go off and marry your rich Foscari, and please him with the tricks you learned in my bed?"

I could have screamed aloud in fury. "Are you *listening* to your own filthy words? You quite literally *told* me to marry him, and now—"

"And yet there you were in that box, dressed like a queen, your hand in his and the two of you staring at each other like you would never look away," he said. "Just what manner of woman are you, Adriana? How am I to know?"

Rage nearly blinded me, and my entire body shook.

"*Parlar non vuoi?*" he demanded. "Why do you not speak?"

"Because I have no desire to waste my breath on you ever again, you bastard!" I shrieked.

"Keep your voice down, lest you want the whole city to hear you!"

"Let them hear!" I cried. "Let them hear how you speak to the woman who gave herself to you out of love, only to have you shame her with that very fact!"

"What do you—"

"And do not attribute your own fantasies to me," I raged. "You with the wealthy, forbidden virgin in your bed before you send her off to marriage, always knowing that you were the first. And what of you? How many have there been before me?"

Now it was his turn to look shocked, horrified. I knew that I had crossed a line with my words, that what I had said was unforgivable, but I could not stop myself. All I wanted was to hurt him as much as he had hurt me.

"Surely you cannot think—"

"I know not what to think!" I exclaimed. "The man I love would never have spoken to me thus, and so I know not what to make of the man who stands before me now!"

His mouth hung open as he stared dumbly at me.

I had arrived so excited to put to rights the dissonance that had slithered between us last time. Yet now I saw this serpent of discord had already struck and left its poison behind, when neither of us noticed, and now all that was left was for the wounds to fester. "I am leaving," I said. "No doubt it will not bother you if I never return."

With that, I turned and stalked out the door before he had a chance to respond.

In spite of it all, though, I could not resist one glance back. Through a parting in the curtains, I could glimpse him standing completely still, his face buried in his hands, body rigid with tension. Then, in a sudden burst of rage, he reached out and swiped one of the empty wineglasses off the table, sending it shattering against the stone of the hearth.

21

CURTAIN

The light of dawn was just beginning to leach away the darkness when a hiss in my ear awoke me. "Madonna. Madonna, wake up. Adriana!"

My eyes snapped open and I sat up in my bed quickly, only to see Giuseppe standing over me, looking slightly embarrassed. "*Dio*, Giuseppe, did you think to frighten me to death?"

"My apologies, madonna," he said, "but I thought it best that we speak before the rest of the house is about." His expression changed to that of a schoolmaster about to scold an errant pupil. "What could you have been thinking, cavorting around Venice alone at that hour?"

"Please, Giuseppe," I said, pushing the covers aside and getting out of bed. I took my robe from my wardrobe and pulled it on over my night shift, so that I did not feel quite so naked beneath his disapproving stare. "I could not stay, and I had not the foggiest idea where you might be."

"And is Madonna going to tell me *why* she had to depart her lover's house so suddenly and so unexpectedly?" Giuseppe asked.

I gave him a sharp, quelling look. "You must know, if you went to his house to seek me. Surely he told you. You will not make me recount it, I hope."

"I know only what Don Vivaldi told me, and he was not all that intelligible."

I started slightly. "What do you mean?"

"He was drunk," Giuseppe said. "By the time I arrived, he was so deep in his cups that it was clear he had been drinking for hours."

"I see." I turned away from Giuseppe and made a pretense of studying the early morning sky from the window.

"Very well. Since you are apparently too proud to ask, I will tell you what he said—or what I could gather, at any rate," Giuseppe said. "You and he got into quite the argument, something about his father discovering you, and . . . it seemed one moment he was swearing he would never forgive you, and the next he was swearing before God that he could not go on until you had forgiven him." He paused. "I would never have guessed it," he said, more to himself than to me.

Tears stung my eyes, and out of habit I forced them back as I kept my face turned resolutely to the window.

"And so?" Giuseppe said, after a moment had passed. "Would you care to elaborate, madonna?"

I sighed, composing myself, and turned to face him. "It is just as he said. When I arrived, his father was there." I told Giuseppe of our lie, and how Signor Vivaldi had not seemed to believe us. "Then he left, and . . ." I bit my lip. "Antonio said horrible things to me, and I said horrible things to him. And I left."

Giuseppe studied me carefully. "And so it is over?"

Over. The word seared, as though I had passed my hand through a candle flame. The blister that was left behind throbbed and swelled until it threatened to drive me out of my mind with pain.

Over. The word I had not thought once, not through the entire night before, even though I knew it was the word to explain the sickening weight in my stomach. How could it not be over, after the things he had said?

I heard Giuseppe sigh, tentatively speaking up. "Adriana, perhaps it is not so dire as all that. You did not see him afterward, and I—"

"No," I cut him off. "Do not say anything. There is nothing you can do."

He did not move for a moment, then I heard him leave the room, closing the door behind him.

I stared toward the Grand Canal, where it snaked its way among the houses and bridges of Venice, leading to the lagoon and eventually to the sea. How I wished I could follow it; let it take me far from this city of so much music and so much pain.

Not long after Giuseppe left, I crawled back into bed and fell into a deep sleep. I was awakened again a bit before midday by Meneghina, who came in to dress me. "Shall I send for some food so that Madonna can break her fast?" she asked as she walked around the bed to the wardrobe.

I could feel the events of the night before nibbling around the edges of my mind like rats with a crust of bread. I felt the urge to let them devour me, to remain in this bed for as long as it took for my memories to be eaten away entirely. But I pushed the thought away. "That sounds wonderful, Meneghina," I said, sitting up.

Meneghina cast me a curious look—I was not usually so effusive in the mornings, or ever, to be truthful—but did not comment as she began pulling out clean underthings and a warm day dress. The December air had finally turned cold, and with a vengeance. Soon it would be Christmas and, the day after the holiday, Carnevale would begin again.

Some bread and cold ham was brought up so that I could break my fast, after which Meneghina helped me to dress and tied my hair back with silk ribbons. "Thank you, Meneghina," I said, smiling warmly at her.

"Will there be anything else, madonna?" she asked, still looking puzzled.

"Yes," I said. "Send Giuseppe Rivalli to me when you leave, if you please. I have a mind to go out and take some air, and would have him accompany me."

She bobbed a curtsy and left to fetch him. I pulled one of my warmest cloaks from the wardrobe and went out into my sitting room to wait for Giuseppe to arrive.

He did, within minutes. "You sent for me, madonna?" he asked formally. He lowered his voice slightly. "How are you this morning, Adriana?"

"I am quite well, Giuseppe, never fear," I said. "I wish to go out, and take the air."

He eyed me quizzically. "And shall we be taking the air at your . . . er . . . favorite spot?"

"Somewhere new this time, I think," I said, deliberately avoiding his eyes. "Perhaps to . . ." I cast my mind about, searching for a proper distraction. "Piazza San Marco, to take a turn about the square."

Giuseppe stared at me as though I had taken leave of my senses. "It is December, madonna. The piazza will be flooded—the *acqua alta*."

Mentally I cursed myself for a fool—perhaps I *had* taken leave of my senses. What Venetian could forget about the high tides that flooded the city on winter mornings? "To Santa Maria della Salute, then," I said irritably. I had not been to the church in years, not since my mother died. She had loved to attend Mass there—when we did not attend at the Pietà—or would often take me there to pray even when Mass was not being held. Ironic that a woman who so loved to pray at a church named for Our Lady of Health would die of a fever.

The poor man seemed quite thoroughly confused, but he nodded. "Very well, madonna. I shall call for the gondola."

He returned to fetch me a few minutes later, and as we made our way down to the dock I chattered mindlessly about a party Tommaso had mentioned taking me to during Carnevale, and how I hoped Father would let me attend. I cannot imagine that Giuseppe cared in the slightest—I scarcely thought it of any import myself. I only knew that I had, desperately, to fill the silence.

Giuseppe helped me into the gondola, and I huddled into the pillows and cushions within the *felze*, pulling my cloak tighter about me. By the Blessed Virgin, what had I been thinking to come out in this cold?

It was a short ride to the church from the palazzo, and soon Vincenzo, our gondolier, docked near the church steps to let us off. I handed him a coin so that he could step into a nearby tavern for a glass of mulled wine, if he so chose. I had half a mind to follow him.

Giuseppe trailed behind me as I entered the church, the weak winter sunlight trickling through the windows just underneath the massive dome. I sank down into a pew near the back, not bothering to kneel and pretend to pray. All I wanted was the silence and stillness and flickering candlelight to dull and quiet my mind, to wash it clean. I tried to remember how it had felt to come here as a girl with my mother, how I had watched her pray with such devotion that she seemed like the very Madonna herself. It had been so much easier—then—to be happy.

But my peace was short-lived. Giuseppe sat next to me, clearing his throat. "So?" he said, glancing at me. "I take it you have something to say?"

I didn't look at him. "I do not know to what you are referring, Giuseppe." I shivered and pulled my cloak tighter—it was scarcely warmer in the church than out.

"Stop it, Adriana," he said, his sharp tone echoing off the walls and ceiling high above us, as though the very stones were reprimanding me. "Pretend to the rest of the world if you must—and you must, it is true—but you need not maintain this façade with me."

"I do not know whatever—"

"Why did you drag us out in the cold to freeze our arses off, then?" he demanded. "If not to speak freely?"

I shifted in my seat to face him, my chin raised haughtily. "We will not speak of the events of last night, Giuseppe," I said. "Not now and not ever. I dragged us out here so that I would not have to think about it. It seems you are determined that I not get my wish, however."

"I think it might help you to speak about it, Adriana," he said.

"You forget yourself, Signor Rivalli," I snapped. "It would do you well to remember that it is I who am the mistress and you who are the servant."

As soon as the words left my mouth, I regretted them. I could have wept at the shocked, hurt expression on Giuseppe's face. *Good God, can I say nothing that does not hurt those I love best?* I asked myself. "Giuseppe, I am sorry—" I began.

"No," he cut me off, getting to his feet. "You are quite right. I should remember my place." He nodded to the door. "I will just wait there for you then, madonna."

"Giuseppe, please," I said, reaching out and grabbing his sleeve. "Do not . . ." I released him and looked down. "Without you, I am all alone," I said softly. "Do not you, too, forsake me."

Giuseppe sighed and sat down again. "Is that what you think he has done, madonna? Forsaken you? Adriana, perhaps I have been wrong all along, for it seems to me that both of you—"

I held up a hand to silence him, unable to bear the bitterness of hearing him concede now, of all times. "Please. I was very much in earnest when I said I do not wish to speak of it."

"Adriana, I only wish to help you."

"Then help me forget," I said.

I knew Giuseppe so well that it seemed I could read all of the words he wanted to say as they chased each other across his face. In the end, he only sighed and said, "As you wish, madonna."

He rose and began to walk about the church, leaving me to my thoughts. After a time I knelt on the cold stone floor and tried to pray. But at first I could not think what to pray for. It seemed to be sin upon sin to beseech God to bring my lover back to me, to send him to beg forgiveness—though I could think of nothing I wanted more. The longer that I thought about it, the more it seemed that I might better ask God to help me become someone who was worthy of being forgiven.

As poor a distraction as my outing had proved to be, it was far better than sitting listlessly in the palazzo all day. Eventually, however, we had to return, and I was again confronted by the problem of how to fill so many empty hours, empty days.

I returned to my old refuge of my mother's library, reading many of the books I had not encountered before, including a few volumes of history of the Venetian republic. I delved deeper into the writings of Christine de Pizan, the Frenchwoman whom my mother had greatly admired, and reread Dante's *Divine Comedy,* which I appreciated far more than I had as a girl of fourteen. I studiously avoided the love poetry of Dante and Petrarch, however.

Giuseppe did his part as well. He had found a new bookshop deep in the Rialto district, and took me there one day when the weather was slightly more hospitable. I spent several happy hours browsing the stacks, and bade the bookseller to send the bill to my father.

Even so, I found reading all the time was soon no longer sufficient distraction. In desperation, I began spending time playing the ancient harpsichord that was housed in the small parlor on the *piano nobile.* I could not remember ever hearing anyone play it; perhaps that was why my father had not felt it necessary to remove this particular trace of music from the house. He came upon me playing it one day; I could hear him enter the room and stand in the doorway but did not turn until he spoke, his voice laced with disapproval. "Adriana—"

I stopped, turning to face him. "Yes, Father?"

"I think you know by now that I feel it inappropriate for a woman to study music," he said dangerously.

Accomplished liar that I had become, a lie sprang to my lips instantly. "I know, Father," I said, "but I did not think that you would mind in this instance, for you see, Tommaso Foscari mentioned that he plays the harpsichord, and so I thought to surprise him by learning to play a bit myself."

"Hmph." My father's two greatest desires were at war on his face: his desire that I be obedient to him in everything, and his desire that I wed Tommaso Foscari. "I suppose if you are just playing for your own amusement, and his, there is no harm." With that he left the room, closing the door behind him, and I had one small refuge left to me.

The harpsichord was not an instrument I had learned in depth. I sat before it and plinked away at the keys, trying to remember which keys were which notes, and trying to string them together into something like a song. It was certainly nothing like playing the violin, but at least I was playing music, however paltry. I discovered some yellowed pages of sheet music beneath the lid of the bench, and tried my best to play them. I marveled at my lack of coordination with the instrument, yet could hear myself improving after the long hours I spent at it each day.

Tommaso Foscari invited me to dine with him, his brother, and his sister-in-law one evening, and of course I went, doing my best to smile and act carefree. Tommaso was just as charming and attentive as he had been at the opera—and just as handsome.

I suppose I may as well fall in love with him, I mused after he had returned me to my palazzo. *For what else do I have left?* Yet just the thought was like a dagger being plunged into my breast.

22

SERENADE

About two weeks after that unspeakable night, something extraordinary happened.

At first I thought it was merely a dream, for all too often lately my dreams had been filled with such violin music, music that could only be played by one person. Yet soon I stirred into wakefulness and realized that the music was coming from outside the palazzo.

Quickly I got out of bed, pulled on my white silk robe, and ran to the window. Drawing the curtains aside, I peered out into the darkness.

It was hard to see, but I caught a glimpse of a gondola out on the Grand Canal, just beneath my window. Heedless of the cold, I unlatched the door and stepped, barefoot, out onto the balcony. There I could see—and hear—clearly.

The gondolier waited patiently in the back of his craft as his passenger—who was wearing a heavy black cloak with a hood, as well as a black half mask such as was popular during Carnevale—stood in the prow and played his violin. Played for me.

I knew without a doubt it was him.

It was a slow melody—something I had never heard before—yet

somehow wild and wistful at the same time, as though he were pleading with me, desperately begging me to hear him, to hear all that he could not put into words.

I stood stock-still on the balcony, my hands gripping the frozen rail, and watched his fingers dance across the strings in spite of the bone-chilling cold. The ice that was inside me—the frozen mass of anger and pride and sorrow—began to melt.

When he finished playing, he lowered his violin and bow and looked up at me. He held my gaze for a few moments, then turned away, motioning for the gondolier to take him home.

I watched him until the gondola was out of sight, but he did not look back. I went back inside and closed and latched the balcony doors behind me before climbing back into bed. Even with the heavy covers pulled over me, it was hours before I stopped shivering.

Vivaldi's nighttime serenade had not gone unnoticed, least of all by my father. Meneghina woke me early the next morning with a summons commanding that I break my fast with him.

For once I was not in the least concerned. I could claim that I had not known who the mysterious musician was, and with such gestures of courtly love being all the rage among Venetian high society—according to Tommaso, in any case—such an event would hardly be to my detriment. Perhaps quite the reverse.

Meneghina dressed me, and I hurried down to the dining room, where I found a place set for me and my father already eating. He rose as I entered and motioned for one of the footmen to serve me.

"Well, daughter," he said, sitting back down as the footman began to fill my plate, "I see you have made quite an impression on the young Foscari."

"Perhaps," I allowed. "I know that Don Tommaso is no violinist himself, so he may have sent or hired someone."

My father smiled. "Indeed. This is most promising." Abruptly his expression changed. "Unless last night's performance was the work of someone else entirely?" he asked, his expression darkening dangerously. "Have you been encouraging anyone else of whom I am not aware?"

His implication behind the word "encouraging" was plain enough. "Why, no, Father," I said innocently. "The only other young men I know are those I met at the ball, and I only spoke to them there. I suppose one of them may have decided to make a bid for my attentions, but I did not think that any of them seemed particularly taken with me. Other than Don Tommaso, of course."

My father chuckled. "They were all excessively taken with you, *figlia.*" He mulled this over for a moment. "Perhaps. Perhaps it was one of the others. We shall see." He smiled at me again. "Endeavor to discover the truth next time you see Don Tommaso."

"Of course, Father," I said.

"Good. *Eccellente.* I must be off, then. And, Adriana—whatever you have done to make that boy so besotted with you, mind that you keep doing it."

With that, he took his leave. I remained at the table, finishing my meal and trying to decide what to do next.

In the end, I did nothing. Despite the softening I had felt toward Vivaldi last night as he played, my anger and hurt were still too great. His words—"ashamed" and "whore"—still stuck in my skin like pins, and I could not pull them out, no matter how hard I tried.

How could I ever face him again?

All day, Giuseppe watched me expectantly, waiting for me to give the order that we were to go to Vivaldi's house that night, but it never came. I could tell he was perplexed, but he knew far better than to ask or offer his opinion.

As it turned out, the day after my serenade, an invitation arrived from Tommaso Foscari to be his personal guest at a party being given by his parents on Christmas, just a few days away. His timing impeccable, and my father was beside himself with glee.

There would be no time to have a new dress made, so my dar green velvet one trimmed with lace would have to do. My father directed Meneghina to remove the existing lace trim and replace it with silver lace that he procured immediately from a merchant friend in the Rialto.

On Christmas Eve, my father and I shared a grand meal together—a tradition my mother had instituted upon her marriage to my father, and one that we kept to this day, in her honor. After dinner, my father left to attend a party given by someone important; I did not know and cared less exactly who.

In keeping with another custom my mother had begun, the servants were given a feast of their own and liberal amounts of punch, wine, and spirits, and were relieved from their duties until after Christmas. The only exception would be Meneghina, who would need to ready me for the ball at Ca' Foscari the following night.

I retreated to what had become my customary refuge before the harpsichord in the small parlor. Having learned to play all of the music I had found in the seat correctly—if not beautifully—I had begun to devise melodies of my own and, once I had done that, to create a proper left-hand part to accompany the melody. Lacking any blank staff paper on which to record these creations, however, they usually vanished as soon as I finished playing them, gone to whatever lost place my violin melody had all those months ago.

It was nearing midnight when I heard a rap on the parlor door. I turned to see Giuseppe step inside. "Madonna?"

I smiled. "Giuseppe. I thought you were celebrating with all the others. Would you—"

He shook his head, cutting me off. "I have a confession to make, madonna," he said, standing stiffly in the doorway.

I frowned. "What is it, Giuseppe? What have you done?"

"Once your father left I went to Don Vivaldi's house."

I gasped, rising from my seat. "Why?"

He fidgeted uncomfortably. "It is plain that you have been miserable without him, madonna. It pained me to watch it go on. I thought that you would go to him after he came here, but when you made no mention of it, I . . . well, I took the liberty of going to see him."

"On my behalf," I finished, "even though I did not send you."

He nodded unhappily.

"How dare you—" I began, but Giuseppe interrupted me one more time.

"At least hear his message, madonna, I pray you. Then you can reprimand me all you wish."

I fell silent.

"He was in quite a state when I arrived, madonna," Giuseppe began. "He asked me if your father had punished you for what he had done, then he despaired that you would never forgive him. I told him—"

"You told him *what?*" I demanded.

Giuseppe continued. "I told him the truth. That you had been distraught for weeks, that you would not speak of it to me—of any of it. That you had been trying to hide how wretched you felt with your false cheerfulness and your belabored harpsichord playing—"

"Beg pardon?" I demanded, feeling a bit offended in spite of myself.

A flicker of a smile appeared on Giuseppe's face. "I do not think you need me to tell you that you are a much better violinist than a harpsichordist, madonna."

"Yes," I said, "these liberties you have taken are all very well, but I have yet to hear any message from the man himself."

Giuseppe's smile returned. "He said he has wanted you to come to him more than he has wanted air in his lungs; that he would give his soul to know he had not dreamt you, that the last few months had been real, and not some fantasy of paradise. He said that it was worth his life for him to know that you forgive him, and for you to know that he forgives you."

"Why does he not tell me such fine things himself, then?" I asked, taking refuge in haughty anger, the only refuge I could find.

A wide smile split Giuseppe's face, and he threw open the door behind him. "Ask him yourself."

23

CROSSING THE RIVER STYX

I could not move as a cloaked figure stepped into the room and past Giuseppe. He pulled down his hood so that I could see his face, making flesh the words I had scarcely dared believe.

I gasped, fighting back the urge to cry. "Did anyone see him?" I demanded.

Giuseppe shook his head. "No, Adriana. The rest of the servants are in the kitchen celebrating the holiday—and with liberal amounts of liquor and wine, I might add. Even if someone sees him, they will be too drunk to think anything of it or even to remember."

But I had stopped listening. I just stared at Vivaldi, the man I had thought I might never see again.

"I will excuse myself, then," Giuseppe said, backing toward the door. "I will keep watch not too far away." He closed the door behind him.

I scarcely registered his departure. Vivaldi and I simply stared at each other, unable to believe we were actually in each other's presence, and here, of all forbidden places.

Suddenly I found I could not bear to look at him. I buried my face in my hands, an involuntary sob escaping me.

"Cara," he whispered, his voice ragged with fear and hope, joy and sorrow, "why do you not look at me?"

"I . . . I cannot," I choked out. I opened my mouth to speak again but could make no sound. How could I ever explain that I feared to look at him, was afraid to see either love or hate on his face?

"Per favore, mia carissima Adriana," he pleaded.

After I took a moment to master myself, after I finally gained the courage to face this man who had come across such a great distance for me, I found I could not look away from him, from the desperate longing and love in his eyes.

"We have both said terrible things to each other," I said, my voice heavy with tears. "But if you can forgive me, then, my love, I can forgive you."

"I have," he rasped. "I *have* forgiven you."

Still neither of us moved. "And did you mean those things?" I asked. "The things Giuseppe told me you said?"

He nodded, his eyes never leaving mine. "Oh, yes." He removed his cloak and flung it over the back of a nearby chair, crossing the room toward me. "All of that and more."

He took me in his arms, his fingers twining through my hair as he kissed me. We drew apart, and he turned me swiftly so my back was pressed against his chest. "Shall I tell you?" he murmured, brushing my hair aside so that he could whisper in my ear. His hands moved down my back and began to unlace my gown. "I was not able to compose a single measure without you," he said. "When I would try to play, every note sounded as though it were made of stone. Do you know why?" He undid the last of the laces and pushed my gown down to the floor. "It is because you are the violin, and I am the bow. Without one, the other is useless." He bent his head to kiss my neck, his thumb brushing the top of my breast.

"I love you as Dante loved Beatrice, as Petrarch loved Laura, as Orfeo loved Euridice." He ran his hands slowly up over my hips, my waist, my breasts. "I would descend into the underworld for you," he whispered, "and play before the King of Hell himself until he released you."

"I love you." I sighed against his mouth as he turned my head to kiss me.

He moaned in response, quickly working to undo the laces of my corset, and then lifted my shift over my head. I waited patiently for him to remove his own clothes, then sank down onto the very conveniently placed daybed, which we put to a use for which I doubt it was ever intended.

As we made love, I held him as tightly against me as my strength allowed. I was determined to never let him go. It did not matter that the world we lived in was an imperfect one, cruel and conniving, and would seek to tear us apart. There was only perfection then, in that room, between the two of us, and I could not remember ever being happier in my life.

"I quite forgot," I said lazily, my head resting on his chest, "that Giuseppe had said he would be keeping guard just outside."

Vivaldi chuckled. "No doubt he knew to make himself scarce." His fingers traced swirling, circular patterns on my bare skin.

We fell silent for a time before I spoke again. It was not something I wanted to say, not in that idyllic state which we had carved out, but I knew I had to.

"And so," I said, propping myself up on an elbow so I could see his face. "Where do we go from here?"

He drew me tighter against him. "We go on," he said. "For as long as we can."

I nodded. "Yes."

After that, he was quiet for so long that I thought he had fallen asleep. Then he said, "I am given to understand that your harpsichord playing leaves something to be desired."

I laughed so hard I nearly fell off the daybed.

Reluctantly, we soon rose and dressed, and Vivaldi helped lace me back into my corset and gown, a task at which he had grown quite proficient.

"Meneghina shall have to find another position, I fear," I teased him. "You would make a fine lady's maid, *caro*."

He drew my hips tightly against his own. "As it would require me to spend a great deal of time in your bedchamber, I think I should enjoy it very much."

I had not even finished cursing the clothing we had just donned again when he released me. I turned to face him, and he gently took my face in his hands. "Come to me the night after next," he said. "We will spend the first night of Carnevale together."

"I would like nothing better," I said.

Just then, there was a knock at the door. A few moments later, Giuseppe stuck his head into the room. "Madonna, Don Vivaldi," he said. Plainly relieved to see we were both fully clothed and not in any sort of compromising position, he stepped fully into the room. "I hate to interrupt, but I think it time that Don Vivaldi takes his leave. Some of the servants are beginning to disperse from the kitchens, and we cannot have anyone discover you."

Vivaldi kissed me once more, then reluctantly released me. "*Buon Natale, cara mia.*"

"*Buon Natale,*" I said in reply.

He picked up his cloak from where he had dropped it and pulled it on. "Thank you, my friend," he said to Giuseppe.

Giuseppe nodded.

With one last look at me, Vivaldi followed Giuseppe out of the room.

Once they had left, I climbed the stairs to my bedchamber, though I knew it would be hours before I could sleep.

What need I with sleep, I mused, my lips curving into a smile as I watched the sky slowly begin to lighten over the Grand Canal, *when life itself has become like a dream?*

MOVEMENT THREE

ORFEO E EURIDICE

December 1710–April 1711

24

SECRETS

Christmas Day passed in a haze, as did the party with Tommaso. My father returned home in the morning only to go out again as evening fell; I did not see him once. Meneghina dressed and polished me appropriately for the party, and Tommaso came to escort me in his gondola.

"You look ravishing," he said, kissing my hand as I met him in the foyer. He led me down to the dock and into his gondola, where glasses of mulled wine were waiting for us inside.

We had scarcely pulled away from the dock when Tommaso said, albeit good-naturedly, "So I hear that I have a rival."

I nearly choked on my wine. "You do?" I asked, employing the same innocent look I used on my father. "Whatever do you mean?"

He took a sip from his own glass. "Your mysterious midnight serenade," he said. "It is the talk of Venice."

I pulled my features into an astonished expression. "Do you mean to say that you did not send that musician?"

He grinned ruefully. "No, though I wish I had thought of it."

I slapped him playfully on the arm. "Do not demur for my sake, Don Tommaso. You can admit it to me. I thought it was lovely."

Tommaso shook his head. "I swear to you, it was not I."

I furrowed my brow. "Then who could it have been?"

"You would know the answer to that better than I, I should think."

"Truly, Tommaso, I am at a loss. Here I was all this time thinking that you were behind the whole thing!" I giggled girlishly.

"Hmmm." His eyes searched my face, looking for truth. He must have found it, for he relaxed. "It should not surprise me. It is too much to hope that I should be your only suitor." He smiled, his eyes sparkling. "I shall simply have to increase my efforts to capture your heart, then."

His words set a stream of panic flowing in my stomach. "I suppose you must," I said, returning his smile.

"I shall begin my endeavors in that regard immediately, then," he said, taking a small wooden box from beneath one of the cushions and handing it to me. "I have a Christmas gift for you."

"How kind of you," I said. I opened the box to find a lovely bracelet nestled on a bed of green silk. It was gold, with emeralds set in a second gold band that twined around it. "Oh, Tommaso, it is beautiful! And it matches my gown exactly!"

He smiled. "It is my good fortune that you chose to wear green tonight," he said. "Here. Let me."

I handed him the bracelet and extended my left arm. He carefully clasped it around my wrist and, once the task was complete, did not remove his hands; they were warm and soft against my skin, contrasting with the cold, hard gold of the bracelet. Then, swiftly, he leaned in and kissed me.

I scarcely had time to respond before he drew back, smiling sheepishly. "Forgive me, madonna," he said. "I found I could not help myself."

"You have done nothing for which I must forgive you," I said, leaning back against the cushions and trying to still my pounding heart.

The party was much like the last, except that Tommaso rarely left my side. I confess that his devoted attention went quite to my head, for he was far and away the most handsome of all the men present.

Don and Donna Foscari greeted me warmly, as did Tommaso's brother and sister-in-law. I spent some time in conversation with Beatrice; she was, I found, an extremely learned and well-read woman.

I also crossed paths once again with Senator Baldovino, who insisted upon speaking to me for upward of ten minutes about his work in the Senate, while sneaking glances at my bosom. I had never been so glad to see Tommaso as when he came to rescue me from the old lecher.

I endured it all in the only way I knew how: with memories of the night before burning brightly in my mind, with the knowledge that the next night I would be with Vivaldi again.

The next day dawned cold and bright and clear: perfect for the first day of Carnevale. When I rose in the morning and went to look out my window, I could see revelers already crowded into boats on the Grand Canal.

Let the debauchery begin, I thought, smiling as I turned away from the window.

When night finally fell and my father had departed for his own Carnevale engagement, it was time for me to dress and be off. The act of dressing was a bit awkward; as I had no choice but to have Giuseppe help me. The gown I had chosen was a rather anonymous black dress I had not worn in several years; the sort worn by noblewomen on those occasions when they dressed in compliance with the sumptuary laws. It would suit my purposes of disguise well enough. And as I had not worn it for some time, it fit almost scandalously tightly, showing off my figure to the best possible advantage.

"Most of the servants have either left or will be slipping out soon, so we should not need to worry about them," Giuseppe reported as

I pulled out the corset I would need, stockings, the gown, and my mask: a silver half mask covered with black lace and adorned with black feathers and black and silver glass beads. He cast a nervous eye over my woman's gear.

"Very well," I said, turning to retrieve my cloak from the wardrobe. "I do not see why you cannot return to Antonio's house to fetch me at, say, dawn—it is Carnevale, after all."

Giuseppe did not answer. I frowned and turned to face him. "Giuseppe?"

The word all but died in my throat as I saw him staring, open-mouthed, at the door to my bedchamber. At Meneghina, who had just walked in, carrying a basket of freshly laundered linens.

Her face was frozen in surprise as she took in the clothing on the bed and the damning words she had certainly overheard.

"By the Virgin," I swore under my breath. This would be the ruin of us all.

Giuseppe, thankfully, came to his senses and took command of the situation. "How much did you hear?" he demanded, taking a step toward her.

"I . . ." Meneghina looked wildly back and forth between Giuseppe and me. "Madonna said you . . . you should return to fetch her at dawn, from—"

A small noise escaped my throat, and I sank down onto the bed, feeling faint. She had heard enough. Enough to tell my father, enough to have him put together the whole sordid picture.

"And how much will it take for you to hold your tongue?" Giuseppe asked.

My head snapped up at this. Giuseppe's gaze was focused, hard, on Meneghina.

"I do not understand," she said, glancing at me.

"How much must I pay you," I said, finding my voice, "for you to swear that you will tell no one what you heard, least of all my father?"

"Oh, madonna." Meneghina put the laundry down and took a

hesitant step toward me. "You need pay me nothing; I will not tell a soul, I swear—"

"And can I trust you with my skin? With my life?" I demanded. "I have heard you gossip many a time, Meneghina. You know, I am sure, what my father would do to me if—"

"I would never betray you!" she said, her large brown eyes shining fiercely. "How could you think I would do such a thing?"

"Because you will lose your position if Don d'Amato finds out you kept such a secret from him," Giuseppe pointed out coldly.

"Even so," Meneghina said. "I . . . oh, madonna, I must confess. I have known for some weeks now that you have been leaving the house in secret, and I . . . well, I assumed you have been going to a lover."

She looked back and forth between the two of us for confirmation, and apparently took our silence as such.

"I have not said anything to anyone—I would never!—because . . ." She hesitated. "Well, because I am happy for you, madonna!" she declared. "You have seemed so happy, and after the way your father has treated you all your life—" She clapped a hand over her mouth and immediately dropped a curtsy. "*Mi scusi,* madonna."

A small smile stole over my face. "You have nothing for which to apologize, Meneghina, I assure you."

"Thank you, madonna," she said, looking relieved. "All I meant to say was that you deserve to be happy. To choose for yourself."

For a moment I was humiliated, that my own maid should pity me. Yet then the simple truth of her words struck me: *You deserve to be happy. To choose for yourself.*

"Thank you, Meneghina," I said finally. "As you are here, you may as well help me dress for Carnevale, and spare poor Giuseppe the indignity."

Giuseppe looked as though he wanted to protest—strenuously—but did not say anything.

"Wait just outside for me, Giuseppe," I said. "I shall not be long."

He frowned, but left quickly to wait in the sitting room.

Meneghina hesitantly crossed the room to me, and I turned my back to her so she could unlace my day dress. "You can trust me, madonna," she said softly. "I swear it, on the Holy Virgin."

"I do not know that I deserve such devotion," I said. "But I thank you, and can only hope that I may repay you one day."

She laced me into my corset, then my dress, as she had done hundreds of times before; but this time was different. Now we were confidantes, coconspirators—more like friends than maid and mistress. She did not ply me with questions, but seemed to trust I would tell her my secrets if and when I chose.

I could see her smile in the mirror as she finished lacing the gown. "You look ravishing, madonna," she said. "I do not know this man of yours, but I should think he will be quite pleased. Now, sit," she said, "and I will pin up your hair quickly."

She used pins set with diamonds that had been a Christmas gift from my father, and then tied on my mask. When she was finished, she placed both hands on my shoulders and leaned in close, so that her face appeared in the mirror beside my own, bright with excitement.

"Now go, madonna," she said. "And happy Carnevale."

I rose from my seat and drew her into a brief embrace. "Thank you," I whispered again into her ear.

25

MASQUERADE

We had not even left the house when Giuseppe started in on me. "What can you be thinking, madonna?" he hissed as we made our way down the servants' stairs. "Do you truly think we can trust her?"

"We do not have a choice," I said as we stepped outside. We paused briefly for Giuseppe to don his own mask: a simple white *bauta,* which covered the entire face, leaving holes for the eyes and with a jutting chin that allowed the wearer to easily breathe as well as eat and drink while remaining disguised.

"Perhaps," Giuseppe grumbled. "But she is a gossip, as you said."

"She has managed to hold her tongue thus far," I said as we set off, "if in truth she has noticed my disappearances before now."

"Let us pray she is the only one who has noticed."

I winced. "No one has occasion to be near my rooms save you and Meneghina," I said slowly.

"And what of—"

I sighed. "Please, Giuseppe. It is Carnevale—my first Carnevale, and I would like to enjoy it. I believe she will keep my secret. We must trust her." Even as I spoke, nervousness gnawed at me—there were too many people now who knew. Like a true Venetian, though, I vowed not to think of such things tonight. "It is Carnevale!" I said again, laughing and skipping on ahead of Giuseppe.

I could hear the smile in his voice. "So it is, madonna. You are right. I will try not to worry."

Soon enough, we had melted into the crowds that had taken to the streets that night. I felt an irrepressible smile stretch across my face. What freedom a mask provided, that anyone could look at me and not guess the face beneath. I had never experienced anything quite so liberating. *Such is the magic of Carnevale!*

I studied my fellow revelers as we passed them, wondering where they were going to spend this most joyous of nights. *Perhaps some of them use their masks to hide secrets, as I do; not just because it is tradition,* I thought.

As we reached Vivaldi's house, I found myself thoroughly enamored of Carnevale—and it had barely begun. I stepped inside, Giuseppe behind me, to find Vivaldi waiting for me.

"You are as beautiful a seductress as Carnevale has ever seen," he said. I could see from the look in his eyes that he was contemplating not leaving the house at all, but instead having a very private sort of celebration. I stepped into his arms and kissed him boldly, heedless of Giuseppe's presence. I drew back after a moment, determined that we should not be tempted to miss out on the fun to be had in the streets of Venice.

Vivaldi was dressed in a suit of simple gray damask, with a lace cravat and lace at the cuffs of his sleeves. He also wore a white powdered wig to conceal his red hair, and in his hand was a white *bauta* mask just like Giuseppe's, anonymity being even more important to him than it was to me.

"I shall leave you, then, madonna," Giuseppe said.

"Very well," I said, turning back to him. "Remember: dawn."

"Indeed."

"Go out, Giuseppe," I said, tossing him a smile. "Enjoy yourself."

He bowed. "Your wish is my command, madonna," he said, a hint of laughter in his voice. With that, he turned and went back into the boisterous night.

Vivaldi chuckled. "He does not strike me as one to revel in such debauchery as he is likely to find out there this night."

I smiled. "No. But he is a man all the same, and no doubt that is prerequisite enough. Besides," I added, my tone becoming a bit more somber, "he needs a bit of respite from worrying about me."

"Then we shall give him nothing to worry about tonight," Vivaldi promised. He settled his mask into place, donned his cloak, and put a simple tricornered black hat on his head. "What say you? Am I sufficiently disguised?"

He was, in fact; to a degree that surprised even me. His fiery red hair was completely hidden, as was his face, and the mask slightly distorted his voice when he spoke. Had I not known that it was him, I would never have guessed it. "Perfect," I said.

He offered me his arm. "Very well, then. Shall we go?"

I placed my hand on the crook of his elbow, and for the first time, we stepped outside together, welcomed into the night that seemed so full of promise.

"To where are we bound, my lady?" he asked.

I hesitated. "I would hazard that you are rather more familiar with the city and its many Carnevale spectacles than I am," I said. "Therefore I shall allow you to lead the way."

"Very well. To Piazza San Marco, then," he said. "There we shall see spectacles enough."

We made our way to the square, where all the merrymakers were out in full force. I peered interestedly at each mask I saw: there were many of the anonymous *baute;* some wore masks of the characters from the *commedia dell'arte;* and still others had more elaborate masks like mine, with lace and feathers and jewels.

There were any number of women dressed in the attire of a courtesan, with their dresses cut so low that their bare breasts were exposed for all to see, even in the winter cold—though their faces were, of course, masked. But it was impossible to tell the true courtesans from those who were simply taking advantage of the license and freedom that Carnevale provided.

Nothing, tonight, was as it seemed.

Then there were those in full costume: figures from Greek and Roman mythology; people dressed in Turkish robes; others still in costumes in the English or French or Spanish styles. There were even a few dressed in the robes of priests, bishops, and cardinals who, it was not difficult to deduce, were certainly not clerics.

Overhead, fireworks lit the sky, enormous splashes of white and red and blue and green.

As we walked into the crowd in Piazza San Marco, Vivaldi wrapped an arm around my waist and drew me close against him. I smiled, dizzy and exhilarated by such contact and affection while in public. It went to my head just like a fine wine.

The piazza was thronged with so many people, I thought half the city must be crowded into its confines. A strange mixture of smells, from unwashed bodies to heavy perfumes to roasting meat to spiced wine, mingled in the sharp winter air. In every corner there were street performers: a group of three men who could contort their bodies into seemingly impossible positions; two men juggling flaming torches; a small group of musicians struggling to make themselves heard over the din. There were also vendors every few feet, selling spiced wine, roasted nuts, ale, and chocolates, as well as those selling masks, comical hats, and other novelties.

Vivaldi bent down to speak into my ear. "Would you like some wine?" he asked, forced to nearly shout to make himself heard.

I nodded, and he led me over to a cart where a man wearing the long-beaked mask of a plague doctor was selling mulled wine, as though dispensing remedies. He handed me a cup and said, "May this protect you from all ills and maladies on this fine Carnevale night, signorina! For the affliction of drunkenness, however, I would suggest you seek a cure elsewhere!"

I laughed and took a sip of the wine, letting it warm me from the inside out.

We walked away, stopping to listen to different musicians that were performing, discussing the flaws and merits of each. We also watched a pair of acrobats execute a series of quite astonishing feats: one would stand on the other's shoulders and launch himself into the air, performing two somersaults in midair before landing safely on his feet. The other strolled casually about on his hands, with the rest of his body straight up in the air, for such a prolonged period that he elicited gasps and murmurs of appreciation from those who had gathered to watch.

As we moved away from the acrobats, I felt a hand clutch my arm and draw me away from the crowd, into the shadowed space between two of the columns that ringed the piazza. Immediately my heart began to pound, and a film of sweat broke out on my skin, despite the light snow that had begun to fall.

I relaxed only slightly when I saw my apprehender: a bent, wizened old gypsy woman. She was dressed in a loose, flowing dress that had once, no doubt, been colorful and vibrant, but was now faded and dirty. Over that she wore a wool shawl, equally dirty and worn, and a striped kerchief bound her stringy hair back from her face. She wore no mask. Her face was a maze of lines and wrinkles; yet her eyes, deeply set in her face, were a blue so bright that they almost seemed to glow in the dim light.

"Beg pardon, signora," I said, catching my breath, "but I do not believe I know—"

She waved my words away imperiously with her free hand, her other still clamped tightly about my arm. "Never mind that," she said, her voice low and accented. "I would tell you your fortune, signorina."

"With respect, signora, I do not hold with such things," I said, my eyes frantically darting from one masked figure to another as I searched for Vivaldi. He saw me before I saw him, and was soon moving quickly through the crowd toward me.

The gypsy woman snorted derisively. "That may or may not be true," she said. "But you should listen all the same. There are things you need to know."

By this time, Vivaldi had reached us; but the gypsy held up a hand to prevent him from coming any closer. He stopped just outside of the gateway created by the two columns, the gateway between the raucous world of Carnevale and the mysterious world of shadows I had been pulled into against my will. "Stay back, padre," she said, her voice as unyielding as stone. "This is none of your concern."

The mask he wore hid his reaction, yet I knew he was as dumbfounded as I. He did not come closer. "Come, *cara,*" he said, reaching for my hand. "Come away. We shall return to the festivities; you need not stay here."

Yet I was shaken. How had she known who he really was? "Very well," I said tentatively. "I will listen to what you have to say." I turned back to Vivaldi. "Wait for me. I shall not be long."

The gypsy woman drew me farther into the shadows. "Give me your palm. Your left," she instructed, and I silently obeyed. She took my soft hand in her gnarled, knotted ones, splaying my fingers apart so that my palm was exposed to her sharp gaze. She ran her fingers lightly over my fingertips, making note of the calluses that had formed there from my violin playing. She studied the lines of my palm intently, tracing them with a clawlike finger while making low, undecipherable noises in her throat.

The rational part of me was nearly bursting with impatience; yet another part of me was apprehensive at what she might find. *Is it so impossible that there might be those who can see beyond the ordinary?* I asked myself. *She did, after all, somehow know Antonio's identity.* I waited in unsettled silence for her to finish.

She let out a low chuckle. "As I thought," she said. She took her gaze from my hand and met my eyes. "You already know your fate. Although it will not come about in quite the way you think."

I stared at her, my mind reeling. What could she mean?

"There is more," she declared, glancing back at my palm, "more that you do not know." Once again her eyes met mine as she imparted her prediction with unwavering certainty. "You will bear the child of the man you love."

It felt as though I had swallowed fire, and it raced through my veins, my blood alight. *So this, then, is my fate . . . the one I have wanted but thought I could never have. Yes, perhaps I do know, have known, though I scarcely dare believe it.*

"Does this mean—" I began, wanting her to confirm this joyous, beautiful future she was suggesting.

She shook her head. "I can tell you no more," she said. "Perhaps you know what it means, perhaps you do not. It will still come, in its time."

Sensing the interview was over, I extracted a coin from the purse at my waist and placed it in her grubby hand. "Thank you," I said. "I think."

She gave a quick nod. "Mind you do not tell anyone what you have learned here tonight," she said, her tone almost threatening as she pointed a stern finger at me. "It is for your ears alone."

"Of course," I said. "I shall speak of it to no one." And I knew that I would not, for what would I say? "Farewell, signora." I turned and walked out of the shadows as quickly as I dared, away from that strange place and back into the world of light and color and sound, of voices other than the ones I heard in my own head.

The noise of the square seemed strangely loud as I stepped back through the columns, as though the sound had been somehow deadened within the fortune-teller's realm. I placed my hand on Vivaldi's shoulder; he jumped slightly, then turned quickly to face me. Sensing something was amiss, he asked, "What is it, *cara*? What's wrong?"

"More wine, I think," I said, searching for a vendor through the crowd. It had suddenly become painfully and obviously apparent to me that my wine had long since been consumed.

"Adriana," he called, hurrying after me. "What on earth did she tell you? Why did you follow her?"

I found another vendor selling wine, handed him a coin, and wordlessly took the cup he offered me. I took a generous sip before turning to face Vivaldi. I found that I had no desire whatsoever to repeat the fortune-teller's words to anyone, least of all to him. The certainty I had initially felt at her prediction was gone now, its fires dampened and extinguished by the December cold, leaving me feeling foolish for having played along, for believing. "She told me nothing of import," I said, trying to still my trembling hands. I smiled widely. "Nonsense, truly. I only listened because I felt there was no harm in it, and she was quite insistent." I shrugged. "A silly Carnevale game, nothing more."

He knew me too well to be put off by such an explanation: he knew that I had been unsettled, if only for a few moments. But to his credit, he did not comment further. Rather, he handed the vendor another coin and took a cup of wine for himself. Offering me his arm, he said, "Well, *mia bella donna*? Shall we rejoin the festivities?"

I placed my hand on his arm and let him lead me back into the throng, where further fantastical displays awaited us.

Several hours later, I realized—dimly—that I was quite drunk. I rather liked it. My head felt lighter than usual, although the ground beneath my feet kept shifting rather disobligingly. I stumbled a few times, each time becoming consumed with laughter.

"Too much wine, *cara*," Vivaldi said, wrapping an arm around my waist to steady me as we left the piazza. I heard the smile in his voice; he, too, had had more to drink than I had ever seen him have, though not as much as I—not that I could be sure of that, having quite lost count. "It has happened to the best men and women before, and will again, I fear."

I giggled. "Where shall we go now?" I asked, throwing my arms into the air. "Venice is ours for the taking!"

"Back to my house now, *cara*, to wait for Giuseppe," he said. "Or perhaps . . ." He hesitated a moment. "Perhaps I should take you right back home."

I wrenched away from him. "No!" I cried. "Do not dare! I do not ever want to go back there!"

"*Cara*, maybe—"

"No!" I stamped my foot childishly. "Take me back to your house and make love to me!"

A burst of laughter sounded nearby, and I saw a group of masked men walking past us. "If you do not oblige the lady, I will be happy to take your place, good signore," one of them called, prompting whoops of laughter from his companions.

Vivaldi stepped closer to me, sliding both arms around my waist to draw me tightly against him. "Oh, I shall oblige you," he said softly. He quickly pulled his mask off and kissed me, hard, on the mouth, right in the middle of the street, where the magic of Carnevale enfolded us in its protective embrace once more.

26

REST

Due to the license and effortless methods of disguise that Carnevale provided, for the duration of the season—and, now, with Meneghina's assistance—it was much easier for Vivaldi and me to meet—when we both had the time, that was. The Carnevale season brought with it, as always, an increased number of opera performances at theaters throughout the city, and the Teatro Sant' Angelo was no exception. Vivaldi was occupied more evenings than not playing at the theater, performing before native Venetians and tourists alike. We took to meeting during the day again at times, though even this was not always possible.

Nor was I entirely idle. I spent many evenings being escorted about by Tommaso Foscari, either to one of the countless parties taking place each night of Carnevale, or to the opera. We went to the Teatro Sant' Angelo again—much to my delight—and also to the more upscale Teatro San Giovanni Grisostomo, where his parents owned a box. We saw an opera there called *Agrippina* that was all the rage, by some German named Handel of whom I had never heard.

And so January arrived, and the weather grew colder. Sometimes a week or more would pass without Vivaldi and me meeting.

Giuseppe became accustomed to carrying messages back and forth between the two of us, arranging or canceling a meeting. I missed him more than ever; sometimes it felt as though he were hundreds of miles away instead of in the same city.

I envied him—that he was a man, a musician, that his life was his own to order. He was busy with his performances, with writing music, with learning new music for the opera. He had plenty to keep his mind occupied, whereas I languished in my palazzo, like a lethargic princess in some old fairy story, with only a dusty harpsichord and some books to divert me.

It was this dread of empty days—and also the ghost of that melody I had played once and lost—that prompted my subterfuge on one of the rare nights when we were together.

As he stepped into the back room, looking for the pages of a sonata he wished to show me, I took several sheets with blank staves drawn on them from his desk and hid them inside my cloak. I knew I could have just asked; but I did not want Vivaldi—Vivaldi the genius composer—to know I wished to try my hand at composition. He would want to hear what I had written, and I was not ready for that.

And so I had a new pursuit to occupy me. I would sit at my writing desk, my hands and clothes ink-splotched, the pages in front of me, and try to compose something, anything. I began with a violin melody, hearing the notes in my head even as my fingers burned to play them, to draw them from the strings, these notes that I myself had found and assembled. I had to resort to the harpsichord—a poor substitute. I soon came to be glad of it, however, when it came time to sketch in the orchestral accompaniment. I would play a chord out loud—usually several times—before putting it to the page and assigning its notes to the other instruments: second violin, viola d'amore, cello—or sometimes the *basso,* depending upon my mood. I began to see that each composition—however short and juvenile—was incrementally better than the last.

During the third week of January, I received an unexpected visitor. I was set to accompany Tommaso to a party being given by one of his friends and, having dressed and had Meneghina arrange my hair, I went to the *piano nobile* to await him. As I left my rooms, however, I encountered the butler, Signor Fiorello. "Ah, Madonna Adriana," he said, bowing. "I was just coming to find you. You have a visitor."

"Don Tommaso Foscari? I have been expecting him," I said, slightly startled at his early arrival.

"No, madonna," Signor Fiorello said apologetically. "Your caller is one Senator Baldovino. He is a friend of your father's, and said he has previously made your acquaintance."

It took me a moment to summon a reply to this unforeseen turn of events. "Yes, I daresay he did," I managed.

"Yes, well. He is awaiting your presence in the parlor, madonna," Signor Fiorello said. Left with no choice, I followed him down the stairs to greet my caller.

The senator rose from his seat as I entered. I pointedly left the door open behind me. "Senator Baldovino," I said evenly. "This is an unexpected honor. Please, do be seated."

"I thank you, Donna Adriana," he said, lowering himself back into his chair. "And may I say you are looking exceptionally lovely this evening." As he spoke, his eyes swept over me in his usual lecherous manner.

"*Grazie*, Senator," I said coolly, smoothing my skirts and taking a chair at an angle to his.

Neither of us spoke for a long, awkward moment, and I felt irritated impatience prickling at me. He was here uninvited, and now he could not be troubled to get down to the purpose of his visit?

"You must forgive my rudeness in dropping by uninvited like this," he said at last. "I have sent several letters to your father, requesting permission to call upon you again, and yet every time he has replied that you have another engagement for the evening—which I do not doubt, as your company is obviously much desired."

"I thank you—" I began.

"Yes," he said, waving away my words. "In any event, I decided I would presume to call upon you in person, and ask that you do me the honor of accompanying me to a ball at the doge's palace this evening."

I wondered what my father would say. Would the honor of his daughter being seen at the doge's palace outweigh the potential advantages of an evening with Tommaso Foscari? "I thank you for the honor of your invitation, Senator," I said. "Truly, I do; and I know my father will be honored as well when I tell him. However, I must decline, as I am already engaged elsewhere for the evening, and could not now go back on my word."

"I might have expected as much," he said. "Very well. But might I not persuade you to tell me who my rival is?"

Good Lord, had he not heard the gossip? "It is Tommaso Foscari with whom I will be spending the evening."

The senator laughed shortly. "I might have known. I will not trouble you further. After all, what young lady—and what father, for that matter—would prefer an aging patrician over a young, handsome, unspeakably wealthy one?"

"I—and my father as well—are certainly flattered by your attentions—" I began uncomfortably.

"Please," he said, rising from his chair, "do not bother. Rest assured that I understand completely." He bowed. "It is my sincerest hope that you should enjoy your evening, Madonna Adriana." With that, he walked past me and out the door, and I could hear Signor Fiorello offering to show him out.

I sagged against my chair, feeling flattered and sorry for him and as though I had only narrowly avoided a rather great misfortune all at the same time.

27

SHADOWS

The parties and performances continued on into February, keeping Vivaldi and myself occupied and therefore separated more often than not. I was out more and more with Tommaso Foscari, and yet no proposal of marriage had been made.

"What in the name of God and Mother Mary can the boy be waiting for?" my father fumed one day as another note from Tommaso arrived, inviting me to the opera—again at the Teatro San Giovanni Grisostomo. "He continues to seek out your company—and exclusively, I might add—and yet he has not made you an offer." He turned to look hard at me where I sat sedately in my sitting room. "You have not been allowing him improper intimacies, have you?"

"Of course not," I said, offended in spite of myself.

"Hmph," he said, pacing before me. "What, then, is the problem?"

"Perhaps . . ." I began hesitantly.

He stopped pacing and looked eagerly at me. "Yes?"

"Perhaps the problem is his family," I said. "Perhaps they object to a match with a girl who is not of noble blood."

"Outrageous," he scoffed. "We come from old Venetian stock, and what is more, we can far outstrip most noble families in the republic in terms of wealth. No family will turn their nose up at a girl with a large dowry in favor of an impoverished noble one."

I remained silent. Truthfully I had asked myself the same question. Why had Tommaso not asked for my hand? Betrothals were arranged every day between brides and grooms of far less acquaintance than we had. Somehow, I was both relieved and worried that he had not proposed. After all, had I not become painfully aware on that first night at the Teatro Sant' Angelo how well suited Tommaso and I were for each other? I might not relish the idea of marriage, but I relished far less the idea of my father being forced to find a replacement for Tommaso, should things not work out as he planned.

Before long, Shrove Tuesday came and went, and the Lenten season was upon us. The city, deprived of parties, excesses, and pleasure for forty days and nights, sank into a gray, lifeless sort of melancholy. The weather seemed infected by the same listlessness, and turned damp, gloomy, and chill.

Relieved as I was that things had quieted down—at least for a time—I soon descended into my own personal dejection, for an entirely different reason. One night not long into Lent, I arrived at Vivaldi's house to find him in a frenzy of activity. A trunk filled with clothes sat open on the floor, and on the table was a worn leather folio with scores spilling out of it.

"What is going on?" I asked, my heart in my throat. For a moment, I thought with dreadful certainty he was leaving Venice for good. After all, what was truly keeping him here? What man would let himself be bound by a woman who was going to leave him as soon as her suitor asked for her hand in marriage?

"I received an invitation to play at several churches in Brescia during Lent, so I depart the day after tomorrow," he explained as he shuffled through his music. "My father is to accompany me."

I let out a shaky breath, relieved.

"Your father?" I asked cautiously. Neither of us had brought up our horrible fight since our reconciliation, but I wondered what had passed between him and his father afterward.

"Yes," he said, distractedly, hunting about his desk for something. "He is to play as well." He glanced up, caught sight of my expression, and straightened. "He is—we have nothing to fear from him, *cara,*" he said. "The day after he . . . discovered us, he returned, and I told him that it was over, because . . ." He trailed off uncomfortably and looked away. "At the time, I thought it was." He smiled tightly. "That did not stop him from reading me quite the lecture, however. He is very pious."

"I see." I looked away, feeling as if Signor Vivaldi's disapproving gaze had fallen on me again. "And how long will you be gone?" I asked, changing the subject.

"I am not certain yet. Two weeks, perhaps? Maybe a bit more."

"Oh," I said. "Well. I shall miss you."

Finally he stopped rummaging and turned to face me, giving me his full attention. "I shall miss you as well, *cara,*" he said. "I wish you were coming with me—for more than the obvious reasons," he said, catching the playful smile that slid across my face. "It is at times like these that I wish women performers could be heard somewhere other than from behind the curtains and screens of the *ospedali.*" He gave me a smile so full of warmth and pride I felt as if I could accomplish anything, if only he would keep smiling at me like that. "Truly the bigots are punishing themselves, for they are depriving themselves of the pleasure of hearing you play."

"Even you cannot change the world that much, *caro mio,*" I said. "No matter how badly you may want to."

His eyes searched mine for a moment. "I want it for your sake more than anything else," he said. "If there is one thing I still pray for, it is that there may be another way out for you."

I did not know what to say to this. "Maybe I should go," I said finally, glancing once more around at the general disarray of the room.

Is this how the ending begins? I wondered, the heat of his smile just moments before having vanished as surely as winter chases away the summer sun. I sighed. "You clearly have much to do, and I—"

"No," he cut me off. "Please stay. I wanted very much to see you before I left. And," he added, brightening, "I have something new I would like you to play. If you are willing, that is."

"And when have I not been *willing*?"

His smile widened at the suggestive double meaning of my words. "*Eccellente*." He crossed the room to me and removed my cloak, his fingers brushing briefly over my collarbone, my breast, my hip. He draped the cloak over the back of a chair and plucked a few sheets of parchment from his desk, placing them on a music stand. I fetched my violin, tightened the bow, and applied rosin to the bow hairs. When he saw that I was ready, he gestured to the pages. "Go on, then. Play."

Two days later he was gone.

"He will be back, madonna," Giuseppe assured me, on a day when I could not seem to hide my misery.

I did not reply, nor could I explain to him that my sorrow was over more than Vivaldi's mere absence. *This is how my life will be. Someday soon we will be apart permanently, and I will live in these suffocating shadows forever.*

I returned to the harpsichord, painstakingly hunched over my splotched and smeared staff paper, which I had been forced to begin drawing myself. Each time I began a new composition, I would think, *Perhaps this is the one that I finally show to Tonio.* Yet inevitably, the tightly woven tapestry that each composition began as, with each note precisely placed and agonized over, would begin to unravel, starting to seem trite and uninspired. I was a merciless critic of my work, even as I was forced to concede that I was consistently improving.

Everything I wrote while Vivaldi was gone was in a minor key—A minor, G minor, E minor, B minor—until even I grew weary of my own melancholy and forced myself to write something in A major. It sounded forced, unnatural; and so I learned to let the music come out in whichever key it chose.

In my darkest moments, I angrily wondered why I bothered at all. There were even fewer opportunities for female composers than there were for female musicians—indeed, I had never heard of a female composer before; not one whose music was performed in public, anyway. My music would never be played from behind the grille at the Pietà, or in an opera house, or in a church or anywhere else. Indeed, no one but I would likely ever know of it. Why, then, did I waste my time?

All women, I realized, on one such dark day, *are shadow creatures. We all stand in the shadows of our fathers, our brothers, our husbands, our sons, our lovers. The sun shines only upon men. And a woman who would play or write music is in the deepest shadows of all, for her existence is usually not even acknowledged.*

The violin was the voice I had been given; yet that voice was doomed to be silenced. And I came to realize that was what bothered me the most about my life, as a sheltered, supposedly privileged Venetian woman. Not marriage, not childbearing, not the inability to choose my own husband; all of these things could be borne, if only there was music. If only I might choose that much, at least, for myself.

28

DYING IN YOUR ARMS

At the beginning of March, Vivaldi sent word of his return to Venice through Giuseppe, and we arranged a date to meet. When the day came, I arrived at his house, ready to throw myself into his arms. Instead he simply looked up from where he was seated at his desk when I entered and smiled enormously upon seeing me. "There you are, *cara,*" he said, before turning back to his work. "I am almost done with this, I promise."

Disappointed, I removed my thick fur cloak and went to stand beside him, peering over his shoulder. Unsurprisingly, a page covered with staves and notes leaping across them met my eyes. He signed his name at the top with a flourish and then, opposite his signature, he wrote *For Signorina Anna Maria.*

Jealousy, hot and potent, seared through me. "Who is this Anna Maria?" I asked.

He started slightly. "Anna Maria?" he asked, sprinkling sand on the parchment to help the ink dry. "What of her?"

"Who is she?"

"One of my former students from the Pietà," he said, rolling up the sheaves of parchment and tying a ribbon around them. He smiled up at me, his eyes looking into the past. "She is an incredibly talented violinist, even more so because she is so young. She is gifted at many other instruments as well. I have scarcely heard anything like it in my life—nor will I, I do not suppose." He sighed. "She—"

"And you still send her music, even though you are no longer her teacher?" I asked.

He frowned. "Yes. I have ever since I was dismissed. I cannot let a talent like hers become dull due to a lack of challenging music. I send the most difficult of my compositions to her, so she does not waste her time on music unworthy of her."

"I see," I said.

Catching sight of my expression, he scowled. "Surely you do not think—"

"Of course not," I said, not wanting him to believe that I would imagine such things.

"And so?" he demanded.

I bit my lip. "It is just . . . is she . . ." I sighed, realizing that now that I had begun, I must proceed, no matter how foolish it made me seem. "Is she more talented than I am?"

He stared at me in disbelief for a moment, then began to laugh as he realized the true reason for my distress. "I am sorry, *cara,*" he said. "I do not mean to laugh." He placed his hands on my waist and drew me onto his lap. "It is not a fair comparison," he said. "She has had much more formal training than you—her musical instruction has been uninterrupted since the age of seven or so. You, on the other hand, have a natural gift that is rarely seen. You do not require so much practice, perhaps, to play well." He smiled. "Though I know that, if you had your way, you would do little else. But that is the best answer that I can give you, I am afraid."

I nodded, accepting that.

"You must not trouble yourself about such things, *amore mia,*" he said softly into my ear. "Let us talk of other things." He bent his head and kissed the side of my neck. "Such as how much I missed you."

I smiled and closed my eyes. This was rather more the way I had imagined the afternoon progressing. "And I missed you," I murmured, the feeling of his lips on my skin making it difficult to string words together. "You have no idea how much."

"I wish you could have been there with me," he went on, his hands now seeking the bare skin beneath my many layers of clothing, as I shifted so that I straddled him. "You would have loved it."

"I love you." I sighed as he began to undo the many hooks and laces of my clothes. I reached down and began to unlace his breeches.

"We are going to break this chair," he murmured in my ear, his breathing growing heavy.

My fingers went still, just barely brushing against him. "Do you want me to stop?" I breathed.

"*Dio mio*, no," he said, abandoning his quest to unlace my corset and simply pushing up the skirt of my shift, which was perfectly effective for our purposes.

We lay in bed together afterward—once we made it to the bed—talking idly as the pale March sun tried its best to shine feebly through the drawn curtains of the bedchamber. I wished we could fling open the drapes and let all the light in, bathe ourselves in what sunshine there was to be had. I could not wait for spring to come chase away the gray of winter.

"Did anything interesting happen while I was away?" he asked, after he had told me all about his trip.

"No," I said. "My life has been as uneventful as ever."

"No swarms of suitors coming to call?" he teased.

I looked up at him, surprised, but he was smiling. "Just the one," I said, "now that Senator Baldovino has finally given up."

"Baldovino?" Vivaldi's brow wrinkled. "I have heard the name," he said. "But he is an old man, is he not? He must have been courting you for his son, no?"

"Not at all," I said, grinning anew at the thought of my thwarted suitor. "He has no son; I do not believe he has ever been married, though he is at least fifty." I told him the story of Senator Baldovino's brief and uninspired courtship of me.

Vivaldi chuckled. "The poor, besotted old fool. Surely he cannot have thought your father would take him seriously, with him old enough to be your grandfather?"

"Can you imagine?" I asked, laughing.

Vivaldi smiled. "No, I cannot imagine, and thankfully the good senator seems to have given up imagining as well." He wrapped his arms around me, drawing me closer. "Though I can certainly understand why he is so smitten," he murmured in my ear. "At the very least, he shows himself to be a man of exquisite taste."

"Naturally."

"Ah, well," he said. "It will give you something to think of and be grateful for when you are married to Tommaso Foscari."

My eyes flew up to meet his, shocked. "It is going to happen, *cara*," he said softly, without bitterness. "I have accepted it."

Rage and anguish and sorrow ripped me apart in an instant. I wanted to shove him away, to leap from the bed and scream at him, to demand what he meant by saying he had *accepted* it.

What about all those things you said, those things you promised me? I wanted to shout at him. *You say that you need me, that you would save me from death itself, from the very underworld, from across the river Styx. Do you not see that I am dying here in your arms, Orfeo? Save me! Save me, and do not look back!*

Instead, I began to cry.

"*Cara*—" He looked down at me in surprise. "*Cara*, please do not cry. Surely you know that—"

Yet once the tears finally found their way out, there was no stopping them, it seemed. Slowly, that word, "acceptance," slithered its way through the cracks and crevices of my mind, lodging itself there, carving its brutal letters just behind my eyes.

He was not going to fight for me. He was going to let me go.

This was how it would end.

Eventually he stopped trying to comfort me, and just held me tightly as I cried.

29

COUNTERPOINT

A few days later came my nineteenth birthday. My father presented me with a strand of fine pearls that had belonged to my mother, but otherwise did not remark upon the occasion.

Tommaso, determined to celebrate with me despite the strictures of Lent, invited me to dine with him at his family's palazzo, where we ate a sparse Lenten meal of plain fish, bread, and pasta. We had a pleasant enough evening; then in the gondola as Tommaso escorted me home, he finally brought up that most elusive of topics.

"I want you to know," he said suddenly, reaching across the intimate space of the *felze* to take my hand, "that I have wished to ask your father for your hand these many weeks past."

I was so taken aback by his raising of the topic, after months of silence on the matter, that I had no idea what to say. "I—you have?" I asked.

"Yes," he said, his eyes shining with resolve and determination. "You must know, Adriana," he said, his grip on my fingers tightening, "you must know I adore you, that I have eyes for no other woman except you. I want nothing more than to make you my wife, as soon as I may."

So this is it, I thought, my whole body feeling heavy. *This is the end. It has finally come.* "I am honored, to be sure, Tommaso," I said, trying to inject the proper enthusiasm into my voice. "But you should be saying these things to my father, not me. It is he who must give his consent for us to wed, as you well know."

He released my hand and sat back. "If only it were that simple," he said. "If it were, I would have done so long ago. Yet my family . . ." He glanced at me nervously. "My family has yet to give their permission."

"Your family does not approve of me?" I asked, sparing him the need to say it aloud.

"No, no," he hurriedly assured me. "It is not that. They simply wish to be sure that I am making a prudent decision. They wish to know you better, and your father. My family," he went on, a hint of excitement in his voice now, "is going to invite you and your father to spend the summer at our villa, so that we all may become better acquainted. My parents will send the formal invitation to your father after Lent."

I was surprised. "That is very generous," I said. "We will be honored to be your guests."

Tommaso paid no attention to these courtesies. "Do not tell your father that we have spoken of marriage; it would not do for him to hear of it before it is proper. I only wished to set your mind at ease, to let you know that my intentions are honorable." He kissed my hand, joy alight in his eyes. "Hopefully we can be betrothed by the end of the summer."

"That sounds wonderful," I said, unsuccessfully trying to sound excited.

He eyed me worriedly. "This is what you want, is it not?" he asked. "You do want me as your husband?" His gaze probed mine. "I know that you are a modest woman, Adriana, but I confess that I thought—hoped—that you felt as I did, that you would be more excited . . ."

Thinking quickly, I learned forward and boldly kissed him on the mouth.

His response was instantaneous. His arms went around me as he deepened the kiss, keeping it gentle yet insistent. He need not know I was imagining that he was someone else.

The next day, I sent Giuseppe to Vivaldi's house, asking if I could come to him that night. He replied in the affirmative, and if he wondered why I should want to return now, after what had passed between us last time, and our lack of communication since, I had no way of knowing. All that mattered was he still wanted me to come to him.

When I arrived that night, I threw myself into his arms without so much as a word of greeting. He was surprised at first, but within seconds his ardor rose to match mine, and no words were needed.

After we made love, he drew me tightly against him, my back to his chest. He was silent a long time before finally speaking. "You will always be mine," he whispered. "You will always be a part of me."

And I knew, for better or worse, what he said was true.

30

COMPOSITION

The beginning of April brought with it Easter and the end of Lent. Unfortunately, the end of the gloomy season also brought with it a fresh start to the opera season, and Vivaldi was again much occupied.

It was all too much—that I would likely be betrothed to Tommaso by summer's end, that I would lose Vivaldi, that I barely even saw him. And since I had no other outlet for my turmoil, I poured my anguish into the music I wrote. I spent every moment I could on it, and soon it seemed that my time and suffering had paid off: finally, one day just after Easter, I finished the first movement of a concerto that I was ready to show to Vivaldi.

Despite my newfound confidence, my thoughts stumbled when it came to how I would present my work to him. Much as I would like to play it for him—or so I told myself—I had never played it on the violin myself, nor could I while in my father's house.

I also thought of handing it to him one night and asking him to play it, without explaining further. Almost instantly I rejected that idea as well.

Yet once I had thought that this one, finally, I would show him,

I could not change my mind. It was a challenge, one from which I could not allow myself to shrink.

Finally, I decided subtlety was best. One night, while Vivaldi was not looking, I slipped the pages onto his desk. I had signed my name across the top, so as to leave him in doubt as to what it was.

I was even more anxious than usual in the next few days—mercifully only three, this time—that passed before we could meet again. Surely he had seen it, but had he played it? Did he like it? Or was he trying to think of the kindest way to tell me that I should keep to playing the violin, instead of writing for it?

As Giuseppe and I approached Vivaldi's door at last, I could not decide whether I would rather run inside or turn and dash in the opposite direction. I had not even been this nervous the night I first offered myself to Vivaldi. Showing him my work was somehow far more intimate and dangerous than making love.

"I shall return in a few hours, madonna," Giuseppe said as he left me outside the door.

I nodded briefly, barely hearing him.

As I stepped inside, Vivaldi came down the stairs almost instantly. *"Buona sera, cara,"* he said, and I stepped gratefully into his embrace, some of my nervousness ebbing away at his touch.

Luckily, he did not keep me in suspense for long—I probably would have thrown myself into the canal outside his door if he had. "I believe you left something on my desk when last you were here, no?" he said, releasing me and taking a step back.

"I did," I said to the floor. "What did you think?"

"I will not tell you unless you look at me," he said, his voice that of the maestro, the teacher. I dragged my gaze up to his. "Why do you act ashamed, *cara*? It was quite well done."

"For a woman, you mean," I said, immediately wishing I had not.

He eyed me sharply. "For anyone," he said. "Do you think I would lie to you? Do you think that I would say it is well done if it is not?"

I wrung my hands. "No," I said. "I did not know what you would say, if you would simply try to be kind, or if you would be harsh, or—"

"I will be honest, if that suits," he said, and—damn him—there was a touch of amusement playing at the corners of his mouth.

"You are laughing at me," I accused.

"Not at all, Adriana," he said. "Forgive me; I only remember the first time I showed one of my compositions to someone else—my father, in my case. You are comporting yourself better than I did, I must say, but only just."

I decided to stop speaking and simply listen to what he had to say. He drew another chair to his desk and slid his own chair over so that there was room for me beside him. The pages of my concerto were already there, waiting.

"Now then," he said, casting his eyes over the pages. "B minor." He flashed a smile at me. "The same as our favorite concerto, yours and mine."

I returned his smile. "I know. I did not realize it until after I had written it. It simply came from my quill in B minor."

"I know just what you mean," he said. "But to business. Let us start with your violin melody. The backbone of any concerto, and the strength of yours, as I might have expected." He drummed his fingers on the desk. "I think I see some influence of my own work here, if I may presume."

"Naturally," I said.

"Yet altogether . . ." He shook his head as though words failed him. "Very different from anything I would write. I could not have written this, Adriana."

I frowned, unsure of his meaning.

"I have never seen or heard anything like it before. It is . . . wild, like a storm on the sea. Beautiful." He looked up at me with pride, respect, and—did I imagine it?—a trace of awe as well. "What you have written here, this melody . . . this is something new. Something I do not think anyone has heard before."

"Surely—" I began to protest, but he cut me off.

"I mean what I say, Adriana. I told you I would be honest, and so I am." He smiled ruefully. "Now I must continue to be honest, and give you some constructive criticism, if I may."

"Of course," I said, feeling foolish at my hope he would adore it unequivocally.

"Your orchestral parts are in need of some adjustments, and understandably so, for when have you worked with a full orchestra?" He smiled. "Here, for example, you have the viola d'amore playing a lower note than the cello; a simple mistake, I am sure. All you will need to do is switch the two, and—"

"I did that deliberately," I interrupted.

He raised his eyebrows. "You did?"

"Yes," I said, my voice smaller now, hoping I had not committed some grave compositional error. "From what I know of it, I like the viola d'amore. It has a very rich, somber sound, but passionate in a way. And this piece . . ." I gestured to the pages. "It is about suffering, about anguish, about screaming . . ." I trailed off as we each caught the other's eye and quickly looked away. "I wanted to explore the fullness of the viola d'amore's range, to the very bottom end." I shrugged, suddenly unsure of myself. "I know it is not what is usually done, but it made sense to me when I wrote it."

"Hmmm." He looked at the score again, considering this. "Indeed. I see now why you made such a choice." He smiled. "In truth, I am quite eager to hear it aloud. We may need to hire ourselves an orchestra."

"It sounded well enough in my head, though I know that that does not necessarily mean much."

"Often that is all we have to go on, at first. Very well, we will leave your crossing parts alone for now. On to your modulation." He indicated a few measures on the second page. "You slip very briefly into major mode here, then go right back to minor. The major section needs to be fleshed out a bit more. I know it may seem counterintuitive, given your subject matter, but as it stands, it will be a bit jarring to the listener, when all the parts are played together. You see?"

"Yes, I think I do," I said, studying the measures.

He shrugged. "It should be an easy correction; insert a few more measures, perhaps. You have the same problem here." He indicated a spot on the following page.

He also pointed out a few places where he had made suggestions for the redistribution of the orchestral parts. I scribbled furiously on a piece of parchment as he spoke, impatient to get back to my harpsichord and consider it all anew.

"And when may I expect to see the second and third movements?" he asked, once he had finished.

"The second is almost complete," I said. "I should have it ready the next time I see you."

"Excellent." He swiftly rose from his seat, taking his violin from its case. "And now, maestra," he said, sweeping me a bow, "I presume you would like to hear your work?"

A shiver went down my spine. *Maestra.* "You have played it?" I asked.

"I took the liberty, yes," he said. "It is my hope that you will teach me how to play it properly."

For a moment, I was taken aback. "I, teach *you* how to play it?"

"Of course," he said. "Who better?"

"But I have not even played it myself yet."

"That is of no consequence," he said. "You know how it is supposed to sound in a way that I cannot."

I shook my head. Me, teaching Antonio Vivaldi how to play something? What strange, wondrous new world was this? "If you insist," I said. "But first, play on."

So he did.

It sounded better than I ever could have imagined, this melody that I had conceived and given birth to. I knew, suddenly, how he had felt all those times, when he told me I had played something just as he heard it in his mind. It was thrilling, beautiful, eerie, and frightening all at once.

But even so, the more analytical part of me remained apart, revising the melody as I heard it, adjusting a note here and there that was out of place.

Yet by the time he finished, I was close to tears. I felt as if I had created some living thing that now had a life of its own, apart from me. How was that even possible?

"It . . . it is beautiful," I said. "I did not think . . ."

He set his violin on the desk and knelt before my chair. "It *is* beautiful," he affirmed. "And if I have taught you nothing else, remember this: we will never, ever find enough beauty in this world to satisfy ourselves. And so we must make our own, and never stop making it."

I could not speak; I only nodded. A single tear slid down my cheek as he cupped my face in his hands and kissed me.

31

THE SIREN

The rest of April passed with my head in a cloud of music. Within two days after working on the first movement with Vivaldi, I had finished the second, and sent a copy to him via Giuseppe. I could not wait until the following night's visit to show him.

The second movement had the same "voice" as the first. In truth I had come to think of the violin part as a character all her own, like the *prima donna* in an opera. She seemed to me to be a water nymph, a mermaid, singing her song of sorrow and longing to the untamed sea.

It began softly, then eventually the cantabile melody would grow louder and higher in pitch, only to suddenly fall off in volume and move back to the lower end of the violin's register. I meant it to mimic the rhythm of sobbing, almost as if the strings of the violin were saturated with tears. The tutti sections, where the entire orchestra joined in, were quiet and hushed, attempting to console this bereft siren. Or so I thought in my more fanciful moments, and so I settled on *La sirena*—The Siren—as a title for the work.

Vivaldi was equally enthusiastic about the second movement, declaring it to be just as fine. He had some comments for revision as well, which I was already using to rework the piece even as he spoke them. Now I understood how he could compose hours into the night without being aware of the time; how he could write so many new works so quickly. Once I had entered into this haze of creation in earnest, it seemed endless melodies and harmonies drifted through my mind, and all I wanted to do was write them down.

I finally had the chance to play my own compositions, with Vivaldi looking on. The two movements were both easier and more difficult to play than I expected. Though I had virtually every note committed to memory, to actually execute those notes upon the violin was another thing entirely. Now I was back in the role of player, of performer: my fingers needed to commit the notes to memory, to find the best way to get from one to the next, an action that I found I had not considered during the composition process.

It embarrassed me that I could not play my own compositions flawlessly, but Vivaldi saw nothing odd in it. "Just because you wrote it does not mean you do not need to learn to play it," he said. "You did not write it in one sitting without error, did you? Why should your playing of it be any different? And consider, you wrote all this without benefit of a violin beside you to test out certain sections. I have never written that way myself—not for the violin, in any case."

Quickly enough, though, I could play both movements with a level of competence that satisfied me, and I soon gave in to Vivaldi's demands that I teach him. I was certain that the entire thing was an exercise in futility—surely he could already play them both better than I—but, to my surprise, this was not always the case.

"You are dotting that rhythm, Tonio," I interrupted, for what felt like the tenth time.

"Yes, but does it not sound livelier that way?" he asked, stopping.

"Yes, but the dotted rhythm comes in the repeat of that section, not here. The contrast is important, as the listener will not expect it."

He sighed but did not protest further.

"Now back to the beginning of the solo section, if you would," I said.

In the second movement, I was forced to criticize him for playing too stridently.

"It is a lament, like weeping, do you see?" I said. "Gentler, *caro*."

When he finally played it as I intended, the result moved me to tears—something that had been happening all too frequently for my comfort of late.

"I hope the next piece you write will be happier, *cara*," he told me later that night, as I was curled up next to him. "Something bright, and not so full of sorrow."

But we both knew the true sorrow was yet to come.

I had been delaying telling Vivaldi about my impending summer visit to the Foscari villa, the official invitation having been tendered and accepted long ago. Yet as mid-April came, I knew it could be put off no longer.

He remained silent for a moment after I explained the Foscari family's desire to get to know me—and my father—better. When he looked up and met my eyes, there was a strange, wistful half smile on his face, as though he were already missing me. "And by the time you return to Venice, you will no doubt be betrothed." It was not a question, and he did not phrase it as one.

"Tommaso has told me that is what he wishes."

He looked at me for a long while with that heartbreaking expression on his face. Finally, he asked, "Do you love him?"

Reeling, my breathing quickening, I turned my back to him, under the guise of situating my violin in its case.

"Do you? Even a little bit? I would know the truth, Adriana." He paused. "It is just . . . this would be easier, if you loved him."

My eyes were filled with tears, making the pane of glass in his front window look as though it had dissolved into a sheet of water. "I cannot love him," I said. "I love you."

He stepped close behind me, wrapping his arms around my waist and drawing me close against his chest. I covered my mouth with my hand, trying futilely to hide my sobs from him.

"I am sorry," he whispered in my ear.

He held me for a long time. And even as I clung to him like a castaway to a rope, part of me wished that he would let me go, so that I might get on with drowning.

32

WILD ROSE

The Festa di San Marco came on April 25, sending all of Venice into a frenzy of celebration as she honored her patron saint. There were boat races on the Grand Canal, musicians and performers and dancing in the streets, and parties—*in maschera*—held by all those who could afford them.

I was, of course, on Tommaso's arm as we attended a party hosted by his friend Paolo. As soon as we were seated in the gondola, Tommaso took my hand in his. "I had hoped to be able to present you with a betrothal ring by this time," he said, smiling ruefully. "But I fear I must settle for something more traditional." He produced a single red rosebud, such as men typically give to the woman they love on the Festa di San Marco.

I smiled as I moved to take the flower from his hand. "Oh, Tommaso. Thank you."

Instead of handing it to me, he slid closer and tucked it into the curls of my elaborate coiffure. His hand trailed down the bare skin of my neck and shoulder, causing me to shiver. He turned my chin toward him and kissed me, gently forcing open my lips with his tongue.

I tried to relax my body into his, as a woman in love would. In response he deepened the kiss, pressing closer to me, pushing me back so that I was falling back, slowly, onto the seat. His hand trailed down my neck to my chest, and his fingers spread out to cup my breast in his hand.

"The gondolier," I gasped, when he removed his mouth from mine.

"We need not worry about him," Tommaso whispered, trailing kisses down my neck. "Gondoliers are honor-bound not to breathe a word of what happens in their craft."

"Yes, I know, but—" He stifled my words by kissing me again, and his distraction was so effective that I did not immediately notice he had removed his hand from my breast and slid it underneath my skirts—not until his fingers brushed against the inside of my thighs and began to probe at the most intimate part of my body.

"*Dio mio,*" I breathed.

"Yes, *cara,*" he said, smiling. "It feels good, *sì?*"

May God and the Holy Virgin forgive me, but it did. I was nearly completely seduced. *Would it be so wrong, truly, if he is soon to be my husband? And Antonio all but gave me permission . . .*

The thought of Vivaldi wrung the desire from my traitorous flesh in an instant. "No," I said, wriggling away from him. "Stop." I moved back, putting as much space between us as possible. I drew a deep breath. "Really, Tommaso," I said, readjusting my clothing, my skin flushed with shame and guilt. I patted my hair back into place, my fingers brushing the satin softness of the rosebud. "Do you wish for us to arrive at Paolo's party quite disheveled? What will everyone think?"

"This is a day for lovers," he said, turning my face back toward his. Breathing heavily, he reached out to put his hands on my waist. "They will think that we have been putting it to good use."

"Tommaso, please," I said, removing his hands. "I cannot."

"Adriana," he said, his voice heavy, "I am nearly dying for want of you."

I looked away from the pleading in his eyes before I gave in. "I cannot," I repeated. "Please understand."

He ran his fingers through his mussed curls, sighing. "You are right," he said. "I am sorry."

Stupidly enough, I found myself hoping I had not ruined the entire night. "I thank you for inviting me out this evening," I offered lamely.

He smiled broadly, as though his disappointment was already forgotten. "And who else would I spend this evening with? Our first Festa di San Marco together," he said, taking my hand and squeezing it. "The first of many."

The next night, I went to Vivaldi—could not help myself, could not have stayed away for anything in the world. When I stepped inside, I found him waiting for me at the door, and before I could speak a word he had me in his arms, his mouth against mine. As he kissed me, he slipped a red rosebud into the bodice of my gown. We did not speak as he led me upstairs to his bedchamber.

I gasped as I stepped into the room. Many a sweetheart must have languished without a rosebud on the feast day, for Vivaldi had surely ransacked all of Venice to gather them: there were dozens, hundreds, scattered over the bed and all about the room.

"The day for lovers," he said, wrapping his arms around me from behind. I could not help a shiver at the way his words echoed Tommaso's, but I pushed that aside.

"Yes," I said, lying across the bed and drawing him down atop me. "Now let us not delay our celebration any longer."

MOVEMENT FOUR

THE END OF TIME

May 1711–September 1711

33

THE CHILD

It was mid-May when I realized my monthly courses were over a week late. I knew what this likely meant but—God help me—I cast about for another explanation with all my might. I had heard that they sometimes came late in times of distress, and that was something of which I had plenty. We were due to leave for the Foscari villa in a few weeks, and then everything would be over: I would spend the summer away from Vivaldi, and I would return betrothed.

But soon enough it was June and they had never arrived. By the time I awoke one morning, queasy enough that I was forced to vomit into my chamber pot, I had no choice but to acknowledge the truth. I had not thought it possible; had trusted in the herbs the wise-woman had given me and taken them faithfully. But they had failed, and I was with child.

I placed my hands wonderingly on my belly, the prophecy of the gypsy woman at Carnevale vivid in my mind: *You will bear the child of the man you love.*

And even though I knew that this would be the end of everything, the tears that sprang to my eyes were tears of joy.

Meneghina, it seemed, was well aware of the truth of my condition, perhaps before I was. When she came into my room that morning to take the chamber pot for emptying, she did not seem surprised at its contents. She glanced at me where I had gone to lie back down in bed until I felt better. Softly, she asked, "How long has it been since you bled, madonna?"

My eyes listlessly sought hers. "Two months."

She drew her breath in sharply. *"Dio mio."*

"Yes." I drew myself into a sitting position. "I do not suppose that I need to say you must speak of this to no one."

She nodded fervently. "Of course not, madonna. But . . ." She eyed me worriedly, biting her lip. "What will you do?"

"I do not know," I said, falling back against the pillows.

What followed the rest of that day, as I lay wretchedly in bed, was something akin to a blizzard of thoughts raging inside of my head.

My first instinct was to tell Vivaldi right away. Yet I fought off the urge to summon Giuseppe to take me to him immediately, forcing myself to ponder what this news meant. What was I expecting of him?

We had both known the days of our romance were numbered, that we must let go eventually. But surely he would not—could not—leave me to simply fend for myself. This child would bring us to our moment of reckoning: would he throw everything away—his reputation, his position in the Church, his place in the musical society of Venice—for me, for our child?

He might think I was trying to entrap him. I gritted my teeth at the thought—I had not wished for this any more than he had. Suddenly I found myself prepared to fight for this child—this child that

I was certain had been conceived the night of our private celebration of the Festa di San Marco—with my very last breath, if need be.

No, he must be told as soon as possible, so we could make plans. Whatever we were going to do, it must be soon, before I left for the Foscari villa at the end of June, not to return until September.

As if Vivaldi knew I needed him, Giuseppe appeared in my rooms with a message for me. "He has sent word to you, madonna," he told me, his voice low as he handed me a piece of folded parchment. "He asks if you will meet him tomorrow night."

It took all of my self-control not to swear, out loud and fluently. Tommaso had invited me to the opera at the Teatro San Giovanni Grisostomo tomorrow evening, and I could not cancel now without arousing his suspicion or my father's. "I cannot," I said, schooling my voice to remain steady. "Take him my reply, and ask him if I may come tonight instead."

Giuseppe nodded hesitantly. "Is there not an opera at the Sant' Angelo tonight, madonna?"

"No doubt, but ask him anyway."

"Very well." He hesitated as he moved toward the door. "Are you quite all right, madonna?" he asked. "Is anything amiss?"

"Amiss? No," I answered quickly. "Why?"

He shrugged. "You simply seem out of sorts."

"I am fine."

"If you say so." He studied me a moment longer before exiting the room. "I shall not be gone long," he called over his shoulder as he left.

I lay back down again, my hands shaking. I could not lie to Giuseppe for much longer.

Hopefully I need not lie to anyone for much longer, I thought, trying to slow my racing heart.

The next night not even the opera could hold my attention. Vivaldi had, in fact, been engaged at the Sant' Angelo the night before, and had sent Giuseppe back with no further message than he would send word when next he could meet. I wanted to break things; to scream, to tear at my hair.

I spent the entire evening trying to think of the best way to tell Vivaldi once I *did* get to see him. Even Tommaso noticed my distraction.

"You do not seem quite yourself, Adriana," he said during the intermission. "Are you feeling quite well? We can leave at once if you are not."

"No," I assured him. "Quite well, just tired. I have not been sleeping well these past few nights."

He covered my hand with his. "I hope it is not concern for our future that is keeping you awake, *cara mia,*" he said. "For you may rest assured, I would move heaven and earth to make you my wife."

At that moment I felt very ill indeed. Still, I forced my stomach to behave itself, reassured Tommaso that I had complete faith in him, and we went on with our evening.

Have I not learned to be a better actress by now? My audience must believe me completely, or I am done for.

34

ORCHESTRATION

Days passed, with more messages carried between Vivaldi and me, still without an agreed-upon time and date. This was nothing unusual; we had been forced to go a week or more without seeing each other in the past. But this was different. This was urgent, and I could not tell him what I needed to say in a letter.

Toward the end of June, Giuseppe finally brought a letter to me after several days without a reply. He waited by the door, in case he needed to return with my response. I went to the window of my bedchamber to read it, letting the late morning sun fall upon the hasty scrawl on the page:

Mia carissima Adriana—

I am sorry to have not replied to you sooner, and you will have to forgive me for giving you such short notice of my news. Even as you read this, I am on my way to Amsterdam. There is a publisher there who is interested in L'estro, *and I thought it best to go meet him without delay. This may be the opportunity I have been waiting for, so I know you will understand. I wish that I might have seen you before I left, but it was not possible. I promise we will meet again as soon as we are both in Venice once more. I beg you to wish me luck in my venture.*

A.V.

I let the letter fall from my hand. "No," I murmured. "Please, no. Not now. He cannot go now, of all times. He cannot!"

I bent to pick up the letter and turned to face Giuseppe, almost accusingly. "Did you have this from his own hand?" I demanded. Maybe, if he had not departed yet, I could intercept him. Maybe he would take me with him . . .

Bewildered, Giuseppe shook his head. "No, he sent it via a messenger, as he often does. I have told the other servants that I have a sweetheart on Burano, to explain why I receive so many letters."

I stared through him. "He is gone," I whispered. "He has left for Amsterdam, to meet with a music publisher." My whole body began to tremble. "He cannot, not now! I must—"

Giuseppe crossed the room and placed his hands on my shoulders to steady me. "Madonna, please! What is the matter? He is planning to return, is he not?"

"Yes," I said. "But by then, it may well be too late . . ." I pulled away, sinking down onto the edge of my bed. "What am I going to do?" I whispered.

"Do about what? Why will it be too late?" he demanded.

I met his worried eyes. "I am with child," I said.

Giuseppe staggered back as the news—and all its potential consequences—became clear to him.

"He does not know," I went on. "I have not been able to see him to tell him. And by the time he returns, it may be too late. My condition may become apparent before . . ." I trailed off, unable to put into words the fate we were both envisioning.

Giuseppe's mouth opened and closed soundlessly several times, as though no words could be found. "How far along are you?" he asked at last.

"Almost three months," I said.

"And he does not know."

It was not a question, but I answered anyway. "No, he does not."

"Then you know what you must do," Giuseppe said.

I gasped and jumped up, backing away from him. "No."

"You must, Adriana," he said. He stepped closer, taking me by the shoulders again. "You must. You have no other choice. He does not know; he need never know. By the time he returns, you will be at the villa. And once you come back to Venice, it will be too late. He will no longer be able to do anything for you. And if your father finds out . . ." He did not finish the sentence, but neither of us needed him to.

"I cannot, Giuseppe," I said, my voice breaking. "Do you not understand? This is the child of the man I love. I would do anything to keep it safe. I could not . . ." I was unable even to speak the words.

"But you must, Adriana!" he exclaimed, releasing me and furiously turning his back on me. He took a moment to regain control before facing me again. "I will go seek out a wisewoman myself, if you wish," he said. "I will get whatever herbs or mixture you need to take so that this can all be over with now. Women do it all the time, Adriana," he added, trying to reason with me. "You will be neither the first nor the last."

"I will *not* rid myself of my child," I said through clenched teeth as I pushed him away. I pressed both hands to my belly.

"It is the only way!" he shouted.

"Keep your voice down," I hissed. "Do you wish the rest of the household to hear you?"

He sighed. "Can you really be so foolish, Adriana?" he asked. "Can you really be so hopelessly, foolishly blind?"

"I am not blind," I said. "I know the consequences just as well as you do."

"And even if you do tell him before it is too late?" Giuseppe asked. "What can he do to save you? He cannot marry you. You could run away and live together in shame, but how will he make a living then? Unless he were to leave the Church—"

Giuseppe broke off and stared incredulously at me. "That is it, is it not? You are planning to ask him to leave the Church for you, and for the child."

"In a way," I admitted, unable to meet his eyes. "Not *ask* him, per se. But surely he will see that it is the only way for us." I grew more confident as I spoke. "He will not abandon me. He loves me."

"I know he does," Giuseppe conceded. "But Adriana, what if he is not willing to destroy his life and his reputation for you? Everything he has worked for, everything that he hopes to achieve, would be undone." He looked at me closely, a hard, scrutinizing stare, the one I had so far been able to avoid when I looked into the mirror but could not turn away from now. "And you would ask him to do all of that for you?"

"I should not have to ask him anything!" I burst out. "He should do it because he loves me and because it is what is right. I did not want this to happen either, but it did. We have both made choices that brought us here; neither one of us is solely to blame, and so we both must make sacrifices."

"And what sacrifice will you be making, Adriana?" Giuseppe demanded. "If all of this goes according to your plan, then you will have everything you have ever wanted, and he will be ruined. What exactly will you be sacrificing, pray?"

I opened my mouth to protest, but found I could not. Giuseppe, damn him, was exactly right. All I stood to lose was a place in society that had never meant anything to me. It would be Vivaldi, and only Vivaldi, who would lose everything. *Can I really ask that of him?* I wondered, guilt creeping in to settle in the pit of my stomach. *And if I do, might he not grow to resent me, someday?*

"It does not matter," I said aloud. "We have no other choice, Giuseppe. We will go someplace far away, far from Venice—far from

Italy, if need be—where the scandal cannot follow us. And then we will begin again."

"Is there nothing I can say that will dissuade you from this folly?" he asked.

"It is not folly."

"It is," he countered. "For what are you going to do when everything you are hoping for falls to pieces?"

"I do not know," I said. "It cannot go awry. It will not."

"Adriana." He groaned, sitting down heavily on the bed. "Even the best-laid plans can go awry, and this one is folly. It is. Folly and madness."

"Stop speaking thus!" I cried. "My life is unraveling, and—"

"But it is not just your life!" Giuseppe exploded, with a vehemence that made me jump. He rose to his feet. "*Dio mio,* for once, will you stop being so selfish and open your eyes? Your life is not the only one at stake! If you fall, we all fall with you: the maestro, your child, Meneghina, and . . . and me."

"If you wish to leave," I said slowly, "then go. Go to my father and ask for the rest of your wages, and leave. I will not stop you, and I do not wish you to suffer for me. Surely you know that is the last thing I want."

He sighed. "I know," he said. "And I would not abandon you, now or ever. Do not think that I care for myself more than I care for—" He stopped, the words he had not spoken hanging in the air, as audible as if he had said them aloud: *for you.* "Damn Enrico," he snarled under his breath, turning away from me. "He is like a great filthy spider, and we are all caught in his web. Damn the old bastard to *il inferno* and back . . ."

I listened, fascinated by his rant, and had to stop myself from questioning him.

"So what will you do?" he asked finally, turning back to me. "You will wait for him?"

I nodded. "I will pray that he is here when we return from the villa, and that we can be gone quickly."

Giuseppe sighed. "I know that I should tell you I will not help you." He hesitated. "But I cannot. For better or for worse, madonna, I am, as ever, at your service."

"And I thank you," I said. "More than I can say. I know that I have a large debt to repay someday."

He waved this aside. "There are no debts between friends," he said. "And I have been wrong before where Maestro Vivaldi is concerned. He does love you, very much. I can only pray that it will be enough to see you through this."

I nodded. "Have faith, Giuseppe."

"And you. You will need it."

I smiled weakly. "I will. I do. For I know no other way, now."

35

GOING UNDER

Having faith, however, became more and more difficult. At the end of the month, we set off for the Foscari villa, and I climbed aboard the boat that would take us there with the feeling of one who was being taken to her execution rather than being spirited away for a restful sojourn in the country.

Three months gone with child, I had gained a bit of weight, but thankfully it was not obvious. Meneghina would be accompanying me, so she would be able to assist me in continuing to hide my condition.

Upon our arrival, we were welcomed with the utmost courtesy by Don and Donna Foscari. Tommaso's brother Alvise was his usual quiet self; however, Beatrice greeted me warmly, as an old friend. She did much to put me ease, and I returned her greeting with equal enthusiasm.

Tommaso was alight with joy, and he made no effort to dampen his excitement. He bowed deeply, kissing my hand, and only then turned to address my father.

"I echo my parents, dear signore and signorina, in welcoming you to our house," he said, his eyes already sliding back to me. "We are honored that you are here."

"The honor is all ours," my father replied.

I smiled at Tommaso, and as a result his own grin widened until he positively beamed.

Dio mio, *he is in love with me beyond all reason,* I thought uneasily to myself. *He deserves better than this.*

As I beheld Tommaso's adoring gaze, it suddenly felt as though, instead of a child within me, there were a mass of writhing serpents.

If you fall, we all fall with you, Giuseppe had said, and only now did I realize that his words included Tommaso as well.

I wish there was some way to explain it to you, amico mio, I thought as I watched Tommaso direct the servants to see to our baggage. *I wish I could tell you everything, and let you know that it is not about you. It was never about you.*

I started when I felt Tommaso's hand on my arm. "You are no doubt weary from your journey, Donna Adriana," he said. "Allow me to show you—and Don d'Amato—to your rooms, so that you may rest and refresh yourselves."

"A rest would be most welcome, I thank you," I said.

"We shall see you at dinner this evening," Don Foscari said as Tommaso led us up the stairs.

He led us to the wing of the villa that housed the guest rooms, and showed my father his quarters. With him thus installed, he led me to my suite, which was at the end of the hallway. He flung open the door in dramatic fashion and waited for my reaction.

The outer sitting room was immaculate; the walls were covered in white and pale green striped silk, and the furniture upholstered to match. An Oriental carpet of various shades of green covered the floor, and white silk drapes fluttered around the open windows, which afforded a beautiful view of the countryside and let in a sweet, fresh breeze.

I turned to face him, impressed. "Oh, Tommaso, it is lovely," I said.

"I am glad that it pleases you," he said. "I thought it might."

We stood facing each other in silence for a moment, and I had the uncomfortable feeling that he was waiting for something, for me to kiss him as I had that night in the gondola, perhaps.

Finally I spoke. "Would you be so kind as to have the servants leave my bags in this room, and ask them to unpack later?" I asked sweetly. "I should like to rest before dinner; I am quite weary from the journey, as you were so solicitous to notice."

"Of course," he replied. "It would be my privilege." He bowed and backed toward the door, not taking his eyes off me. "Sleep well, *mia cara* Adriana."

As soon as he was gone, I went into the adjoining bedchamber and closed the door. Hardly noticing my surroundings, I removed my traveling dress, loosened the laces of my corset as best I could, and let myself fall into the soft mattress. Soon I was drifting off to sleep, and did not even hear the servants leaving my bags in the outer room.

Dinner that night went well enough. I dressed in a newly made summer dress, one of many new items of clothing my father had had made for me specifically for our stay. I could only pray that they continued to fit me for the rest of the summer.

I tried as best I could to put my worries from my mind. Despite myself, I did truly enjoy the company of the Foscari family—even if Don Foscari was a bit pompous, and Donna Foscari a bit vain. A part of me was disturbed at finding such pleasure in their company, since soon I would no longer be able to claim their acquaintance.

Don and Donna Foscari seemed rather impressed with me now that we had a chance to converse; throughout dinner they asked me casual questions about my education, what pastimes I enjoyed, what I thought of some of the operas I had recently been to see. I had to carefully guard each word that came out of my mouth, so that I did not betray my violin playing or composing, and once, when asked how I liked the Sant' Angelo, almost spoke Vivaldi's name. Yet no one seemed to notice my struggle.

When they learn my secret, when they learn what is truly in my heart, they will turn on me and tear me to shreds, each and every one of them. Even Tommaso. Perhaps especially Tommaso.

The days flowed by in a leisurely manner very different from the pace of the city. We dined on exquisitely prepared food, sometimes as a collective group, sometimes just Tommaso and I, or even Beatrice, Donna Foscari, and I without the men. There were picnics and excursions into the countryside, by boat and on foot. There were moments when I was even able to forget the impending disaster hanging over my head. But after a month or so, the idle sameness of the days began to chafe on me.

I had Meneghina lace my corset as tightly as I dared to conceal my expanding waistline. My condition was easier to hide than I had anticipated because even as my belly grew, I became thinner everywhere else. I found it difficult to eat and was only able to force myself when others were watching. The more time passed, the more the dread seemed to snake its way around my heart and constrict my lungs with every breath I took.

I also missed Vivaldi terribly. This was the longest I had been without him, and it was more difficult than I had dared to imagine. The mere thought of him was enough to cause my eyes to well with tears.

Giuseppe could not look at me without worry creasing his brow, and I kept catching Meneghina sneaking scared, pitying glances at me. But none of us dared speak freely within the villa; indeed, I barely spoke to Giuseppe for most of the time we spent there.

Even in my dreams I was unable to escape. They became nothing more than tortured visions of being discovered, of confrontations with my father, with Tommaso. I would wake gasping for breath with my heart pounding. I knew all too well that such fears might not be confined to my dreams for much longer.

"I have the very best news for you, *cara mia*, the news you have been waiting for," Tommaso said one day near the end of our stay, as I opened the door to admit him to my rooms. He stepped inside, shut the door behind him, and took both of my hands in his. "I have just this moment come from speaking with your father. I have asked for your hand in marriage, and he has enthusiastically given his consent."

I was unsurprised by his news, but the finality of it made me feel as though I had been doused in cold water. "Truly, Tommaso?" I exclaimed, with what I hoped seemed like happiness. "Oh, how wonderful!"

"It is, is it not?" he said, grinning. "This is all I have wanted, all I have been able to think of and dream about for months."

"And I," I said, forcing a smile.

"Oh, Adriana, *mio amore*." He sighed, lowering his voice. His hands trailed down to my waist, which was thankfully securely laced into my corset. "You are going to make me the happiest man in the world."

Quite the opposite, I am afraid, I thought, waves of sorrow crashing against me, threatening to drown me, to pull me under. "And you will make me very happy," I said, lowering my eyes so that he would not see the tears forming there.

Tommaso, however, was not interested in such modest, aloof responses. He placed a hand beneath my chin and raised my face. Apparently taking my tears for those of joy, he slowly brought his lips to mine, kissing me gently, then more passionately, parting my lips with his tongue.

I tried to respond as best I could, yet even as he kissed me, panic began to squeeze me tightly in its grip. *I cannot do this. I cannot.* I tried to subtly withdraw, but that seemed to only increase his ardor. He thrust his hands into my hair, loosening it from its pins, his tongue now boldly exploring my mouth. At the same time, he managed to all but carry me into the bedchamber.

"Tommaso—please—" I protested.

"Yes, *cara*," he murmured, misunderstanding, one hand gently cupping my breast as he pushed me back onto the bed. "All in good time."

Summoning all of my strength, I shoved against his shoulders, pushing him off. "No!" I cried.

He withdrew from the single, sharp syllable as though it were a knife I had slipped between his ribs. I rose to my feet, breathing heavily, and tried to compose myself. "Really, Tommaso," I said. "We are not wed yet. It would not be proper."

"You are right. I am sorry. Please forgive me," he said, sounding abashed. "It is just . . ." He sighed. "How can you be so cold to me, Adriana?" he burst out. "I am mad with love and desire for you, and most times you act as though you care no more for me than for any other man!"

Guilt tore at me as I sputtered, "Simply because I do not think it right for you to have me before our wedding night does not mean—"

"It is more than that," he interrupted. "Sometimes I feel as though you look at me and do not even see me!"

"How can you think such a thing?" I demanded. "I do love you, Tommaso. I want to marry you. You know this."

He gave me a rueful look. "You say these things, Adriana, but your actions say otherwise." He fell silent, and when I did not reply, he began to look like a dog that has been kicked by its master. "I would not have you marry me against your will."

"Tommaso, if I have given you cause to doubt my affections, I apologize. I was raised to be a modest woman, so I have acted in the only way I know how," I said.

"I know you have," he said. "I am the one who should be apologizing. The last thing I want is for our life together to begin with an argument. I hope that you may forgive me."

"Of course," I replied. "You need not even ask."

If only I would be able to win his forgiveness so easily.

"I thank you," he said. "I will leave you now, but I shall see you at dinner in a few hours. Everyone will be abuzz with the news, no doubt."

"No doubt," I echoed.

He closed the space between us further, kissing me chastely on the lips. "I do love you, Adriana," he said. "I do. I want to make you happy and give you everything you might possibly want."

"And I love you," I answered.

He smiled, the same brilliant smile he had been wearing when first he entered my rooms. "Until tonight, then, *mio amore*." He kissed my hand and departed.

As soon as the door closed behind him, I let myself collapse onto the bed. If I had only let him have his way with me in his gondola on the eve of the Festa di San Marco, I would have a way out if everything fell to pieces. In the next instant I hated myself so much for the very thought that my stomach turned, roiling in a sickening stew of guilt and remorse and anguish. Yet very quickly I realized that this sensation was none of those things.

It was my child, moving within me.

36

MOLTO AGITATO

We stayed at the villa until the first week in September. In our final days the mood was one of celebration and anticipation of the upcoming nuptials. Though the official contract had yet to be negotiated—my father and Don Foscari having decided to wait until our return to the city—it had been determined that after Easter would be the most suitable time for the event: Lent would be over and the celebrations of Carnevale would be beginning again, allowing for a most extravagant occasion.

Thankfully, Tommaso did not attempt to make love to me again and behaved like a perfect gentleman, taking only as many liberties with me as was considered proper with a woman to whom one is betrothed but not yet married.

By the time we finally returned to our palazzo, it felt as if we had spent an eternity away. I forced myself to be patient as our trunks were unloaded from the boats, as mine were taken to my rooms so I could supervise their unpacking. As soon as that was complete, I shut myself into my bedchamber alone, claiming weariness.

But rest and sleep were the last things on my mind. I paced across the room, unable even to sit down. I knew Giuseppe would come to me as soon as he deemed it prudent, and with his help I would decide how to proceed.

After about twenty minutes, I finally heard a knock on my outer door, and rushed to open it. However, my visitor was not Giuseppe but my father.

"Father," I said, trying not to sound surprised as he stepped inside. "Is something amiss?"

He frowned. "Amiss? Why would anything be amiss? I have merely come to see my daughter."

I said nothing, not pointing out that he usually only sought my company to lecture or reprimand me.

"I thought you should know that the Foscari family will be returning to the city tomorrow, and then the betrothal negotiations can begin."

"I am pleased to hear it," I said.

"Yes, I thought that you might be," he said. "I have also come to give you this," he added, handing me a small wooden box.

I opened it to find a ring, one large diamond set in a gold band—my mother's betrothal ring. She had once told me my father had chosen it for her—rather than a gaudier ring with a small constellation of diamonds—because he thought she should have just one diamond as beautiful and rare as she.

"No doubt Tommaso will be presenting you with a betrothal ring of your own," my father said, "but I thought you might wear this on your other hand. Your mother would want you to have it, and . . ." He trailed off, his eyes—to my shock—misting over. "She would be so proud of you, and so happy that you will be wed to a man who loves you."

I clutched the box in my hand, looking down at the floor so he would not see my tears.

He put a hand awkwardly on my shoulder. "I understand," he said, his voice heavy. "Rest now."

I could do nothing but nod as he left, closing the door behind him.

Giuseppe, when he finally arrived about a half hour later, counseled further patience. "You are now the affianced wife of a Foscari," he reminded me. "There will be more eyes on you than your father's now. We must tread carefully, for we cannot afford a misstep this late in the game."

I agreed to allow him to go and seek Vivaldi that night, rather than risk going myself. If he was home alone, Giuseppe was to tell him I needed to speak to him about a matter of great urgency, and then return to fetch me directly.

I suffered through dinner alone with my father, all the while wondering where tomorrow would find me.

Giuseppe returned from his errand around midnight. "He was not there, madonna," he reported in a low voice, dropping wearily into one of my chairs.

"He has not yet returned from Amsterdam, or he was not home?" I demanded.

"I cannot say, madonna. I banged on the door several times, and waited, but did not see any sign of him."

"He must have returned to Venice by now," I reasoned. "So tomorrow we try again."

Giuseppe nodded. "Tomorrow we try again."

For the next few nights, I continued to send Giuseppe to Vivaldi's house, and each time he was never home.

Perhaps he has not returned, I thought on yet another sleepless night. *Oh, God, perhaps something has happened to him . . . or perhaps it is no more than some foolish new opera.*

It was not until nearly a week after our return that Giuseppe went to Vivaldi's house—in broad daylight, and without waiting for me to send him—and finally found him.

"He looks haggard, and quite exhausted," Giuseppe reported. "He did not say where he has been, nor did I ask. I gave him your message, and when I told him you needed to speak with him immediately, he seemed rather concerned. He said you can come to him tonight." Giuseppe smiled slightly, thinking that, at last, our problems were resolving themselves.

I groaned aloud. "I cannot see him tonight."

Giuseppe's face fell. "After all this? Why ever not?" he demanded.

I sank down onto my bed and put my head in my hands. "My father is giving a dinner party tonight for Tommaso's family," I said. "God only knows how late they will all stay, and I cannot make some excuse and attempt to slip away—not tonight, not with all of them here."

Giuseppe's shoulders sagged in defeat.

"Did he say anything about tomorrow night?" I asked.

"No, he did not," Giuseppe said. "Fortuna is playing a cruel joke on us, it seems," he added, referencing that capricious goddess of gamblers, merchants, and statesmen alike.

"Yes," I replied. "I hope that she is enjoying herself."

37

STAND MY GROUND

The next morning, I rose and waited for Meneghina to come help me dress. As I was pulling on my white silk robe, the door to my bedchamber banged open unexpectedly. I turned, expecting Meneghina or perhaps Giuseppe. I froze as I beheld my father, his eyes fixed in shock on my protruding belly beneath my shift. I quickly pulled my robe closed, but it was too late. He had already seen what he needed to see.

In an instant, his expression changed from shocked to enraged, though I could tell that he was trying to keep his anger under control. "Please tell me," he said through gritted teeth, "that is Tommaso Foscari's child."

Suddenly there seemed to be a new way out. What if I lied and said yes? What could my father do? We were engaged to be married, after all, and once we were, it need not matter to anyone again.

But Tommaso would know the truth. And love me though he did, he was not so mindlessly besotted that he would consent to raise another man's child as his own. Nor could I ask such a thing of him.

But it did not matter. My hesitation had been the giveaway. My father had seen the calculation in my eyes, as I tried to decide the best answer to give. And in that one moment, he knew everything that I had tried so hard, for so long, to hide.

In a few quick, long strides, he crossed the room, and the back of his hand came crashing against the side of my face, sending me tumbling to the floor.

"You disgusting hussy!" he yelled, standing over me. He reached down, grabbed a fistful of my hair, and used it to haul me to my feet. "You filthy whore! How . . . who . . ."

But his anger was so great that words failed him. He struck me across the face again, harder this time. Black spots began to dance across my vision, and I could feel my lip split open and begin to bleed.

"How could you be so stupid, you slut?" he demanded, shoving me into my wardrobe. I fell against it, striking my head and back so hard that I cried out. I huddled against it as he came to tower over me again.

"Tell me his name!" he demanded, spittle flying from his mouth. "Tell me the name of the depraved bastard who dared defile you, or so help me God—"

"I would sooner die!" I flung my head back and shouted at him.

He struck me across the face again. "Tell me his name!"

But beating or no beating, I was through cowering in fear of him. Even as I knelt on the floor, my body curled around my belly to protect my child, I refused to give in. "You are not fit to touch his shoes!" I cried. "Your filthy, foul lips are not fit to speak his name!"

He dragged me to my feet by my robe, and I could feel the thin cloth tear under his violent grasp.

"How dare you speak to me that way!" He shook me roughly. "You will burn in hell for this! For your harlotry, for lying to your father, for your disgusting lust!"

"Oh, yes," I choked out. "And the man who beats his pregnant daughter will have a seat in heaven just below the throne of God!"

"Damn you!" he shouted, shoving me away from him. "Damn you to hell!"

"I will see you there, Father," I shot back.

"It is the violin teacher, is it not?" he demanded, causing the air in my lungs to desert me yet again. "He has been your lover all along; you have been going to him all this time, and you have let him have you."

I tried to get around him to the door, but he caught my face in a crushing grip. "I told you to stay away from him! Now for the last time, tell me his name!"

"No," I bit out. "I will not."

He struck me again, a stream of insults spilling from his mouth. "Stupid bitch . . . whore . . . slut . . . harlot . . ."

He had backed me up against my dressing table, and my hand scrabbled over the surface of it, finding a pair of shears Meneghina had left there with one of my gowns she was letting out. I grasped them behind my back as he withdrew, ready should he try to strike me again.

"And to think," he said, extracting a small box from his pocket, "I came to bring you your betrothal ring from your fiancé, and to tell you the negotiations are complete and everything is settled." He flung the box at me, overcome by his wrath again. "Do you realize what you have done, you insufferable whore? No one will want to marry you now! You have ruined yourself, and you have ruined me! I am going to be shamed before all of Venice by you, the whore with the bastard child whom no one will ever marry . . ."

He raised his fist to hit me again, but this time I was ready. Gripping the handle of the shears so tightly that my fingers ached, I brought them up in an arc above my head, intending to plunge them into whatever part of his body I could, to save myself and my child.

A hand seized my wrist in a crushing grip. "No, Adriana!" Giuseppe shouted in my ear. "Stop! Give me the shears, for God's sake!"

I struggled, but Giuseppe was much stronger than I. He wrested the shears from me, pushing me away from my father as he did.

"The bitch tried to kill me," my father said, staring at me in wonder. Quickly his shock dissipated, and he lunged at me again. "You bloodthirsty demon, I shall teach you!"

Giuseppe caught him and forcefully shoved him back. He leveled the point of the shears at the older man's chest. "You stay away from her!" he shouted. "As God is my witness, Enrico, if you lay another finger on her, I will kill you myself!"

"You!" my father seethed. "You knew! You have been helping her in her harlotry! Helping her to deceive me, after all I have done for you!"

"I am my own man, Enrico," Giuseppe said. "You do not own me."

"How dare you, you ungrateful wretch!" My father looked wildly back and forth between us. "I am betrayed not only by my daughter, but by my son as well!"

Silence fell as the truth was spoken aloud at last.

Finally I had the answer to the question I had asked so often.

"Is this true?" I asked aloud, even though I already knew it was.

"I am not about to answer to you, you murderous bitch—" my father began, but Giuseppe cut him off.

"Yes," he said, turning to look at me, all the while keeping the shears pointed at my—*our*—father. "It is true."

And even in this most dire moment, as my life lay in pieces around me, I could not help but study his familiar face anew, seeing things I had never noticed before. His hair was the same dark brown—almost black—as my father's before it had begun to gray. Their skin was the same color, a shade lighter than mine. And Giuseppe and I had the same dimples at the corners of our mouths . . .

"Are you going to stand there brandishing those shears at me forever?" my father demanded imperiously, yet there was fear on his face.

"That depends," Giuseppe said. "Because I am not going to let you hurt Adriana again. Ever. I have stood by enough times in the past, but no more." He jerked his head toward the door. "Now get out."

He did as he was told, glaring all the while. Yet he stopped just inside the doorway to my bedchamber. "You have ruined everything, you know," he told me, almost conversationally. "You might have had everything any woman has ever dreamed of, and you threw it all away to be some common musician's whore."

Rage nearly blinded me, but I would not give him the satisfaction of showing it.

"The Foscaris will never have you now, of course," he went on, "but perhaps I can find someone else who will still have you. Either way, do not expect to keep that bastard you are carrying."

I could no longer restrain myself. "You despicable excuse for a man—"

"You shall see, you worthless whore," my father said, his eyes glittering dangerously. "You will not defy me again."

"Enough!" Giuseppe yelled. "Get out, Enrico!"

This time he obeyed, but not before slamming the door with an earsplitting crack.

Giuseppe put the shears back on my dressing table and turned to me, his expression almost fearful at what he might find. "Come and sit down," he said, taking my arm and leading me gently to the bed. I complied, beginning to tremble as my exhilarating rush of anger began to fade. Suddenly I was fully aware of each bruise, each ache—and there were many.

"I will send for Meneghina to bring some cloths and warm water, madonna," Giuseppe said, moving toward the bellpull that rang in the servants' quarters.

I nodded, still trembling. "But you must never call me madonna again," I told him, my tongue feeling thick and awkward in my swollen mouth. "How can you have condescended to be my servant, to be Claudio's servant, all these years, when the whole time you knew . . ."

He shook his head. "It does not matter. I was watching over you—the best I could, in any case. What do you think has kept me here all these years?"

I merely stared at him in wonder, silently willing him to continue, greedy for the whole truth now that I had had a taste of it.

"I stayed," he said, "because of you. Enrico was good enough to give me a place in the household—"

"As a *servant,*" I spat. "And you his own son!"

Giuseppe shrugged. "It could have been much worse. He could have thrown my mother and me out and washed his hands of us. Instead, he saw that I was educated, and had a roof over my head and food in my mouth. The only condition was that I never reveal the truth to you or Claudio."

"Who was your mother?" I asked. I was far beyond being shocked that infidelity was also on the long list of my father's crimes; yet a part of me felt what my mother's pain must have been at discovering such a thing.

"A kitchen maid," he said. "Her name was Maria Rivalli. Your father kept her on after I was born, but she died of a fever when I was only five. Your mother, angelic woman that she was, never once took her hurt out on me. She loved me as if I were her own." He smiled sadly. "When she knew she was dying, she made me promise I would always look after you. As if she needed to ask." He sighed, and after a moment chuckled. "I always knew the day would come when I would have to protect you from Enrico, but I never expected I would have to protect him from you."

"You should have let me kill him," I snarled. "I would have done all of us a favor."

"No," he said. "That is not a road you want to travel, Adriana."

Meneghina came in just then, stopping dead when she saw the state I was in. Giuseppe told her quickly what we would need, sending her scurrying off again. She soon returned with a basin of steaming water and strips of clean cloth. She efficiently set about cleaning the blood from my face and applying the warm cloths to the ugly bruises and lumps forming on my skin. *"È il lavoro del diavolo,"* she whispered as she inspected me. "How did he find out, madonna?"

I laughed mirthlessly. "He came to bring me my betrothal ring and saw me in my robe," I said. "After all this time, it was naught but a moment of chance that has undone me."

"What will you do now, madonna?" she asked.

"You must rest," Giuseppe said, before I could answer.

"No," I protested, moving to get up from the bed.

"Please," he said gently, placing his hands on my shoulders to prevent me from rising. "You must think of the child."

"I am thinking of the child!" I retorted. "I must get both of us to its father at once, or else . . ."

"Oh, Adriana," he said, in a voice so full of sorrow that my heart nearly broke. "Do you not think we have finally lost?"

"No!" I shouted, pushing him away and sitting upright. "To give up now would be to lose all!"

"Please, Adriana," he said. "You must rest! You will think more clearly if you do."

"What are my choices, Giuseppe?" I asked. "What would you have me do?"

"I would have you sleep, restore yourself," he insisted, getting to his feet. "We will leave you now, so that you may do so."

"Giuseppe," I whispered. "Please. Do not you abandon me, *mio fratello*."

Tenderness, joy, sorrow, and pain all warred on his face as I addressed him, for the first time, as *fratello*. Brother. "I am not abandoning you," he said. "I would never. And so long as you promise me that you will rest, I will take you to him tonight, I swear it on my life. But after this . . ." He gestured at the vicious bruises that covered me. "I no longer know what we are fighting for." With that, he turned and left, and Meneghina silently followed him, looking back at me sorrowfully.

I lay down and rolled over onto my side, curling my body into as tight a ball as my swollen belly would allow. *It will be just as Giuseppe said,* I told myself, letting the thought gently lull me to sleep. *I will go to Antonio tonight, and then we shall flee together.*

Despite my initial resistance, I fell asleep almost immediately. I was exhausted from so many things, including relief. My father's wrath had been horrific, but it was over, and I had nothing further to hide. And soon all of this—this house, my father, my betrothal, Venice—would be behind me.

When I awoke, it was evening. Meneghina had left food for me beside my bed. It was not much—stew and some bread—but I bolted it down, famished. Then I strode to my wardrobe, pulled out a simple dress that I could lace easily myself, and donned my cloak. I went to the door, prepared to walk out of these rooms for the last time, but as I seized the handle I found that it was locked. I twisted the knob again and again, staring at it in disbelief, as if it might open under my incredulous gaze.

But it did not. I was locked in.

38

LOST

Morning dawned to find me still locked in my rooms. I had paced them all the night, certain Giuseppe would come set me free, but he did not. No one did.

It was beneath my dignity—only just—to pound at the door and demand to be released. It would have been an exercise in futility in any case. The order to lock me in had surely come from my father, and none but Giuseppe would dare to defy him. Which could only mean that Giuseppe had been similarly incarcerated, to prevent him from coming to my aid.

The sun rose, and lingered in the sky, and still no one came. I had finally succumbed to exhaustion and was sleeping atop the coverlets of my bed when I heard voices outside my door.

"Let me pass, please," an unfamiliar female voice said. The door swung open, and I was on my feet as quickly as my condition would allow. A woman whom I only vaguely recognized as a kitchen maid came in with a tray, set it on my sitting room table, and moved to leave.

"Wait!" In an instant I caught her arm in a tight grip. "What is the meaning of this? Why is the door to my rooms locked? Where is Giuseppe? Where is Meneghina?"

"The master commanded it, madonna," the woman informed me, looking almost apologetic. "I know not where they are; only that I was told to bring you this to break your fast." Quickly she slipped from my grasp and went out the door. I heard the lock click back into place behind her.

I stood, dumbfounded, staring at the closed door.

For over a week I was trapped in my rooms, seeing no one except the servant from the kitchen—whose name, I learned, was Teresa—who brought me my meals three times a day, helped me dress, and drew me a bath every other day. For the first few days I continued to ply her with questions, until I came to realize that even if she did know something—and how could she not?—she was not about to share with me.

My father I saw not at all. He had found the perfect punishment for me, worse than a beating, and he knew it.

On the third day of my imprisonment, I hit upon the idea of bribery. I took a pair of small diamond earrings set in gold that my father had given me and had them ready when Teresa arrived with my midday meal. "Come look, Teresa," I said, making my voice as cheerful as possible.

Glancing at me wearily, she set the tray down and came to where I sat, in a chair by the window. I opened my palm to show her the earrings. "Lovely, are they not?"

She nodded, still not sure of my aim.

I held one up to her ear. "They would look marvelous on you. That lovely dark hair of yours would set them off quite well."

"I would have no use for such things, madonna," she said, but I could see from the gleam in her eye that she was rather taken with the idea.

I extended my palm again. "They will be yours if you help me leave this house."

For a moment she hesitated, looking covetously at the baubles in my hand. Then her face closed off, and she shuddered slightly. "I dare not, madonna," she said. "The master has said if you were to be found missing whilst I am attending you, it will go worse for me than it did for Meneghina . . ." She trailed off, eyes wide. "I mean to say—forgive me, madonna . . ."

"What has happened to Meneghina?" I asked, feeling slightly sick, Giuseppe's words echoing in my mind: *If you fall, we all fall with you.*

"Forgive me, madonna, I am not supposed to say."

"And who is to know if you do say?" I asked, standing to block the door that led from my bedchamber to the sitting room so she could not leave. "One earring if you tell me what has befallen Meneghina," I said, holding them out to her again, "and the other if you tell me where Giuseppe is."

Her meaty shoulders sagged in defeat. "Very well," she said. She reached for the earrings, but I curled my fingers into a fist over them.

"Speak first."

"Very well," she said again. She lowered her voice. "Meneghina was dismissed."

"No!" I cried.

"*Si.* The master assumed she knew of your . . . that you had a lover," she said awkwardly. "Nor did she deny it."

"*Dio mio,*" I murmured, the guilt tightening like a noose around my throat. "Here," I said, dropping one of the earrings into her hand.

"If it please you, madonna, you did promise me the other one as well . . ."

"First tell me of Giuseppe."

"He is locked in his room," she said, admiring the diamond in her hand. "Under guard, as well. All of the servants have been forbidden from carrying messages between the two of you, under threat of dismissal."

He was still in the palazzo at least; our father had not turned him out as I had at times feared. Yet that may have been preferable, for now he was in no position to help me, nor I him. I gave Teresa the other earring, as promised, and she scurried from the room, her new treasures hidden in a pocket of her worn apron.

Despite everything, I smiled. My jailer was susceptible to bribes.

Each day, I tried to tempt Teresa into releasing me, first with a strand of pearls—another gift from my father—and then with the emerald bracelet Tommaso had given me on Christmas. I was rather fond of it, but I did not see that I had a choice. After a week had passed since my door was first locked I offered her both, in desperation.

Each day she refused, though not without some hesitation. When she refused both the pearls and the bracelet I snapped, screaming at her to get out of my sight.

Finally I pulled out the strands of silver set with dozens of diamonds that my father had ordered for my coif on the night I attended the Foscaris' ball, the night I first met Tommaso. It was obscenely valuable; I had more costly things still, but I refused to part with anything that had been my mother's, or that I might need later. When Vivaldi and I made our escape from Venice, we would need everything of value we had. Those pieces were packed away in a purse I had secreted in my wardrobe.

On the ninth day of my incarceration, I was ready. I let the chain slip through my fingers as Teresa came in with my evening meal. Her eyes locked on the gleaming silver, the sparkle of the diamonds.

"It can be yours," I said. "You know what you need do."

"But madonna, I would lose my place," she protested, her eyes never leaving the jewelry.

"And how much would that matter?" I asked. "How long could you live off the money that this would bring you?"

Her silence told me that I had finally won. "Distract the guard tonight, and then return when he is away," I said. "I will hand this to you and then be gone."

"Very well," she said, her voice low. "Consider it done." With that, she set down the tray and vanished, leaving me to prepare myself for my flight.

I was ready when Teresa returned later that night to unlock the door, wearing my plainest dress and cloak and with the purse of gold and jewelry slung across my chest. In one hand was the strand of diamonds, in the other the pearls.

I did not know or care how she got the guard to leave his post. I know only that I heard the key turn in the lock, and that she opened the door for me, her palm outstretched as she stood alone in the hallway. "Thank you," I said, placing the diamonds in her hand.

She did not speak, merely stepped aside to let me pass.

I went immediately to the servants' quarters. A tall man I had never seen before slouched beside the door to Giuseppe's room, head bowed. When he heard me in the darkened hallway he straightened up, wary.

I approached him and handed him the strand of pearls. "Be gone," I admonished him. To my amazement, he did as I asked, even handing me the key. He was clearly some hired hand that had no loyalty to my father and no real need for this position.

I unlocked the door and slipped inside, shutting it behind me. Giuseppe bolted upright at my entrance. "Adriana?" he asked. He leaped from the bed and embraced me tightly. "How did you—"

"Bribery," I explained. "Listen to me, Giuseppe. I am going now."

He moved toward the door. "I will come."

"No," I said. "You must stay here, at least for a bit, so that I will not be found missing right away. If we are both gone, they will know. You can make your escape afterward. Once I am gone, our father will no longer feel any need to keep you here."

"Adriana." He put both hands on my shoulders. "Are you sure this is what you want to do?"

I laughed mirthlessly. "It is all I have thought about these days past. And I have had much time to think." I embraced him, tightly, aware that if all went as I hoped, it would be some time before I saw him again. If ever. "Good-bye, *fratello,*" I whispered into his ear. "*Grazie mille.*"

He held me close, not speaking. "Godspeed, Adriana," he said. "*Mia sorella.*"

It took all I had not to break down at those words, so I turned quickly and left, left Giuseppe, left the palazzo, and made my way to Vivaldi and to my future.

39

NOTHING LEFT

I tried the door of Vivaldi's house and unsurprisingly found it locked. Peering in through the part in the curtains, I could see him seated at his desk, candles blazing around him as he composed some new masterpiece. The sight of him made me want to weep with relief, but there was no time for that.

I pounded on the door. "Antonio!" I hissed loudly. "It is I! Open the door!"

Hearing me, he quickly unbolted the door, and I stepped inside. "Adriana!" he exclaimed. "*Cara*, you cannot know how happy I am to see you! There has been no word for days, and I was worried."

"And I am happy to see you," I interrupted. "But there is no time for such now."

His brow creased. "What is it, Adriana? What is wrong?"

Now that I was finally here, finally near enough to touch him, finally where I had wanted to be for so many interminable weeks, I found I did not know how to ask him to uproot his life. "I . . . we are undone," I stuttered at last. "My father has discovered that I have a lover, but I would not tell him your name."

As I spoke, I moved into the light so he could see the last traces of the bruises on my face, now an ugly yellowish color; the remnants of my split lip. His eyes widened. "It was worse still," I said. "He has kept me barricaded in my rooms for over a week now. Giuseppe was similarly imprisoned."

"*Domine Deus,*" he whispered. "So this is why there has been no word. Oh, *cara.*" He reached out and cupped my face in his hands. "How could I not have known? Please forgive me somehow."

I shook my head. "There is nothing to forgive. My father's spite and hatefulness are no fault of yours." I took his hands in mine. "But there is good news, too, *mio amore,*" I went on, "beautiful news." I placed his hands on the swell of my belly beneath my cloak, looking up into his eyes. "I am carrying your child."

He did not speak for a long time. I felt his fingers stretch slowly over the curve of my abdomen as his eyes widened further in shock and wonder.

Suddenly, he drew his hand back sharply as though he had been burned. "*Mater Dei,*" he breathed, "this cannot be. How? I thought you said . . ."

I shrugged. "I had begun to think it impossible as well, yet clearly I was wrong. But none of that is important." I stepped close to him, again taking his hand. "This is our chance, Tonio." When he did not respond, I went on, trying to quell the uneasiness I felt growing within me. "We can leave tonight, before anyone knows we have gone. We can be together; have what we always thought we could never have. We can raise our child together." I paused to clear my dry throat. "Come with me, *amore.*"

Again he was silent. "I . . . I have just been reinstated at the Pietà," he said finally.

I could not fathom what this had to do with anything I was saying. "You . . . what?"

Silence.

His head was bowed, so I could not search his eyes for the truth I was so desperately afraid I would find there. Yet when he did look up at me, I wished he had not. "I . . . I cannot, Adriana. I cannot. May God forgive me." He paused, voice ragged. "May you forgive me as well, though I have no hope of either."

My breath caught in my throat. I pressed a hand to my chest and stumbled away from him, trying to steady myself, to convince myself that I had not heard those words from his lips. When I finally looked back at him, I could only manage one flat syllable, a wish and a prayer and a question and a denial: "No."

Hurriedly he crossed the room to me. "Adriana, please. I never intended for things to happen this way—"

"But it *has* happened this way!" I said, staring hard at him. "All of it has happened, and you cannot now undo it. The child—*our* child—cannot go away at your whim!"

"Adriana," he said, lowering his voice. "Think of what you are asking me to do."

"Think of what you are asking *me* to do!" I shot back. "You are abandoning me! You are flinging me to my father's mercy, and an abhorrent marriage."

"Marriage?" he asked, almost hesitantly. "To whom?"

"Not that it makes any difference to you," I said, "but Tommaso Foscari asked for my hand several weeks ago. Now he and his family will surely call it off once my father tells them I am with child. If he has not told them already." I laughed harshly. "He thinks he can still find someone who will have me, and with the king's ransom of a dowry he will give me simply to be rid of me, no doubt he is right."

"And . . . what will become of the child?" Vivaldi asked.

I turned on him anew. "I have not the slightest idea!" I cried. "Do you not see what you have done? What you are doing? Can you not see the devastation you will wreak in my life, our child's life?"

"I am not the only one who has made choices!" he all but shouted. "I would do anything to set this right, anything, but—"

"You could set it right," I said. "You could, but you will not." I turned my back to him and pressed my trembling hands to my forehead. "This is not how it was supposed to happen," I whispered. "You were supposed to agree to come away with me, and everything would have been perfect." I squeezed my eyes shut, hoping that when I opened them something, anything, would have changed. "This is a dream, a nightmare," I murmured. I opened my eyes. "Please tell me this is all a dream. Please."

"I wish it was," he said, looking away from me.

"Why?" I asked. "Why, Antonio, why?"

"I have already told you," he said. "The governors of the Pietà have—"

"I *know* that," I said. "What I do not know is why that is worth abandoning your child, and the woman you claimed to love."

"Surely you see how many doors this opens for me, and for my music," he said. "It is only because I am a priest that I can be given a position at such an institution, and there are many more opportunities available to me if—"

"If what?" I interrupted. "If you cease to love anyone save yourself?"

"That is not fair."

"Fair or not, it certainly rings true."

He fell silent then.

So that was how it was going to be. He was choosing his music over me.

And yet . . . was that not why I had fallen in love with him in the first place?

This thought was unpalatable to me just then, so I let it drown in my sea of sorrow and self-pity and fear. I drowned with it, sinking to my knees onto the weathered floorboards. "Tonio," I whispered. "Please. Will you make me beg you?"

"Please, *cara,* no," he said. He moved to help me to my feet, but I shoved him away.

"Can you still call me so?" I cried. "I believed more in you than in God, and now both have forsaken me!"

"I . . . I will make this right someday, Adriana," he said. "I swear I will, no matter what it takes."

I laughed as I got wearily to my feet. "What can you possibly do that will make this right?"

He opened his mouth, but I put up my hand to stop him. "Please. Save your breath. Maybe saying such things will help you sleep well at night, but they can do nothing for me."

"What in God's name makes you think that I shall ever sleep well again?" he burst out.

"And yet you shall never suffer half so much as I," I replied. I looked around me, at the room in which I had known so much joy, the room in which I had come to life and fallen in love and played the most beautiful music I had ever heard.

I never thought it would end this way, I thought, taking in the permanent clutter of parchment, of ink and quills and instruments. *I have always known that it must end, but I was meant to leave him; never did I dream that he would leave me.* "I suppose it is time for me to go, then," I said aloud as tears filled my eyes.

"You cannot walk home all by yourself," he said.

"*No!*" I choked out. "Do not dare tell me what I can and cannot do. Do not dare think of following me home." I moved to the door, knowing that if I remained in his presence one moment longer, I would come completely undone. "Good-bye, Antonio," I whispered. Then, while I was still able to do so, I tore myself away and went out the door.

On my walk home, I became aware of a second set of footsteps, following me. I did not have to turn around to know that it was him, that he was seeing that I got safely home despite my protests. Orfeo following Euridice back to the underworld, in a strange inversion of the tale.

I let the tears fall.

40

GOOD-BYE

As I neared the palazzo, I noticed that light streamed from a great many windows; too many for such a late hour. Surely I could not have been discovered missing already?

It did not matter, I decided wearily. I had nothing left.

As I approached the servants' door, I whirled around to see the cause of my anguish still trailing behind me. "Why are you still here?" I spat. "You have made your choice, now leave me in peace!"

Even as I spoke, the door suddenly flew open, banging against the side of the house with a hideous cracking as my father stormed outside.

He stopped abruptly when he saw me, his surprise quickly hardening into rage. "Here she is!" he cried. "How good of you, signorina, to deign to join us and save me the trouble of rousing the whole of Venice to find you!"

I watched as his eyes moved from me to Vivaldi, still standing several paces behind me. Every bit of me ached with this final defeat.

"So this is him, is it?" he demanded.

"Let me pass, Father," I said, deliberately ignoring his question and trying to push past him. His hand came down and clamped onto my shoulder so tightly that I had to grit my teeth to keep from crying out.

"You will go nowhere until I allow it," he said coldly.

"How do you know I do not have a pair of shears, Father?" I asked.

He released me instantly, fear flashing across his face.

"Coward," I spat.

But he ignored my taunt. Instead, he was staring hard at Vivaldi. "You," he said suddenly. "I know you. You are that man they speak of . . . the violinist. *Il Prete Rosso.*"

Without warning, my father turned and struck me full across the face. I cried out as my knees buckled beneath me, and I dropped to the wet, dirty cobblestones. "You brazen slut!" he shouted. "How can you possibly have been so wanton as to seduce a priest?"

He raised his hand to strike me again, but Vivaldi stepped forward and caught his arm, shoving him backward against the wall of the palazzo, and held him there with one arm across his throat.

I heard the door bang open again and turned to see Giuseppe. He quickly helped me to my feet.

My father managed a disdainful laugh at Vivaldi. "You would strike me, padre? You, a priest, would deal in violence?"

"In your case, I would consider it," Vivaldi growled. "But I can promise you one thing: you will have to kill me where I stand before I will allow you to harm Adriana again." Abruptly he released him, glancing at me where I stood shakily, Giuseppe supporting me. "And I am not much of a priest, after all."

Yet my father recovered his bearings quickly. "How dare you," he said. He stalked over to me, shoving Giuseppe roughly aside, and seized me by the hair. "Not only have you defiled my daughter, but you dare to speak to me in such a manner?"

"Release her, Enrico!" Giuseppe said, moving toward him.

"As you wish," he said. He flung me away from him with enough force to send me stumbling to the ground, but Vivaldi stepped forward and caught me tightly in his arms, cradling me against his chest.

What little pride I had left demanded that I pull away from him, but I could not force myself to move. This would be the last time he ever held me in his arms, and I could not bear to ruin it with spite and pride. I closed my eyes and rested my head against his chest, breathing in his familiar scent and reveling in this one last, deeply flawed moment of intimacy.

Dimly, I could hear Giuseppe. "Leave her be, Enrico," he said. "Sell her in marriage if you will—I cannot stop you—but this abuse must stop. And I warn you, I do not make threats in vain."

As Giuseppe went on, Vivaldi brought his lips to my ear, whispering, "I will make it right, somehow, someday, *mia carissima* Adriana. I swear that I will, even if it takes my very life."

He moved to release me, but my arms tightened around him. "Do not leave me," I whispered, making my final, futile plea.

He did not reply, only gently extracted himself from my arms. "Take care of her," I heard him murmur to Giuseppe, "for I cannot." Then his footsteps began to move away from me, fading into the night.

I remained rooted to the spot, trembling, my eyes closed so that I did not have to see him leave.

"Adriana," my father's cold voice bit out. Slowly I opened my eyes to find that Vivaldi was gone, had vanished into the fog that had begun to rise off the canals, and that this awful, endless night had been all too real. "Get inside. *Now.*"

I swayed on the spot, remaining for a moment longer before obeying. As I turned to go inside, I became aware of moisture on my cheek. Touching my fingers to the damp spot, I realized that they were not my tears—they were his.

MOVEMENT FIVE

WITHOUT YOU

September 1711–September 1713

41

MY HEART IS BROKEN

As my father had commanded me, I went straight inside. I did not stop walking until I had reached my bedchamber and barricaded myself inside. He did not follow.

Giuseppe did, however. I had only just turned the lock in the sitting room door when he began to pound on it. "Adriana!" he called. "Open the door! Please, tell me what happened! Are you all right?"

"Leave me be, Giuseppe!" I screamed at the door, finally beginning to unravel, and at a speed I could no longer control.

"Please, Adriana!"

"No!" I shrieked. "Leave me! There is nothing you can do for me now!" My ragged voice caught in my throat as I fled into my bedchamber, closing that door as well to stifle Giuseppe's shouts. "It is over," I choked out, though I knew he could not hear me. "It is over, it is really over. And you were right: we have lost."

Consumed by grief, it was all I could do to pull my heavy, ungainly body up onto the bed, burying my face in the coverlet as sobs shook my aching body.

So this is what it feels like, this heartbreak about which the poets write and the singers sing. You taught me so many wonderful and beautiful and difficult things, Antonio. Perhaps it is only fitting you would teach me this as well.

But there was nothing lovely about this despair, no music or poetry in it. It was a night without stars, a sea without bottom, a hellfire without hope of salvation.

I had not thought that anything could be as consuming as the love I had for him, until I knew the anguish of losing him. And was there anything as tragic as the fact that sorrow should be a deeper ocean in which to drown than love?

I could only let the tears come and wonder when it would be over.

I must have fallen asleep, for at some point in the early dawn I woke suddenly, roused by a dream, a fading melody. I rose, lit a candle at my desk and sat, grabbing the first quill and parchment with staves on it that I could find. I began to write, scribbling down this swirling, tempestuous melody that was storming through my head, harsh like the waves of the sea and jagged as the rocks that lay hidden near the coast. On and on for pages it went, sliding into a slower movement, and then back into fury. The siren was raging now, raging at the sorrow and pain of her heartbreak, and her force could not be contained.

I do not know how long I wrote; only that when I finished I was breathing heavily, staring down at the angry ink marks that chased each other across the pages. Almost in a trance, I got up from the desk and went back to bed, where sleep claimed me again almost instantly.

42

SINS

It had to be near to midday when I heard pounding on the outer door of my rooms. I squeezed my eyes tightly shut, wishing that whoever it was would go away.

"Adriana! Open this door right now!" my father called.

Still I did not move. Let him break the door down, if he would.

"Adriana! Open the damned door, or so help me God . . ." He trailed off.

As abruptly as it began, the pounding stopped. Moments later I heard the sitting room door swing open; he must have obtained the key. The door to my bedchamber slammed open, and he stormed through it in all his wrathful glory.

"Get up," he barked. "A maid is coming in to dress you."

I stared back up at him impassively. "Why?"

"Because I commanded it," he retorted. His hands were clenched into fists, but they remained firmly at his sides. Yet another debt that I owed Giuseppe.

"Why?" I asked again. "I have no plans of leaving this room in the near future."

"Oh, no?" he said. "That is too damned bad, as I have different plans at the moment."

Just then, a girl a few years younger than me entered the room—another of the kitchen girls—and looked questioningly at my father. "Get on with it," he said. "Dress her hair and put some powder on her." He stalked to my wardrobe, pulling out a gray silk gown. "And put that on her," he ordered, flinging it at the maid. "If you can get it over her stomach with that filthy bastard she is carrying."

My face burned, but still I did not speak, nor did I resist as the girl washed my face, removed my dirty dress and undergarments, and dressed me in a clean shift and petticoat. After pulling a comb roughly through my tangled hair, she pinned up the top sections. Lastly she applied powder to my face, to cover my bruises. Once all that was complete, she laced me into the dress.

"Good enough," my father said, and the girl curtsied to him and left, having never spoken a word. He threw my cloak at me. "Now let us go and get this over with."

Not having the energy to fight another battle with him, I followed him quietly through the house and out to the gondola. "Move," he said to the gondolier as soon as we were both aboard.

"In case you were wondering," he began as soon as the gondola was moving, "I am taking you to Ca' Foscari."

I gasped.

"They are expecting us, though I have not told them why we wish to see them," he went on. "*You* are going to tell them. You are going to tell them about your condition—not that they will not be able to see it for themselves—and beg for their forgiveness and discretion."

A chill washed over me as I thought about having to look into Tommaso's eyes as I took apart his every dream for the future, destroying the last of his illusions about love.

"Never before have I thought it a mercy that your mother is gone; yet at least she did not live to see the depths to which you have lowered yourself," he said. "She would be ashamed of you."

"I think she would not," I said, finding my voice. "And you dishonor her memory by saying so."

His face turned scarlet. "How dare you!"

"You told me she would have been happy I found a man who loved me," I said. "And I did. Is that so terrible?"

"Yet he did not love you enough, did he?" my father snarled.

I flinched and fell silent, as he had known I would.

Not another word passed between us as the gondola continued toward Ca' Foscari. Upon arriving, the gondolier leaped to the dock to help me out. His eyes flicked briefly to my swollen belly as my cloak parted, but there was no surprise in his gaze. I could not stop my lip from curling with bitterness that everything I had struggled so long to keep secret should now be laid bare before so many.

My thoughts were interrupted by the cruel grasp of my father's hand on my shoulder. He steered me along the dock and into the entryway of the giant palazzo that loomed before us.

How I dreaded what was about to take place within these walls.

A servant greeted us, showing us into a small, elaborately furnished room on the floor above the *piano nobile*. I drew the folds of my cloak around my belly as we sat, hoping to hide it for as long as possible. My father chortled.

It was not long before Donna Foscari swept into the room, elegantly dressed in a simple silk dress, followed by her husband and Tommaso. "Now, what is all this fuss about, Enrico?" she asked, patting her hair, no doubt just pinned into place by her maid. "What is so urgent that you must call on us at this dreadfully undignified hour?"

"It is my great regret that I have been forced to do so," he said. "Yet I regret even more what you shall be forced to hear next."

Tommaso's parents looked at us quizzically. "What can you mean, Enrico?" Don Foscari asked.

Tommaso kept his eyes fixed on me. "What has happened, Adriana? Your father sent word that you have been quite ill . . ."

"Yes, Adriana," my father said. "Tell your betrothed about your *illness.*"

I could not bring myself to meet Tommaso's eyes. I knew of no way to lessen the pain of what I was about to say, so I took a deep breath and stated the facts as plainly as I could, with no mincing of words and no attempt to make it sound better than it was. The sooner I said it, the sooner it would be over. "I am with child," I began, my eyes fixed on a spot on the far wall. Don and Donna Foscari gasped, their eyes darting questioningly to their son. But no one looked more shocked than he.

"I had a lover for quite some time," I continued, growing angry as I spoke. The only person to whom I owed an explanation was Tommaso. His forgiveness I would readily beg, but only his. Yet here I was, explaining myself to all of them. "But that is over now. And I . . . I am sorry," I said, at last meeting Tommaso's eyes, flinching at the anger and hurt I saw there. Yet I held his gaze, so he would know my apology was for him alone. "I am sorry to cause you pain. That is the last thing I wanted. If you think me a fool, then you are right. And that is all I have to say."

I do not think I have ever heard a room so silent, before or since. The silence was physical in its presence, separating me from everyone in the room. I was on an island, alone.

"Well," Donna Foscari said at last, the one word as sharp and corporeal as the silence had been. "This changes everything."

"I should say so," Don Foscari growled. "You may consider our offer of marriage revoked and the betrothal contract null and void. And if you should try to fight it, Enrico, so help me—"

"Father," Tommaso interjected in warning, surprising me.

"Rest assured I shall attempt nothing of the sort," my father replied, humbly. "I would expect nothing less on your part. No one is more deeply shamed than I by my daughter's disgraceful conduct."

I lowered my head to hide my burning cheeks. *What is this*

Venice we live in, where love is dirty and unspeakable and marrying for wealth and power is the highest virtue?

"How could you do this, Adriana? You selfish girl!" Donna Foscari exclaimed. "After all that our family has done for you! After all that my son has done for you!"

She was right. Tommaso had been good to me, better than I deserved. He had been honorable throughout our courtship. He had asked for my hand; he had been willing to give me his name, make me his wife, be a father to my children—much more than the father of the child I was carrying was willing to do.

I looked at him, leaning forward in his chair with his elbows on his knees, his eyes growing red. He looked up suddenly and saw me watching, visibly flinching as our eyes met.

"Answer her, Adriana," Don Foscari prompted me. "I think we would all like to know."

I took my gaze from Tommaso and raised my chin defiantly. "I have no answer which you will find acceptable, madonna, and so I choose not to give one."

"Why, you impudent, foolish tart!"

"*Enough!*" Tommaso said, cutting his mother off and standing. "Everyone out! Everyone except Adriana."

His parents and my father stared at him, dumbfounded.

"*Now!*" he cried. "I would speak with Adriana *alone*. I think I am entitled to that much."

A moment passed; then Don Foscari rose from his chair, followed by my father and, eventually, Donna Foscari. She threw me a scalding look before following the men out. "Do be quick about it, Tommaso," she told her son. "She deserves no sympathy or forgiveness from you." She closed the door behind her.

Once we were alone, Tommaso did not speak for a long while; rather, he sat back in his chair and looked at the floor. When he finally looked up, the tears he had been fighting were now visible. "Adriana, why?" he asked, in a voice so lost and forlorn I felt what remained of my heart crack a little more. "Why would you do this? How could you lie to me this way?"

"I . . . I did not mean to," I said. "I did not want to. But I . . . oh, Tommaso, I knew him long before I met you. And I fell in love with him before I met you. It was not anything I could change. But . . . I meant what I said before, though it does not mean much now. You are a good man, Tommaso. You deserve better than this. But everything . . . got away from me. It did not go how I planned, not at all."

"And what did you plan, then?" he asked, the bitterness in his voice lashing across my skin. "You would use me and toy with me until your lover decided to do the honorable thing and marry you?"

"No," I said. "I was going to end it once you asked for my hand. I would not have married you and been unfaithful."

"And yet . . ." He trailed off, letting the question hang unspoken in the air.

"Yet by the time you did ask for my hand, I was already with child," I answered. "And I . . . I was trapped. I *am* trapped." I looked away. "I am sorry, Tommaso. I do not expect you to forgive me. Only that . . . one day you may understand."

He laughed bitterly, a harsh, unnatural sound of which I would not have thought him capable. "I do understand, Adriana, better than you will ever know. I understand, and I wish to God that I did not."

I looked up at him curiously.

"You loved this man as I love—loved—you," he said. "And wherever your life takes you after you leave this room, I would beg you to think on that. I think you owe me that much, at least."

With that, he turned abruptly on his heel and left the room. I remained in my chair, unable to stop the silent tears that had begun to stream down my face.

43

CHAINS

When we finally returned to the palazzo, I was immediately locked in my rooms again. One of the servant girls came to wait on me, though it appeared my father had dispensed with posting a guard at my door.

He need not have bothered with locking me in, for I had nowhere to go. All that was left for me, it seemed, was to contemplate my bleak future.

Fearing I would go mad, I distracted myself by returning to the new composition I had begun on that fateful night, fleshing out the orchestral accompaniment but trying to leave the raw pain of the melody alone. It was not as polished as *La sirena*, but it was, perhaps, more powerful for it.

I had not seen Giuseppe—no doubt he was similarly confined once again—but when I did, and when this new piece was done, he would have one last message from me to take to Vivaldi.

When my father finally saw fit to release me from my imprisonment, it was in much the same manner as he had prepared me for Ca'

Foscari. This time, however, my father directed the maid to take even greater care with the arrangement of my hair, and he personally looked through all my jewels to select just the right ones for me to wear.

He nodded approvingly as he studied the finished product. "Good," he said. "I will send for you when our guest has arrived." Then he turned and left, with the maid following him out, leaving me alone to wait.

It was not long before Signor Fiorello came to fetch me. Moving woodenly, I followed him to the large parlor to find my father conversing with Senator Baldovino. Dread drenched me just as surely as if I had taken an icy bath.

When the two men noticed my presence, they rose to their feet politely. "Daughter," my father said. "You remember Senator Baldovino, surely."

"Indeed."

The senator approached me and lifted my hand to his lips. "A pleasure to see you again, signorina," he said, with surprising sincerity.

"Be seated, Adriana," my father said.

I took a chair, opposite the two men who held my future between their fingertips.

"I have no doubt you can deduce why Senator Baldovino is here," my father began. "He has expressed his willingness to marry you, even in your . . . condition."

The way he said "condition" made it sound as though I suffered from leprosy. "Is that so?" I asked snidely.

My father shot me a warning look. "Yes."

"She is quite far along, as you said," Senator Baldovino interjected, studying me.

"Yes," my father answered. "How far along exactly, Adriana?"

"About six months now."

"So she will be delivered sometime in December, or perhaps January," the senator said.

"So it would seem," my father replied.

"And how old are you, signorina?" the senator asked me.

"Nineteen," I replied. "I will be twenty come March."

"March, eh?" the senator said. "Perhaps an April wedding, then. A lovely spring wedding. What would you say to that, Enrico?"

"That sounds like a marvelous idea, Giacomo," my father said, smiling.

I began to feel as if every part of my body were growing cold, as though I were a walking, reanimated corpse that wanted only to be returned to the grave.

"Very well, then," Senator Baldovino said. "We will draw up the betrothal papers before I leave." He turned his gaze back to me. "Would it suit you to be a senator's wife, signorina?"

I could not speak, but Senator Baldovino did not wait for a reply.

"Rest assured I will not hold your past indiscretions against you. Quite the reverse, in fact." A lecherous grin spread across his face. "I rather prefer a woman who knows what she is doing during the act of love."

His use of the phrase "act of love" caused me to physically shudder. *It will never be so for me, never again.*

"Nor shall I question you as to the father," he went on, in what he no doubt felt was a benevolent tone. "I do not care, quite frankly. This is in the past, or soon will be. God willing, you will be carrying a child of mine before too long."

I froze in horror at these words.

"Do we understand one another, signorina?" he asked.

There was nothing I could do but nod.

"*Benissimo.*" He turned back to my father. "I am well pleased by our business here today, my friend."

"As am I, Giacomo," my father said.

"Perhaps you had best inform her of what we discussed earlier."

"Ah, of course." My father turned his gaze on me, his expression hardening. "Listen carefully, Adriana, so that you understand what is going to happen."

I sat in silence: a condemned prisoner waiting for her sentence.

"Next month, I am sending you to my sister's house in Mantua, where you will spend your confinement," he informed me. "You will give birth there, and once the child is born, it will be given to a family in that city to raise as their own."

At this, my chilly composure cracked; I whimpered slightly.

My father scowled. "I told you that you would not be allowed to keep the child."

"Please," I whispered, glancing from my father to my future husband. "Is there no way that I might . . . ?"

Senator Baldovino shook his head. "No," he said. "I will forgive your past, signorina, but my money will not be used to bring up another man's bastard. It will be better put toward the care of our own children, would you not agree?"

And what makes you think you will even be able to father children at your age, old man? I thought viciously. I gasped as a new idea came to me. "What if the child were to be reared at the Pietà?" I asked. "As my mother was?"

While my father looked enraged at this, Senator Baldovino appeared intrigued by the suggestion. "I would not be opposed to such an idea, Enrico," he said, leaning back in his chair. "The Pietà is a fine institution; as you know, I have been one of their benefactors for many years. Adriana could rest assured that her child was well cared for, and given a good education."

My heart began to pound wildly as hope sprang to life once again within it. *The child's father will be able to watch over him or her . . . he surely owes me that much, at least.*

But my father shook his head. "Out of the question," he said. "It will present far too great a temptation for Adriana. I know my daughter, Giacomo. She will want to visit the bastard, send it gifts and so on. Would not that time and attention and money be better devoted to your own children, as you so rightly said before?"

"I suppose you are right," Senator Baldovino said, shrugging.

All hope drained out of me. My life would go from being under the control of my father to being under the control of my husband, as I had always known it would. It was shocking, after all the upheaval and destruction that had been wrought in my life, to realize how little had actually changed.

"We shall abide by the original plan, then," my father said. "You shall go to your aunt's house, and the child shall be adopted by a suitable family as soon as we find one amenable to the arrangements. It should not be too difficult, for I will make it worth their while."

I bowed my head so that neither of them would see the tears gathering in my eyes.

"Do you understand, Adriana?" my father demanded.

"I understand," I said. "I suppose I have no choice, do I?"

"No," he bit out. "You do not."

To my surprise, Senator Baldovino rose from his chair, crossed the room to me, and patted my shoulder. "Do not fret, signorina," he said. "In a few months' time, all of this will be behind you. I am sure you will find nothing to object to in your life with me." He turned back to my father. "Shall we adjourn to your study, Enrico, and draw up the papers?"

"Certainly," my father said, rising from his chair. "Right this way, Senator." He tossed me a careless glance over his shoulder. "Please return to your rooms immediately, Adriana."

After they left, I remained seated, trying to absorb what had just happened to me. I was not surprised by my new betrothal, as I had known that my father would do his damnedest to find *someone;* yet I had found that imagining a blank future with some faceless husband had been ultimately more palatable than knowing exactly who I would be forced to spend my life with.

Just as I was about to rise and obey my father, Giuseppe slipped into the room and closed the door behind him.

"Oh, *Giuseppe*!" I cried, leaping to my feet and flinging myself into his arms. "Oh, where have you been? What has Father done to you?"

Giuseppe smiled. "He has done nothing to me, yet. But please, Adriana, sit. It cannot be good for your condition to be so excited."

I obeyed, and he drew up another chair beside me. "I doubt I shall ever have occasion to be excited again."

"So you are betrothed, then," he said.

"You know?"

He shrugged. "I knew Baldovino was coming today, and I saw him and Enrico leave the room looking quite pleased with themselves." He paused. "So you are to marry him?"

I nodded. "They are drawing up the betrothal contract. And the child—" I broke off, not sure if I could speak the words.

"They will not let you raise it yourself, will they?" he asked.

Taking a deep breath to steel myself, I told Giuseppe of our father's carefully laid plans.

"Despicable," he said when I had finished. "The two of them. But in truth I expected nothing better."

"Nor did I," I said. "But even so . . ." My eyes filled with tears. Dear God, would I ever stop weeping?

"Would that I could come with you to your aunt's house, but Enrico would never allow it," Giuseppe said. "He would no doubt think we were plotting an escape."

"Would that I could escape," I said. "But he need not fear, for I have nowhere left to go." I changed the subject. "But what of you, Giuseppe? Where have you been?"

"I have been here, in the palazzo," he said. "Enrico has not thrown me out, but he has forbidden me to communicate with you in any way. The servants have been warned not to carry messages between us, nor admit me to your rooms."

"Oh, Giuseppe," I said. "I have brought all of this upon you. It was all just as you said."

"Do not trouble yourself about that, Adriana, do you hear me?" he said. "I have no desire to stay here in any case, since you will soon be gone."

I reached out and took his hand. "I do not know how I can bear to be parted from you, especially now."

"Do not fear, *mia sorella*," he said softly. "We will still be a part of each other's lives. I will not allow it to be otherwise."

I smiled. "Nor I."

"You should get back to your rooms soon, should Enrico decide to look in on you," he said. "But first, I have something for you." He rose, opened the door, and picked up something he had left just outside. I froze when I saw what it was: a violin case. "What—where did you get that?" I demanded.

He held it out to me, and when I made no move to take it, set it on the floor at my feet. "He sent it," Giuseppe said. "It is for you."

I did not reply. Slowly, I leaned down and lifted the case onto my lap. I opened the lid and gasped. It was not my violin that he had sent me: it was his.

Gently I lifted the instrument out of the velvet-lined case, hoping, fearing he had included a letter. But there was nothing. He knew there was nothing left to say.

But I had one last thing to say to him, in the only way I knew how—and the only way he would understand. "Follow me to my rooms, please, Giuseppe," I said, my voice wavering as I closed the lid. "I need you to take something to him in return."

"A message?" Giuseppe asked, somewhat incredulously. "Adriana, what can you possibly—"

"Not quite a message," I said. "It is a piece of music."

44

THE GREATEST PAIN

All went according to my father's plans. The betrothal terms were finalized, and my affianced husband presented me with a heavy gold betrothal ring set with a large diamond and bordered with smaller diamonds. It had belonged to his mother, which accounted for its old-fashioned design. I wore it whenever I knew I would see him or my father; otherwise it remained in its case on my dressing table. My mother's ring I wore every day, if only to feel that she was with me.

I was sent to Zia Gianna's palazzo in Mantua at the end of October, as planned. The maid who had been seeing to my appearance, Agnese, accompanied me.

My stay with Zia Gianna was just as odious as I had anticipated. She was as disagreeable and miserable as ever; more so, in fact, due to the shameful circumstances of my visit. She wasted no opportunity to say that I was a common slut, no better than the whores who sold their bodies on the bridges of Venice—or worse, since I had always acted so modestly and properly, thus deceiving everyone as to my true nature. She was shocked that any man would stoop to make me his wife. I got into the habit of sitting on my hands whenever she would launch into such a tirade so as not to reach out and slap her smug, sanctimonious face. One day I finally broke down and screamed at the old harpy to be silent. I was locked in my room the rest of the day as punishment; but being confined was something to which I had grown quite accustomed.

A few weeks after my arrival, she informed me that a family had been found for my child. Their name was Girò, they already had one daughter, and owned a wig-making shop. That was all I was told; and none of it told me what I most needed to know: Were they good people? Would they treat my child well? Would they love him or her?

My questions were destined to go unanswered.

And so I waited, as I had been doing for so long now, for the birth of the child, for this phase of my life to end so the next could begin. Some days I could not help but think that this limbo in which I existed was perfect, for I wanted to go neither forward nor back.

The day after Christmas—a joyless and somber feast, so completely unlike the previous Christmas—I awoke in the dead of night to find the sheets of my bed soaked through. As I went to get up, a clenching pain caused me to double over, as though an enormous hand was wrapped around my innards and was squeezing tightly.

Within half an hour, I was installed in a chamber that had been prepared especially for the birth. My aunt was striding about the room giving orders as we waited for the midwife to come from town. It seemed as if all the servant women in the house were crowded into the room, carrying pails of hot water and piles of linens or herbs or medicines that were supposed to aid in the birthing process, or prevent childbed fever from setting in afterward. Somehow it had never occurred to me I might die during the birth, but I could not bring myself to be afraid. I could only wonder how Vivaldi would feel if he were to learn that I had died in childbirth.

When the midwife finally arrived, she ordered the servants out, save two older women—experienced in delivering babies—and

Agnese. Zia Gianna remained as well, pacing and wringing her hands nervously. I wanted to ask her what she was so concerned about, considering the stain I was on the family name. But it occurred to me that perhaps she did not relish the thought of informing my father that his daughter—the intended bride of a senator—had died under her care.

The midwife, Pietra, had me lie on the bed and lifted the hem of my linen shift up past my waist. She instructed me to bend my knees and spread my legs, so that she might check on the baby's progress, which I did.

When she was done, she replaced my clothing and looked at me with a faint smile. "You are in for a very long night, I am afraid," she said. "This is your first child, is it not?"

I nodded.

"And do you know when, precisely, you conceived?"

Even then, my face flushed with heat as I remembered that April night, and the rose petals against my skin in Vivaldi's bed. "I believe it was April 26."

"A few weeks early, then," the midwife said. "Yes, it will be quite a long night. The first child always takes the longest, for your body must perform a task with which it is not yet acquainted. And since the child is coming early, it will be harder to expel from the womb."

She told me to walk about the room, the better to help the child shift into the proper position. Meanwhile, she had Agnese fetch me some broth from the kitchen. "Drink it," she admonished me. "You will need your strength."

I paused in my pacing long enough to obey, then resumed, back and forth, back and forth.

The pains were still few and far between when I began to grow weary. My eyelids began to droop, and my footsteps slowed.

"Might I not rest now?" I asked the midwife.

Pietra shook her head. "You must continue to walk about," she said. "It will make it go faster."

Obediently I continued to shuffle back and forth.

The sun had long since risen by the time my pains began to come closer together. They lasted longer and were more forceful; each time it was like a wave breaking over me, and I had to double over and squeeze my eyes shut until it passed, leaving me weakened and drained.

Finally, Pietra gave me permission to lie on the bed, which I did gratefully. She pulled up my shift again to inspect me, her fingers gently probing.

"Your body is opening to push the child out," she told me. "The hardest part is still before you."

I stared at her in wonder, hardly believing I could be any more tired than I already was.

As the pains began coming faster, Pietra instructed me to push each time they were upon me. Before long, each pain brought with it the utter certainty that I was being ripped in half; but I would do my best to push with the strength I had left, which was not much.

"You must push, signorina!" Pietra told me, crouching down to peer between my thighs.

"I cannot!" I cried, lying flat, my eyes closed.

"You must!"

"Please, signora, I cannot!"

In that moment, I was so full of hatred for everyone who had brought me to this place: Vivaldi, God, my father, Baldovino, even Giuseppe. Even if I did succeed in giving birth to this child, I was certain it would be formed of rage and loathing instead of flesh and blood.

"Signorina, you must not give up now!"

Why not? What do I have to live for? And how do I know things will be any better for my child?

My eyes fluttered open, and I fought to sit up.

I will not abandon my child as everyone else has abandoned me.

Teeth gritted, I commenced pushing, with Pietra urging me on. "I can see the head, signorina," she told me. "Nearly there!"

I scarcely noticed the woman standing next to me, wiping my sweat-drenched face with a cool, damp cloth. The pain was relentless now, and I knew, with some basic, primal female instinct, that this meant it was almost over.

I pushed, harder, crying out in pain as I felt a rush of blood come from between my legs.

What strange, foolish creatures we women are, some numb, detached part of me mused. *All of this blood and suffering for the love of a man.*

"Once more, signorina! Almost there!"

With one last excruciating push, I gave the last of my strength and fell back against the pillows, utterly exhausted; so much so that I wondered if I had, in fact, died.

But then I heard my baby cry, and my eyes flew open, new life filling me.

Pietra was holding the small, red, blood-covered thing in her arms, smiling down at it. "A girl, signorina," she said, looking up and transferring her smile to me. "A beautiful healthy girl."

I reached out my arms, and Pietra, after severing the cord that still connected her to my body, gave her to me without hesitation.

She was the most beautiful creature I had ever beheld in my life. Each part of her tiny body was perfectly formed, a replica in miniature of my own.

"She has a good set of lungs on her," Pietra remarked.

Indeed she had, for she scarcely seemed to pause in her wailing to breathe. I moved to bare my breast for her.

My aunt gasped in shock and disapproval. "Take the child from her at once," she ordered Pietra. "We have a wet nurse who is to suckle the child, and go with her to her new home. Adriana is to have no further contact with the child."

I clutched my daughter as tightly as I dared. "No! You cannot take her from me yet! Please, just give me a little time!"

But Zia Gianna was shaking her head. "You will only grow attached to her." She motioned again to Pietra. "Take her away. Now."

"No!" I screamed. "Please, I beg of you! Just give me an hour—not even that! Half an hour only!"

I broke off as Pietra approached me. "Please, signora," I whispered, tears streaming down my cheeks. "This is the child of the man I love. She is all I have left."

"Pietra!" my aunt barked, seeing her hesitation. "If you do not do as I bid you, I will see to it that you do not find work in this city ever again. Am I understood?"

At that, Pietra stepped closer, gently taking my daughter from my arms. The child began to wail anew, only this time her cries were like knives upon my ears. "What is her name, signorina?" Pietra whispered.

I looked for the last time upon my daughter's face. In that moment I feared that, should I name her after her father as I had wanted, someone might guess his identity. "Anna," I said aloud. "Her name is Anna."

Pietra nodded once, then stepped away from the bed. I fell back and closed my eyes.

Once I heard the door close behind her, I began sobbing. "You evil, hateful witch!" I screamed as my aunt made to leave the room as well. "How could you—why—" But I could no longer speak, my words dissolving into screams, but of a different, far greater pain this time.

45

DARKNESS BEFORE THE DAWN

By two days after the birth, Pietra proclaimed me perfectly healthy. She also assured me—and my aunt, who would report to my father—that I should have no trouble bearing children in the future.

Tossing and turning, I tried to get some sleep. Despite my exhaustion, I wondered if I would ever be able to sleep again not knowing where my daughter was, or if she was safe.

I must have drifted off at some point, however, for the next thing I was aware of was being gently shaken awake. "Adriana," a voice whispered in my ear.

"Who is there?" I mumbled, rolling over toward the voice, still half asleep. I opened my eyes to see Giuseppe's face, dimly illuminated by the light of a single candle. "Giuseppe!" I gasped, pulling myself into a sitting position. "How did you get here? How did you get in?"

"Shhh," he hissed, sitting on the edge of the bed. "I got on a coach that was headed here, of course. And as to how I got in . . ." He smiled mischievously. "You underestimate my effect on the fairer sex, Adriana. I spoke for a time with a young maid, who was kind enough to let me in once I explained."

"Does Father know you left?" I asked, fully awake now. I pushed my heavy hair off my face, anxiously searching his eyes. His silence, however, told me all that I needed to know. "*Dio mio,*" I breathed. "He has not thrown you out?"

He nodded. "Told me I was no longer welcome in his house because of my betrayal. He gave me a small fortune before I left, though." He chuckled darkly. "My inheritance."

"Oh, Giuseppe. Whatever will you do?"

He shrugged. "Do not worry about me, Adriana. What of you? How are you faring here?"

I looked away. "I gave birth two days ago."

His eyes widened. "Are you well? And what of the child?"

My eyes filled with tears. "I am not well, not at all. It was a girl, and they took her from me at once. Her name is Anna."

"Oh, Adriana." He enfolded me in a tight embrace. "I am so sorry."

"There was nothing I could do, Giuseppe," I said, sobbing. "Yet sometimes I think that if I really loved her, I would not have let them take her. That I should have died first."

"Do not blame yourself," he said. "You were caught in a web of plans laid by powerful men. There was nothing you could have done."

"Perhaps," I said. I knew he was right, yet I also knew that a mother's guilt would never cease to hound me.

"And when do you come back to Venice?"

I wiped away my tears. "No one has said. As soon as I am recovered enough to travel safely, I suppose. But what of you?"

"It was suggested that it would not go well for me if Enrico were to find me hanging about you, causing trouble," he said, smiling. "So I have a mind to see more of the world, outside of Italy. With Enrico's money, of course."

"I wish that I could keep you with me always," I said, crestfallen. "But perhaps you are right, and this will be best for now."

He squeezed my hand. "I will return to Venice soon enough," he said. "In plenty of time for your wedding."

I chuckled. "Father will be thrilled."

"He cannot stop me. What will he do, throw me out of the church?"

I laughed at the image: my aging father, formidable though he might be, attempting to bodily expel the young, robust Giuseppe from my wedding ceremony. "It is to be in April, I believe," I said. "After Lent."

"I will be there," he said. "No doubt I will be homesick before long, in any case."

I smiled. "Come home with a lovely French wife, Giuseppe. They are said to be the most beautiful women in the world."

He leaned forward and kissed the top of my head. "No, *cara sorella,*" he said. "*Le donne italiane sono.*"

As he rose to leave, I clutched at his sleeve. "Wait," I said. "Where do you go from here?"

He paused. "Back to Venice, I suppose, to find passage from there."

I hesitated only a moment. "There is one thing I need you to do for me," I said. "I have no right to ask, not when you have already done so much for me, but . . ."

"Anything," he said, sitting back on the edge of the bed. "Just tell me what it is, Adriana."

"Will you go to him?" I asked. "Tell him he has a daughter, and her name is Anna."

"Oh, Adriana." Giuseppe sighed, running his fingers through his dark hair. "What good can it do now?"

"Would you not want to know, if you were in his position?" I asked.

He was silent. "Very well," he said. "I will go. Yes, of course I will go." He rose to leave. "I promise I will find him before I do anything else."

"I will repay you someday, Giuseppe," I vowed. "For everything. I know not how, but I will, I swear it."

He shook his head. "You need do no such thing." Before I could protest, he moved toward the door. "*Addio,* Adriana. I will see you at your wedding."

Tears stung my eyes again. "*Addio, mio caro fratello.*"

And then he was gone, and I was alone in the darkness of the cold room.

46

RECAPITULATION

I returned home to Venice at the end of January, without having heard any more of my daughter's fate. I was not such a fool that I did not realize this was how it would be, for the rest of my life: Anna would be the child I could never admit to having borne, and everyone around me would pretend these events, which had shattered my entire life, had never happened at all.

Plans for the wedding were well under way by my return. My father and my affianced husband had apparently disagreed over the size and style of the event: the former wanted the large, lavish wedding that would normally accompany the union of a senator and a daughter of a wealthy family and, as such, quash any rumors of scandal. The latter, however, in a turn quite uncharacteristic of a Venetian nobleman, did not want much made of himself. My father was not happy, but he was forced to hide his displeasure.

I did not care either way what people might think and doubted anyone would ever guess the whole truth. After all, besides myself, only my father, Vivaldi, and Giuseppe knew everything there was to know—Meneghina had never even asked my lover's name—and we would all remain silent unto the grave, if for very different reasons.

I had resolved to be as stoic as possible regarding the wedding arrangements and the marriage itself. I had lost and I knew it.

Yet there was one crucial detail of the arrangements that, when revealed to me by my fiancé, nearly caused me to lose the composure I had just barely achieved.

Several days after my return, I was informed the senator was waiting in the small parlor for me. I went down to see him in the graceless, listless manner I had adopted since giving birth. It was as though my body could not seem to remember how it ought to move without the added weight of a child within me.

He rose when I entered, his eyes moving over my form probingly. I had lost all of the weight I had gained while carrying the child, and then some. "You are thin, Adriana," he said, in lieu of a greeting. He lowered himself heavily back into his chair once I was seated. "You have not been eating well, I take it?"

I shrugged. "I do not have much of an appetite of late," I said.

"You must try to eat more to regain your health," he instructed. "You do not want to be a pale, wan bride, do you?"

I do not want to be a bride at all.

He leaned toward me. "If you think to discourage me with your indifference, you are destined to be disappointed," he said. "I care very deeply for you, and nothing would induce me to part with you, when I am so close to making you mine."

You care for me as you would a prized possession, not a woman.

To my surprise, his tone grew gentler. "All I ask is that you give me a fair chance," he said. "I know I am not the young, gallant knight errant that young ladies dream of marrying. But I cannot make you happy if you do not let me try."

In spite of myself, my heart softened ever so slightly. "You are a man of sense, I see," I said, glancing up to find him smiling at me. A bit more at ease, I prompted, "And to what do I owe the pleasure of your visit today, Senator?"

"Wedding plans, what else?" he said. "The dressmakers and

jewelers and what have you—since I know not what gear a woman needs for her wedding day—will be coming here in the next few days to consult with you. Spare no expense, my dear. Choose anything and everything you desire. Though it is to be a small wedding, I want it to be as beautiful and luxurious as you wish."

I nodded, touched by his heartfelt words. "I thank you very much, Senator. And has a date been chosen?"

"It has. The happy day is to be the thirtieth of April, at the church of the Pietà. There should be enough of spring in the air by then, would you not say?"

I scarcely heard his last words. "It . . . what? Where?"

He gave me a puzzled look. "At the church of the Pietà," he repeated. "Adriana, whatever is the matter?"

"I . . . I . . ." I stuttered.

How can I be married in that church, where I will see him everywhere?

"Please, I beg of you," I began. "Might we not be married somewhere else?"

"No," he said, still looking perplexed. "I have been attending Mass there since I was a boy and I am one of their benefactors. And I confess I do not understand your reluctance, my dear. I thought it would please you to be married in the same church as your parents."

"Please," I repeated. "Please, Senator, anywhere but the church of the Pietà."

His expression darkened. "No, Adriana. I would give you your head in anything else, but I am quite set on this, and it is already arranged. You are being quite unreasonable, especially as you have yet to explain your objections."

"I will not ask you for anything else," I said. "Just, please . . ."

He rose to his feet. "Out of the question," he said. "I have decided, and so it shall be. I hope you are not planning to make a habit of questioning my decisions in such a way. Good day to you, Adriana." With that, he moved crossly past me and out of the room.

Once alone, I buried my face in my hands. Fortuna was, no doubt, once again laughing loudly at my expense.

The wedding preparations seemed to go on around me, as though I were standing in the middle of a river and simply letting the water flow past me, neither helping nor hindering the current. I made decisions when I was asked to, but did not offer an opinion otherwise; yet somehow, no one seemed to notice.

My twentieth birthday came and went, lost in the wedding plans, almost as unremarked upon as the previous one. My father invited Senator Baldovino to dine at our palazzo, but it was a rather subdued, joyless affair. After dinner, my future husband presented me with a heavy gold necklace set with an enormous diamond, saying he would be most pleased if I would wear it on our wedding day. I did not know if I would be able to hold my head up with such a thing around my neck, let alone stand through the entire ceremony, but I said I would.

The date of the nuptials quickly approached, and I heard nothing from Giuseppe. He had sent me several letters since his departure, telling me of the things he had seen and the people he had met. His first letter came from Milan, the second from Vienna, the third from Barcelona, and the last from Paris. The first letter had informed me he had succeeded in delivering my message to Vivaldi, but gave no further details.

The letter from Paris was dated in late March, and as the beginning of April came and went, I had no further news of him. I began to worry that Giuseppe—the only person I truly wanted at my wedding—would not return to Venice in time.

My other, incessant worry was for my daughter. I worried that she was not being properly cared for, that the Girò family did not love her, did not want her. I worried, foolishly, that she somehow knew I had abandoned her. And as I had no one in whom to confide, these worries bled and festered within me, a wound that everyone chose not to see and so could not be healed.

47

B MINOR

As soon as I heard the first notes of the music, I knew it was his. My steps slowed as I tried to catch the breath of which the music had robbed me. My father turned his head ever so slightly to glare at me, as though he thought I had some dramatic notion of releasing his arm and running away. As if I could move at any but the slowest of paces, weighed down as I was by the senator's diamond necklace and this gown with its stiff bodice and ten-foot train.

Thank God that, at just that moment, I caught sight of a familiar face in one of the back pews: Giuseppe, grinning at me like a boy who had just succeeded in playing a trick on his nursemaid. I smiled back. Now I knew there was one person, at least, in the church who loved me for myself and truly wished me well.

I collected myself, gave my father a reassuring smile, and we continued our procession to the altar.

The music played by the orchestra, which was soon joined by the choir, was a joyous, vibrant piece, glorifying God. *He may as well have written me a requiem Mass,* I thought, *for I am only twenty years old, and already my life is over.*

Yet as I reached the altar, the music changed, so drastically

I thought my own thoughts had summoned what I was hearing. It was in B minor—of course. Urgently tolling strings climbed higher and higher before the choir came in, each voice part layering on top of the next, moving upward by half steps. Tears filled my eyes even as I quelled the urge to laugh.

I took my place before the priest, and beside Senator Baldovino, looking as old as ever. My father released me and went to his place in the front pew beside Claudio, come from Florence for the wedding, with what I fancied was a rather self-satisfied smirk on his face.

The priest waited for the music to finish before commencing, and I could not help but notice that this movement was longer than the one before. A reprieve. I closed my eyes and let each chord wash over me, tears streaming freely down my face. If either the priest or my intended noticed, no doubt they simply attributed it to happiness.

Once the music—both gift and cruel reminder of what I could not have—ended, the priest began. I scarcely listened to what he was saying, my eyes and attention drawn to the choir loft above and to the left of us, obscured from view by a high metal grille that served to protect the *figlie di coro,* as they were called, from the eyes of outsiders. I could just make out the red of the robes they wore to perform, or on the extremely rare occasions they went out in public. My mother had told me this, I realized; I had only just now remembered.

Was he there, as well? Was he watching? Surely he was, directing the orchestra and choir in his work. Perhaps it was merely my imagination wishing to at once torture and soothe me, but I was sure I could feel his eyes on me from somewhere in the sanctuary.

I hope you are seeing this, I thought, as though he could hear me. *I hope you are seeing the wreck you have made of my life. I hope it was worth it, Antonio. I do.*

"I do," Baldovino suddenly declared, tearing me from my reverie.

"And do you, Adriana d'Amato, take Giacomo Piero Baldovino to be your husband?"

"I do," I said dully.

More joyous music rang out as my new husband led me away from the altar, though this time I scarcely heard it, nor did I hear the good wishes being shouted to us by the smattering of people in the pews. I blinked as we stepped outside into the mocking sunlight and into the decorated gondola that would carry us back to the senator's—and now my—palazzo for the wedding feast. I felt heavy with the weight of this new life, of all the lives I had lived before, and all the ones I might have lived; so heavy that it was a wonder I did not sink the gondola straight to the bottom of the lagoon.

Our wedding night, after I suffered through the banquet in stony silence, was rather what I had anticipated. In the master bedchamber, *mio marito* clumsily removed my cream-colored, lace-trimmed shift—created especially for this night—then gestured for me to get into the bed, where he nearly crushed me with his weight as he pushed himself roughly inside me. I could not even draw breath to cry out in pain. I simply lay there, unmoving, enduring his short, jerky thrusts until he finally moaned aloud in his release and then rolled off me. I curled myself into a ball, facing away from him, trying and failing to hold back the tears that stung my eyes.

Once he had regained his breath, my husband placed a gentle hand on my shoulder. "You are doubtless weary from the excitement of the day, and perhaps a bit nervous and anxious about this first bedding, as well," he said, in what he no doubt believed was a reassuring tone. "So I will make allowances. But for the love of God, Adriana, surely you know that a man wants a woman to do what she can to please him?"

I would have murdered him right there in our marriage bed had I been in possession of a weapon. I wanted to scream at him. *There are only two kinds of women who seek to please men in bed: whores and women who are in love. I have been both, but now I am neither.*

Instead I closed my eyes and prayed for sleep to come as quickly as possible.

Yet before I could retreat into the security of slumber, the gypsy's words whispered themselves across my mind again: *You already know your fate, although it will not come about in quite the way you think . . . you will bear the child of the man you love.*

It had come true, all of it, every word. I laughed silently at the foolish, naïve girl who had first interpreted these words as a blessing, a benediction, a sign that she was going to get everything she had ever wanted; the girl who had then told herself that it was all silliness and superstition.

If only she had believed that tragedy could actually befall her.

48

INTERMEZZO

The ocean breeze somehow smelled different here than it did in Venice—sweeter, warmer, fresher. I could leave the villa—loaned to us for our wedding trip by a friend of Giacomo's—and wander down to the shore in nothing more than a shift, for there was no one else on this small Greek island to see us. I spent many enjoyable days exploring the beaches and forests, as I was usually left to my own devices.

The evenings were another matter.

As I watched the fiery sun sink beneath the waves, Giacomo came up behind me, wrapping an arm around my waist. "Beautiful, is it not?" he asked, as if he had commissioned the entire spectacle for my pleasure and now expected to be thanked for it. "Beauty seems to flourish here." He bent his head and kissed the side of my neck, while slipping my shift down my shoulder. I did not move, keeping my eyes on the fading horizon, until he took my hand and placed it over his hardening manhood beneath his breeches. I forced myself to pull away slowly.

"Here, *marito*?" I asked. "Surely the marriage bed is a more appropriate place for such . . . activity."

"We are newlyweds," he reminded me. "A bit of adventurousness is to be expected, *si?*" He reached for me again, but I instinctively took a step back.

"A wife's duty is to please her husband, in *every* way," he reminded me with a growl. "God knows I am not some handsome young swain, but I *am* your husband, and so you might think about resigning yourself to that, Adriana. A bit of gratitude would not be wanting, either."

The more I help him along to his pleasure, the less time it all will take. "I am sorry, *marito,*" I said aloud, looking up at him through my eyelashes. "Of course you are right. Let us only go inside to the bed, where we will be more comfortable."

His annoyance melted away at once. I let him take my hand and lead me inside.

Gloomy autumn rain splashed against the windows and high stone ceilings of the church—a far cry from the weather on that lovely island paradise, which I still thought of longingly from time to time. The humidity made my mourning wear—a heavy black velvet gown and black lace veil—difficult to bear.

On my left side, Giacomo listened stoically to the funeral Mass, while on my right, my father was—uncharacteristically—weeping. I had never been under the impression that he loved Claudio all that much, but rather only saw him as a successor to the business. Yet apparently I was wrong.

Earlier that month, we had received news that Claudio had been found stabbed to death in an alley in Florence—outside of a brothel, where there had been an altercation between Claudio and another patron. The murderer was not apprehended; likely the culprit was someone of far greater wealth and influence than my brother.

It was a fitting end for Claudio, really, I thought ruefully. Yet tears sprang to my eyes as I contemplated how devastated my mother would have been, had she lived to see the mess her son had made of his life.

As everyone rose to receive the Host, I surreptitiously glanced around the church from beneath my veil. The pews were full of people I did not know. I had been hoping to see Giuseppe, but he did not appear to be present. I wondered if he had even heard the news, though there was no love lost between him and Claudio in any case.

Giuseppe and I corresponded regularly by letter—he had found employment as a secretary for one of the members of the Council of Ten—but we had not seen each other since my wedding. Giacomo's and my first true argument as a married couple had been when he had forbidden me from inviting Giuseppe into our house.

"Your father warned me about this friend of yours," Giacomo said as I broached the subject over dinner one evening. "I know he was the one who helped facilitate your trysts." He shook his head and reapplied himself to his meal. "No. I shall not have him in my house."

"And did my holier-than-thou father also inform you," I asked, "that this same Giuseppe Rivalli is also his bastard son, and therefore my half brother?"

The look of surprise on my husband's face was quite gratifying. Giuseppe may have sworn not to reveal the truth of his parentage, but I had taken no such vow.

Giacomo recovered rather quickly. "Most men of privilege have at least one bastard somewhere," he said. "It is the way of the world." He glanced up at me. "You should know that better than anyone, Adriana."

That put a quick end to our discussion on the matter.

After the requiem Mass, we accompanied Claudio's coffin out to one of the islands in the lagoon for burial, and then returned to the city. We had offered to return home with my father and spend the evening with him, but he had declined rather brusquely, saying he preferred to be alone.

"A sad state of affairs," Giacomo said as our gondolier rowed us back. "But in truth it seems your brother had no one to blame but himself." He quickly crossed himself. "Not to speak ill of the dead, of course."

"I do not believe the dead can hear you, husband," I said, smiling slightly, "nor do I think they can take offense at an utterance of the truth."

He smiled back, changing the subject. "As to happier thoughts, can we expect the renovations to be finished by the end of the month, as projected?"

"We can," I told him. "The new carpets I ordered are set to be delivered tomorrow, and the last few pieces of furniture by early next week."

"Excellent."

Just as Giacomo had told me on the night we first met, his palazzo was very much in need of renovations when I moved in: the furniture was both old and old-fashioned, scratched and worn; the curtains were oppressively thick and heavy; the carpets had grown threadbare.

He had told me to spare no expense in the renovations and to choose whatever pleased me. Glad to have a project to distract myself from the memories that resurfaced upon our return to Venice, I summoned the finest furniture makers, upholsterers, and carpenters in the republic to remake the old bachelor's house into a home fit for a patrician and his wife, and perhaps someday children as well.

Giacomo had also allowed me to hire whatever additional servants I might need, and my first act had been to find and rehire Meneghina as my personal maid, for which she seemed both grateful and happy.

"Home we go, then," he said, smiling at me.

"Yes," I said, realizing that I was beginning to think of his palazzo that way. Ahead of us, Venice rose out of the waters of the lagoon to greet us, as if by magic. "Home."

49

PERFORMANCE

The renovations were finished by the end of October, as planned, and Giacomo was more delighted with the finished product than I could have imagined. I went from room to room with him, pointing out everything that had been done and explaining my choices.

"This is excellent," he marveled, taking everything in. "You have marvelous taste, Adriana."

"I am glad you like it," I said genuinely. He had been most generous in giving me free rein, and I was happy that he was so pleased.

"And it is finished just in time, for I am planning to give a party," he informed me.

"Oh?" I asked. I had been under the impression that Senator Baldovino did not cut a large, dashing swath through Venice's social scene. "I thought that you did not like parties," I ventured.

He chuckled. "I have never had a particular fondness for them, it is true," he said. "But I have this lovely house which looks as if it were new, and a beautiful wife whom I am eager to introduce to society."

"That sounds wonderful," I said, finding his enthusiasm was

catching. And I was hardly opposed to having company; surely there would be *someone* among Giacomo's circle of friends who would be pleasant enough. "I should like to meet more of your friends."

"And so you shall," he said. "But I had something else in mind for this particular *festa* that I think shall be most pleasing to you." The smile on his face was almost boyish, and I was touched he should be so happy at the thought of pleasing me.

"Do tell, *marito,*" I said. "For pity's sake, do not keep me in suspense."

"You know that I have long been a benefactor of the Pietà," he began. My stomach clenched at that word. "It is a most worthy institution, as you know. So I thought that we might invite the orchestra of the Pietà to come and give a concert for us and our guests. And of course we would make a suitable donation to the *ospedale* in return."

He watched me eagerly for my reaction, which I was trying desperately to hide. "What say you?" he asked. "I know you played the violin when you were younger, and I am told that you love the opera. I thought it something that you would especially enjoy."

I looked into his gentle, doughy face and knew that I could not break his heart. *As in Scripture, I must forgive him, for he knows not what he does.* "Oh, Giacomo," I said, smiling widely. "That would be wonderful! Why, that you should go to such lengths for my sake!"

He slipped an arm around my waist, drew me against his hip, and kissed my lips lightly. "It is no trouble at all. I would gladly do so much and more for a chance to see one of those rare smiles of yours."

Before I could recover from his tender declaration, he was already moving off to inspect the newly carved moldings in the dining room. "Lovely," he murmured. "Exceedingly lovely. Fine work, indeed."

As he stepped into the next room, I sank down into one of the newly upholstered chairs, burying my head in my hands.

I was going to have to face Antonio Vivaldi again.

The invitations to the party went out a mere two days later, and Giacomo assured me that I was not to trouble myself over the arrangements. He would see to everything, he promised.

The powers that be at the Pietà were thrilled to receive such an invitation from a senator of the republic. Giacomo promptly delivered half of his promised donation, and there was the prospect of more to come from our wealthy guests. The Pietà was sending an orchestra comprised of their finest musicians, they promised us, under the direction of the reinstated Maestro Vivaldi.

"This man they call *il Prete Rosso* is remarkable, truly," Giacomo said as he read me the reply to his invitation over dinner. "I am sure you of all people will appreciate his talent."

I kept my gaze fixed determinedly on my plate.

"And I have no doubt that the orchestra will be playing some of his own compositions," Giacomo went on. "He is rather good at that sort of thing. Strange to think the Pietà parted with him for so long. No one seems to know what he got up to during that time, other than playing at the Sant' Angelo."

I drowned my wry smirk in a sip of wine. *I can tell you exactly what he was doing during that time. I can also tell you that he wishes he had not done it.*

"They say he is now trying his hand at opera—and no wonder, for it certainly pays better than writing music for the Church," Giacomo added. "I believe he published some concerti not long ago, as well."

This was news to me. So he had managed to get *L'estro armonico* published, then. And opera, well, that only made sense financially, as Giacomo pointed out. That Vivaldi would distinguish himself well in this new field I had no doubt. Whether I could ever bear to attend an opera he had written would be another matter entirely.

Fortunately, Giacomo changed the subject to something about a dispute two other senators were embroiled in, but I scarcely heard him. *Dear God and Mary Virgin,* I thought, *if I can barely keep hold of myself when I hear him mentioned, how in the name of heaven will I manage when I am faced with the man himself?*

50

LONG-LOST LOVE

The best I would be able to do was avoid Vivaldi as long as possible, though eventually we would be forced to come face-to-face. When the musicians from the Pietà arrived several hours before the party was to begin—along with their maestro and a few nuns as chaperones—I sent Giacomo to greet them, telling him I still needed a great deal of time to dress and ready myself for the evening. This was to diverge slightly from what was expected of me as a hostess, but I could not bring myself to care. Not tonight.

In truth, dressing did not take all that long. I wore black, with a single strand of pearls, as all patrician women did in the first year after marriage. But as though she sensed how much I wanted to look beautiful on this day, Meneghina took extra care with my hair. She pinned it back—leaving a few strands down to soften the effect—and wound through it a strand of diamonds and pearls set in gold which had been a wedding gift from my father to my mother, and which he had given to me on my wedding day. Finally, she applied a light touch of cosmetics to enhance my eyes and lips.

When she was done, I hardly recognized the woman in the looking glass. Her glossy hair shone nearly as much as the diamonds nestled in it, and her large, luminous eyes gazed seductively back at me.

Meneghina met my eyes in the mirror with a satisfied smile. "Every man in attendance tonight will fall madly in love with you," she said. "You shall break a great many hearts tonight, madonna."

In spite of all that was weighing on me, I laughed. "Perhaps I shall make that my goal for the evening."

When the time finally came for me to go greet the guests who were beginning to arrive, I was relieved to learn the orchestra was setting up in the *piano nobile,* where the concert would take place before dinner. Though Meneghina had painted confidence on my face, I could only thank God that my skirts hid my shaking legs as I stood beside Giacomo in the entrance hall and was introduced, one by one, to his friends and acquaintances. The man whom I had loved with all my heart, whom I had trusted with my life and more and who had betrayed me, was in a room just behind me, living and breathing and real and not at all like my pale remembrances of him. I could *feel* him. I could just barely admit to myself the foolish fantasy I harbored, the fantasy of a naïve girl: when he saw me, he would draw me away into another room, and fall to his knees, begging me to forgive him, telling me that he had made a terrible mistake, that he could not live without me after all, and ask me to leave Venice with him this very night. My face heated with embarrassment for even allowing such a scene to play out in my head. I had not learned much this past year after all.

"Ah, here is a very dear friend of mine," Giacomo said, breaking into my self-pitying thoughts. I looked up to see a short, somewhat rotund man, his face doughy and flushed, though the white wig that sat atop it was immaculate, as were his expensively tailored clothes. On his arm was a petite yet shapely and very fashionably dressed young woman, with a lovely, heart-shaped face and what seemed to be yards of silken blond locks. "Adriana, this is Senator Roberto Grimaldi, whom I have known since I was a boy. It was in his villa that we stayed on our wedding trip. Roberto, may I present my wife, Adriana."

I smiled at him, extending my hand for him to kiss. "I must thank you for your generosity, Senator Grimaldi," I said. "It is a most lovely house."

"Not at all, Donna Baldovino," he said. "It was my pleasure to be of service, and it is my hope that you and your esteemed husband will be our guests there again in the future." He gestured to the blond woman beside him. "Donna, may I present to you my wife, Giulietta Grimaldi."

"It is an honor and a pleasure, Donna Grimaldi," I said, nodding.

"Oh, no, the honor and pleasure are all mine," she said, her voice remarkably strong and animated coming from such a small frame. "I have been much looking forward to making your acquaintance, Donna Baldovino—why, I came this close to simply climbing into my gondola to come call on you, but Roberto insisted I wait for a formal introduction, as no doubt your husband was not through keeping you all to himself!"

As she spoke, something about her face, her figure, and her name jarred my memory. "Why, Donna Grimaldi," I said, "forgive me, but I just realized I have seen you before. I was in a gondola passing your palazzo some time ago, and a young man was outside singing to you. You came out to blow him a kiss."

She laughed. "That was my dear Mario, no doubt," she said. "He is a most charming and devoted *cavaliere servente*. We shall have to find you one just like him, and I have no doubt the young men will be falling all over themselves for the honor!"

I laughed. "I shall trust your judgment in this matter, donna," I said.

She smiled warmly. "I have been so hoping for someone marvelous and diverting among all of my husband's stuffy friends, and you are just such a person!"

I laughed again, startled and refreshed by such frank speech. Senator Grimaldi chuckled tolerantly. "My wife is quite outspoken, you will find, Donna Baldovino," he told me.

"Indeed." I tossed a conspiratorial smile to her. "I, too, have a bit of outspokenness in my nature."

Grinning back at me, she reached out and briefly clasped my hand. "I think that we are going to be great friends," she said. "But for now, I shall let you continue greeting your guests. We will have more of an opportunity to talk later."

"Indeed." I smiled at her as she took her husband's arm again, and they moved past us into the *piano nobile*.

I greeted the rest of the seemingly endless procession of guests with an easy charm that surprised me; such pleasantries had never come easily to me. I flattered myself that I was acting the perfect Venetian hostess, though I knew I scarcely remembered anyone's name.

Finally Giacomo turned to me. "I believe that just about everyone is here," he said. "Should we not perhaps begin the concert soon?"

My already rapid heartbeat doubled its pace. "Yes, I suppose," I answered.

"Very well. Perhaps a bit of wine first."

I took his arm, and we went into the *piano nobile*, where our guests were mingling cheerfully. Across from the double doors was the semicircle of chairs and music stands where the orchestra would be seated. The musicians—no more than girls—were already in their places, tuning their instruments and practicing a passage here and there. I quickly looked away, lest I catch sight of their maestro, and grabbed the nearest glass of wine I could find.

What if I faint dead away when I see him? I wondered, suddenly panicked. *Yet . . . why am I so fearful? It is* he *who wronged* me; *it is he who should be afraid to meet my eye.*

Yet any sort of logic left me just seconds later, when I finally saw him. He was standing off to one side of the orchestra, sifting through a pile of scores. My stomach lurched violently, and my head swam. If not for a deep, well-timed breath, I no doubt would have fainted.

He looked as I remembered, albeit thinner. As though he sensed my eyes upon him, he looked up, causing me to look quickly away, my heart pounding and my breath coming in short, shallow pants.

But there were guests to attend to, and Giacomo and I threaded our way through the throng, drifting apart from each other and trying to speak to everyone all over again. I made certain that my voice was light and my laugh bright and genuine, should Vivaldi still happen to be observing me.

I was engaged in conversation with Donna Barbo, a lovely, silver-haired older woman who was the wife of Senator Barbo, when my husband approached us with another couple whom I could not remember greeting earlier. "I will perhaps speak with you at greater length during dinner, Donna Baldovino," Donna Barbo said, nodding regally to me and returning to her husband so that I might greet the newcomers.

The man was tall and thin, and had eschewed the fashion of wearing a wig, having combed back his own iron-gray hair and tied it with a ribbon. His clothes were simple but made of the finest stuff. Beside him stood a slender young woman who looked to be about my age. She was tall, easily Giacomo's height, with a perfect oval-shaped face that featured high, delicate cheekbones, cream-colored skin, and wide green eyes. Her long, wavy brown hair, a shade lighter than mine, was bound at the nape of her neck, with a few strands loosened to frame her face. She, too, wore the black gown and pearls of a newly married woman. She was perhaps the most beautiful woman I had ever seen, but beautiful in a different way from Giulietta's sensual, seductive charms: this woman may well have posed for an artist's portrait of the Blessed Virgin, so pure and serene was her beauty.

"Adriana," Giacomo said, "this is another dear friend of mine, Francesco Cassenti. Francesco, my wife, Adriana."

We exchanged pleasantries, and then Don Cassenti indicated the woman next to him. "May I present to you my wife, Vittoria."

"A pleasure, Donna Cassenti," I said, smiling.

"Likewise, Donna Baldovino," she said warmly, her voice smooth and sweet.

"Donna Cassenti was formerly at the Pietà," Giacomo informed me. "She was a singer, if I am correct, just like your late mother."

I appraised her with new interest. "Truly, Donna Cassenti? That is most fascinating! You must tell me all about it!"

She laughed, a musical sound that instantly made me wish to hear her sing. "I would be glad to do so, certainly. But please, you must call me Vittoria." She smiled shyly. "Actually, it is Maria Vittoria, but there were so many Marias at the Pietà that I was always called by my second name."

"With pleasure," I said. "But you must call me Adriana."

"Of course," she said. "But if you all will be so good as to excuse me, I must go and greet Maestro Vivaldi. I remember him well from my days there."

"Very well, my dear," Don Cassenti said. I peeked in the direction of the orchestra to see Vivaldi now seated in the first violinist's chair. He looked up as Vittoria approached, his expression one of excited surprise and pleasure. He rose quickly, and soon the two were deep in conversation.

A hot surge of pointless jealousy swept over me. Did he think Vittoria more beautiful than I?

Almost instantly I was ashamed of such thoughts, especially about a woman I hoped would be a friend.

I turned back to hear Giacomo addressing me. "Francesco and Vittoria were married just after us; in fact, we were on our wedding trip at the time, and so could not attend. May, was it not?" he asked Francesco.

"It was indeed."

"Perhaps, Giacomo," I interrupted, "it is best that we begin the concert." God help me, I could not take another moment of mindless pleasantries. *Let us get this over with.*

"Yes, yes, you are right, as always, my dear," Giacomo said. "Let us take our seats, then."

We moved to our seats in the front row of chairs that had been arranged to face the orchestra; Giacomo on the end and I beside him, uncomfortably aware of how close I was to Vivaldi. I did not look directly at him, nor he at me, yet neither of us could escape the fact that the other was there.

Fortunately, Vittoria Cassenti came to sit in the seat next to mine. "I hope you do not mind if I sit beside you," she said, arranging her skirts in the artful manner of someone who has been wearing them all her life, rather than only just becoming accustomed to costly garments.

"Not at all," I replied. "It is a privilege."

She smiled. "So you enjoy music, then, Donna Baldovino?" She blushed slightly. "Excuse me. Adriana."

"Very much," I said.

"And are you a musician yourself?"

I hesitated. I could tell that although Vivaldi seemed intent on tuning his violin, he was actually listening to the conversation between Vittoria and myself. "I was," I said. "I played the violin."

"That is wonderful!" Vittoria exclaimed. "I tried to learn it once, but I have little skill for that sort of instrument, I am afraid. God in His wisdom put my instrument within my body."

I smiled. "There you have the better of me by far. I should very much like to hear you sing."

"And I should like to hear you play your violin, if ever you decide to play again."

Thankfully, I was spared the need to respond to this by Giacomo rising from his chair to perform the introduction.

"My wife and I would like to thank all of you for being here this evening, during which we hope you will join us in lending support to one of the republic's worthiest institutions, the Ospedale della Pietà." He gestured toward the orchestra. "With that said, I shall now take my seat without further ado and allow the performance to begin." The guests applauded, and Giacomo sat down beside me again. He took my hand, squeezing it affectionately. I squeezed his hand in return, hoping it was enough to hold me steady through the next few hours.

And just before the orchestra began playing, just when I thought I might survive this evening after all, I had to bow my head to hide the tears pooling in my eyes. Vivaldi's violin was not some new one he had bought to replace the one he sent me; nor was it one of the other ones, of lesser quality, that he kept in his house.

No. It was my violin.

51

FOR YOU

The concerto the orchestra began with was one in D major that I did not recognize. The melody and the first violin part were relatively simple, and in spite of myself I realized I was working out the fingering in my head while I listened. The second movement, a larghetto, was equally simple, though pretty. When the third movement continued on in much the same vein, disappointment washed through me. I had been hoping—in spite of everything—the music today would be like the music I had played with Vivaldi: different and lively and exciting. Yet as I glanced around me, seeing the approving nods of the guests, I realized Vivaldi had started with this concerto deliberately. It was safe, what listeners would expect; he would not challenge them yet.

The second concerto—which I recognized right from the opening notes—proved I was right. It was one he had been teaching me just before I had discovered that I was with child, with a first movement that rose in pitch and intensity until it seemed that the notes were bouncing right off the ceiling. For a moment it was almost as if I were standing in Vivaldi's front room again, squinting at the music on the stand, trying to play it with the technical prowess and emotion he required.

I was thankfully pulled from this reverie when the concerto ended, and the audience began applauding. I tried to steady my breathing, but it was not easy; so much of what I had been trying to repress had come flooding back, as vivid as ever. And all it had taken was a few bars of music.

The next concerto, in E minor, was one I did not know. The opening movement had a dark, foreboding edge to it, a warning of danger. The second movement was painfully beautiful, and sounded as though the violins themselves were weeping. I could not help but wonder when he had written it, and about the thoughts that plagued his mind as he had done so. Inwardly I wept that I would never learn it, that there was so much music I would never be able to play with him in those glorious stolen hours.

The next concerto was one I did not recognize until the second movement. It was for two solo violins, with the first part being played by Vivaldi, and the second by a slender girl with plain brown hair and a light dusting of freckles across her pale face, seated beside him. She played extremely well, so I deduced that this must be his protégée, Anna Maria. She had certainly earned his praise.

The first movement began with a bold, rapid tutti section, the two solo violin parts circling and dancing around one another, now in a duet, now competing, now plunging quickly back down the scale, then back up, growing louder in volume, then softer.

At the very first chord of the second movement, I felt myself dragged down deep by the undertow of memory. It was all I could do to keep from gasping for air. It was none other than the duet we had played together on that September day over two years ago. It was the same day, the same moment, that the attraction between us had first manifested itself physically, but only just, only in something so light as the touch of his fingertips on my cheek and the ghost of a kiss that had never truly lived. And even as I sat beside my husband, lifetimes away from that day, I suddenly felt a girl of eighteen again, knowing nothing of love or desire until this music, his music, had begun to teach me of them.

I barely heard the third movement, or the concerto for *il violincello* that followed. I was too busy flailing about in a sea of memories, trying not to drown. All I could do was wonder why he had chosen to play that piece, if he was trying to tell me something.

It would not be long before I had an answer.

When the violincello concerto ended, Vivaldi rose, facing his listeners. "For our next piece, we have something a bit unusual to present to you," he said. "This is a piece that reached me recently, by a composer who wishes to remain anonymous. What you are about to hear will be the premiere performance of this work."

I barely heard the murmurings of surprise and excitement from our guests. My heart was pounding so loudly in my ears as to nearly drown out everything else. *No. He cannot mean what I think he means.* I could not tell, in that moment, if I was more hopeful or afraid.

The orchestra began to play my concerto—the one I had written on the darkest night of my life, the one I had Giuseppe take to my former lover as my final farewell. The excruciating, intimate story of my heartbreak filled my ears as Vivaldi's violin sang with my rage in the first movement, a song of passion and pain and betrayal. The rest of the violins played a slow, languid part in support, while the violas, celli, and violincelli stormed along with the solo. It was exactly how I had heard it in my head, but at the same time greater, larger, more alive and terrifying.

Chills raced up and down my body, so that every hair, every last inch of me, felt alive. Tears pooled in my eyes, and I had to fight to stop them from falling.

Come the second movement, my resolve broke. The voice of the first violin sang on, weeping now, and asking why her lover had betrayed her so, how she was supposed to go on without him. The rest of the orchestra played only the barest traces of accompaniment. I no longer cared who might see: I buried my face in my hands and wept.

At the movement's end, I managed to compose myself, but only just. As I lifted my head, trying to dab discreetly at my tears, I noticed Vittoria brushing away a tear of her own. A sudden surge of pride filled me. Perhaps my music really did mean something.

The third movement was of a faster tempo, with a more balanced, traditional string accompaniment, but the same sadness and wistfulness of the previous. It was a song of letting go.

Wiping the rest of the tears from my eyes, I drank in the enthusiastic applause of the audience as the piece finally concluded. Though I could not stand up before them all and claim my work—not that any of them would believe me even if I were to do so—I knew, all the same, they were applauding for me. And that would have to be enough.

Again, Vivaldi stood. "My thanks to you all for being such a gracious and attentive audience," he said. "We have one more piece to perform, and I would like to dedicate it to our host and hostess"—he turned to where Giacomo and I were sitting, his gaze fixing on mine—"in thanks for welcoming us into their home." With that, he resumed his place, and immediately the orchestra broke into the opening bars of their final piece.

I knew it instantly, would never be able to forget it. And I knew he was playing it for me and only me.

It was the piece he had played for me at our first lesson, when I had boldly asked to hear him; the piece he had later told me was his favorite, among everything he had ever composed. I had dreamed of what it would sound like when played by a full orchestra, and now I had my answer.

The majesty and passion of the music was only enhanced when played by the orchestra, as well as the four solo violins who shared the melody. I think I ceased to breathe altogether for a moment.

And just then, in that beautiful, flawless, enlightened place to which his music took me, I felt that it had all been worth it. All the pain, the suffering, every last sacrifice I had made had been worth it, because it made possible this glorious music we were hearing.

Then it was over, and just like that, I went back to being a woman still hopelessly in love with the man who had rejected her.

There were two more movements to the concerto, but neither could equal the power and splendor of the first, which I was sure Vivaldi knew better than anyone. However, I was grateful for the extra time to compose myself. It was hardly enough time, but had I been expected to rise and resume my duties as a hostess immediately after such an intense flood of emotion, I would have failed miserably, ripping apart like a ship dashed on the rocks, unintentionally laying bare my deepest secret.

It was a gift that only he could give me: the chance to hear my own music played, by a full orchestra in front of an audience, and to hear a piece that held so much meaning for us both. He had performed the best of both of our works, set them side by side; and though it could never make up for the wrong he had done me, there was nothing he could have done that would have meant more.

When the final movement ended, the applause was almost deafening, in sharp contrast to the second of complete silence after the final notes had faded. All the audience members rose to their feet, and I shakily did the same. The musicians took their bows, and the applause continued, second only to the pounding in my ears.

"A wonderful performance, truly," Giacomo said, once the ovation had ended. "I heartily thank our performers for bringing this wonderful experience to us, and I thank our guests again for attending. Dinner will be served shortly; our servants shall lead you all into the dining room when the time comes."

As the guests resumed their mingling, I quickly turned to Giacomo and laid my hand on his sleeve. "I think, *marito,* that I shall go and check on the cook's progress."

He frowned. "You need not trouble yourself, my dear. I can send one of the servants to do that. Stay here and chat with our guests."

I shook my head. "It is no trouble. In fact, I think I should like some air . . ." Before he could protest further, I turned and left the suddenly cramped, close room, making for the stairs that led down to the kitchens.

Pausing by the staircase to collect myself, I decided that I might as well go down to the kitchens to check on the feast. When I arrived, the cook assured me everything was going perfectly, looking somewhat confused as to my presence. Feeling slightly foolish, I climbed back up the stairs to the *piano nobile,* only to find a figure awaiting me at the top of the steps.

Vivaldi.

He froze when he saw me, his expression uncomfortable, as though now that he was with me, he did not know what to say.

I stopped several steps from the top, chin raised defiantly, and waited for him to speak.

He opened his mouth, but no sound escaped. "Adriana," he said finally. "I saw you leave, and I thought that if I followed you, I might have a word . . ."

In a voice stronger than I felt—and before I could think better of it—I said, "Not here. Follow me," and led him down to the mezzanine, where he followed me into one of the storerooms.

"The concerti," I said, turning to face him. "Mine and yours." I stopped, uncertain of what else I meant to say.

"Yes," he said. "I played them for you. You deserved the chance to hear your work as it was meant to be played, and I . . . I think perhaps I needed to hear it, as well. I wanted to—"

"I know," I said. "I . . . I know. And I thank you for it."

He nodded.

"And your concerto," I said. "Our favorite."

"Did you . . . what did you think?" he asked.

"It was . . . glorious. Magnificent." I looked away. "There are no words. You must know that, Tonio."

I started at my old, affectionate name for him coming from my lips. He, too, looked surprised, but did not comment. "It seems that I have given you my message, then," he said. "There are so very many things for which there are no words."

"Yes."

We stared at each other in silence. His eyes swept upward over me, drinking me in. "You look beautiful," he said. "Beyond words."

"Apparently sorrow agrees with me," I said, with the fierce resolve of a soldier in battle who knows he is doomed, but will fight to the death anyway.

"Adriana." He moved toward me, but I stepped back. Hurt flashed across his face at this, and I told myself that I did not care. "Do not think that you can possibly reproach me more than I have reproached myself this past year."

"And yet you were not there when they took our daughter away, and so you do not know—" I stopped abruptly, the tightness in my throat making it impossible for me to go on.

"Yes, Giuseppe told me," he said. "I am—"

"Please," I cut him off. "Do not say that you are sorry. It is such an empty word that has the power to change nothing."

I could see in his face that he wanted to press me, ask me more about the child—our child. However, when he said nothing further, I moved to walk past him and out the door. "I must go—I have a lot to do, and—"

He placed a gentle hand on my arm, causing me to flinch. "Please, Adriana," he said. "I only wanted to—"

"To what?" I demanded, suddenly angry again.

"To see how you fare. Please, no," he said, when I opened my mouth to retort angrily. "If I thought it would make you feel better—if I thought it would make any of this better—I would go drown myself in the Grand Canal right now."

His words so shocked me that I could think of nothing to say in reply. He, however, took advantage of my silence and changed the subject. "And what is he like?" he asked, nodding in the general direction of the *piano nobile*. "Your husband?"

I laughed. "He is an old man."

"Is he good to you?"

"He treats me well enough in that he leaves me mostly to my own devices," I said.

He studied me with sympathy. "That sounds very lonely."

"I am quite accustomed to being lonely, I am afraid," I said. "And perhaps I am now paying for having stolen so much joy, once."

We were both silent for a long moment, the uncomfortable silence of two people who know everything there is to know about each other, and who can speak of none of it.

It occurred to me that dinner was surely about to begin, and that my absence must have been remarked upon, and Vivaldi's as well. But something prompted me to make one last confession. "I cannot play anymore, Antonio, let alone write. The music . . . I have lost it."

He smiled. "That is not true, Adriana. It cannot be. You have more music in you than anyone I have ever known. You wrote that spellbinding concerto everyone just heard, did you not?"

To my horror, tears stung my eyes. "I did, but . . ."

He moved to place his hand reassuringly on my shoulder, but then thought better of it. "You shall find the music again, eventually. Inevitably. I know you will."

The tears were flowing freely now; I would have given anything to make them stop. "I cannot. Not without you."

"Oh, Adriana," he said. "I was never that important. You never needed me that much. Maybe you could not see it then, and cannot yet, but—"

"You do not know," I whispered. "You do not—" I broke off. Oh, God, why had I let him follow me here? Why had I thought that I could bear it? "I am sorry. I should not be . . . that is, as I said, I have much to do."

He nodded uncomfortably. "Yes, of course. Your guests."

"Yes," I replied. I took a deep breath. "*Addio,* Antonio." This time when I walked past him, he let me go.

I could hardly return to my guests in this state, so I climbed back up the stairs and ducked into the small parlor outside of the main room of the *piano nobile*. I sank down onto a daybed, doing my best to stitch myself back together.

A few moments later, the door opened slightly and the elegantly coiffed head of Vittoria Cassenti appeared. "Why, Donna Baldovino," she said, stepping fully into the room. "Everyone is quite at a loss as to where you vanished to."

We were both silent as she took in my appearance. "Are you quite well, Adriana?" she asked, lowering her voice.

"Yes," I answered quickly. "That is, no, I was feeling unwell, and so I stepped in here to collect myself . . ."

She crossed the room and sat beside me. "I understand," she said, sliding an arm around my shoulders, and I found myself leaning into her strong yet slender frame.

"There are so many things in a woman's heart of which she can never speak," she said gently, without accusation or curiosity.

And as I accepted her comfort, I wondered, fleetingly, how a girl who had grown up hidden away in a cloister could be so very wise.

52

CONSONANCE

I managed to get through dinner without further incident—a dinner at which many of the guests expressed their admiration for the mystery concerto.

"Whoever that composer is, he has quite a career ahead of him, should he choose to reveal himself," Don Cassenti said.

I felt Vivaldi's eyes on me, and allowed myself a small, secret smile.

Thankfully, both Vittoria Cassenti and Giulietta Grimaldi were seated near me, and I was able to pass some of the meal in conversation with them—as much as my duties as hostess would permit, anyway.

I was not sorry when the evening came to an end, though it had not been without its happier moments: Vittoria promised to call upon me at my earliest convenience, and Giulietta Grimaldi and her husband extended an invitation to a party they were giving on the first night of Carnevale. I had not realized how my life had suffered all these years without female companions whose company I enjoyed and looked forward to.

So excited was I by the idea of having friends that I could scarcely wait to take Vittoria up on her offer. Only two days later, I sent her a note, saying that I hoped she might be able to pay me a visit that day. I received a speedy reply, telling me she would be along within the hour.

I received my guest in the same small parlor where she had happened upon me the evening of the party. The servants prepared some mulled wine for us to ward off the November chill. There were two steaming glasses waiting when she arrived.

"I thank you for your kind invitation," Vittoria said, gratefully accepting the glass. "These empty winter days have made me rather melancholy. At the Pietà we were always so busy, or at prayer. Though I am very much looking forward to fully experiencing Carnevale for the first time."

"They do not celebrate Carnevale at the Pietà, then?" I asked teasingly.

She laughed. "Hardly. We were never allowed outside the cloister except under close supervision, and they took even more care with us during Carnevale, for obvious reasons."

Vivaldi's voice rang in my head: *I did not much care for their rules . . . rules for performing, for practicing, for the types of music that could be performed . . .*

"You were much bound by restrictions there, then?" I asked.

She laughed again. "That is putting it mildly," she said. "There were rules for everything: speaking, praying, eating, rehearsing, even sleeping." She shrugged. "But it was not that bad. After all . . ." A dreamy look came over her face. "There was music, always music. Glorious music, especially once Maestro Vivaldi began composing for us." She sighed. "And even so . . . the rules, the confinement, they did chafe on one. All I could think of was the freedom of the outside world; I did not think long enough on what I would be giving up when I decided to leave and marry. I miss singing, performing; miss it more than I think I would miss one of my limbs if it were to be cut off."

Her choice of phrase shocked me, not for its passion and severity but because I had once had the very same thought about the violin. "And your husband?" I asked, without thinking. "Do you not love him?" I blushed. "I do beg your pardon. I should not have asked you such a question. It was unspeakably rude of me."

"No, no," she assured me. "It is a fair question. In fact, you do me a great service by allowing me to unburden myself. My few friends are all still at the Pietà, so I have no one to whom I may speak freely."

"You may speak freely with me," I said.

"Francesco . . . he is not the dashing, fairy-tale prince I believed him to be when he first asked for my hand," Vittoria said, after a moment of reflection. "But he never claimed to be anything other than what he is. I allowed myself to be caught up in the romance of it all: a man asking for my hand even when he had never seen my face, only heard me sing from behind a grille. It was so easy to imagine he was a knight out of an old tale of courtly love, come to rescue me. When I married him, I was madly in love with this vision I had of him, but not with him." She shook her head and laughed sadly. "What a naïve fool I was."

For a moment, it seemed that I was looking at a younger version of my mother. Had she, too, been disappointed by the harsh indifference of reality to a young girl's dreams? Even I, who had been no virgin in a cloister, who had known more of the world than either of them, had allowed myself to believe in a love so absolute it could destroy all other realities, or at least make them no longer matter.

"Not a fool," I said at last. "Not at all. Very few of us end up living the life of which we may have dreamt." I looked down at my hands. "No doubt you have gathered that my marriage to Giacomo is no grand love match, either."

"I had guessed as much, yes," Vittoria said. "You have too much spirit for an aging gentleman like him."

I smiled at her delicate phrasing.

Impulsively, she reached out and squeezed my hand. "Do not worry," she said, before releasing me. "You are not alone."

"Thank you," I said, smiling. "It has felt that way, all too often."

A companionable silence stretched between us before Vittoria spoke again. "I must apologize. I have quite dominated our conversation with my past, which can hardly have been interesting."

"On the contrary," I said. "I have always been curious about life within the Pietà. My mother was a ward there before she married my father."

"Ah, yes," Vittoria said. "I believe your husband mentioned that. She was a singer as well, is that what he said?"

"Yes, a soprano. Her name was Lucrezia della Pietà, and she became Lucrezia d'Amato."

"Lucrezia della Pietà!" she exclaimed "She was one of the best ever to sing there, or so the *maestre* used to say."

"Yes. She would sing to me when I was a child, and I remember thinking an angel must have lent her that voice."

"I can imagine," Vittoria said. "Well, then, perhaps now you are better able to picture what her life would have been like as a girl—no doubt it is a world that seems very foreign to you."

I laughed. "Some of what you have described is more familiar to me than you can perhaps guess."

"Oh?"

I nodded. "There were many rules confining me as well. After my mother died, my father became very strict, protective . . ." I trailed off; how to describe something that I still did not understand myself? "I was not allowed to go out into society until I came of marriageable age, each invitation carefully scrutinized. And he stopped my violin lessons and forbade me to study music."

Vittoria looked at me closely, then raised an eyebrow. "And now?"

"What do you mean?"

She gestured to the room around us. "You are mistress of your own house. Who would stop you if you wish to play again?"

I had no answer for her. Giacomo would not deny me such a simple thing if it would bring me joy. And, I realized with a shock, I *was* my own mistress now.

But the thought of playing the violin again caused an uncomfortable twisting in my stomach.

"I do not know," I said finally. "I could, I suppose, but it has been so long . . ."

"Perhaps someday, then," Vittoria said, in a tone that indicated she would leave the topic if I wished.

I forced a smile and took a sip of my wine, thankful our talk then turned to other things. Vittoria and her husband had also received an invitation to Giulietta Grimaldi's party, much to my excitement. "Francesco has promised to accompany me, even though it is not fashionable for a husband and wife to appear in each other's company." She rolled her eyes. "He tells me he cannot wait to introduce me to my first Carnevale."

"There *is* something about one's first Carnevale," I said wistfully, remembering. Vittoria raised her eyebrows expectantly; blushing, I quickly returned to the topic at hand. "Yes, Giacomo will be accompanying me as well. He is not the most sociable man, as you no doubt know, but he would not fail to attend a party given by such a close friend."

"I shall look forward to seeing you there, then," Vittoria said, rising from her seat. "Now I pray that you will excuse me, as I must be on my way home. Francesco and I will be dining soon."

I rose as well. "Of course. And thank you for calling on me. I have not . . ." I bit my lip, somewhat self-conscious. "I have not had many good friends in my life."

She smiled. "Nor I. I shall be glad and honored to call you my friend, Adriana."

"The honor will be all mine," I said. And with that, Vittoria departed, leaving me happier than I had been in a long time.

I had to lean in close to hear Giulietta Grimaldi over the noise around us: other guests of the Loredan family talking, laughing, the music of the orchestra. "And then, if you can believe, she said to me—"

A woman behind me in a blue and green peacock's mask, with feather plumage to match, let out a shrill laugh just then, drowning out Giulietta's words. "*Che?* I did not hear you, *amica,*" I said, nearly shouting.

She pursed her lips in a pretty pout, one she had perfected to the devastation of many a Venetian gentleman. "It is *far* too crowded in here, and we cannot even hear one another gossip! Shall we go to the Ridotto, then?"

"Because the Ridotto will not be crowded at all," Vittoria said, rolling her eyes behind her mask. "And honestly, Giulietta, I do not know how you can gamble so much."

"Where, then? It is too early to eat dinner— Oh, for the love of God and all the saints, it is so *hot* in here," Giulietta complained, snapping open a fan and flapping it vigorously. "Where *has* Mario gotten to? Ah!"

Giulietta broke off when she saw Mario Albonini across the room. She waggled her fingers at him, and he excused himself and began to move toward us.

"We need some air, *caro,* and we have quite tired of this crowd," she said when he drew near enough. "Do come fetch us when the gondola is ready, *si?*"

Mario nodded, kissing Giulietta's hand, and went off to do her bidding.

Mario was Giulietta's *cicisbeo:* a lover whose name was included in the marriage contract as part of the arrangement between husband and wife. I had heard of this practice before; it was quite fashionable among a nobility comprised of aging men who took young wives. In such cases, the older husband was often glad his wife had someone nearer her own age to squire her to parties and other entertainments. It was a strange arrangement, but Giulietta and her husband were both perfectly comfortable with it, and she and Mario seemed to care a great deal for each other. Mario would take Giulietta wherever she wished to go, bring her gifts, and write her poems, while she would repay him with certain favors which—as she told Vittoria and me in a giggling whisper—she was only too happy to provide.

"We still have not decided where we are going," Vittoria pointed out as we began to move toward the door.

Giulietta smiled. "Do you mean to tell me the convent girl has not yet had her fill of merrymaking for the night?"

Vittoria laughed, a light, carefree sound. "Hardly!"

I had been surprised to learn that Giulietta and Vittoria were already friends; I would not have expected the pious, introspective Vittoria to get along so well with someone like the outgoing, flamboyant Giulietta, but I was wrong and gladly so. Giulietta had taken it upon herself to serve as our guide into the tangled thicket of the Venetian nobility, a jungle which, she informed us cheerfully, we were both novices at navigating.

"Let us go to Piazza San Marco!" I said suddenly.

Both of my friends stopped, looking at me quizzically. "Have you never been to Piazza San Marco during Carnevale?" I asked Giulietta.

"When there are parties to go to? No," she answered. "Whatever is there to do in *la piazza?*"

"Oh, you will see!" I said excitedly. When Giulietta still looked doubtful, I added, "There are wine vendors."

"Well, in that case," she said. "I suppose it is worth a try. Leonardo, *andiamo*!" She waved to Leonardo Franchetti, a friend of Mario's and another member of our party. Leonardo joined us, wrapping one arm around my waist and one around Vittoria's. "Where are we off to, my lovelies?" he asked.

"Piazza San Marco, apparently," Giulietta said.

As Giulietta had Mario, Leonardo fulfilled the more chaste role of *cavaliere servente* for Vittoria and me: he accompanied us to all social functions, brought us flowers and little gifts, and even wrote us a terrible poem or two, as in the game of courtly love. He had become a good friend, and was the final member of this merry group of ours that had formed over the course of the Carnevale festivities.

We left the palazzo and the party and climbed into our gondola. The other houses we passed were all brightly lit, with the noise of parties and dinners and concerts pouring out of each one. My eyes drank it all in hungrily. Even this late in the Carnevale season, the unbridled excess and scandal and pleasure of my city still fascinated me. Tommaso Foscari had been careful only to escort me to events of which my father would approve, never keeping me out too late. I had never truly experienced the freedom of Venice until now.

As we passed one of the palazzi along the Grand Canal, I peered at a man in a black cloak with a familiar hawk mask helping a woman—a courtesan, judging by her breast-baring neckline—into a gondola. Giacomo.

I looked away, pretending I had not seen, as any good Venetian wife was expected to. I knew that when we went out separately—as we often did—he enjoyed the company of the occasional courtesan, but it did not bother me, as I hardly envied any of them a place in his bed. There were, of course, times when we both returned early in the morning from our respective entertainments and he exerted his husbandly privilege, bolstered by the wine he had consumed. It appeared this evening I would be spared.

When we reached Piazza San Marco, Giulietta and Vittoria were just as enchanted as I had known they would be. There were no fireworks this night, but the jugglers and tumblers and magicians were out in force, and my friends gasped and whooped at their exploits. We moved through the crowd, each with a cup of mulled wine in our hand. We had quite misplaced Mario and Leonardo, but I could not say that we minded.

Just as Giulietta was suggesting we adjourn to a restaurant for dinner, I thought I saw the old gypsy fortune-teller lurking behind one of the pillars that ringed the square. But when I turned to look more closely, there was no one there.

I put my back to the columns and joined my friends' conversation again, letting the past retreat back to the shadows, where it belonged.

53

STABAT MATER DOLOROSA

I was quite sad to see Carnevale end. There would be no more entertainments for the next forty days, while Venice began the tedious process of repenting of our sins during Lent's somber season.

I further lamented when Giacomo made a most unwelcome announcement at dinner on the first Saturday after Ash Wednesday. "We will be attending Mass tomorrow morning at the Pietà," he informed me. "So be sure to rise and make yourself ready."

"Oh?" I asked, raising an eyebrow with practiced composure. "Suddenly so pious, *marito*?"

He chuckled. "I have neglected piety a great deal of late, it is true," he said. "But I mean to begin attending again with you. No doubt you will find the music the *coro* performs during Mass just as enjoyable as their performance here. Also," he added, "tomorrow the *coro* is to premiere a new work by *il Prete Rosso,* and I mean to hear it."

I felt that old vibration of longing, as though someone had taken a bow to the strings of my heart. "As you wish, *marito,*" I said, bowing my head to hide my discomfort.

The chapel was crowded when we arrived, but Giacomo seated us in one of the first pews, reserved for the nobility. I cast my gaze at those sitting around us, hoping that perhaps Vittoria might be among them. I did not see her.

Sighing, I turned my attention to the simple beauty of the chapel. I had been far too distraught on my wedding day to appreciate the painting of the Blessed Mother over the altar, and the high, graceful dome with windows beneath it allowing sunlight to spill in. To my left was the choir loft, where the members of the *coro* filed onto the balcony and took their places behind the grille in a blur of indistinct shapes and colors.

Just then, the Mass began. The words of the priest and the mumbled replies of the congregation faded into a dull blur of sound as I tried to regulate my breathing. The past few days had found me quite ill in the morning—a pattern I knew too well and couldn't bring myself to think on just yet. It was an unseasonably warm, muggy day, and as such the air inside the chapel was heavy from the closely packed bodies within, oppressively so.

When it came time for the psalm, it seemed as if the congregation drew in a collective breath of anticipation. I realized that this must be the expected new work of *il Prete Rosso* as the strings struck up a beautiful yet heartbreakingly somber melody. After several measures, a mournful contralto voice rang out from the balcony.

"*Stabat mater dolorosa,*" she sang, managing to convey so much sorrow in her rich, low voice it seemed as though she were actually weeping as she sang. "*Juxta crucem lacrimosa, lacrimosa.*"

I broke out into a cold sweat, feeling as though the close air was smothering me. The psalm was of the Virgin Mother standing before the cross, sobbing as she looked up at her crucified son, her sacrificed child.

"*Stabat mater dolorosa, dolorosa,*" the soloist sang with heightened urgency. Then she backed away, her voice becoming softer, as though her anguish were such she could not muster the strength to be any louder: "*Juxta crucem lacrimosa, lacrimosa.*"

My breath came in shallow gasps. Never before had I thought of the Holy Virgin as a mother like any other, who had surely raged against the divine plan that took her beloved child from her. How she would weep to find that the world had not changed, that mothers and children were still being separated by the plans of those more powerful than they.

And I was going to bring another child into this world . . .

I tried to stand, pulling myself up using the back of the pew in front of me, but found my legs would not support me. The heat was overwhelming; the altar and the crucifix swam before my eyes. *If I could just breathe, breathe past this sorrow . . .*

Vaguely I heard Giacomo's urgent whisper: "Adriana! Be seated!" I opened my mouth to reply before collapsing against him, surrendering to the blackness that was waiting to catch me.

When I awoke, my breathing came easily, and the air around me was cool and clean. I slowly opened my eyes to find myself lying on a narrow bed in a small, plain room with feeble sunlight trickling in through a window.

I sat up, leaning against the wall, and discovered that I was dressed only in my shift. My gown, petticoat, and corset were draped over a nearby chair.

The chapel . . . that music . . . the heat . . . then nothing.

Evidently I had fainted dead away.

I breathed in sharply, my hands going to my abdomen: the child. Was the child well?

In the space of only a few seconds, I felt myself become fiercely protective of the child about whose existence I had been somewhat ambiguous—so much so that I had not yet told Giacomo.

I began to take inventory of my ailments. But other than a minor and persistent ache in my head and what felt like a bruise forming on my hip, I felt quite well. There was nothing leading me to believe that the tiny child within me was any the worse for wear after its mother's unexpected adventure.

Just then, a nun entered my chamber, carrying a tray with a bowl of soup on it. Her face brightened. "Donna Baldovino! You are awake, praise the Virgin!" She set her tray down and laid a hand on my forehead while peering into my eyes. "There is no fever, so that is well," she said. "How do you feel, madonna?"

"Well enough, if a bit embarrassed," I confessed. "But Sister . . . ?"

"Sister Graziella," she supplied. "I am the nurse and apothecary here."

"Sister Graziella," I repeated. "I must ask . . . that is, I am with child, you see, and I hope my fainting spell did not harm the baby."

An excited yet knowing look came into her eyes. "Why, *congratulazioni,* madonna! You need not worry; I saw nothing to indicate that the child would have suffered any ill effects. And this quite explains your spell."

"Good," I said, relieved.

"But, madonna, does *il senatore* your husband know?" she asked. "He did not mention anything of your condition when he brought you here . . ."

I was somewhat touched by the implication Giacomo had carried me to the infirmary himself. "No," I said. "Not yet, I fear. It is early days yet."

She nodded. "Of course. Well, I have brought you some soup to help you regain your strength, and I shall send for your husband. I am sure he will be overjoyed at your news!"

After she left, I obediently ate my soup, pondering the best way to tell Giacomo. Then I wondered whether Vivaldi had seen me fall in the chapel, whether he had known it was me. Whether he had worried. Whether he cared.

54

LULLABY

Giacomo was overjoyed and puffed with pride at my news. As soon as the Lenten season ended he threw a large, lavish party in honor of the forthcoming birth of (he hoped) his son and heir.

The spring and summer that followed were wonderful: Giacomo saw to it that I had everything I could possibly need or desire—from fresh fish, fruits, and vegetables to pastries and even a new, softer coverlet for my bed—brought to me without question or delay.

As my belly grew and my time neared, I went out in public less, depriving my friends of my company on their excursions—something they lamented very loudly. But much as I missed accompanying them out, I had begun to anticipate the birth of my child with unabashed joy. This child would never be able to replace my Anna, but here was a chance to start again, and to have a son or daughter that would be mine to love, bring up, and care for as I saw fit.

We went to Giacomo's villa for June and July, but returned in mid-August as my confinement drew nearer. And so I waited, without dread, only happiness, and perhaps a little impatience.

"A girl," Giacomo said, trying and failing to hide his disappointment as he looked down at the squalling infant in my arms.

"But look at her," I said testily, lifting her up. "Is she not beautiful?"

"Oh, beauty she has in abundance," he said, displaying the first genuine smile I had seen since he entered the birthing chamber. "Just like her mother."

I smiled.

"Still, she is a girl, so I cannot make her my heir."

"I would love her no more if she were a boy," I said defiantly. "I am going to call her Lucrezia, after my mother." It was a statement, not a request. Her full name would be Lucrezia Giuseppina, but I chose to omit the second name for now.

"As you wish, my dear." He moved to the door, then stopped and turned back to me. "This has only strengthened my resolve to beget a son," he informed me. "We must continue our efforts as soon as possible." He closed the door behind him with a decisive click.

I cringed but put our conversation out of my mind as I found myself alone with my daughter for the first time.

I do not know how long I spent marveling at her. She was perfect. As she drifted into sleep, a look of contentment came over her face, and I felt as if light shined down upon us from heaven itself, bright and warm.

And she was all mine. There was no one hovering at my bedside, ready to snatch her away. I would have a lifetime to watch every exquisite change that she went through, from babyhood to childhood to womanhood. And never, I vowed, would I let her father or anyone else sell her in marriage or lock her in a convent against her will. Her choices would be her own, and if she chose to marry, it would be for love.

She soon woke and began to wail. At the sound of her cry, the midwife appeared from the next room. "Let me take *la bambina* to the wet nurse," she said, moving to take my daughter from my arms.

I shifted my body slightly, moving little Lucrezia out of her reach.

"Certainly not," I said, my voice coming out sharp. "I am her mother. I will nurse her myself."

The midwife gasped in horror at such a flouting of convention. "But madonna, surely *il senatore* your husband would prefer—"

"These are women's matters, signora, and not something over which my esteemed husband has dominion," I told her. "I pray you send the wet nurse away with some coins for her trouble."

And with that, Lucrezia latched onto my breast, and I blissfully allowed my eyes to drift halfway closed. I was wonderfully, completely happy.

Lucrezia's cradle was placed in my room, so that I might tend to her during the night if need be—though a young maidservant by the name of Giovanna slept in the nursery adjoining my bedchamber, should I need assistance. Exhausted, I immediately fell into a deep sleep the night following her birth, only to awaken with a suffocating sense of urgency in the dark hours of the morning.

For a moment I thought Lucrezia's crying must have woken me, but all was silent. Rising, I crossed the room to peer into her cradle. She was perfectly well, her chest rising and falling as her tiny lungs settled into their task.

Yet as though she could sense her mother nearby, she soon woke and began to fuss. I lifted her out of her cradle and sat in the chair beside it, tugging down the shoulder of my shift to offer her my breast. But Lucrezia was having none of it. I waved away Giovanna, who had stumbled sleepily into the room when she heard the baby's cries. After unsuccessfully trying to persuade my daughter to feed, I checked her swaddling clothes, but they were dry, leaving me at a loss as to why she continued to wail.

I tried humming to her, a lullaby I vaguely remembered my mother singing to me. But that did nothing to calm her—small wonder, my vocal talents being quite nonexistent.

"Please, madonna." I jumped, startled, when Giovanna slipped back into the room unnoticed. "You need to rest. Let me take the child."

"No!" I insisted. "I will tend to her. Go back to bed."

The timid Giovanna sighed but did as I commanded.

In my mind, it had become a test: only if I could find the source of Lucrezia's distress and soothe it was I fit to be her mother.

Standing, I began to pace, hoping the movement would lull her back to sleep. In this, too, I was disappointed.

I placed her back in her cradle, hoping that she might fall asleep again if she were lying down. Still I did not meet with success.

I wrung my hands, almost frantic. Could she be ill? Should I send for a doctor? Was she in some sort of pain that I could not detect? Did infants simply cry for no reason?

Wait, I thought suddenly, *maybe . . .*

Kneeling down on the floor beside my bed, I reached underneath and pulled out the violin case that had sat there, untouched, since I had moved into the palazzo. Vivaldi's violin.

Lucrezia's cries faded into the background as I took the instrument out and beheld the polished wood, worn but still gleaming in the dim light. I ran my finger over the strings, listening to them hum. I reached for the bow, tightened it, and ran it slowly over two strings at a time, my fingers automatically moving to tune it. Then I played a long, glorious, drawn-out E, just to hear the music in the air, just to hear the instrument sing. A smile tugged at my lips.

I moved to the side of Lucrezia's cradle, took a deep breath, and began to play.

Slowly and awkwardly, then more smoothly, the second movement, the largo, of Vivaldi's A-minor concerto from *L'estro armonico,* came spilling from the strings. I had always suspected, hoped, he had written it as a love song for me. Now it became a different sort of love song, a lullaby for my baby. My fingers were stiff from lack of practice, and I stumbled over sections that I had forgotten, but it did not matter. Lucrezia's crying slowed to a stop as I played, as though she were as transfixed by this piece of music as I had once been.

Once I reached the end of the movement, she was drifting off to sleep again. Afraid to stop for fear she would wake again, I quickly began to pick out my mother's lullaby on the strings, smoothing it out, embellishing and rearranging as I went.

I do not know how long I played, but when I stopped Lucrezia was sleeping deeply once more. I lowered the instrument, my heart racing. The temptation to keep playing, to reach back into the memories I had walled off for any scrap of music—Vivaldi's or my own—was almost more than I could bear. Yet I did not want to reach for too much all at once. What if the magic that had returned to me so briefly should disappear if I chased after it too eagerly?

So I put the violin back in its case, returning it to its spot beneath the bed. There would be time enough to rediscover what I had lost. And suddenly I could no longer remember what it was that I had been so afraid of.

MOVEMENT SIX

KEY CHANGE

May 1714–October 1727

55

IMPROMPTU

"Please have a seat, Senator Baldovino, Donna Baldovino."

My husband and I obeyed, taking the two richly upholstered chairs that sat opposite the barrister's desk.

Signor Peri pressed his fingertips together, looking at us intently. "I shall get right to the point," he said. "Your late father's estate is something of a mess, Donna Baldovino. The details are rather . . . murky, shall we say."

I was not altogether surprised to hear this. In the letter scheduling the reading of my father's will, he had warned us of some complications that had arisen with the estate. "How so, Signor Peri?" I asked.

He sighed and picked up a sheaf of papers. "Unfortunately, Don d'Amato never made a new will after the death of your brother, Claudio. The most recent will we have leaves everything—ownership of the company, the palazzo and all its contents, the share in the glass factory, and all financial assets and property—to Claudio. There are a few smaller bequests which he made to several of his servants, which will of course be honored. But his wishes concerning the estate as a whole, of course, cannot be." He handed me the papers so that I might examine them myself.

I was not surprised that I had been left out; even had I not horribly disgraced him, this will had been drafted after my marriage. With my dowry paid and me safely ensconced in my husband's house, there would have been no need for me to receive anything.

Nor did it surprise me that my normally meticulous father had let such an important matter fall by the wayside. He had gone to pieces after Claudio was killed, showing his age in a way he never had before and indulging heavily in drink. I had thought—rather uncharitably—this was less out of distress over his son's death and more for the disappointment of his fondest hopes: to see a d'Amato dynasty established that would rival any of the great families of the republic. That dream had been mortally wounded when I had become the wife of a minor senator rather than Tommaso Foscari, and it had breathed its last along with Claudio.

His death was not entirely a shock. He had been extremely pleased at Lucrezia's birth, and came to see her several times a week. I had just begun entertaining the hope that we might begin to enjoy a more cordial relationship when, just eight months after his granddaughter's birth, he had taken a fever. By then, his health was so ruined by neglect that there was nothing any doctor could do.

Now, several days after his requiem Mass had been sung, we were in the office of Signor Alonso Peri, barrister to both my father and his company, to set his affairs to rights.

"What will be done with the estate, then?" Giacomo asked as I passed him the papers.

"This is where I have good news," Signor Peri said, breaking into a small smile. "My colleagues and I see no problem with the entirety of the estate passing to you, Donna Baldovino, as Enrico d'Amato's only living child; and by extension your esteemed husband as well."

Giacomo looked like a man whose fondest dreams had all come true right before his eyes—and no doubt they had. After all, what more could a patrician with a dwindling fortune ask for when marrying the daughter of a wealthy merchant?

It did not occur to me he might never forgive me for what I said next. All I thought of was the chance to repay a debt that could never truly be satisfied. "And what if my father had another child?" I asked.

Both Giacomo and Signor Peri turned to stare at me.

"Well," said Signor Peri, recovering his voice first, "that would complicate things, certainly. But as your father had no children other than yourself and Claudio—"

"He did, in fact," I said.

"Adriana," Giacomo all but growled in warning.

I ignored him. "My father has another son who is yet living; an illegitimate son, but a son nonetheless, who is older than me by several years. His name is Giuseppe Rivalli, and he currently resides in Venice."

"Well, this is most fascinating, Donna Baldovino," Signor Peri said. "Can you provide any proof of this claim?"

I laughed. "Are my words not proof enough? What other reason could I possibly have to relinquish the fortune I stand to inherit, unless it were to see that fortune come into the hands of a most beloved brother?"

"Adriana," Giacomo said, attempting to sound pleasant and pacifying, "I do not think that this is entirely appropriate—"

"On the contrary, husband," I said. "It could not be more appropriate. You would not wish to wrongly inherit my father's estate, would you?"

Giacomo looked positively apoplectic at my words. "But surely this bastard cannot—"

"Not necessarily," Signor Peri said, somewhat reluctantly. "Again, the fact that we do not have a current will muddies matters. Though this—Giuseppe Rivalli, is it?—man is not Don d'Amato's legitimate son, there would have been nothing stopping him from leaving this son the estate, if he so chose. So we cannot assume—"

Giacomo leaped from his chair with such force that it tipped over. "Like hell we cannot!" he shouted. He pointed one finger at me accusingly. "Your father would never have left anything to that conniving bastard, and you know it!"

"He did not trouble himself to leave it to me, either," I said. "Who are you to say which one of us my father hated more?"

"You will not take this out from under me, Adriana, I swear," Giacomo said.

I rolled my eyes. "Please, husband," I said, placing one hand on my again-growing belly. My pregnancy was already noticeable, although it was only my fourth month; this led Giacomo to hope it would be a strapping son this time. "It does not do to upset a woman in my condition."

Giacomo turned back to a rather embarrassed Signor Peri. "Tell her this cannot be, signore," he said. "This is folly, all of it."

"I am afraid it is not," Signor Peri said. "I will have to have my agents investigate your claim, Donna Baldovino, but if what you say is true, then perhaps we can divide the estate and its assets in half—"

"Half!" Giacomo roared.

"Giuseppe can have it all," I said. "I do not want any of it."

With one last, frustrated scream, Giacomo whirled around and stormed from the room.

I rose to follow him, but Signor Peri lifted a hand to detain me. "Wait, Donna Baldovino. A moment, if you please."

I sat down again.

"Is this truly what you wish?" he asked me. "I do not doubt that you are in earnest, but it is a rare individual who would turn their back on such good fortune."

"Giuseppe is my brother," I said. "I love him more than anyone on earth, save my daughter." *Daughters,* I amended silently. "It is not his fault he was not born in the marriage bed. And I owe him a great debt."

Signor Peri smiled. "I understand, madonna. At least, I think I do." He sighed. "I will do what I can to see that he inherits at least some of the estate—you are entitled to some of it, as well, no matter your preferences." I opened my mouth to protest, but he continued. "Think of your daughter, and the child you are carrying, and their futures, if not of yourself."

I remained silent, knowing that he was right. Giacomo's own estate was not so diminished as that of many other members of the Venetian nobility, but if I wished for there to be enough money for my children—my daughter—to lead lives of their own choosing . . .

"Perhaps you are right, signore," I said. "But we shall leave the details to a later date."

He nodded. "Very good, madonna. I must first seek out this Giuseppe Rivalli, though I fear I will make an enemy of your husband by doing so. You may have made him an enemy as well."

I waved a hand carelessly as I rose. "I will handle my husband," I said. "I look forward to hearing from you soon, then, signore."

"Indeed," he said, rising as well. "And my condolences on your loss."

I smiled briefly. "Thank you, signore."

When I stepped into the hallway, I found a furious Giacomo waiting for me. "What in heaven and hell is wrong with you, Adriana?" he demanded, seizing my arm in a punishing grip. "We were about to inherit a vast fortune! We would have been wealthy beyond imagining!"

I wrenched away from him. "Unhand me," I said. "Think of your child, if nothing else."

"I am the only one thinking of our children, it seems," he hissed. "Do you realize what you have just done? You have deprived them of a future filled with everything they could ever dream of!"

"We shall still receive something, *marito*," I said, with a touch of guilt. "Which you would have heard had you not stormed out of the room like a petulant child instead of comporting yourself as befits a patrician and senator of the republic."

He looked slightly chastened at my words. "You gave everything away, or almost everything," he said through gritted teeth. "How can you—"

I laid my hand gently on his cheek. "I promise that I did not do this to hurt you, Giacomo, nor our children," I said. "But Giuseppe . . . you do not know the extent of the debt I owe him."

He snorted. "Oh, do I not? I know that without him, you would not have been able to carry on your disgraceful love affair."

"He protected me from my own father," I said. "Numerous times. I know you do not want to hear this, Giacomo," I said, as he blanched at my words, "but my father was cruel, violent, and angry from the day my mother died. Giuseppe was my only friend in that house."

"It does not do to speak ill of the dead, Adriana."

"The ill was my father's own doing. I speak only the truth, because I wish you to understand."

"Be that as it may," he said, after a long moment had passed, "you had no right, Adriana—"

"It is my inheritance to give away," I said, lifting my skirts and starting down the stairs that led to the water entrance. "And you would not have come within miles of it had it not been for me."

He said nothing further the entire the trip back to our palazzo.

And so, after several weeks of paperwork, correspondence, and further meetings, a settlement was reached. Giuseppe inherited the d'Amato palazzo and all its contents, ownership of the company and all its assets, and half of the money and other assets my father had left behind, of which there was far more than I realized. Despite the luxury in which I had grown up, my father had spent his wealth far more prudently than the majority of Venice's nobility. And in the interests of Lucrezia and her as yet unborn brother or sister, Giacomo and I inherited the other half of the financial assets.

Signor Peri suggested Giuseppe take the d'Amato name, in order to help smooth his transition into both Venetian society and his new role at the company. After some reluctance, Giuseppe relented partway, taking it as his second name. Thus, seemingly overnight, he became Giuseppe d'Amato Rivalli, one of the richest men in Venice.

Our reunion, once everything was finalized—for, given my brother's new status, Giacomo could hardly continue to deny me his company—was a joyous one. Despite our regular correspondence, I had not seen Giuseppe in the two years since my wedding. I introduced him to his niece, and saw his eyes glisten when he learned that she had been christened not only in my mother's honor, but in his as well.

"Oh, Adriana," he said, once our near-hour of excited exclamations had passed. "How could you do this for me? You might have had everything, for yourself, for your children, and yet—"

"Do not speak of it," I cut him off. "Surely you know that it does not begin to make up for everything you have done for me, Giuseppe."

"I just feel as though I do not deserve it."

"Nonsense," I said. "You are his son, are you not? It is only reparations for how he treated you. Think of it that way."

"Perhaps," he allowed. Then he chuckled. "What would Enrico say to see me sitting atop his throne, and it all your doing? I accepted it just to spite him, you know."

"I suggested it for the same reason," I joked.

Our talk turned to other things then, and it was late into the night when he reluctantly rose to take his leave. "I should return to the palazzo and get some rest," he said. "It has been a trying several days."

"'The palazzo'?" I teased. "Still not home, even after all these years?"

He shuddered. "*Dio mio*, no. Now that all this business is settled, my first act will be to sell it and buy a new one—if you are agreeable, that is, *sorella*. There are more ugly memories in that house than any other kind, I think."

"Yes," I agreed; then unthinkingly added, "Save for in the parlor with the harpsichord."

Giuseppe looked almost dumbstruck at my bringing up such a thing, then he laughed. "Fair enough," he said. "I will have the harpsichord sent to you without delay."

I smiled. "I will be most willing to accept it." I rose and saw him to the door. "I shall see you again soon, *sì?*"

"Oh, certainly. Now that I am a respectable member of society, you will not be able to be rid of me." He grinned. "I suppose I must start participating in all of the required social events: the opera and scandalous parties and I know not what else. If anyone invites me, that is."

"I shall begin by extending you your first invitation," I said, smiling. "You must accompany my friends and me to the opera next week."

"That sounds splendid," he said. "I look forward to meeting these friends of yours." He kissed me on the cheek. "Of everything that has happened in these last weeks, I am happiest of all to have seen you again, and to see that you are doing well."

"I am," I assured him. "I truly am."

56

SOL DA TE, MIO DOLCE AMORE

The following week Giuseppe joined us for an opera at the Teatro San Giovanni Grisostomo. By that time, all of Venetian society was buzzing with the news of Enrico d'Amato's bastard son, raised from obscurity to inherit his empire. Thus, my circle in particular was most excited to meet him.

"So this is your brother, is it, Adriana?" Giulietta Grimaldi asked excitedly, allowing Mario to help her into the gondola that Giuseppe had so graciously volunteered for the evening.

Once she had settled her heavy frame against the cushions—she was well into her seventh month of pregnancy with her second child—she extended her hand, which Giuseppe kissed with a gallant flourish. "Giuseppe Rivalli," he introduced himself. "And you must be the charming Giulietta Grimaldi. My sister has told me much about you."

Giulietta giggled. "Indeed! It seems she must have found *something* good to tell you, for you do not look scandalized in the least." She tossed me a conspiratorial glance. "But you did not tell me he was so handsome, my dear Adriana!"

I laughed. "Then I apologize for being remiss in my description."

Giulietta introduced Mario, and then we made our way to the Cassenti palazzo, where Leonardo would have arrived earlier to escort Vittoria.

Giuseppe had been deep in conversation with me but stopped mid-sentence when Vittoria joined us, his jaw hanging slack. A similar stillness came over her for just an instant upon catching sight of him, before she allowed Mario to help her into a seat—the one on Giuseppe's other side, as luck would have it.

Some light, bright happiness sparked within me as I observed the way they looked at each other. At that moment, nothing mattered other than the fact that two of the people I loved best in the world should be so instantly attracted to one another.

"Giuseppe," I said, as soon as Vittoria was seated, "this is my dear friend Maria Vittoria Cassenti, formerly Vittoria della Pietà."

Giuseppe reached for her hand and brought it quickly to his lips. "Madonna," he said, with as much reverence as if he addressed the Blessed Mother herself. "The pleasure is all mine. Giuseppe Rivalli, your servant."

A blush bloomed in Vittoria's cheeks. "I am delighted, Don Rivalli," she said. "Adriana speaks so highly of you, and yet I see now that her praise was insufficient."

Giulietta tossed me a knowing glance over the folds of her fan as Leonardo plopped down close beside Vittoria and loudly cleared his throat. "Leonardo Franchetti," he said, nodding at Giuseppe. "A pleasure."

"Likewise, Don Franchetti," Giuseppe said.

"Well, we are quite the merry group!" Giulietta broke in, smiling. She looked at Vittoria, then at Giuseppe, then back again. Vittoria's face grew self-conscious, flushing even more. And Giuseppe, engaged in conversation with Mario, kept stealing glances at Vittoria when he thought no one would notice.

That evening at the opera, we broke from our usual tradition, in which Vittoria and I insisted we watch at least a portion of the opera and would sit riveted at the front of the box, whispering critiques of the musicians to one another. In fact, we scarcely saw any of the opera, and were content to have it so. We remained in the rear section of the box, eating, drinking, and playing several hands of cards. I was delighted Giuseppe fitted in with my friends, who had in turn accepted him wholeheartedly—with the exception of Leonardo. Giulietta and I were quite certain Leonardo was in love with our friend, and his behavior tonight confirmed our suspicions.

I watched my brother closely throughout the evening. The two seemed to dance about each other in some strange, unspoken complicity. Giuseppe did not single Vittoria out, nor did Vittoria readily engage him in conversation. Yet their eyes would constantly dart to the other's face, as though trying to memorize each other's features.

Once we had taken the others home at the end of the night, and Giuseppe and I were alone in the gondola, I considered bringing it up, but decided it might be no more than a simple fancy. It was best not to make more of it than it was. After all, Vittoria was a married woman, and hardly one inclined to break her marriage vows.

Our newly enlarged group of six went out together a few more times before the annual migration of Venetian society to the country. Giulietta remained behind, being near to her confinement, and I knew that I would miss her company.

Giuseppe, too, remained in the city over the summer, having many details to attend to as he began to take over our father's business. He was true to his word and sold the d'Amato palazzo within weeks of the estate being finalized and bought a new one, slightly smaller than our father's, that was not far from my own.

Giuseppe wrote me frequently, and spent a few nights with us at our villa. Giacomo treated him courteously if a bit coldly. He was still angry at me for proposing that Giuseppe receive the inheritance, and angry at Giuseppe for accepting it; yet despite some grumblings, he had done nothing to block the process in earnest, which led me to believe that my words outside of Signor Peri's office had reached him.

In August we were forced to return to Venice early, as my pregnancy had become increasingly difficult. My belly had grown quite immense, and I suffered from aches and inordinate exhaustion that kept me in bed much of the time. We decided to make the return journey while I was still able, and once back home I found myself rarely able to leave my chamber. I was too tired even to play the violin, which I had continued to do, slowly, since Lucrezia's birth.

Lucrezia, the joy of my life, brought me even more happiness in those days when I stayed abed. She would curl up next to me contentedly while I told her stories of princesses and genies and angels, until we both fell asleep. Giuseppe was completely enchanted with her—more so, perhaps, than her own father—and often came over to help her toddle about her nursery while I rested.

Yet I was far more impatient for and apprehensive about this birth than my previous two. I tried my best not to worry, as the midwife who examined me upon our return pronounced me perfectly healthy, and assured me my difficulties simply stemmed from carrying a large child. My friends happily came to visit me as I rested, and Giulietta brought her new infant son, named Giulio in her honor.

Giacomo's anger and frustration toward me faded away as his concern for my health grew, and he was even more attentive than he had been during my last pregnancy. As summer cooled into fall, my expected delivery date drew nearer, and it could not come soon enough.

57

DUET

"It is a son!" the midwife cried triumphantly, holding up the red, squalling child in her arms.

I let my head fall back, my body sinking into the mattress beneath me, exhausted, overjoyed, and relieved. I did not want to confront Giacomo's disappointment again, and I was genuinely happy to have given him the son and heir he had wanted so desperately.

I opened my eyes to see the midwife frowning. "You may not rest yet, I fear, madonna," she said, handing my son to Giovanna.

"What?"

"There is a second child," she said, crouching down to peer between my legs again. "Twins."

"Holy Virgin," I breathed, shuddering as another pain racked me.

"Indeed, we shall beseech the Holy Virgin to give you strength, madonna," the midwife said. "You must push yet again!"

Twins. I could hardly believe that I must expel another child from my body, that I would have the strength. Yet a mother's fierce love shot through me, love for this second creature I had not known was there. I did as the midwife bade me and, in relatively short order, gave birth to my fourth child and my third daughter.

This time, when I lay back against the pillows, I did not think I would ever open my eyes. But I was roused when I heard my children crying. "Bring them to me," I said, struggling to sit up.

The midwife hesitated. "You should rest, madonna, and we need to clean them up in any case."

"No," I said. I held out my arms, taking one child in each, with Giovanna hovering nearby should I need assistance.

I studied each of them in turn. My son, I was certain, was the most perfect son ever born, from his tiny toenails to his soft, velvety head.

And my daughter. My unexpected one. She was smaller than her brother, with an impressive head of dark hair, and perhaps feistier, for as he settled comfortably against me, making a strange hiccupping noise, she began to wail, demanding to be fed.

I laughed. "Very well, *figlia*." I handed my son to Giovanna, and set his sister to my breast.

"Shall I send for a wet nurse for the boy, madonna?" Giovanna asked.

"Of course not," I said. "He shall have his turn."

Once both children had been fed, I reluctantly surrendered them to be washed before Giacomo came to see them. He had been informed of the happy news.

"Twins?" he cried incredulously when he was finally allowed in the room. "*Dio mio*, twins! And one of them a son, a son at last!"

I smiled as he sat on the edge of the bed, peering at the children. "They are healthy, yes? A strong and healthy son and daughter?"

"They are," I said. "We are all three of us well."

Giacomo gently stroked our son's head. "Yes, little Giacomo," he said softly, as the baby stirred. "It is your father."

"*Marito*," I began, "I . . . that is, I had a different name in mind."

He looked up. "Why should my son and heir not be named after me?"

"Surely we can be more creative than that," I said. "I have always been fond of the name Antonio."

Giacomo was silent for a moment, and I could scarcely breathe, praying that he would not guess. "Antonio Giacomo Baldovino," he said, testing it. "Very well. Antonio was my father's name, after all."

"But of course," I said, though I had forgotten that entirely. "That is part of the reason I suggested it."

He kissed my forehead. "I can deny you nothing, *mia bell'Adriana*. And our little surprise?" he said, turning his attention to the girl. "What shall we name her?"

"I rather like Cecilia," I said. "For the patron saint of music."

"I think that suits," Giacomo said. "Cecilia Adriana, for her courageous mother."

I smiled, tears stinging my eyes.

He drew me gently against him. "You have made me the happiest man alive, *mia carissima*. I know that our marriage was not your choice, but I fancy that I have managed to make you happy at times, yes?"

The tears spilled over onto my cheeks. "Oh, yes," I whispered. "I am happy at this moment, *marito*. Brilliantly happy."

Giacomo spared no expense on a lavish party to celebrate the twins' birth, and particularly the birth of his heir. Antonio was, as such, the focus of the evening—the early part, anyway. He was carried about by me, by Giovanna, and even by Giacomo, for our guests to admire and croon over. Cecilia, however, was not to be ignored, and took to wailing loudly whenever she felt not enough attention was being paid to her.

Soon, however, they both grew fussy, and I made my escape. As refreshing as the party was after my long confinement and recovery, I still tired easily, even though a month had passed since the birth. I excused myself to put the children to bed, gathered Vittoria and

Giulietta, and we adjourned to my sitting room just as Giacomo was calling for more brandy to be poured.

I sighed in relief as I sank down into one of the armchairs and kicked off my silk shoes. Lucrezia promptly crawled into my lap, peering into the face of the sleeping Antonio, who lay in my arms.

"Shall I take Cecilia to the nursery?" Giovanna asked.

"Oh, may I hold her?" Vittoria asked, her eyes alight.

"Of course," I said, and Giovanna handed the baby to her. "You are dismissed for the evening, Giovanna."

Vittoria cradled my daughter as skillfully as any experienced mother. "What a little angel," she said. "All three of them. You are blessed, Adriana. Truly you are. What I would not give for such beautiful children as yours."

I smiled, stroking Lucrezia's feathery light hair with one hand as she fell asleep in my lap. Vittoria was right: I *was* blessed, in spite of the things I had lost. "Perhaps you and Francesco might yet be so blessed," I said, though even I did not believe my own words. As if Francesco's age were not enough of an impediment to conception, his health had been poor of late. Always thin, his appearance had become almost skeletal, and he was prone to chills and fevers.

Vittoria smiled sadly. "Not now, I am afraid. He was already too old to father children when I first married him, or so it seems."

Giulietta chuckled. "I would have thought the same of our illustrious Senator Baldovino, yet it appears he has more life in him than anyone could have guessed!"

I rolled my eyes. "And he has thrown a party to announce and celebrate that fact."

"As well he should," Giulietta said. "He is apparently so potent that he managed to get you with two children at once!"

"Or such is the story he shall tell," I said, and we all dissolved into laughter.

"If only Roberto could have done the same, I might have been finished with childbearing all in one fell swoop," Giulietta said.

"Perhaps Giacomo can give him lessons," Vittoria said, surprising us so with her bawdy joke that our fits of giggles returned, petering out only when we saw all my children were fast asleep.

"Come, *cara,*" I whispered, nudging Lucrezia awake. She sleepily tumbled off my lap, and I lifted her with my other arm, carrying her and her brother into the nursery. Vittoria followed me with Cecilia.

Once the children were safely abed, Vittoria and I returned to the sitting room. "I was just wondering, Adriana," Giulietta said as I sat down, "why your son is not named after his father."

I froze, just for an instant, yet the look in Vittoria's eyes told me she had seen it nonetheless. "Oh . . . well, Antonio was the name of Giacomo's father," I said. "And he is Antonio Giacomo, at any rate."

Giulietta looked satisfied enough with this explanation, though Vittoria's face remained curious.

"Oh!" Giulietta cried suddenly, heedless of the sleeping children in the next room. "Have you heard who that dreadful Claudia Cornaro was caught *in maschera* with?" She leaned forward, eyes wide. "They say she was found in a very *compromising position,* if you take my meaning, at the *festa* given by the Guicciardi family with—you shall never guess it—her brother-in-law! Her sister Elisabetta's husband! They were found in the mezzanine by a footman! They say it was Claudia, anyway; the mask the lady was wearing was the same as one she has worn. I, for one, believe it, what with the way that girl behaves . . ."

I readily confessed to enjoying the frivolousness of gossip from time to time, but tonight I could not bring myself to pay attention. Instead, my thoughts were on my children, and what their lives would be like in this vain, decadent Venice of ours, and how I could protect and shelter them while still letting them live. And what of my lost daughter? Did the Girò family love her, and treat her well? Had they told her of her true mother, or did she believe herself to be their daughter? Which way was better?

And, in spite of myself, I found myself wondering whether or not Antonio Vivaldi would ever know I named my son after him.

58

HARMONIES

My son's namesake had been anything but idle since last I had set eyes on him. May of 1713 had seen him mount his first opera, *Ottone in villa,* to much acclaim in Vincenza. The gossip said that it had been well received; well enough, at least, for him to return to Venice, the city with the most discerning musical tastes, to continue his new career. He had also begun to gain a reputation as a very shrewd businessman when it came to selling both his scores and his skills to whoever may have need of them.

In November of 1714 he premiered *Orlando finite pazzo* at the Teatro Sant' Angelo, where he was now impresario as well as composer and performer. Still recovering from the birth of the twins, I managed to avoid attending. My friends enthusiastically went, not about to miss one of the biggest operatic events of the year: the premiere of a new work by a native son of Venice, who had gained much notoriety across Europe since the publication of *L'estro armonico.*

Vittoria had been especially eager to see the opera. She came to visit me the following day, imparting the information I both dreaded and hungered for.

"The sets and the costumes were all a bit overwrought, as usual," she said. "But the music," she went on, her expression softening, "the music was *wonderful*. I do not believe that Maestro Vivaldi could write anything that is not beautiful."

I nodded my agreement, not trusting myself to speak.

She sighed, not noticing my lack of response. "It is when I am confronted with such beauty, such music, that I realize anew what I have lost."

My head came up sharply at this echo of my own thoughts.

"He wrote a few pieces of music especially for me," she went on, lost in the past, "for my voice. I do not believe that I shall ever be so honored again in my life."

Suddenly it struck me how deeply one man and his music could touch so many people. He had never, I realized with both sorrow and pride, been mine alone. How selfish I had been, to believe that I could and should keep him for myself.

"I am sorry," Vittoria said. "You did not invite me here to listen to me bemoan the past. I am selfish, I know. I have a wonderful life, and I do it and my husband a disservice by longing for days that are gone."

"And I did not even invite you," I said. "You simply dropped by of your own accord."

Vittoria laughed. "Horribly rude of me, I know."

"I trust you will continue to exercise such rudeness often enough," I told her.

She inquired after the children then, and our talk turned to happier matters. Thus the past retreated to whence it had come—for both of us.

Since Lucrezia's birth, I had continued—hesitantly, sporadically—to resume my violin playing. Giacomo, just as I had hoped, made no comment when he noticed.

On that night when I had played my daughter to sleep I had felt invincible—to fear, to the past's power to hurt me—but that feeling quickly faded. It was a struggle to discipline myself, to regain my technique and to learn, once again, to push aside everything but the music.

It was a slow process. It had been years since I had played with intensity, and my fingers had to once again accustom themselves to their task. And even then, I could only play scales and half-remembered bits of concerti for so long.

Finally I went to a shop that sold scores one day, and selected a few at random for the violin: some by composers I had heard of, such as Arcangelo Corelli, and others I had not. Though much of the music was lovely and challenging, it was not Vivaldi's music. Was it only because he had been my lover that I so plainly preferred his music?

No. His music truly did have something that the music of others did not. I had recognized this within hours of meeting him, long before we had become lovers.

Every now and then, especially once I had started playing again, it occurred to me that I could—I *could,* if I wanted to—slip away to see Vivaldi. Giacomo never questioned my comings and goings; was often not home enough to notice. Vivaldi was so *close,* still in the same city, and would anyone ever know me as well as he had?

Had. Once. And if I were to see him again, what then? Would we play music together as though nothing had happened? Talk about the past? Make love? The remnants of my anger and heartbreak would always come flooding back like the *acqua alta,* and I would wonder what, precisely, I had been thinking.

I had mentioned to Giuseppe one day, rather in passing, that I had begun to play again but did not have enough scores to satisfy me. I should not have been surprised he managed to decipher my true meaning; yet I could not have been more astonished when, one day in late January of 1715, a rather large packet was delivered to me. A small cry escaped me as I opened it, finding the scores for every piece

Vivaldi and I had ever played together, as well as many new works of increasing difficulty that I had never seen before. It was enough to keep me busy for years to come, and to bring me back to virtuoso form.

On top of this pile of treasure was a note, folded in half. I opened it, a slight tremor in my hands, and read:

Adriana—

I saw Giuseppe at the Sant' Angelo two weeks ago, and he mentioned to me that you might have some use for these. I hope that you are well, and that these scores will help you to find the music again, if indeed you still feel that it eludes you.

At the bottom of the parchment it was signed, as he had always signed his missives to me, simply *AV*.

The leaping, acrobatic notes on the staves swam before my eyes. I clutched the packet to my chest and let the tears roll down my cheeks.

I invited Giuseppe to lunch the next day. Once the meal was served and we were alone, I did not mince words: "You saw him."

It was somewhere between an accusation and a question, but Giuseppe needed no further explanation of my meaning.

"Ah." He laid down his silverware beside his plate. "I take it he sent you the scores, then?"

I nodded.

"Yes, I went to see him at the Sant' Angelo after a production I attended there. You had said you needed music to play, and I assumed you would rather have his music than any other, though I knew you would never say it." He looked at me calmly, as though daring me to dispute it. "I had heard he is now quite the music salesman these days, and so I thought to buy some scores from him. When he learned that they were for you, though, there was no mention of payment. All he said was, 'I will see that she gets them.' And I see that he has done just that."

"He copied them himself," I said. "I know his hand. He did not have a copyist do it for him."

Giuseppe held my gaze. "That does not surprise me."

"What . . ." I hesitated. "What else did he say?"

Giuseppe looked away and returned his attention to his pasta, pretending my inquiry was a casual one. "He congratulated me on the change in my circumstances, of which he had heard. I took the liberty of telling him that you are well, and have three beautiful children."

I nodded at my plate but did not speak.

"He looks well," Giuseppe ventured, "if a bit harried."

Suddenly I felt there was nothing more I wanted or needed to say on the subject. I looked back up at my brother, a cheerful smile on my face. "Did you receive an invitation to the ball Leonardo's father is giving on Friday next?"

He looked a bit startled by the abrupt change in topic, but followed my lead, letting me steer the conversation to friendlier shores.

When Giuseppe left that afternoon, I went upstairs to my rooms and pulled out a sheaf of papers from my desk. Sitting, I smoothed them out and began to look them over anew.

Here it was, *La sirena,* my first real concerto. I had feared facing this more than even Vivaldi's music.

I had been certain that when I finally looked at what I had written again, it would pale in comparison to the memories I had of it, of learning to play it myself, of teaching Vivaldi to play it. Or that I would now dismiss it as a juvenile girl's scribbling.

But as I read through each note, sections I had forgotten and those I remembered all too vividly, I felt its power anew, in a way that

I had not before. I could see it as a work of music separate from myself, and not just as something I had created. It was well done; Vivaldi had not been lying to me, nor had I been lying to myself.

Gathering the pages, I placed them on my music stand. Then I got out my violin, took a deep breath, and began to play.

I played the entire thing, and let the memories flow through me. They were infused in the music, had bled into every note as I had written it. There was no parting the two.

But, I knew now, there were new memories to be made, and new music to be written.

When I finally reached the end, I was startled by a light applauding coming from the doorway into the nursery. I looked up to find both Meneghina and Giovanna watching me.

"That was beautiful, madonna," Meneghina said. "Who wrote that?"

A slight smile touched my lips. "I did."

59

RESONANCE

Time passed, in the peaceful and quietly joyful manner to which I had become accustomed since the births of my children. I watched them grow, take their first steps, say their first words. I spent as much time with them as I could, determined that their childhoods should be as happy and carefree as possible.

Giacomo made a point of seeing the children once or twice a day, but only briefly. In that respect he was not different from many patrician fathers, but I could not help feeling slightly resentful toward him. He had been so excited by my pregnancies and the births, especially of the twins, that I had allowed myself to hope that Lucrezia, Antonio, and Cecilia would grow up with the loving, doting father I never had. Still, at least I was able to raise them as I saw fit. Giacomo's only stricture was that they—especially Antonio—be reared as befitted patrician children, and the children of a senator of the republic.

When Lucrezia turned four, I decided it was high time I find a tutor to begin teaching her to read and write, and to teach the twins once they were old enough. My daughters, I determined, would receive the same education as their brother: mathematics, Latin,

French, Greek, philosophy, religion, literature, and—if they so chose—music.

To this end, I engaged a young Jesuit priest, Padre Davide. He began coming to the palazzo every day but Sunday to begin teaching Lucrezia her letters, and soon enough Antonio and Cecilia joined the classroom as well.

From the night she was born onward, Lucrezia became my most devoted audience whenever I played the violin. A generally playful and restless child, she could sit still without fail when listening to me play—her mother's daughter, indeed.

One day when she was five years old, I noticed her humming along with my playing. She matched the pitches perfectly, and her voice—young though it was—sounded melodious enough.

I waited until I reached the end of the piece—not wanting to make her feel self-conscious—before I turned to her. "That was lovely, Lucrezia," I said, smiling at her.

She looked surprised. "What was?" she asked in her high child's voice.

"Your humming. You made a nice accompaniment to my playing."

"Oh, that." She shrugged. "I forget I am doing it sometimes."

I went to sit on the bed beside her. "Do you like to sing, *figlia mia*?"

She nodded. "I cannot do it as good as Zia Vittoria, though."

I laughed. "Few people can, darling."

Only a few months before, Vittoria had finally sung for me during one of her visits. Lucrezia had learned that Vittoria had once been a singer, so she took to pestering her to sing something. Vittoria demurred but Lucrezia insisted just as strenuously as I wished I could. Finally she relented, saying that, after all, her contract with the Pietà did not forbid her from ever singing again, just from performing in public. So she took in a deep, slow breath, and began to sing a beautiful, elaborate piece that sounded as though it were part of a motet. The chatty Lucrezia was, for once, silent. The purest of sounds rang out of Vittoria's mouth, full and lovely. Any opera singer in Venice—in all of Italy, no doubt—would trade all of her jewels and finery for such a voice.

When she finished, we both simply stared at her, awestruck, before I remembered myself and began to applaud, my daughter following suit.

Vittoria blushed. "Maestro Vivaldi wrote that motet for me," she said, confirming what I had already suspected. "*Laudate pueri Dominum*. He would have been disappointed with that performance, I am afraid—I am quite out of practice."

I tried to find the words to properly express what I thought of Vittoria's impromptu performance, but she waved them aside, begging me to change the subject, which I did reluctantly.

Upon learning of Lucrezia's love of singing, an idea struck me the very next day that prompted me to send a note asking Vittoria to pay me a visit.

"I shall get right to the point," I said, as soon as we were ensconced in my sitting room.

Vittoria raised one of her delicately arched eyebrows. "What? You mean this is not a visit to gossip about everyone we know?"

I laughed. "Not today, I am afraid. I have a proposal for you. I was wondering if you might consider taking on my Lucrezia as a voice student."

"Truly?" she asked, surprised.

"Yes. I have noticed her humming to herself often, and she likes to sing. I can think of no one better for her to learn from than you."

"Oh, I . . . I do not know," Vittoria said, looking stricken. "Please, do not mistake my meaning. I would like nothing better. It is just . . . I do not know if it would be allowed."

"Who is to find out?" I asked. "You could come here, as you do anyway, and give Lucrezia her lessons, and I shall pay you. It need concern no one but ourselves."

"Pay me!" she exclaimed. "I could not accept payment for teaching music."

"As I said, who is to find out?"

She vigorously shook her head. "No, no. I could not take payment, not for something I would do gladly."

I sighed. "Then I will not pay you. But please at least consider it. I think it will be good for both of you."

Vittoria promised to think on it, spending several days soul-searching and, no doubt, praying. Ultimately she agreed to teach Lucrezia, though firmly refused payment.

"We will start with scales, and sight-reading, but I will need to get some music for her to learn from," Vittoria mused aloud. "And she must first learn technique, breathing and posture and so on . . ."

"I will pay for whatever music you need," I told her. "Let us see if she has any talent first."

"Oh, I am sure she does!" Vittoria said.

We decided Vittoria would come once a week for an hour to teach Lucrezia. When I told my daughter, she skipped around the nursery in excitement, and I knew I had made a good choice.

As I tended to my children by day, I was more often than not in the company of my friends by night. During such pious seasons as Lent we were forced to forgo our merrymaking; but the rest of the year, Venice offered no shortage of amusements. We frequented a number of the many opera houses—though I carefully avoided seeing any opera written by Vivaldi, which I am certain no one marked, save for Giuseppe. Then there was gambling at the Ridotto, endless parties, playhouses, and the many cafés and restaurants.

One evening, bored with the opera and impatient for our dinner to arrive, I left the box to get some air and stretch my legs.

I had not wandered far when I noticed a man clad in a familiar dark green jacket, intimately speaking to someone in a shadowy, curtained corner. It was Giuseppe; his height and broad shoulders just barely concealed the tall Vittoria. I drew in a sharp breath.

Vittoria saw me before I could speak. She turned a brilliant shade of red and stepped around Giuseppe. "I am sorry to have left you all so rudely," she said, her voice wavering slightly. "Has our dinner arrived?"

"No," I replied, looking from her to my brother curiously. It was plain that they had only been talking, but knowing how modest Vittoria was, I was far more surprised than if I had come upon Giulietta and Mario making love in the same corner. "I merely wished to take a short stroll."

"Yes, of course," Vittoria said. "Well, I should return directly." She swept past us, disappearing back into our box.

"Giuseppe," I began, but he shook his head.

"I know." He sighed. "Let us return to the box as well, before our friends become curious about all these comings and goings."

I acquiesced and followed him back; as if by unspoken agreement, we moved past the back section, where Vittoria had smoothly joined a very rowdy game of cards, and stepped past the curtain into the front section.

Giuseppe fixed his gaze on the extravagantly costumed diva parading about the stage before us, but his interest—real or feigned—was not about to distract me from learning what I could, especially now that we had privacy.

"Giuseppe," I began again in a whisper.

He sighed and turned to face me, his handsome face full of anguish. "Please," he said, "do not judge me too harshly, *sorella*. I know it looked scandalous, but we were doing nothing but talking. That I swear, upon my honor."

"I do not doubt it," I said. "But you are lucky it was I who came upon you, and not someone who might not have been so discreet."

"I know, I know," he said. "But I just had to have a word alone . . . had to know if it was possible that she—"

"Giuseppe," I admonished him, "she is a married woman."

"I know!" he bit out sharply. "I know, and I am in torment! I am all too aware that she is married, and to a powerful nobleman, no less. She is too pious, too good, to violate the sanctity of her marriage vows. Nor would I ever ask her to." He turned to me, his expression nakedly earnest. "I swear to you, Adriana, I would never ask that of her. Never."

"I know you would not, *fratello*," I said, staring in wonder at my levelheaded, reasonable brother, who just now seemed to be tearing at all his seams right before my eyes. "But I would not see her reputation harmed by some misunderstanding. Nor would I see you heartbroken."

"You need not worry for her reputation," he said. "I will not again forgo discretion in such a way. But as for my heart . . ." He smiled ruefully. "That is past saving, dear sister."

"Giuseppe," I whispered. I had not realized his feelings for Vittoria were so strong; had not thought he loved her so deeply, so completely. Yet it was there on his face for me to read.

Sighing, he rose to his feet. "There is nothing to be done," he said. "I shall surely burn in hell for coveting another man's wife, and yet I cannot imagine that Lucifer himself could devise a more painful torment than what I now endure." He parted the curtain and returned to the back of the box, leaving me alone.

No doubt I, too, shall know the fires of hell for lying with a priest, and you are not the only one who knows of such torments, I thought. But no one knew better than I how love robs us of all reason, but never completely of all hope.

60

THE DANCE

Tommaso Foscari was married just before I: to Faustina Barberini, daughter of one of Venice's oldest and most noble families, and whose father was Giuseppe's former employer. The Foscari family was likely more impressed with her pedigree than her fortune, which was dwindling. She was classically beautiful, with pale skin, blue eyes, and long golden hair. She was also reported to be vain, shallow, and even—so some said—rather stupid. She had borne a strong, healthy daughter perhaps a year after their marriage, followed quickly by a son around the time I gave birth to the twins and, the year after that, another daughter.

I only came face-to-face with the couple once, while attending the opera during my first Carnevale after being married. As we were making our way to our box, we passed by Tommaso, his pretty new wife on his arm. The rest of my party continued on without a thought, but I started when he saw me. He froze, his jaw tightening. For a moment I thought he would ignore me altogether, yet he nodded briefly and went along his way. Thankfully, none of my friends noticed, so I was spared the need to explain.

Then, in January of 1720, well into the Carnevale season, my friends and I attended a party being held by Senator Barbo and his wife. I had just begun a dance with Leonardo when someone cut in on him. "I hope I can persuade you to give up the honor, my fine fellow," said a smooth, deep voice that I recognized well, even though the speaker's face was hidden by his mask.

"Of course," Leonardo said, sounding puzzled. He stepped aside, and the newcomer swept me into the circle of dancers. Suddenly I was a girl of eighteen again, dancing with Tommaso Foscari in the ballroom of his parents' palazzo.

"Donna Baldovino," he said as we entered the dance. "I should not presume to use your Christian name, I suppose."

"I see the mask my maid recommended leaves much to be desired," I said, "since you knew so easily that it was me."

"You have not changed all that much."

"I was but a girl then," I said, unsure of his tone.

"And now you are a senator's wife," he said. "You have done very well for yourself, I see."

"Are you mocking me, Tommaso?" I asked, my composure slipping a bit as I used his given name.

"Not at all," he said. "To be the wife of a senator of our fair republic is an enviable position."

"Yes, well," I said. "It is not exactly what my father wanted."

"And you, Adriana?" he asked. "Is it what you wanted?"

I was taken aback by his directness, by the venom in his voice. So disarmed was I that I answered honestly. "You must know that it was not," I said, lowering my voice.

"Ah, that is right. You wanted to run away with your mysterious lover, and be *his* wife and bear *his* children."

"How dare you," I bit out, stopping abruptly in the middle of the dance. Several people looked curiously in our direction. "What gives you the right to accost me on a ballroom floor, and to speak of that about which you know nothing? Is this the behavior of a *gentleman*, then?"

He gaped at me in silence, then guided me back into the dance before we attracted any further attention.

"I am sorry, Adriana," he said, sounding chastened. "Forgive me. I do not mean to be so bitter. It is just that . . ." He lowered his voice to a near-whisper and leaned closer to me. "I do not love my wife," he confessed. "My parents chose her and forced her on me. She is vapid and vain and foolish, and I pray each day that my daughters will not grow up to be like her." He sighed. "Some days I wake up and rage at the mess my life has become."

His bitterness shocked me, but his honesty shocked me more. I could taste the unpleasant burn of guilt in my mouth. *How strange,* I mused, *that a man, too, could end up just as hopelessly trapped as a woman.* "I know well enough how you feel," I said quietly. "It seems neither of our lives went as we might have liked."

"Would you go back and undo it all, if you could?"

His question startled me; it was the question I had danced around but could never bring myself to ask. Now I had no choice but to face it, to dance with it.

On that night Vivaldi and I first made love, I remember thinking that never would I wish it had not happened, despite what consequences might come. Had that been simply the silly, romantic notion of a girl in love? Or had I known then what perhaps I had forgotten since: that it *was* worth any cost to love and be loved in return, to choose and be chosen, to make love with the one person in all the world that you wanted, and to carry a piece of them with you forever after?

And maybe, just maybe, I had been completely wrong this whole time. Maybe fate had not punished me. Maybe I was the luckiest of women: for knowing what it is to be in love, such all-consuming, senseless, heedless love; and now I had three children whom I loved and would not trade for anything or anyone.

Was it worth the price? My innocence, my faith, my firstborn child?

"I . . ." I stuttered. "So much has happened . . . I no longer know . . ."

The music came to an end, and Tommaso executed a perfect bow and kissed my hand. His eyes were sad behind his mask, sad that I had not said that I would have done it all differently, with no regrets, if only to be with him.

"It is all right," he said quietly. "I understand."

61

AVE MARIA, GRATIA PLENA

It was one of those beautiful, early spring days in March, a day completely unfit for the news we received, in the form of a hastily scrawled note delivered by one of the Cassenti servants.

Giacomo was still abed, as he had grown rather older and wearier of late. This left me as the first one to read the message: Francesco had died the night before, after suffering violent chest pains. The distraught Vittoria begged me to come to her as soon as I could.

Tears stung my eyes, thinking of Vittoria now a widow at such a young age—she would be only twenty-six this year, two years younger than me—and alone and adrift in a large and boisterous world where she still struggled, sometimes, to feel comfortable.

"My mistress beseeches you to attend her as soon as possible," the servant informed me. "She said I am to bring you back in the gondola, if it pleases you."

I nodded, taking a deep breath and banishing the tears. "Of course," I replied. "But first I must take the news to my husband, if you do not mind waiting. Don Cassenti was a good friend of his."

I dreaded telling Giacomo. But when I did, he simply remained where he was, silently lying unmoving on the bed, still, not speaking.

Then he rolled over, putting his back to me. "Go to her," he said quietly. "I will remain here."

I left without further discussion, knowing that each must handle their grief in their own way, and allowed the servant to take me to my friend.

Vittoria was much grieved. Despite her occasional disappointment in the life for which she had forsaken music, Francesco had always been so good to her, she said between fits of weeping. He was her protector, her teacher in the ways of the world, her companion.

It was not until some hours later, when I finally persuaded her to rest and left her palazzo, that I thought of Giuseppe. Had he heard? And what would he do now that the one obstacle to his love was gone?

Immediately I reproached myself. He would do nothing; Vittoria was a newly made widow, and must go through the requisite period of mourning. Francesco had yet to even be buried.

Giacomo remained in his rooms for days, emerging only to attend the requiem Mass—during which he promptly dissolved in a shower of tears. Perhaps his friend's death was a dark reminder that his own could not be far to seek. Francesco had been a full year younger than Giacomo, whose own health was not nearly as robust lately. Finding these thoughts disturbing, I pushed them aside.

Vittoria, though looking pale and wan against the black gown and veil she wore, comported herself remarkably well. She stood tall, and what tears she shed were silent ones. No doubt her faith, as strong as ever, was consoling her a great deal.

I had been relieved to learn that Francesco—having no other heir—had left everything he had to his wife. It ensured she would want for nothing, and could live comfortably for the rest of her days, even should she choose not to remarry.

Leaving the church, we encountered Giuseppe, whom I had not

seen enter. He bowed. "Don Senatore Baldovino," he said. He turned to me, a slight smile cracking his otherwise grim face. "Adriana."

Giacomo nodded disinterestedly, walking past him to await our gondola.

"It is a tragedy," Giuseppe said to me, his voice low.

"Yes," I answered, slightly bewildered. Giuseppe had hardly known Francesco, and had obvious reasons to not feel kindly disposed toward the man. "Francesco was a good man; a good friend of Giacomo's, as you know. He has taken the news ill, indeed."

"She is so young, so good," he said, as if he had not heard me. His eyes followed the funeral gondola that Vittoria had mounted, accompanying her husband's body to one of the islands in the lagoon for burial. "And so sad. She is bereft, now, of her protector in the world." He sighed, running his fingers through his dark hair. "I hate to see her in such a state."

I nodded. "As do I."

"I went to her when I heard. To offer my condolences," he said, in the hurried tone of one confessing some damning sin. "Just to do that, nothing more, I swear. And she . . ." He paused. "She cried in my arms, Adriana. And though God will surely punish me for taking such joy in her grief, I have never known a happier moment in my life."

I sighed. A newly widowed Vittoria weeping for her husband in the arms of another man, one who loved her and whom she loved . . . I knew not what to make of that. But in that moment, all impropriety aside, I fervently wished that Vittoria would not spend the rest of her life alone, nor that my brother's anguish would continue without relief.

I was not privy to whatever arrangements were made between Vittoria and Giuseppe, nor to what promises they made each other, but some months after Francesco's death, Giuseppe began visiting

Vittoria at her palazzo. A year and a half later, the pair announced they were to be married. They brought the news to me themselves, giggling and blushing like a couple of love-struck teenagers.

The following week, Giuseppe held a dinner at his palazzo, during which they made the news public. Vittoria beamed with a happiness so great her smile could barely contain it, and Giuseppe scarcely took his eyes off his affianced bride all evening.

"Congratulations again, *cara*!" I cried during a private moment, embracing her and kissing her cheek. "I must confess I have hoped this day would come, ever since the night you first stepped into Giuseppe's gondola and he almost fell overboard at the sight of you."

She laughed. "Just as they sing of on the opera stages. We have loved each other long, but I confess I had some doubts. After my mourning period was over, I did not want to dishonor Francesco's memory or to act in haste, but my prayers and my love made up my mind for me. And we did not want to tell anyone immediately, for fear people would talk—they will still talk, I know, but I will not let the wagging tongues of others stop me from wedding the one man I have ever loved."

She paused, a thoughtful look coming over her face. "Finally I understand what God intended for me in directing me to leave the Pietà," she said. "Finally I understand His plan. There were times when I questioned it, and Him. But I should not have. Now I know why. For such love as Giuseppe and I have . . . it was worth everything. And never again will I wonder, or regret."

Tears sprang to my eyes. "You do not know how happy I am that it should be you two, my brother and my dearest friend," I said. "There are no two people more deserving of love in all the world."

"Oh, Adriana," she said, embracing me. "Perhaps it is wrong of me to hope so," she whispered, "but my fondest wish is for you to know this kind of love yourself."

And suddenly, before I realized it, my secret was spilling from my lips. "I have," I whispered.

She drew back quickly, surprised.

"I have known such love," I said softly. "Long ago, before I married Giacomo. Before you knew me." I looked away from her alert, curious gaze, regretting having said anything. "I am sorry. I should not have spoken of it. This night is about you and Giuseppe."

"No, no," she said, clasping my hands in hers. "Would you like to tell me about it?"

For a moment, I actually considered it. But the overwhelming need for secrecy pressed in around me. Only a small part of me was willing to admit that I feared the censure I might see in Vittoria's eyes if she were to learn who my lover had been, and that I could not bear. "No," I said. "No, I should not. Forgive me. I should not have said anything. And this is not the time. We should rejoin the party, should we not? No doubt your future bridegroom is anxious without you . . ."

Vittoria nodded, her gaze never leaving my face. "I understand, *amica mia*," she said. "I understand."

Giuseppe and Vittoria were wed in a beautiful ceremony eight months later, in early May of 1722. The wedding took place in the chapel of the Pietà at Vittoria's request, and Giuseppe was only too happy to acquiesce to anything his bride wanted. The feast that followed was held at Giuseppe's palazzo, the new couple's home.

Vittoria looked more beautiful, more joyful, than I had ever seen her, and Giuseppe was just as ecstatic. The two could not help but constantly lean their heads in close to whisper to one another, or to steal a kiss.

Other than the congratulations I extended to both outside the chapel, I was only able to speak to Giuseppe briefly during the feast. "*Fratello carissimo*," I said, kissing both his cheeks. "I am sure I need not tell you how happy I am for you."

"I can imagine, *sorella*," he said, beaming. "I know you have only ever wanted my happiness, as I have only wanted yours."

"It would seem your torment is at an end, then," I said.

"I never dared to dream of this day," he said. "I now have more in one lifetime than I would ever have thought possible for an ordinary man."

I embraced him again. "Not ordinary, Giuseppe," I whispered. "Never ordinary."

When the time came for the newlyweds to adjourn to their bedchamber, there was a great deal of the customary ribald cheering and explicit advice for both bride and groom. The ever-modest Vittoria blushed spectacularly, but I could see the excitement on her face all the same. Once they disappeared, I signaled to Giacomo that we should take our leave, and he was only too happy to comply.

"Francesco is rolling in his grave, and no mistake," he grumbled on our way out, as though he did not think I could hear him.

But I had not the heart for arguing, not on that night. I simply ignored him, settling into the cushions of the gondola to take in our dark city. It seemed that true love could thrive in Venice after all, in this city of reflections and hidden depths.

62

ENSEMBLE

My children were growing up healthy, happy, and intelligent as well; the kind of children any mother would be proud of. They all acquitted themselves well in their lessons, even if Padre Davide had to gently admonish Lucrezia for talking too much, and prod Cecilia into completing her arithmetic assignments. I caught her more than once persuading her twin to do her figures for her. Antonio was showing quite the proficiency for numbers, such as Cecilia had for languages—by the age of eight Cecilia could speak her native Italian as well as Latin and French. Her siblings spoke passable French and Latin, and Antonio had a particular fondness for Greek, about which Cecilia teased him—what use was such an old language?

Lucrezia kept on with her singing lessons with Vittoria, and they were the high point of her week. That Vittoria was now truly an aunt to my children only added to my happiness with the arrangement.

Yet never could I forget about the missing child in the schoolroom. Anna's ghost followed me everywhere, and I saw her shadow in every corner of my other children's lives. It was a pain that never ceased; rather, I simply became accustomed to its presence.

Ultimately, it was Cecilia who proved herself to be very much my daughter, in every sense. When she was eight, I caught her in my bedchamber, holding my violin—which was much too large for her—in position, squinting at the notes on a sheet of music.

"Cecilia, child," I said, stepping into the room, "whatever are you doing?"

She faced me, chin held up defiantly. "I wanted to try."

"All you had to do was ask, *cara;* there was no need to go sneaking about," I said. I gestured to the music on the stand. "Can you read it?"

She scowled. "No. I thought it might make sense if I looked at it for a while, but . . ."

"That is not surprising. It takes time to learn." I came around to stand by her, freezing briefly when I saw she had selected Vivaldi's A-minor concerto from *L'estro;* the one he had taught me to play, and played for me at the opera. "I will teach you to read music, if you like."

"Then I will be able to play this?" she asked.

"You have much to learn first, Cecilia. You will have to work hard, just as your sister does with Zia Vittoria. Is this what you want to do?"

"Yes," she answered without hesitation. "It sounds so beautiful when you play. I want to be just like you."

It was one of those unexpected, childish confessions that surprised me every time. "Oh, *cara,*" I whispered, bending down and hugging her to me. "You will be your own person, and a better one than I, I hope."

She was not paying attention. "Did you write this?" she asked, her eyes on the music, in the way children have when they are small and assume that all the world around them is the doing of their parents.

"No, I did not."

"Then who did?"

I took a deep breath. "A man who is a great violinist, and a great composer. His name is Antonio Vivaldi."

"Does he live in Venice? Do you know him?"

"He does, and yes. I do know him."

"Oh." She scowled at the music again. "Someday I am going to play this," she vowed.

I hugged her tighter. "I think you will, *carissima*. In fact, I know it."

And so I began to teach Cecilia—my daughter who was unexpected in so many ways—to read music, and to play the violin. She took to it quickly, soon growing bored with scales and arpeggios. Thus I was forced to find something she might be able to play, something simple that would nevertheless build her skills.

I recalled my mother's lullaby and wrote that down for Cecilia, in a simple form. When she mastered that, I added difficulty with ornaments and embellishments. After that, I was forced to begin writing simple pieces that would be suitable for her to play. I structured them as concerti, and could not always resist the temptation to fill in the rest of the orchestral parts.

The lessons for my daughter became lessons for me, once again, after all this time. The hours spent at the harpsichord—which now stood in my own parlor—came back to me. Over the years I had heard the melodies, heard the chords and harmonies, but had never seemed able to find the time to write them down. But for Cecilia, I made time, even finding time to write down the other melodies I had been hearing, the ones that had found me over the years. They became sonatas and the occasional concerto for two violins. Nothing Cecilia could play quite yet, but for a young woman and her violinist lover, they would have been perfect. And some of them, I was surprised to find, were perfect for a mother who also happened to be a virtuoso violinist, and never ceased to daydream of what it might be like to have a stage to herself.

63

THE FOUR SEASONS

While no great, grievous illness befell Giacomo, over the next two years his health slowly but steadily failed. He was sixty-two, after all, yet it took some time for me to reconcile the robust man I had married with this elderly one, who would take to his bed for days at a time.

For every stretch of days that he remained abed, there would be another stretch when he insisted on being up and about, seeing to his government duties and setting his affairs in order. He had a new will drawn up, the contents of which were nothing extraordinary: I, as his widow, would be given control of his estate until Antonio reached his majority; there were also generous sums set aside for Lucrezia's and Cecilia's dowries.

While I fully supported his foresight and initiative, I believed him a bit overdramatic in his belief that death was imminent. He still had many good years left—provided he minded his physician—yet it did not seem I could persuade him otherwise.

It did not surprise me that once he had seen to his worldly affairs, he would look to his soul, and the no doubt questionable state in which he found it. He resolved the best way to set this right would be to make a donation to some godly institution—and which was more godly than the Pietà? The donation would not be enough, of course; he would also host a concert, so that others might be encouraged to donate as well.

When he told me of this, during the Lenten season of 1724, my only response was to mildly inquire as to whether his health would permit such an endeavor. He indignantly assured me it would.

This time, there was no mortal dread of coming face-to-face with the man who had single-handedly wreaked so much upheaval in my life and my heart. There was a bit of trepidation, but mostly annoyance. Finally I had managed to steady the rolling, heaving ship that my life had been for so many years, found peace and even happiness; and now *he* was going to return, like a storm that had the power to destroy everyone and everything in its path, with only God's will to decide if there would be any survivors.

But no, I told myself firmly. It was *my* will that ruled my life now. And surely I was strong now in a way that I had not been at nineteen years old.

The Pietà responded swiftly to Senator Baldovino's request. They were happy and honored to oblige, and would gladly send their orchestra, under the direction of Maestro Antonio Vivaldi, once Lent had ended.

Indeed, the orchestra was currently putting the finishing touches on an "exceptional" new work by Maestro Vivaldi, and the concert which we were to host would be the perfect venue for the debut of such a work, if we were interested and agreeable.

I was immediately overcome with an almost physical desire to hear it, and to be among the first outside of the Pietà's stone walls to do so.

Within the hour I had dispatched a reply, my irritation gone, and only anticipation remaining.

I debated over whether or not to send an invitation to Tommaso Foscari and his wife. He had, after all, been the one to reinitiate friendly (or friendly enough, anyway) relations at Senator Barbo's ball, long ago though it had been. In the end, I sent him an invitation. It would be up to him whether or not to accept—which he did.

And so everything was set, waiting for the day to approach: the third of May, 1724. It could not come soon enough.

On the appointed day, I could not help but take much care with my dress and appearance, instructing Meneghina to dress me in the gown I had ordered especially for the occasion, having accurately predicted my state of mind on this day. It was of a vibrant, rose-colored pink, with a tight-fitting bodice and voluminous skirts, pinned and tucked just so, and inches of lace on the sleeves. Meneghina wove a strand of large pink diamonds through my elaborately pinned-up curls, and added a pair of teardrop-shaped diamond earrings, also pink. My neck and shoulders I left tantalizingly bare.

Things proceeded much as they had at that first concert: Giacomo welcomed the members of the orchestra as they arrived, directing them to the ballroom. And once I was finished with my toilette, I joined him in greeting the guests.

Though playing the role of the gracious and attentive hostess, inwardly I could think of nothing but the music. I could hardly bear all the polite social trivialities, so impatient was I for the concert to begin.

The arrival of Giulietta and her husband pulled me from my reverie. "My, my, *cara,* how wonderful you look," Giulietta said, eyeing me with approval. She heaved a false sigh and patted her own flawlessly arranged coiffure. "I always take such pains to outshine the hostess at these events, but it would seem that today I have been bested."

I laughed and embraced her, kissing her once on each cheek before she and Roberto moved on to mingle with the other guests.

Not long after, Vittoria and Giuseppe arrived. "I am most excited for this new work," Vittoria said, her smile wide as she looked up at Giuseppe. "I am afraid I have quite wearied my husband with all my talk and anticipation of this day."

Giuseppe smiled in return. "And how can I help but also anticipate with pleasure something which promises to bring you such happiness?"

Their obvious joy and delight in each other had not dimmed since their wedding day. In the almost two years since they had been married, they happily flew in the face of custom by appearing everywhere—the opera, Carnevale festivities, parties—together, despite how unfashionable it was. And now Vittoria was expecting their first child in August.

Giuseppe's smile faded ever so slightly as he turned to me. "And how do you fare this day, *sorella?*" he asked, his eyes asking what he could not.

I smiled. "I am well, Giuseppe, thank you."

He seemed unsure whether he should believe me, but he let it pass. I knew he would be keeping a close watch on me throughout the evening, as he always had, and the thought gave me strength.

Once most of the guests had arrived, Giovanna brought the children, dressed in their finest, downstairs for the concert. I had promised they would hear some wonderful music today—violin music, I had specified for Cecilia's sake—and, true to their mother's blood in their veins, they had been excited for days.

Settling Cecilia on one side of me and Lucrezia on the other, with Antonio next to her, I waved over Vittoria and Giuseppe, who readily came to sit with us. Giuseppe settled himself into the chair next to his nephew, who began to speak animatedly to his uncle. The three children—but Antonio especially—adored Giuseppe, seemingly more than they did their own father. And Giuseppe, bless him, fulfilled his role as someone for Antonio to look up to, perhaps sensing Giacomo fell short in that regard.

Vivaldi's presence was a humming under my skin, without my

looking at him even once. Now I dared to sneak a glance in his direction, only to see him look at me in the exact same moment. I froze as our eyes locked, unable to look away. Mercifully, he broke the gaze, nodding in my direction. I returned the nod, and he continued arranging his scores on the music stand in front of him.

He looked much older than he had the last time I had seen him. I knew that he must be well into his forties by now. His priests' robes hung loosely off his thin frame, and his face had a number of lines I did not remember. A white wig covered his hair, but I would wager there were strands of gray in the fiery red now, as well.

And neither am I as young as that girl who fell in love with him, I reminded myself, suddenly aware of my soft and heavy flesh beneath my gown and corset. *We have both grown older, in more ways than just years.*

Giacomo came and took his seat beside Cecilia. Seeing that their host and hostess were seated, our guests quickly sought the nearest seat, their chatter ceasing. Such was the assembly's eagerness to hear Vivaldi's new music that even the gossip, the one pastime that Venetians sometimes preferred to music, had stopped.

Vivaldi glanced at Giacomo and myself, seeking permission to begin. Giacomo, rather than making a speech of introduction, simply nodded to the maestro to commence. At this cue, Vivaldi rose from his seat and addressed the audience.

"I must first thank our gracious host and hostess"—he bowed in our direction—"for having myself and the orchestra here today. I must also thank all of you for being so good as to attend.

"What you are about to hear is a new work I have spent much time in composing and perfecting, and an equal amount of time rehearsing with these most capable musicians. And it bears a bit of explanation before we perform it for you, the first audience ever to hear it.

"This work is a series of four concerti, each representing a different season," he went on. "We shall go in the same order as does nature: beginning with spring, continuing on to summer and fall, and concluding with winter. The work as a whole is titled, as you might guess, *Le quattro stagioni*. The first concerto, Primavera," he added, fastening his eyes on mine, "we would like to dedicate to our lovely hostess, as thanks for having us here this day."

His eyes lingered on mine just a moment longer, allowing me to hear all the things he could not say. *Are you still writing music for me,* caro mio? I wondered, an almost fathomless well of sadness opening within me. But when he took his seat once again, and the music began, all my sorrow was swept far away.

The opening bars were lively and joyful, an exuberant, fitting herald of the coming of spring. Yet after the opening tutti came the first of many remarkable things we were to hear: Vivaldi sent his bow gliding over the highest string in a series of high-pitched notes and trills, mimicking almost exactly the chirping of a bird. Beside him, the second violinist played a passage that was very similar, an echo and a harmony.

The second movement, a largo, was much more languid and melodic. As I listened, I suddenly found myself carried back to that rainy April night, more than a decade ago, when a rebellious eighteen-year old with music in her heart had sought out the great Maestro Vivaldi. Perhaps he had thought of the same night while writing this.

I was so lost in the past that, when the largo ended and the last movement of the Spring concerto began, I was quite startled. The tone had again shifted to a joyous, celebratory one, with the solo melody playing almost a dance.

The first movement of the Summer concerto evoked the sweltering heat of the summer, heat so heavy and oppressive that one can barely move. The movement was punctuated here and there by bursts of rapid violin passages, perhaps an indication of an oncoming storm, as well as several more tentative sections of birdsong. The second movement continued this, a brief, apprehensive prelude to the storm of the third movement.

With no warning, all the instruments began to play at a frantic pace, with the violins moving to create waves of sound like rolling thunder. Vivaldi's harried, agitated solo evoked both lightning flashing jaggedly across the sky, as well as some poor creature trying to flee the storm. The lower string instruments combined to imitate the ominous rumblings of thunder, with the violins rushing on almost without pause. The harpsichordist forcefully beat out the continuo underpinning it all.

The season of Autumn brought with it joy and festivities again, colored with all the merrymaking of a country harvest feast and its aftermath. I could see people dancing, such was the vividness of the music.

The second movement, however, brought with it the first chill winds of the autumn, when the skies start to turn gray, bearing the melancholy news that winter is coming.

The last movement was again upbeat; one last celebration before winter arrived and drove the world indoors.

Then, finally, Winter came, the opening bars sounding just as a shiver would, if one could hear it. Vivaldi had again a frenzied solo which enhanced the feeling of shivering, of moving about almost frantically to try to keep warm, while the increasingly forceful winter winds of the orchestra blew about.

In the second movement most of the strings, incredibly, played pizzicato, and the sound perfectly imitated a crackling fire in the hearth when the day outside was frigid, and the melodic violin solo contributed to the feeling of warmth and contentment.

In the third movement, it was back out into the cold, to watch the snowflakes glide to earth, to slide on the ice of frozen canals and to fall down.

When this final movement ended, the silence that followed the last crashing chord seemed to stretch on and on. Yet it was broken, all at once, by the entire audience rising to its feet as one and bursting into tumultuous applause. The orchestra rose in acknowledgment, with Vivaldi bowing deeply, happiness and excitement creeping cautiously onto his careworn face.

I had forgotten everything while I had been lost in the music: where I was, with whom, any reason that I should be scared or hurt or hiding. I had even forgotten my children, who were all now clamoring for my attention. Once again, Vivaldi had stretched forth his hand and given me something of glorious beauty when I had needed it most.

Perhaps I should have made some speech of thanks to the orchestra, to my guests, yet I was rooted to the spot by what I had just heard. Giacomo did not speak either, thus our guests began to mingle, talking excitedly about the music.

Antonio had turned to talk to Giuseppe, since I had not responded to his tapping on my arm. Beside me, Lucrezia was much more persistent.

"Mother! Mother! Oh, did you like it? I did, very, very much! It was wonderful! I have never heard music like that before!"

Slowly I was coming back to myself, returning from the world the music had taken me to, a world where birds sang and people rejoiced and I was as beautiful as a spring maiden, as Vivaldi thought me. Yet finally I was forced to acknowledge the reality: that I was a woman no longer young, hostess to a teeming ballroom full of people, with three children needing attention at my side, and that this magnificent, sublime music had been written by a man as full of imperfections as any man.

Drawing a deep breath, I bid farewell to that other world, and turned to address my daughter. "I am glad you enjoyed it, darling. I certainly did as well." An understatement. But there was only one other person in that room who would ever truly understand my feelings.

Or perhaps, I thought, turning to Cecilia, *there is more than one person who understands.* My nine-year-old daughter was staring determinedly at the orchestra, as though trying to unravel their magic.

On my other side, Lucrezia was still chattering away. "I did not know one could play like a bird singing, or snow falling or . . ." she continued on, running through the list of things she had heard in the music.

This seemed to free Cecilia of the spell she had been under. "Have you ever played such music, Mother?" she asked.

"No, *carissima*," I said. "I have played much music in my life, but never any such as this."

Giacomo leaned across Cecilia. "I grow hungry, wife," he said, the touch of petulance that had taken up residence in his tone of late very much present. "Do order the feast to begin soon, won't you?"

Hot anger flared in me. I had been patient almost to the point of sainthood with his moping and mooning about, yet this struck me as blasphemy beyond bearing. *You have not the faintest idea in your thick skull what you have just heard.* "Of course, husband," I replied through clenched teeth. "I shall send someone to the kitchen to see if all is ready."

Once I had accomplished that errand and returned to my children, I saw that Lucrezia had found a new audience for her raptures in Vittoria. I felt a slight tug of guilt as I saw how attentively Vittoria listened.

My gaze wandered, unbidden, seeking the source of my distracted mind; to my surprise, I saw him bending over the harpsichord, explaining something to a small boy seated behind it—my son.

There was no help for it; I had to approach him. "*Figlio*, come away from there," I said, voice calm. "Is my son bothering you, Maestro Vivaldi?"

He looked up at me. "Not at all," he said.

"Mother, can you play the harpsichord?" Antonio interrupted.

Vivaldi's eyes met mine, a smile playing about his lips, and I knew we were both recalling the very same moment. "Not well, I am afraid," I said, feeling hopelessly foolish as a blush rose to my cheeks. "But would you like to learn?"

"Oh, yes," he said, his usually quiet eyes shining with his new discovery. "We have one in the parlor, but I have never heard anyone play it. I like it, I think."

I laughed. "Very well, then, I shall look into it if you promise me you will practice. You must practice just as much as your sisters do."

"I shall!" he promised. "Perhaps I can play for Lucrezia when she sings." Antonio had an almost puppylike devotion to his older sister.

"Perhaps, but you have much to learn before that," I said.

"The harpsichordist who plays at the Sant' Angelo is excellent," Vivaldi interjected. "And I know he takes on students. I can give you his name and direction before I leave, if you wish."

"That would be very kind of you," I said. "Thank you." I looked away again, down at my son, who was carefully pressing the harpsichord's keys, one after another. "I see you have met my son Antonio."

Vivaldi's head jerked up upon hearing the name. I looked up and saw on his face surprise mixed with sorrow and joy, and perhaps a bit of pride in the boy who bore his name. For a moment I thought he would weep; but then he swept my son an exaggerated bow. "A pleasure to make your acquaintance, Don Antonio."

My son giggled at being addressed like an adult. "It is a pleasure to meet you also, maestro."

Jealous of the attention the maestro was paying her brother, Cecilia suddenly appeared at my side. "You are Maestro Vivaldi, *si?*" she said.

He glanced at me with a quick smile before answering. "*Si*, I am."

"My mother plays your music all the time," she announced. "You play as well as she does. I think even better."

"He plays much better than I do, *carissima*," I said. I hesitated. "He always has."

Cecilia studied Vivaldi. "Someday," she said, "I am going to play as well as you, maestro." Then, as if suddenly remembering her manners, she bobbed a small curtsy and said, "Pleased to meet you."

He laughed. "I am very pleased to meet you as well, signorina."

"Both of you run along to your sister," I told them, smiling.

"Antonio's twin sister," I explained. "Cecilia."

"Ah." He was smiling broadly. "She looks very much like you. And is very much like you in other ways, I think."

I smiled. "That she is." I nodded toward the children. "And my older daughter, Lucrezia. I named her for my mother."

"Ah, yes."

When the conversation seemed to end there, I moved to extricate myself. "I must go see to my guests."

"Wait," he said, moving as if to prevent me from leaving, but stopping abruptly. "Am I to have no other word from you, Adri—Donna Baldovino?"

I sighed. "We cannot speak here. Meet me in the small parlor just outside the doors as soon as you may. Dinner will not be served for another half hour at least." Without waiting for him to reply, I swept away from him, stopping to speak with several of my guests so no one would think anything was amiss.

Just as I was poised to head to the parlor, I found myself hailed by none other than Tommaso Foscari.

Mentally I cursed myself; I had forgotten altogether that he was to attend, and he must have arrived after we had all adjourned to the ballroom. Momentarily I panicked; had he seen me speaking with Vivaldi? Had he guessed?

By God and the Virgin, I am too old for such intrigues!

My breathing steadied as I thought of how silly I was being, and I threw him a genuine smile. Whatever had passed between us in years past, he was once a friend to me, and I was glad to see him. "Don Foscari," I said. "I am so glad you could attend. I did not see you earlier."

"I am not surprised, for my wife and I arrived late," he said. "I shall introduce her to you before we dine, if you wish."

"I should be pleased," I said politely.

He nodded. "I remember well that you are a true lover of music," he said. "What are your thoughts on this performance?"

"It was magnificent," I said. "Something entirely new; a way to use the instruments that has never been done before."

"I agree wholeheartedly. It will be the talk of Venice before long." He took a small step closer to me. "You look beautiful, Adriana. But I am sure you do not need me to tell you that."

"And I am sure that you do not need to be told a compliment of beauty is always welcome to a woman—especially an aging one."

"You are as beautiful today as the day that we met."

"As are you," I said, before I could stop myself. Yet it was true. There was a hint of gray among his dark curls, and a few lines in his face, but he was still handsome, perhaps the most handsome man present. Always I had been somewhat dazzled by his looks, from that very first moment when he rescued me from a lecher in his parents' ballroom.

"Adriana . . . may I come call on you?"

Seeing I was rather taken aback by the implications of his request, he hastened to reassure me. "I mean nothing that would bring dishonor upon us, nor call your reputation into question," he said. "Only that we may become friends again. I bear you no ill will for things long past. And I miss your company. Truly."

"And I yours," I said, meaning it. "But for my sake, and yours—and the sake of my children—I would not want to provide gossip for idle tongues."

His smile, charming as ever, stopped my protests. "Have you no handsome young swains coming to engage in courtly love with you, Adriana?"

I laughed. "I do not, I am afraid."

"Then this I shall do, though I am not so young," he said. "It is to a lady's credit to have a devoted *cavaliere servente*, I believe."

"I believe it is," I said, conceding.

He bowed low. "Then I shall leave you to your guests, my lady, and will be glad to call on you as soon as is convenient for you."

I could not help but smile as I walked away from him and slipped through the doors of the ballroom. Hopefully my next encounter with my past would end as well as the first.

Opening the door of the parlor, I found Vivaldi pacing inside. He whirled to face me as I entered, clutching a rosary tightly in his hand.

"Am I a demon from your past that you would exorcise, then?" I asked with a sardonic smile, nodding toward the rosary.

He looked a bit startled by my question, but his face soon relaxed into a wry smile. "Hardly. Yet I might well pray to be delivered from temptation where you are concerned, Adriana."

"Now you would call me temptress?" I demanded, but he shook his head.

"Nothing of the sort. Do not think that I mean to lay any blame at your feet, only at my own where it belongs . . ." He trailed off and looked away. "I only meant to compliment your beauty, which for me will always be far and beyond that of any woman living."

I gazed at him, this man I had loved with such passion it had nearly destroyed us both, my anger and bitterness melting away. This man, flawed as any mortal, had somehow managed to create music beyond what even I had thought him capable; I, who knew him better than perhaps anyone else. Surely that was worth more than all his failures, even if one of them had been that he failed me.

"I am sorry," I said quietly. I sat on the daybed that stood between us and, taking my cue, he sat beside me. My body lurched awake at his nearness.

After a moment of silence, he said, "What did you think?"

"It was—it is—a masterpiece," I said.

"You think so?"

"There has never been anything like it before," I said. "You must know that."

"Yes, but that does not make it a masterpiece," he said. "Perhaps there is a reason there has never been something like it."

"Surely you cannot doubt that the composition of such a work is a remarkable feat, and the performance of it no less so," I argued.

When he did not reply, I spoke again. "Still so unsure of yourself, Tonio?" The old endearment slipped out yet again, but I paid it no mind. "There has never been anything like *Le quattro stagioni* before because there has never been a genius like yours."

"Do you truly believe that?" he asked.

"I always have."

He sighed heavily. "You must know what your opinion means to me," he said. "More than that of anyone else, I think. And you must know . . ." His expression softened, and its tenderness made me want to fall into his arms and run away all at once. "Every time I sit down to compose for the violin—for my instrument and yours—I am writing for you. Always for you. I write as if you are still the same young woman about to appear at my door to play music late into the night."

I bowed my head, hiding my tears. "And I still play, Tonio. I play all the music you sent me, and I write my own. Thus a part of me is still that young girl, after all."

I could sense he wanted to take my hand, but he did not. "Then you have found the music again?"

I nodded. "Yes. Yes, I have."

And then our stolen time came to an end, as it always had, and I was forced to rise, to excuse myself, and leave him.

In truth our lives run in seasons as well, I thought as I left the parlor. *My youth was spring, and my affair with the man I loved was summer, with all its heat. And autumn came as we began to come apart, and winter when we were undone, and I was forced to give up our child. And yet surely that winter has ended long since. Then spring came again with the births of my children, and this peace and contentment I know now is like the beautiful sun of summer once again.*

64

WIDOW'S WEEDS

"Zio Giuseppe and Zia Vittoria are waiting downstairs," Lucrezia said, peeking her head in. I sat motionless at my dressing table, staring down at the black veil that sat upon it. When I did not respond, she stepped into the room. "*Madre?*"

I took a deep breath. "Yes. Of course." Still I did not move to put on the veil. I had waved Meneghina away when she offered to do it for me. This was something I had to do myself, and yet found that I could not. By donning this widow's veil, I moved from one part of my life to another, and there would be no going back.

I was not ready.

And yet I had no choice. It was only two short years after the premiere of *Le quattro stagioni* in our ballroom, and Giacomo was dead. His death was rather like his life, in which he cut no great social or political swaths: he died quietly in his sleep.

I jumped when I felt Lucrezia's hands on my shoulders. "Mama, are you all right?" she asked softly.

I closed my eyes and banished the waiting tears. "I am, I suppose," I said. "But, *cara*, what of you?"

Lucrezia looked guilty as her eyes met mine in the mirror. "I am well," she said. "Perhaps too well." At that, she began to cry.

"Oh, *cara*," I drew her onto my lap, though at thirteen, she was much too big for such things.

"I am *sad*, but I do not know why, Mama," she said through her tears. "If I am sad because he is dead, or sad because I did not know him better, or sad because I think I should be *more* sad . . ."

"I understand," I whispered. The children had cried upon hearing of their father's death, but their emotional recovery was swift. Giacomo had so distanced himself from their lives that they never truly knew him.

When Lucrezia ceased her crying, I squeezed her once, then helped her to her feet. "Now go downstairs to your aunt and uncle," I said. "I will be along directly."

She left the room, and I took one last, long look at my bare face.

My own tears of sorrow for Giacomo were very real. Ours had been a difficult marriage, yet there had been true affection and partnership between us, and he had given me three beautiful children. Even his cruelties were more out of thoughtlessness than malice.

And now he was gone.

I picked up the veil and pinned it into place, letting the gossamer fabric fall over my face.

Mask in place, I stepped off the dock and into the waiting gondola, helped by a warm, familiar hand. "*Buona notte*, Adriana," Tommaso Foscari said from beneath his mask as I settled onto the seat beside him. "How are you faring, *mia cara*? I have missed you these past weeks."

"Well enough," I said. "And the children are well, which is all that matters. It is just strange, without him, even though . . ." I trailed off, and Tommaso nodded, understanding. "I have missed you as well,"

I went on, and he briefly squeezed my hand. "I just do not know how much more mourning I can take. That is, I do not mean . . ."

He shook his head. "I understand. I know all too well the complicated emotions of a . . . marriage of convenience," he said delicately. "But as Giacomo never begrudged your going out while he lived, I hardly think he should do so now." He smiled. "And in Venice, no one need know you have been out rather than home grieving."

I smiled. "And where are you taking me tonight?"

"A small concert I have heard of—some German harpsichordist who is traveling through," Tommaso said. "He is to play some music by this obscure fellow named Bach. A friend of mine with no musical taste finds him deplorable, so I am certain that you and I will enjoy him greatly."

Laughing together, we talked like old friends until we reached the concert. The first few visits with Tommaso had been somewhat awkward: him trying to hide the remnants of his pain, and me trying not to see it. But soon, somehow, it had become easier, effortless. And I saw the man I had known before, but more clearly, now that I was no longer afraid of him.

65

WAYS TO SING OF LOVE

It was my children who concocted the entire scheme. They appeared in my bedchamber one morning, as Meneghina was dressing my hair for the day.

I eyed the three of them in the mirror: devastatingly beautiful fourteen-year-old Lucrezia, with her long blond hair and heart-shaped face; Antonio, nearly thirteen and still a head shorter than his older sister, his light brown hair falling into his eyes; and Cecilia, taller than her twin and as beautiful as Lucrezia, if in a different, darker way. *Vivaldi was right. She does look much like me.* "What is this, my darlings?" I asked aloud. "Are you not due for your lessons now? Must I make excuses to Padre Davide?"

The three shot each other conspiratorial glances. "Yes," Lucrezia said. "But we wanted to speak with you first."

"We wish to put on a concert," Cecilia announced. "We have been practicing, and wish to play for everyone—for you, and for Padre Davide, and Zio Giuseppe and Zia Vittoria, and Zia Giulietta, and—"

"And *everyone*," Lucrezia finished impatiently. "Everyone who wishes to come and hear us."

I turned on my chair to face them. "Are you sure that you a. ready?" I asked. "You have practiced enough, and have enough music to play a whole concert?"

Antonio glanced uncertainly at his twin. "I can play some of the songs Crezia has learned with Zia Vittoria," he said. "To accompany her. And Cecilia—"

"I have made up a violin part for some of them," she said. "I just use parts of the accompaniment and the melody, and—"

"And we are learning more," Lucrezia added.

"Yes," Antonio added. "We need to practice more, but—"

"But if we knew we had a concert to prepare for, it would encourage us to practice," Lucrezia said.

Smiling, I studied the three of them again, only slightly surprised. They were my children through and through, and I was thrilled to see how my blood—and my mother's—had held true. "Very well," I said. "We shall hold a concert here—say the last week of October. That gives you a little over a month to prepare. Will that be sufficient?"

"Oh, yes!" Antonio said.

Cecilia tossed her head. "We could be ready sooner," she said.

"No doubt," I said, my mind beginning to work. "But if, perhaps, you were to have some new music to learn as well—would that still be sufficient time?"

"Yes, certainly," Lucrezia said. "What new music would you have us learn, Mother?"

I smiled. "I have not written it yet."

I began work that day, writing a strange sort of song for voice, violin, and harpsichord. The violin part came first, naturally, and the harpsichord was a great deal simpler to write for than when one had an entire orchestra in mind. Lucrezia's part, however, gave me pause; I had never written for the voice before, though I was certainly miliar enough with my daughter's voice to feel up to the challenge. enlisted Vittoria's help in selecting a text, and in working words and melodies together.

"I have brought a book of Petrarch," Vittoria said, when she arrived at my palazzo to lend her assistance. "Not very original, I know, but I do so love his poetry. I have a few sonnets in mind."

"Yes, of course," I murmured when I saw the first sonnet she had marked. *I would sing of love in so new a way / I would draw a thousand sighs / from that hard heart, and light / a thousand noble desires in that chill mind . . .*

It would be perfect, perfect for the music I was composing, and perfect for Lucrezia to sing; the sweetness of her voice could melt even the hardest of hearts.

"I rather thought that one would be best as well," Vittoria said. "But Adriana, I knew not that you composed so much!"

"I am no Maestro Vivaldi, it is true," I said. "But I have been writing music since I was a young girl. Some of it is passable enough."

"More than that, I should say," Vittoria said, studying the staves of what I had already written for the concert. "Why, you are quite accomplished!"

I smiled. "My experience is rather limited, all told."

"But so you have formed your own *coro* of sorts," she said, smiling. "I think it is lovely. I am so happy your children wish to perform." Her eyes lit up, an idea coming to her. "But Adriana, you must play us something at the concert as well!"

"Me?" I asked. "Of course not. The day will be about the children."

"Do not be silly!" she interjected. "They will love to see you perform, and so will your friends! Why, I do not think I have ever heard you play, not once in all these years!"

I grinned. "Very well, I will play—on one condition."

"Name it."

"That I may accompany you as you sing."

Vittoria's hands flew to her face. "Oh, Adriana! How ca
even suggest such a thing? You know I cannot perform!"

"You must have performed masterfully at one time, for from wha
I hear you commanded many an audience from the balcony of the Pietà," I said.

"You know that is not what I mean! I signed a contract which forbids me from performing in public."

"Vittoria," I said, "my *piano nobile* is not 'public.'"

She paused. "I suppose you are right about that," she said. "But I . . . oh, I just do not know if I can! It has been so long."

"You will have to practice, as the children do," I said.

"I do not know," she said. "I will have to think on it, and consult Giuseppe, and make sure he is comfortable with the idea."

I rolled my eyes. "When have you ever known my brother to deny you anything?" I asked. "He will be more delighted than anyone."

In typical Vittoria fashion, she begged me to give her time to consider it further, and we turned our attention back to Lucrezia's melody.

Later that week, however, Vittoria asked me to tea and gave me her answer.

"I will do it," she said, her eyes shining with excitement. "You were right, Giuseppe is thrilled. And since it will not technically be in public, I do not think it violates the contract."

"Of course it does not," I said. "Oh, Vittoria, this is wonderful! Have you decided what you shall sing?"

"I shall write to Maestro Vivaldi and have him send us something," she said. "Something for soprano and violin; whatever he thinks is best. If that is agreeable to you."

Already my fingers were itching for the strings of my violin, to play something of Vivaldi's I had never seen. "Oh, yes," I said. "I am perfectly agreeable."

ıght of the concert, Vittoria and I had decided that we would ırst, and then leave the stage to the children.

"Oh, I so hope it goes well!" she said, pacing nervously. "Not just for me, but for the children as well!"

"It will all be fine, *cara,*" I promised her. I adjusted the sleeves of my gown. "It is going to be a wonderful evening."

We went downstairs, where guests had begun seating themselves, directed by Giuseppe. The children were waiting in the small parlor of the *piano nobile.*

"Are you nervous, my darlings?" I asked them.

"No," Lucrezia said, though she looked uncertain.

Antonio shook his head, though I noticed he was a bit pale.

"No," Cecilia said, sounding as if she were the only one who meant it.

"Good," I said. "You must play as you do when it is just you three, and forget anyone else is listening."

"The only reason you will ever have to be nervous," Vittoria added, "is if you do not know your music well enough. And you three have it well in hand."

I smiled at her. "Wise words," I said pointedly.

She blushed. "For me it is a bit different."

"Should we begin soon? Is it time?" Although Lucrezia was trying hard to act the poised young woman—dressed in her finest pale pink dress, her hair artfully pinned up like a lady's—she was near to bouncing up and down in excitement.

"I think that it is time," Vittoria said hesitantly. "Shall we?"

We filed out of the parlor and into the main floor of the *piano nobile,* where instruments and music had already been assembled. The audience applauded as we entered. I saw Giuseppe seated in the front with Marco, their oldest son—Adriana (named in my honor) and her baby brother, little Giuseppino, having been left at home with their nursemaid—and a couple of his friends and their children. Donna Barbo and her husband, Senator Barbo, sat in the second row—Donna Barbo and I had taken to calling upon each ot often, and though she was a great deal older than I, she was excellen company, with her sharp intelligence and even sharper wit. Beside her sat Giulietta and Mario, then Tommaso Foscari and his three children, who had become fast friends with my own: Isabella, Andrea, and Pia. In the last row sat Padre Davide, Giovanna, Meneghina, and Antonio's harpsichord instructor, Maestro Ferro.

The children went to sit with their uncle, and Vittoria and I took our places. "Friends," I said, addressing the assembly, "thank you for coming. My children have put together this program all on their own, with little help from me or their teachers. I am so happy you could all come, to hear their hard work and talent for yourselves."

I turned to Vittoria. "I could not, however—and my children agreed—pass up this opportunity to showcase another great talent among us. Without further ado, *signori e signore,* my dearest friend and sister-in-law, Vittoria Rivalli, formerly Vittoria della Pietà."

Everyone applauded, and I took a moment to retrieve my violin—Vivaldi's violin, the one he had given me and which I had played ever since—from its case. I tightened the bow, checked the tuning, then glanced at Vittoria. When she nodded, I began to play.

The lilting yet flowing violin melody seemed to fall from the strings of its own accord. After my few measures of introduction, Vittoria began to sing.

"Domine deus, rex coelestis," she sang, her sweet yet powerful voice filling the whole room. *"Deus pater, deus pater."*

She sang on, her voice tumbling through the long, melismatic passages. I struggled to keep my mind on my own playing, so engrossed was I in listening to her. As marvelous as she had sounded in practice, here she was otherworldly.

Sometimes my part doubled hers, and sometimes I went off on my own, playing little flurries of figures behind and between her singing. It was, in truth, a conversation between soprano and violin, ɪ during practice we had learned to make it so, ensuring that neither part overpowered the other—though in truth I felt certain Vittoria's performance would outshine mine no matter what.

Soon enough we had reached the end of the aria, and I played the final measures, slowly bringing the piece to a close.

The applause was instantaneous. I could see that Vittoria was flushed, and her face almost could not contain her grin.

So this is what she gave up, I mused, looking out at the applauding audience. I felt my own grin stretch wide as I realized that they were also applauding for *me.*

Once the applause ended, we took our seats. "Beautiful," Giuseppe murmured, leaning over to kiss Vittoria. "The angels themselves are jealous," he said, smiling at us both, "for there are no finer musicians in all the celestial choir."

Then the attention shifted to the children, as it should. Lucrezia, dimpling prettily at the audience, explained that their first piece was an old love song that her Zia Vittoria had taught her. Without further ado they began, Antonio playing a short introduction on the harpsichord, joined by Cecilia, who had added trills and ornaments to the simple piece. I thought I caught her throwing a glance at Andrea Foscari, to see if he noticed her skillful playing.

I found myself quite forgetting that I was listening to my own children. While they were perhaps not quite as polished as the musicians from the Pietà, that their skills went beyond their ages was obvious. Although Lucrezia's voice was not as strong or mature as Vittoria's, she projected it well, and had a lovely vibrato. Vittoria was certain that she was a soprano; she said there were certain telltale signs: her facility at handling and sustaining the higher notes, the lighter coloring of her voice.

Next, they moved on to a song by Alessandro Scarlatti, entitled "*Sento nel core.*" Maestro Scarlatti had died just a few years before; a tragedy, to be sure, for having seen many of his operas, I had grown quite fond of his work.

The song—which Vittoria had told me was perhaps more appropriate for an older singer, with a heavier voice, but Lucrezia had insisted—sounded lovely even stripped down to a bare accompaniment. Yet as much as Lucrezia captivated the audience with her shimmering voice, and Antonio solidly provided the basis of the whole endeavor, I found my attention continually drawn back to Cecilia.

She played well, better than I had at her age. She lost herself in the music, played the emotion of it as Vivaldi had always said I must, found the heart of each phrase, each note, and leaned on it until the listener nearly gave way beneath her.

She had much still to learn, but her gift was monumental. If she trained it properly, she would be greater than I ever could be. She could, I realized, tears stinging my eyes, make good on her promise to Vivaldi and someday play as well as he.

But for what? So she could marry someday, and play for and teach her children, and have no one beyond her own *piano nobile* ever know what a talent she was?

In that instant, I was angrier at the injustice of it all on my daughter's behalf than I had ever been on my own. *But,* I thought, *has this not always been enough for me? Is music not an end in and of itself?*

After this song, Cecilia lowered her violin and spoke to the audience, sounding far more poised and mature than her not yet thirteen years would account for. "You have heard, earlier, that our mother is a most accomplished violinist. Yet what most people do not know is that she is also a talented composer. She has written this next piece for us, so that we might share it with you."

With that, she set her instrument into place again and, with a nod to Antonio, began.

This was not like the concerti I had written as a young woman, melancholy and minor and full of despair at the future I knew awaited me. No, this was light and deliberately simple, a song for my children, a song of love.

"I would sing of love in so new a way," Lucrezia began, the lively and vibrant melody falling from her lips like a shower of gentle spring rain. Cecilia's violin part, which I had set to both imitate and embellish the melody, danced with her sister's singing, creating a harmonious counterpoint that rang out more brilliantly than I had ever imagined it could when I placed those blots of ink on the page. Even Antonio's part had an echo of the melody here and there, not just the simple chords that were usually given to the harpsichord.

They performed it just as I had imagined they would, and better. *No, I could not have written that; whatever I did write they have taken and transformed and made into their own, into something better than I dreamed.* And when they finished, Lucrezia was pulling me back up to the front of the room, to bow again. I knew I should say something else, if the applause ever faded; congratulate my children, say how proud I was. But I could not find the words.

My teary eyes flitted from Giuseppe and Vittoria to my nephew to my friends and then to Tommaso Foscari, wearing a huge smile and looking as proud of me as Giuseppe had been of Vittoria.

Surely there are many, many new ways to sing of love; ways that I have yet to discover or even imagine.

MOVEMENT SEVEN

THE RED PRIEST'S ANNINA

November 1727–April 1734

66

ORLANDO FURIOSO

I did not see Anna Girò make her operatic debut in Venice, in Albinoni's *Laodicea*, in 1724. Nor did I go to see her sing in her first role that Vivaldi wrote for her, in his opera *Farnace*, which premiered at the Teatro Sant' Angelo in February of 1727.

In truth, I was torn by uncertainty. The desire to see my daughter—fueled in no small part by simple curiosity—was almost overwhelming. Yet still I resisted.

Anna Girò was slowly becoming the talk of Venice. Her early performances did not receive much praise, when she was noticed at all among the crowd of ostentatious divas and preening castrati. Yet it had been conceded by many of the operatic critics that she was quite young and had potential, once she had learned more about singing and the operatic stage.

However, she remained a relative nonentity in the opera world until she was taken on as a protégée by the great Maestro Antonio Vivaldi.

Vivaldi, it seemed, was both teaching her how to be a great diva, as well as writing roles for her low voice—unusually low for someone so young. And in Venice, where no morsel was too small to make tening meal of gossip, the exclusive attention paid by a well-known composer, impresario, and violinist to a heretofore unknown singer gave society's tongues plenty to wag about.

For a while it was accepted that she was simply the maestro's favorite pupil. Yet by the time it was announced that she was to appear as the sorceress Alcina in Vivaldi's *Orlando furioso,* premiering at the Sant' Angelo in November of 1727, the rumors had begun to brew into the storm that would hang over Vivaldi's head for the rest of his life.

While there was the odd critic who raved about her performance in *Farnace,* most critics and the discerning, operagoing Venetian public seemed to think that while her acting skills were of an extremely high quality, her voice was not. And, everyone was asking, should not Vivaldi know this better than anyone? Why, then, was he devoting so much of his surely valuable time to a rather unremarkable student?

Only three souls living knew the truth: Vivaldi, Giuseppe, and I. I knew without needing to be told that Anna still did not know the truth of her parentage. I also knew Vivaldi would not reveal it to her, out of respect for me and for the secret we had scrupulously kept all these years.

But as far as the rest of Venice was concerned, there must be only one explanation: Anna Girò was Vivaldi's mistress. It was whispered by the most notorious gossips until it became common knowledge. Already they were calling Anna *l'Annina del Prete Rosso:* the Red Priest's Annina.

My initial reaction to the rumors was horror; luckily, it was from Giuseppe that I heard it first, so there was no need to hide my response. Yet eventually—though my disgust with those who delighted in such unproven rumors did not abate—that horror faded, replaced by a rather wry sense of irony.

This was all in addition to the reputation Vivaldi had gained of late for being somewhat grasping, determined to receive his due his art at any cost. He was, it was said, capable of being a most un pleasant man when crossed. I could not quite reconcile these accounts with the man I had known so well. Could he truly have changed so much?

I had found excuses to absent myself when my friends were going to hear Anna sing, yet I found my resolve weakening as they made plans to go to the opening night of *Orlando furioso*. It weakened even more when Giuseppe came to try to talk me into attending.

"I told them that as your brother I would have the best chance of getting you to agree," he said, standing before the fireplace. "They do not know, of course, all the arguments I might present, nor the true reason you are so reluctant."

I did not speak.

"They—Vittoria and Giulietta, and even Mario—are beginning to wonder in earnest why you have not wanted to hear her thus far," he said.

I laughed mirthlessly. "Such a tactic is beneath you, *fratello*."

He shrugged. "You may think so, but nonetheless what I say is true. The pieces are all there for someone to assemble if they may."

"I do not think that anyone living is in possession of *all* the pieces," I said. "Giacomo may have been able to put the picture together, had he lived."

"I do not think you give your friends enough credit," he said. "Especially Vittoria."

My head snapped up. "Has she said something to you?"

"No," he said. "But you know that she is quite perceptive. And I know not the things you may have said to her over the years."

I fell silent, considering all the slips—and near slips—of the tongue I had had.

"You will be able to see her," Giuseppe said softly. "How long have you waited for this chance?"

Am I being a fool? And am I betraying the secret I have tried so hard keep by my reluctance? "By the Virgin, I am too old for such intrigue," I said aloud. "Very well, I shall go."

Giuseppe smiled. "Good. Your friends will be pleased. And I will be there, *sorella mia*. You may depend upon me."

"I know." I smiled at him. "I always have."

67

COSÌ POTESSI ANCH'IO

And so, on the evening of November 10, 1727, I found myself in the Cassenti box at the Teatro Sant' Angelo, from which I had seen countless operatic performances, and followed the careers of singers and composers alike. Yet never before had I seen a performance like this one.

I tried to focus my attention on the stage right from the beginning, but my mind was a blur of thoughts and my stomach was churning. Once the dark and haunting opening *sinfonia* had ended, I could not bring myself to concentrate. Even Vivaldi's music could not drown out the refrain echoing in my mind: *Any moment now, my daughter,* mia figlia, *my firstborn, will appear on that stage.*

Much to my annoyance, my friends were engaging in their usual games and conversation in the rear of the box, and I could hear them even from where I sat at the front. *And they had all been so anxious to attend, or so I thought,* I reflected irritably. Yet to my surprise, it was Giulietta who finally brought everyone to order. "Come, *mieri cari,* we must quiet down and not disturb Adriana. After all, it is the first time she is seeing Anna Girò."

With that, they all filed out to take their seats in the front of the box with me. Giuseppe contrived to sit beside me, swiftly reaching out to squeeze my hand before anyone could see.

I had to fight back the tears that threatened at his gesture. *Oh, what am I doing here?* I cried inwardly. *How can I see my daughter stand upon that stage, open to the criticism and judgment of all Venice, and still retain my composure? I should leave, leave now, plead some illness and not put myself through this . . .*

Then she swept onto the stage, and every last thought fled so quickly that I could not hope to recall them.

Even at the young age of sixteen years, her body was that of a woman: she had inherited my curvaceous figure and full breasts, displayed to their best advantage by the low neckline of her costume. A long, braided black wig concealed her true hair color, but I began to imagine that it was dark brown, like mine.

So lost was I in studying her that I scarcely noticed she had begun to sing. Gradually I came to realize that what so many had said of her voice was true, and the knowledge was a dull, blunt blade between my ribs. As much as the mother in me wished otherwise, the musician in me could not deny the truth.

Anna had not inherited her grandmother's gift, then. Yet it could not be denied that she was the most commanding actor on the stage. Every gesture, every movement, every facial expression drew the eye and brought to life the words that she was singing, so that she seemed a sorceress, indeed: one who could make the audience believe entirely what was happening before them.

In between picking out more points of resemblance—*she has my nose, though her skin is paler, like her father's*—I listened closely to her singing, and a number of good qualities began to emerge. When she created more space within her mouth to let the sound resonate, for example—a technique I knew from sitting in on some of Lucrezia's lessons with Vittoria—the result was a big, rich, darkly textured sound that sent chills through me. Yet despite the heaviness of her voice, she moved with ease through the ornaments and trills as the opera went on.

The height of her power over the audience—myself included—came during what was Alcina's most beautiful and sympathetic aria, in act two.

"Così potessi anch'io," she sang sorrowfully, wrapping her arms around herself in a gesture of desolation. *"Goder coll'idol mio, la pace che trovar non può il mio cor."*

The words of the aria—and her masterful singing of it, as if she had been saving all that she had for that moment—caused me to tremble. *If only I, too, could enjoy with the one I love the peace my heart cannot find . . .*

The words reflected my own fragile hope of so many years ago. And Vivaldi's marvelous music, his melody and skillful word painting—which made it seem as if Alcina were alternately weeping and raging—only served to heighten this effect, creating more truth than words by themselves ever could.

Selfishly, I could not help but wonder if this, too, Vivaldi had written for me. Was he trying to say to me that he, too, wished for the same things, had always wished for them? After all, how better for him to ensure that I hear his message than by putting it in the mouth of our daughter?

True to custom, Anna added a great deal of embellishments and ornaments as the first section of the aria repeated again, showcasing a technical virtuosity which I had not heretofore glimpsed. *Surely now no one can doubt what he sees in her.* And indeed, the applause at the conclusion of the aria was quite robust.

As soon as the applause ended, I rose from my seat and exited the box, so swiftly that no one had time to question me. I walked out to the foyer of the theater, where I hoped no one would happen upon me, and finally let loose the tears I had struggled to hide.

I was trying to compose myself when one of the theater's servants hesitantly approached me. "Madonna? Is there any way in which I may assist you?"

"Yes," I replied, without thinking on it further. "Please bring me a bit of parchment and a quill, if you would."

The servant hurried to obey, and when he returned, I leaned the parchment against a small table in the foyer and wrote my message: *I must see her after the performance. Arrange it any way you must.* I signed it with only my given name, folded the parchment into four sections, and handed it to the servant. "See that Maestro Vivaldi gets this as soon as possible," I instructed him.

The servant bowed. "Very good, madonna." He disappeared to deliver my message, and I made my way back to the box.

68

FORGIVEN

"This way, madonna." A servant led me through the maze of the backstage area, past immense pieces of painted scenery, past singers still in costume and garish stage makeup, and piles of props.

We turned down a quieter hallway, and I saw Vivaldi waiting for me outside of what I presumed was Anna's dressing room. The servant bowed to us and departed.

"Adriana," Vivaldi said. He looked even older than he had the last time I saw him, as though he had aged more than three years since then. But there was no trace of the abrasive character of which the gossips spoke. "I . . . your note surprised me."

"Did you think I would not be here?" I asked.

"I was not sure." He paused. "I had hoped you would come."

"And here I am."

"Yes," he said. "Well, then, let me present you to her." He stepped forward and knocked twice on the door, then opened it.

As we stepped into the room, Anna rose from her seat at the dressing table. "Dear maestro," she said happily. "Did you hear how they applauded after the aria? I do not think I have ever sung better!"

"I do not think that you have either, *cara*," he said, surprising me by using the endearment so openly.

"Do you think—oh." She broke off as she saw me. "*Mi scusi*. I did not realize that you had brought a visitor."

"Yes. Anna, may I present Donna Adriana Baldovino, wife of the late Senator Baldovino," Vivaldi said. "She sent me a message expressing a desire to make your acquaintance. Donna Baldovino, Signorina Anna Girò."

Anna curtsied and I nodded in acknowledgment. The desire to gather her into my arms and clutch her to me was nearly overpowering.

She was looking at me expectantly, yet now my tongue felt like a massive, immovable rock, unable to rouse itself and speak.

Now that she had removed her wig, I saw her hair was, indeed, similar in color to mine, save for the red that laced through it, turning it a rich auburn. Her eyes were dark, and fathoms deep, like her father's. She was beautiful, as beautiful as I had been at her age, perhaps more so.

Remembering myself, I managed to speak. "Signorina Girò," I said. "I wished to compliment you on your performance. I was much moved by your aria in act two."

"I thank you, madonna," she said, perfectly poised and gracious. "I do believe that is my favorite aria of those the maestro has written for me thus far."

"Indeed," I murmured, continuing to study her. I glanced at Vivaldi; he seemed to be fighting back tears. My own eyes began to well. *He and I and our daughter are all in the same room. Together. When will this ever happen again?*

"*Allora*, I shall impose on you no longer, signorina," I said. "I merely wished to give you my compliments." Before turning to leave, I added, "I wish you only success in your career and your life."

She curtsied again. "Thank you, madonna." I could see she was weary from performing and relieved I was leaving; I tried not to let it sting.

I walked past Vivaldi and exited the small room; he pulled the door closed behind me and followed me. A lone tear slid down my cheek.

"I know," he murmured, as if I had spoken. "I wish that you could know her as I do, and spend time with her."

"There is nothing on this earth that I wish more," I said. "And yet it is impossible, I am afraid."

"Yes, I suppose it is. Adriana." He grasped my arm, drawing me away from the door. "The rumors . . . you have heard them, surely?"

I nodded.

"God, how they torture me, how they pick at my soul!" he burst out. "And I cannot contradict them, for I cannot reveal the truth!" He sighed. "Does it not pain you as well?"

I did not know how to answer. The gossip did not particularly upset me, not any longer. And it did not seem to bother Anna. It would not, after all, be the first or last time that scandalous tales were told about a famous opera singer.

After all, the things of which they were accusing Vivaldi now he had, in fact, done—but years ago, and not with the woman they thought. But I could not say any of this.

"Adriana, you must know, for you heard . . . her voice, it is not the best," he said, speaking even more softly now.

I nodded reluctantly.

"And I know that—how could I not? Perhaps I should not blame them for what they say. Short of the truth, what other explanation could there be? Unless everyone is to believe that I have lost my ear, my skills."

"Venetians will always find something to talk about," I said. "You told me that, once. In a few months, no one will think of it more."

"Perhaps. But Adriana, surely you can see why?" he asked.

"What do you mean?"

"Why I have brought all this upon myself." He released my arm, which he had still been clutching. "I sought her out when I was last in Mantua. I knew that was where she was; it was not difficult. And she wished desperately to be an opera singer. How could I deny her, when it was within my power to give her what she most wanted? I swore I would teach her as best I could, so as to know her, be near her, even if she never knows the truth."

"Why have you not told her?" I asked.

"I have been tempted," he confessed. "But I knew it would be a selfish act, for my benefit and not hers—and not yours, either."

"Rest assured that I know, even if no one else does, that everything you do for her is because she is your daughter, and you love her," I said.

"But it is more than that," he said. "I would do anything for her, yes, but this is also for you."

Final words, a farewell, whispered into my ear: *I will make it right somehow, someday,* mia carissima *Adriana. I swear that I will, even if it takes my very life.* I heard his words again with such clarity that for a moment I thought that he had spoken them aloud again.

"It is all for you, Adriana. I swore to you, and everything I have done has been to fulfill my vow. I have done everything I could—even some unscrupulous things at times—to ensure that my career would be successful, for if it is not, then all I did to you was done for nothing. And this—supporting Anna—this is the best way I know how to fulfill my vow." He paused and looked away. "Perhaps it is selfish of me, but I wanted to make sure you knew. That you knew I had not forgotten." He sighed. "You must have hated me all these years. As well you should, but I—"

Trembling, I reached out and laid a finger against his lips. "Please, *caro.* No more. It is forgiven."

He looked at me, disbelieving. "Truly, Adriana?"

I stepped closer, pressing my mouth to his and, though surprised, he responded quickly, and for a moment we were the young lovers we had been, one last time.

I drew away. "It was so long ago, Tonio," I said, struggling to steady my voice. "But know that I have forgiven you for all long since."

It was only when I spoke the words that I realized they were true.

69

RITORNELLO

Though my renewed friendship with Tommaso Foscari had at first been a matter for secrecy, it was no longer the case once he appeared at the concert given by my children. Wondering what our need for secrecy had been—Giacomo was dead, and there was no love lost between Tommaso and his wife—we began to venture out openly in public together. Tommaso joined our group on outings, as my *cavaliere servente,* and everyone seemed glad of the addition. He also came frequently to dine at my palazzo—the better to avoid his wife, he always said—and as our children were by this time good friends, he would bring them along and the arrangement suited everyone.

But in 1729, when Tommaso's wife died, everything changed.

She died in childbirth, bearing a second son, who survived and was christened after his father. Tommaso observed the customary period of mourning, during which time we deemed it prudent not to be seen in public together, though we still met privately. His children, whom I had grown to love, were saddened by her death, but as she had not been a great part of their lives—much like Giacomo, who had involved himself very little with our children—their lives continued as before, save for the addition of their new baby brother.

Perhaps we had both been waiting for the death of his wife, in a way. For before his period of mourning ended, our relationship changed.

I had come to dine with him one evening, alone. After dinner, we adjourned to his private sitting room, still discussing a recently published book of poetry we had both read and finishing our dessert wine. The hour grew late, and the wine dwindled, and still I did not take my leave.

At a pause in the conversation, Tommaso reached out, brushing away a stray curl that had fallen in my face. His hand lingered on my cheek for a moment, then trailed down my neck before abruptly pulling away. "I am sorry," he said, moving so that he sat farther from me on the daybed.

I leveled my gaze at him. "You should be."

His expression was absolutely stricken. "You should be sorry that you stopped," I said, a smile playing about my lips.

"Adriana . . ." He slid closer, cupping my face in his hands. "Do you mean it?"

I took a deep breath. "I have wanted it for some time now." I smiled. "I do not usually make a practice of seducing mourning widowers, but you are just so *handsome*—"

His mouth covered mine then, cutting me off, and we did not speak again for some time. His hands explored beneath my bodice, and began to push up my skirts.

"Yes." I sighed, reaching for him, beginning to unlace his breeches.

He drew away. "No."

I stared at him in wonder.

"Not here." He smiled, stood, and helped me to my feet. "I have waited this long. I can wait the few more minutes it will take me to remove all of your clothes, and make love to you in a proper bed."

It was Tommaso who taught me that love between a man and a woman can take many forms. It need not be a grand, sweeping passion that can carry you to ecstasy and also destroy you. Instead it can be a quieter love, mingled with friendship and respect and desire and a wish to make the other happy.

We carried on with our affair unashamedly; he would stay at my palazzo, or I at his, and our children grew so used to our comings and goings that they soon ceased to comment altogether: an unspoken sort of approval that meant a great deal to me. Once Tommaso took me to one of the small islands in the lagoon after nightfall, and we made love on the beach, with not a soul to see us.

"I am the luckiest man alive," Tommaso murmured in my ear one night, drawing me tight against him in his bed, his skin warm against mine. "It has taken me years, but finally I have the woman I love in my arms."

I arched my neck to smile up at him. "And she is not going anywhere."

I was so wrapped up in my own romance that when trouble began to brew, I did not notice until it was too late.

It was Cecilia's lady's maid, a girl named Laura, who discovered my daughter's secret. "She has been ill in the mornings, madonna," Laura reported nervously. "I have twice this week cleaned the vomit from her chamber pot, and more times before that. And she . . ." Her face turned red as she looked down at her shoes.

"Go on," I encouraged, thanking the Blessed Virgin for loyal servants who would bring me such information about my children, though in truth they were children no longer: Lucrezia was a woman of nineteen, and Antonio and Cecilia had just turned eighteen. God help me, but perhaps there was a bit of my father in me after all.

"She has not bled these two months past, madonna," Laura said.

"I change her linens and take her clothing to the wash, and there has been no blood."

"Mother of God," I whispered.

"I cannot be sure, of course, madonna—she does not discuss such things with me—but the signs are there," Laura said.

"And who—" I shook my head, cutting myself off. "Never mind. Thank you, Laura. You have done the right thing in coming to me. I will see that a bit extra is added to your wages this month."

She curtsied. "I hope it may all end well, madonna," she said, turning to leave the room.

So do I, I thought, the dread in my belly so heavy that I could barely rise from my chair.

I summoned Cecilia to my sitting room immediately.

"Cecilia," I said, as she entered and sat. "I have heard some disturbing news this morning."

Her face remained impassive. "Oh? And what might that be?"

"I think you know."

She grew a bit paler. "I have not the slightest idea, Mother."

"Do not play the coy maiden with me, girl," I snapped. "It is rather too late for that, or so I hear."

In an explosion of rage, she rose from her chair. "Laura!" she cried. "I might have known that minx could not keep a secret—"

"Sit down," I commanded, rising to my feet as well. "Your maid did right, coming to me as soon as she did, so that we might take this in hand. Sit *down,* Cecilia, *now.*"

But she just stood there, chin raised defiantly, her eyes boring into mine. "It does not matter what you think," she informed me. "I love him, and he loves me."

God and Mary Virgin preserve me, I thought, a freezing chill sweeping over me, as though I beheld a ghost. *I have given birth to my own image.* "Who?" I asked aloud.

She raised her chin higher. "Andrea," she said. "Andrea Foscari."

"Dear God," I whispered, and shame washed over me. What manner of mother was I, that I had not seen it? "How long has this been going on?"

She took a deep breath and looked away. "Since Carnevale," she said. "At the party Don Foscari gave."

Lord, Holy Mother, forgive me. I had been there, we all had, and I had not noticed that Andrea Foscari had led my daughter away—or the reverse, knowing Cecilia as I did.

I had been rather occupied that night, when Tommaso—disguised so well that I almost did not recognize him—had led me away from the party and down to the mezzanine, where he had pressed my back against the wall, hiked up my skirts, and taken me swiftly and almost roughly, as if we were a pair of servants trying to escape the master's eye. I had returned to the party flushed and with a grin I could not entirely hide, prompting Giulietta to wink at me and say, "You are not a true Venetian until you have made love to a masked man during Carnevale."

If only we had known, that night, that we were not the only ones behaving like fools in love . . . I shook my head in disgust at myself. "Andrea cannot marry you," I said aloud. "He is betrothed to Elena Corner. And yet he says that he loves you, dishonoring you when he cannot act as a gentleman and ask for your hand?"

"He does not love her, much less wish to marry her. I would not expect you to understand," Cecilia shot back. "What would you know of love, married all those years to my father?"

"Do not dare to speak of what you do not understand," I replied. "I know more than you do, it seems, about what befalls young women who give away their hearts and their maidenhead."

"How? How would you know?" she demanded scornfully.

"How do you think? Because I, too, fell in love with a man who could not marry me, and found myself with child as a result!"

The shock on Cecilia's face made me realize what I had said. Just like that, my greatest secret, the one I had guarded so closely all these years, was secret no longer.

"*What?*" she cried.

I looked down. "That is neither here nor there."

"What do you mean? What happened?"

"I am not here to answer to you for my actions, you foolish girl," I said. "Quite the reverse."

"But then . . . surely you must understand . . ."

"Better than you can imagine," I said. "And I also understand that my daughter has repeated my mistakes, which was the last thing I ever wanted."

"Maybe if you had *told* us of your mistakes," she retorted, "we may have learned from them."

I had no answer for that, but I would be damned if I admitted it. "Go to your rooms and stay there," I said, "while I see what can be done about this mess."

"What do you mean? What are you going to do?"

"Go see Andrea's father, of course."

Her face paled. "You are going to tell him?"

"Of course. He must know, so that we may deal with this." I stared hard at her. "Go. Now. And do not make me lock you in your rooms, as my father once did to me."

This time, sullenly, she did as she was told. When I passed by her door on my way down to the dock, I could hear her within, weeping.

I arrived unannounced at Tommaso's palazzo, and he came to greet me with a wide smile, removing my damp cloak.

"Adriana, this is an unexpected pleasure," he said. His hands slid down to the laces on the back of my gown. "Let me help you remove a few other things as well . . ."

I frowned. "Would that this visit were a pleasurable one, Tommaso."

His smile fell away. "What has happened?"

"It is best that we talk in private," I said. Without delay, he led me up the stairs to his sitting room. He called for the servants to light a fire and bring wine, then settled into a chair beside mine. "Tell me, Adia," he said softly, calling me by the pet name that only he ever used. "Whatever it is, we shall face it together."

"My daughter Cecilia," I said. "She is with child."

He drew in his breath sharply.

"Like mother, like daughter," I said, causing him to blanch. We had never spoken of our painful past since that night when he had sought me out for a dance, but it could no longer be left to lie. "She is, Tommaso," I said, tears beginning to fall. "She is just like me: impulsive and headstrong and impervious to reason when her heart is involved. I should have seen that this would happen, and told her of my mistakes so she would not repeat them . . ."

"Shhh," he said, taking my hand, stroking my fingers lightly. "It is not your fault, Adriana. Our children grow and become adults, doing what they will." He squeezed my hand. "Anything that I can do to help, I will."

I laughed through my tears. "How I wish you meant that, Tommaso."

He looked startled. "Why do you think I do not?"

"I have not told you who the father is."

At first he seemed puzzled, then all at once the truth became apparent. "No," he whispered. "Andrea."

I nodded.

"Damn the fool!" He rose and began angrily pacing the room. "Does he not know better? Have I not raised him to comport himself better than this? He has a duty, to me and to his family—"

"She told me they love each other," I said.

"They are neither of them twenty years old!" he exclaimed. "What do they know of love?"

"As much as we did at that age, I expect."

He paused, acknowledging the many truths behind my words. "And what is to be done now?"

"I came here to ask you that very question," I said.

He spun away from me. "*Damnation!* What are we to do, Adriana? They cannot marry. I am sorry, but they cannot. He is already contracted to Elena Corner; his mother made the match, it was her wish—"

"I am not asking you to break the betrothal," I said. "I am asking you to consider whether you are willing to do to our children what our parents did to us."

"This is not the same, Adriana," he said, his voice heavy with warning. "I would remind you of that."

"You are right, it is not," I said. "All I am asking is that you let them choose for themselves."

Silence ensued. After a long while, Tommaso stalked to the door, opened it, and stuck his head out, calling for one of the servants. "Bring Andrea to me," he said. "Immediately." He returned to his chair, spinning his wineglass in his fingers. He did not look at me or speak further.

After a few moments, Andrea entered the room. He froze as he saw both of us sitting there.

"Sit," Tommaso said, gesturing to a chair across from us.

Andrea sat, his back straight, his head held high.

He was a handsome young man, I thought, studying him. It was easy to see why he had turned Cecilia's head.

"No doubt you know why you are here," Tommaso said. "I expect you to answer for your actions as a man would."

"You know, then," he said, glancing at me. "That Cecilia and I . . . she told you."

"Her maid did, rather," I interjected. "She discovered that my daughter is with child." I noted the lack of surprise on Andrea's face. "As you know."

"Damn it, Andrea!" Tommaso burst out. "Have you no sense? What can you have been thinking, to so dishonor the daughter of a patrician, of a senator?"

"I love her," Andrea said quietly. "As she loves me. There is no dishonor in that."

"And your betrothed?" Tommaso demanded. "What of her?"

Andrea shook his head. "I do not love her," he said. "I do not even particularly like her. She is vain and foolish, and all her conversation is malicious gossip. Not like Cecilia." As he said her name, his whole expression changed. "She is intelligent—more so than many men. And beautiful, and the music that she plays . . ." He shook his head. "Any man would be honored, should she agree to be his wife, were she the daughter of a senator or a gondolier. I wonder that she ever even looked twice at me."

That was enough for me. I saw it then: he loved my daughter; she was not just sport or a dalliance. He was a good man, just like his father.

"And so you expect me to break your betrothal?" Tommaso asked. "The Corners are a family not easily slighted, *figlio*."

"You need break nothing, Father," Andrea said. "Cecilia and I have been discussing it. We will elope, and leave Venice together. My honor is better served by doing right by my child and the woman I love than it is standing by a promise my mother made on my behalf."

Silence. After a moment, Tommaso looked at me. "And would your daughter consent to wed my son, then?"

A smile broke out on my face. "I believe that she would, yes."

Tommaso sighed. "Well, then, yes. God forbid that I should stand in the way of a young couple in love. There is enough of that in this Venice of ours as it is."

70

MY CONFESSION

And so it was settled. Andrea and Cecilia would be married in April of 1734, two months before the child was due, thus allowing it to be born in the marriage bed, even if it was not conceived there.

Tommaso and I gave a grand party to celebrate the betrothal of our children. No one but our families knew Cecilia was with child; though no doubt Venice would find out soon enough, for the moment it was a secret. And whatever people chose to think later, no one who saw the couple that night could doubt that they were very much in love—and that their parents were very pleased to have it so.

I learned that Lucrezia had known of Cecilia and Andrea's affair all along, and of her sister's pregnancy. I could not find it in me to fault her for not telling me; after all, who better than I to understand the bond between siblings?

The night of the party, Vittoria and I looked on as Andrea made a toast to his bride-to-be, declaring himself the happiest and most fortunate of men, and heaping boundless praise upon the blushing Cecilia—good heavens, when had I ever seen the girl blush, of all things?

"They are a lovely couple," Vittoria murmured to me. "Oh,

Adriana, I am so happy for them, and so glad you and Tommaso were able to come to an accord. Not that he set himself against anything you wanted, I will wager," she added slyly.

I laughed. "You may or may not be right about that, *sorella*. But all we want is our children's happiness."

"Then you are successful." She watched the couple kiss, to the applause of those present. "There is nothing like one's first love," she said. "I am lucky enough to be married to mine, and so will Cecilia."

"Yes," I said. "Not all of us are so fortunate, and it has always been my fondest wish for my children."

Out of the corner of my eye, I could see Vittoria studying me as the speech ended and the crowd began to disperse. Softly, so softly I was almost not sure I had heard her, she said, "It was Maestro Vivaldi, was it not?"

I could only stare at her, dumbstruck with horror.

Apparently I had not kept my secret as well as I thought.

I grabbed her arm and drew her out into the hall where there was no danger of being overheard. But once there, I still could not speak.

"Oh, Adriana, forgive me," she said. "Forgive me for prying; it is a sin I will readily confess. I have been curious, and I thought . . . it seemed to me that everything fit together, over the years."

When still I remained silent, she said, "Please forgive me. I should not have said anything."

She made to return to the ballroom, but I reached out, stopping her. "I can only imagine what you must think of me," I said.

To my surprise, she smiled slightly. "I admit, I was a bit shocked when first I thought I had stumbled upon the answer. But . . . he was always a rather difficult man to work with; at the Pietà he demanded perfection at all times. Yet we all adored him just the same, perhaps because of that." She studied my face. "So I can see how easy it must have been for you to love him. And just as easy for him to love you."

"It was," I whispered. "It was easy to love him, and yet painful at the same time." I cleared my throat. "Did Giuseppe—"

"No," she hurriedly assured me. "Giuseppe never breathed a word. I asked him once, after we were married, if he knew who your great lost love was. He tried to avoid the question, but I . . ." She smiled ruefully. "I pressed him, which was wrong of me. It was the only time in our marriage that he has ever spoken sharply to me. He said that it was your secret to tell, not his."

"I am sorry to have caused discord between you," I said.

Vittoria smiled. "Do not be. It is one of the things I love most about him—his loyalty." She paused, studying me. "There is one thing I still do not understand," she said. "Where does Anna Girò fit into all this?"

I took a deep breath. "She is our daughter. Mine and Maestro Vivaldi's."

Vittoria threw her arms around me. "Oh, Adriana," she whispered. "I will not tell a soul. I will take it to my grave, I swear."

That night, after the party had ended, I went into Cecilia's room. She was still awake, though dressed for bed. "Mother," she said, surprised. "What is it?"

I sat on the bed beside her. It had taken me until tonight to realize how heavy secrets are, and how much heavier they grow over the years. And if there was one person I would have know the truth—other than Vittoria—it was Cecilia, the child who was most like me. My unexpected one. "I told you," I began, "that as a young woman I fell in love with a man who could not marry me."

She nodded, her eyes wide.

"It has been a secret long enough," I said. "I will tell you everything, if you are willing to hear it."

"Of course, Mother," she said.

I smiled. "You met him once, you know," I said. "If you recall, when you were much younger. His name is Antonio Vivaldi."

And then I told her all.

71

DA CAPO

Cecilia and Andrea were married in April, in as beautiful and festive a ceremony as anyone had ever seen; and in June my Cecilia gave birth to a son, who was named Andrea Tommaso.

Once the newlyweds were settled, Tommaso began asking me to accompany him on an extended tour of Europe. He wanted to show me the world before we grew too old to travel. While a part of me longed to go, I always refused. At first my excuse was baby Andrea; I could not imagine missing any part of his childhood. Then there were my other children to think of; but they, too, were growing up. Lucrezia, who had become society's reigning eligible beauty, had scandalously turned down an offer of marriage from the doge's son and instead married Rafaello Marino, son of Giuseppe's friend Baldassare. Giacomo, I knew, was rolling in his grave, but I gave my daughter a sizable dowry and my blessing.

Just as he had been a serious and studious child, Antonio grew into a serious and prudent young man. He retained his excellent head for numbers, and occupied much of his time with making wise investments with the money from his father's estate—mostly in property, though his love of music shone through when he bought a share in the Teatro Sant' Angelo.

My children were prospering, as were my nieces and nephews; I could very well have left Venice, but for whatever reason, I did not. If ever the time became right for me to leave, I thought, I would know it.

And so I remained. And I remained happy. And perhaps there are as many kinds of happiness as there are love, for each time I felt that I might lay claim to the word, it never felt quite the same. *Perhaps,* I mused one day, as I sat in my gondola on my way to meet Tommaso, *that means that I have tasted much of life.*

CODA: ON THE OTHER SIDE

Vienna, July 28, 1741

I stepped out of the hired coach, looking up at the building before me. It was nondescript, even shabby; the windows were shuttered, and the stone façade was dirty and crumbling. But I gave all of this only a passing thought as I knocked on the front door and waited to be let in.

In my hand I clutched the much-folded parchment that had been delivered to me about a week ago. The words on it were imprinted on my mind as well as my heart.

Adriana—

I am dying. I have no right to ask this of you, but all I want is to see you one more time.

If you do not come, I will understand.

A.V.

Below his initials was an address in Vienna before which I now od.

I had deliberated briefly upon receiving the letter. In the end, though, I had left the next day. How could I do anything else?

Tommaso had come to call as I was in the midst of preparations. "What is this, my love?" he asked in confusion, as I directed the servants in packing a trunk.

"I have received a letter," I told him. "From a . . . very old friend. He is in Vienna, and he is dying. He has asked that I come to him, and so I am going."

I could see from the look in Tommaso's eyes that he knew exactly who this "friend" was, had been, to me. "Very well," he said. "You are right to go, I think." He kissed me. "When you return," he murmured, "I shall have a very particular question to ask you."

I was pulled from my memories by the opening of the door. I looked up to see Anna standing before me.

I was so taken aback that I did not immediately know what to say. I had heard that Vivaldi came to Vienna to seek the patronage of Emperor Charles. Things had gone sour for Vivaldi in Italy; in 1738, the Cardinal of Ferrara had denied him entrance to that city for the opera season for being a priest who traveled openly with his mistress. Only years of hiding my emotions had allowed me to remain composed when Giulietta had related that piece of gossip.

However, the Emperor Charles had died not long after Vivaldi's arrival. And I did not know Anna had come with him. What to say?

In the name of God and the Holy Virgin, Antonio is dying. Can it possibly still matter what I tell her? I asked myself impatiently.

"Donna Baldovino," she said, surprised. I was stunned that she remembered me.

It was plain she had been doing much weeping of late. She was dressed in a plain linen dress with her hair pulled back from her face, looking very different from the last time I saw her.

Dear God, she is almost thirty years old.

This reminded me that I was nearing the age of fifty; therefore I decided that it was high time to push such thoughts aside and deal with the matter at hand. "I do not mean to be rude," Anna said, "but what are you doing here?"

"He sent for me," I said, holding up the letter. "I am an old friend of his."

I could see she wanted to question me further, but realized that now was not the time. "Then you have come just in time," she said, letting me in. "I fear he has just hours left." With that, she burst into renewed sobs, pulling a handkerchief from her sleeve. "Oh, my poor maestro!"

I was surprised to feel a prickle of irritation. *Silly girl, at your age I had been married ten years, borne four children, had one of them taken from me, and lost my lover long since. Death is death; there are greater tragedies in life, and by the time you are my age you will not fear death in any case, but respect him so that he will treat you kindly when he comes for you.* "There, there, all will be well," I said. "Now please take me to him."

She led me into a darkened bedchamber at the rear of the small house. I entered, and she shut the door softly behind me.

I stood, frozen, looking at the thin body stretched out beneath the coverlet.

Yet then he stirred, slowly lifting his head. "Adriana?" he asked, his raspy voice no more than a whisper. "Is it you? Or do I but dream . . ."

His words trailed off into a fit of coughing, and I moved swiftly to his side, sitting in a wooden chair beside the bed and taking his hand. It was all I could do to contain my cry of shock as I looked into his face.

His skin had a deathly pallor, and he was skeletally thin. His famous red hair was now all white.

"Tell me, *caro*," I said, "what ails you?"

He groaned. "I am not certain. Annina had a doctor in here, but he could not be sure . . . it may be my lungs, or my heart, or . . ." He broke off, beginning to cough again. "Or simply that I am old."

I squeezed his hand gently, painfully aware that his brittle fingers could no longer play the violin with the speed and dexterity that had once seemed like magic to me. "We are both old, I am afraid," I said, fighting to keep my tone light.

He looked at me, his gaze still clear. "You are as beautiful today, Adriana, as you were on that night when you first walked into my house."

"If you persist in this flattery, I shall be forced to tell you how old I really am," I said, tears threatening to choke me. "Know you not that our daughter is nearly thirty years old?"

"Our daughter," he repeated, smiling faintly. "I told her, you know."

I froze. "Told her?"

"That I am her father. She wept—I think she is upset with me for keeping it from her all these years." He shifted slightly, as though seeking some small scrap of comfort that eluded him. "I did not tell her who her mother is. That is for you to do. If you choose."

I remained silent, mind racing.

"Adriana." His voice, softer now, drew me back to him. "I was not sure that you would come."

"And how could I do otherwise, *caro mio*?" I asked, tears flowing freely now.

He sighed. "I can die in peace now that I have seen you once more." He let his eyes drift closed. "And I . . . I am sorry, Adriana. For all the wrong I have done you. For everything I did to hurt you."

"Shhh. No more talk of that. I told you years ago, Tonio, I have forgiven you all."

"I have always loved you," he said, briefly tightening his grip on my hand. "I never stopped."

"I know, *carissimo*," I said, unable to see him through my tears. "I know, *amore mio*. Go to sleep now. Go with my love."

I sat beside him, keeping my grip on his hand as his breathing slowed and grew ever shallower.

It was early evening when he breathed his last.

After, it was as if a light had been extinguished inside me, one that had always been there but that I only noticed now that it had vanished. I realized then how much comfort I had taken in simply knowing that he was out there, somewhere, in the world.

But now he was gone, taking with him a part of me he had had all along, changing me forever one final time.

I do not know how much time passed before I rose and left the room. Anna was sitting in the front room, and when I appeared, tears began to trickle down her face anew, realizing what my emergence meant.

"He told me he was my father," she said, her face grief-stricken. "He said that he had a love affair as a young man, and that I . . . I was his daughter." She shook her head. "Sometimes even I wondered why he was so devoted to me. I knew what people said, of course, and I knew it was not true. But it never did fit together until now."

"He loved you," I said. "That was plain to see."

"But you . . ." Her eyes brightened somewhat. "You said you are an old friend of his. Do you know who my mother is, madonna?"

I had imagined this moment for thirty years: the moment when I could finally claim my lost daughter as my own. Never had I given up hope that it would come, one day. And here it was, and I was not ready.

What, in truth, could I gain by telling her? She would never think of me as her mother, not a stranger whom she had only met twice.

And, much as my heart broke to admit it, I had difficulty thinking of her as my daughter. Lucrezia was my daughter, Cecilia was my daughter; the daughters I had suckled and raised and watched grow, day by day. Anna, my lost child, my firstborn, was a stranger to me and always would be. Even if we were to begin now, we could never make up for what we had missed.

Everything had happened as it had happened, and it was not for me to say that there was not a reason for it all.

The girl had enough havoc wreaked in her life this day. Let it remain at that. No doubt she would draw her own conclusions, but I would let it be.

"No," I answered her finally. "No, he did not confide such in me. I am sorry."

She studied me for a moment, then bowed her head. "Very well. It may be that I am not meant to know." She rose. "If you will excuse me, I must . . ."

"Yes, you see to him, signorina," I said. "It is for you to do, now."

"Will you stay the night, madonna?"

I shook my head. "No. I must return to Venice. There are those who are waiting for me."

She nodded and turned to go into the bedchamber, leaving me.

I saw myself out.

As I stepped out of the house into the heat of summer, I thought that when Tommaso asked me to marry him, maybe I would say yes. And maybe . . . maybe I would let him show me the world, after all.

Maybe the time had come.

HISTORICAL NOTE

Antonio Vivaldi was well-known in eighteenth-century Europe as a virtuoso violinist and composer. But he was in fact ruined later in his life by his relationship with the young opera singer Anna Girò. The common gossip, as portrayed in my novel, was that she was his mistress, an accusation which he always vehemently denied. In the end, he died impoverished in Vienna, and was buried in an unmarked pauper's grave.

I came across the theory in several places (one of which being Barbara Quick's phenomenal historical novel *Vivaldi's Virgins*, about Anna Maria dal Violin of the Pietà) that Anna Girò was perhaps Vivaldi's daughter, not his mistress. The idea fascinated me, and it also begged the question: if this were the case, who was Anna's mother?

We will likely never know the true nature of Vivaldi's relationship with Anna, but it was this "what if" idea that led me to write *The Violinist of Venice*.

Adriana d'Amato is a fictional character, as are her family and friends. While Adriana's mother, Lucrezia, and best friend and sister-in-law, Vittoria, are not based on any real figures, they faced the same choice as many real wards of the Pietà did: to stay in cloistered seclusion and continue their (often celebrated) musical careers, or to leave for marriage and the outside world. Marriage indeed meant signing a contract stating that they would never again perform in public.

The Foscari family was a real Venetian patrician family of considerable wealth and power, and Ca' Foscari still stands on the Grand Canal in Venice to this day. Tommaso and his family specifically are my inventions.

Each piece of Vivaldi's music I describe here is real; each concerto that he and Adriana play together is one that I chose carefully to fit the mood and needs (and the era) of a particular scene. I hope that, after reading this book, you will seek out some of Vivaldi's music if you are not already familiar with it, whether it is the music described here or other works.

I tried to bring the backdrop of sensual eighteenth-century Venice alive as much and as accurately as possible. Baroque Venice was a city long past the economic and military glory of the Renaissance; the discovery of the New World had made Venice's formerly prime position as a trading empire between East and West irrelevant. As such, by Vivaldi's lifetime what was once the richest and most powerful state in Europe had been slowly crumbling for years. The wealth of the great patrician families, originally amassed from trade, was quickly dwindling. Yet almost in defiance of this fact, eighteenth-century Venice was more decadent and hedonistic than ever. What money the wealthy had left they spent quickly, on lavish parties and costumes and clothing, on food and wine. Carnival (or *Carnevale*) went on for months at a time, and with the whole city going around masked for so long, the results were just as scandalous as you would expect.

Eighteenth-century Venice was, as modern Venice is today, a major tourist destination. Young aristocrats from around Europe would visit on the grand tour, and notable figures such as Jean-Jacques Rousseau and Lord Byron also spent time in Venice. Tourists would partake of the city's many delights: the architecture; the artwork; musical performances both at the many opera houses and at the

Pietà and other institutions like it; traveling by gondola; and, of course, the famed Venetian courtesans.

Venice is a wonderful place to visit, to read about, and to imagine. I hope I have accomplished my goal of bringing it to life for you, and giving you an entertaining and meaningful story at the same time.

ACKNOWLEDGMENTS

They say writing is a solitary endeavor, and yet I count myself fortunate in that I do not always find it so. I have been so lucky to have so many wonderful people in my life who have inspired me, championed me, and believed in me and this book all along the way.

Bear with me, because it's a long list.

I would be remiss if I did not thank, first and foremost, Lindsay Fowler, my critique partner, one of my closest friends, and a mind-blowingly talented writer herself. She read each draft of this book (and is to this day the only person besides myself to have seen the messy first draft, a dubious honor) and gave me excellent notes, suggestions, and criticism at every step of the way. Thank you times infinity for your patience, your support, for endless conversations talking through plot points and characterization and themes, and for putting up with all my two A.M. freak-out texts.

Thank you to my fabulous Canisius Alumni Writers (aka CAW), without whose enthusiasm this book might still be languishing on my hard drive: Joe Bieron, Cara Cotter, Brittany Gray, Caitie McAneney, Ryan Nagelhout, and Ryan Wolf.

Showers of gratitude upon my amazing, fabulous agent, Brianne Johnson: for taking a chance on a cold query by a first-time author with a crazy-long manuscript, for helping me improve said manuscript exponentially, and for finding it a wonderful home and making my dreams come true.

Millions of thanks (and brisket tots!) to my gem of an editor, Vicki Lame, for giving me this chance, for your love and enthusiasm for this story, and for making this book so much better than I thought it could be. I've already learned so much from working with you—can't wait for round two!

Thanks to the wonderful team at St. Martin's Press for their work on this project, and for the absolutely gorgeous cover that I am so in love with.

Thank you to all my wonderful English and creative writing teachers at Canisius College, especially Janet McNally, Jennifer Desiderio, and Eric Gansworth. And, above all, thanks to Mick Cochrane: mentor, fellow writer, and friend, for making me the writer I am today. I'll never forget the day, a few years after I'd graduated, when he took the time to meet with me at a point when I was feeling particularly lost and talked through my writing-career options with me. Thanks to his advice and wise counsel, I decided to really give this book a shot, and it worked out.

Thank you to Karla Manzella, my ninth-grade English teacher, who knew I was writing my own stories during her class and let me keep doing it.

Thank you to piano teacher extraordinaire Karen Schmid, for all those wonderful and inspiring conversations about music. Thanks to my voice teacher, Melissa Thorburn, for not batting an eye when I showed up with obscure Vivaldi arias to learn. Thank you to the wonderful and wise Maestro Frank Scinta, who taught me more about music than I can possibly say.

Thank you to all the rocking musicians whose music I listened to and drew inspiration from while writing this novel, namely Nightwish, Lacuna Coil, Evanescence, Within Temptation, Delain, Stream of Passion, Epica, Florence + the Machine, Serenity, Tori

Amos, and Icon for Hire. A special thanks to Lindsey Stirling for giving a voice to Adriana's violin inside my head.

Heaps of thanks with sprinkles on top to my BFF and partner in frozen-yogurt crime, Jen Hark, for letting me babble at her about all kinds of historical subjects.

Thanks and virtual hugs to #TeamWritersHouse for reaching out via Twitter and Facebook and welcoming me to the family, and for all their support and wonderful bookish conversation.

Thanks beyond words or measure to my family. To my grandparents, Mike and Kathy Zimmerman, who read early drafts of this book and brag about me all the time. To my brother, Matt Palombo, for making me laugh and for always believing I could do it (even if this book has no duels, car chases, or explosions. Maybe next time!). And thank you, thank you, thank you to my parents, Tony and Debbie Palombo, for never doubting me for an instant, for supporting me in everything I've ever wanted to do, for instilling in me a love of reading and of history, for teaching me the value of hard work, and for their unconditional love every second of my life. Without them I would not be here, nor would I be a writer.

And last but certainly not least, thank you to Antonio Vivaldi. *Grazie mille per l'ispirazione, maestro.*

1. Both Adriana and Vivaldi reference the myth of Orpheus and Eurydice several times throughout the novel—also a brief, fateful love affair. Do you see parallels between this myth and *The Violinist of Venice*?

2. At the beginning of the book, Adriana is blinded by her passion for Vivaldi to such an extent that she often cannot fully comprehend the risks that others take on her behalf. But, by the end of the book, she is a complex woman full of great warmth and compassion for others. How might Adriana have been different if she had never ignored her father's rules and taken violin lessons from Vivaldi?

Discussion Questions

3. Taking into consideration the time period of the novel, do you see Adriana as a feminist character? Why or why not?

4. Throughout the novel, Adriana has several relationships with men that evolve significantly over time, most especially Vivaldi and Tommaso, but also Senator Baldovino. How do you think becoming a mother—someone responsible for the life of another—might have changed these relationships or led to more understanding within them?

5. Though Adriana raised her children with more freedom than she had growing up, her daughter, Cecilia, ends up pregnant out of wedlock, much like she did. Cecilia confronts her for not telling them her mistakes so that they might learn from them. Does nature vs. nurture have a role here, or as humans are we always destined to follow our hearts regardless of the consequences? Discuss.

6. At the end of the novel, Adriana chooses not to reveal to Anna that she is her birth mother. Did you agree with this decision? Why or why not? What might have happened if she had?

7. Do you feel that Adriana, and the story as a whole, ultimately has a "happy ending"? Why or why not?

8. Wards of the Pietà, such as Adriana's mother, Lucrezia, and her best friend, Vittoria, could marry if asked, but were force to give up their (often celebrated) musical careers in order to do so. What choice would you make in that position?

9. Were you familiar with any of Vivaldi's music before reading *The Violinist of Venice*? How did this prior experience—or lack thereof—affect your reading of the novel?

10. Adriana, who was, among other roles, Vivaldi's muse, was a fictional character sprung from the author's imagination. How do you think a figure like Adriana might have altered his work if she actually existed?